DEVDUTT PATTANAIK

JAYA

AN ILLUSTRATED RETELLING OF THE

MAHABHARATA

Illustrations by the author

PENGUIN BOOKS

An imprint of Penguin Random House

PENGUIN BOOKS

USA | Canada | UK | Ireland | Australia
New Zealand | India | South Africa | China

Penguin Books is part of the Penguin Random House group of companies whose addresses can be found at global.penguinrandomhouse.com

Published by Penguin Random House India Pvt. Ltd
4th Floor, Capital Tower 1, MG Road,
Gurugram 122 002, Haryana, India

Penguin Random House India

First published by Penguin Books India 2010

55 54 53 52

ISBN 9780143104254

Typeset in Garamond by Eleven Arts, New Delhi
Printed at Replika Press Pvt. Ltd, India

www.penguin.co.in

I dedicate this book to all the scholars, authors, archivists, playwrights, film-makers and storytellers, both ancient and modern, who have worked towards keeping this grand and ancient epic alive through their songs, dances, stories, plays, novels, performances, films and teleserials for over 3000 years

Contents

AUTHOR'S NOTE

What Ganesha Wrote

They were perhaps whispers of God, or maybe insights of the wise. They gave the world meaning and life a purpose. These chants relieved vedana, the yearning of the restless human soul, hence became collectively known as the Veda. Those who heard them first came to be known as the Rishis.

Based on what the Veda revealed, the Rishis created a society where everything had a place and where everything changed with rhythmic regularity. The Brahmans were the teachers of this society, the Kshatriyas its guardians, the Vaishyas its providers and the Shudras its servants.

Thanks to the Veda, everyone in this society knew that the life they led was just one of many. In other lives, past or present, the Shudra of this life would be a Vaishya, and the Kshatriya would be a Brahman, or perhaps a rock or plant or beast, maybe even a god or a demon. Thus everything was interconnected and everything was cyclical. The point of existence in this dynamic, ever-changing world then was not to aspire or achieve, but to introspect.

Then there was a drought, a terrible fourteen-year drought, when the river Saraswati dried up, the society collapsed, and the Veda was all but forgotten. When the rains finally returned, a fisherwoman's son, born out of wedlock, took it upon himself to compile the scattered hymns. His name was Krishna Dwaipayana which means the dark child who was born on a river island. His father was Parasara, grandson of the great Vasishtha, one of the seven Rishis who heard the Veda first. In time, Krishna Dwaipayana became known as Veda Vyasa, compiler of the books of wisdom.

Vyasa classified the hymns and created four collections—Rig, Yajur, Sama and Atharva. On completing this monumental task, Vyasa had this inexplicable urge to write a story, one that would convey the most abstract of Vedic truths to the simplest of men in the farthest corners of the world in the most concrete of forms. The gods liked the idea and sent the elephant-headed Ganesha to serve as his scribe.

Ganesha said, 'You must narrate without a pause.' This would ensure that what Vyasa dictated was not adulterated by human prejudice.

'I will,' said Vyasa, 'provided you write nothing unless it makes sense to you.' This ensured that all that was written appealed to the divine.

The characters of Vyasa's tale were people he knew. The villains, the Kauravas, were in fact his own grandchildren.

Vyasa called his tale Jaya, meaning 'the tale of a victory'. It had sixty portions. Of these, only one part reached humans through Vyasa's student, Vaisampayana. Thus no one really knows everything that Vyasa narrated and Ganesha wrote down.

Vaisampayana narrated Vyasa's tale at the yagna of Janamejaya, the great grandson of the Pandava Arjuna. This was overheard by a Sauti or bard called Romaharshana, who passed it on to his son Ugrashrava, who narrated it to Shonak and the other sages of the Naimisha forest.

Vyasa also narrated the story to his son, the parrot-headed Suka, who narrated it to Parikshit, Janamejaya's father, comforting him with its wisdom as he lay dying.

Jaimini, another of Vyasa's students, also heard his teacher's tale. But he was confused. Since Vyasa was not around to clarify his doubts, Jaimini decided to approach Markandeya, a Rishi blessed with long life, who had witnessed the events that had inspired Vyasa's tale. Unfortunately, by the time Jaimini found Markandeya, the sage had renounced speech as part of his decision to renounce the world. Markandeya's pupils then directed Jaimini to four birds who had witnessed the war at Kuru-kshetra. The mother of these birds was flying over the battlefield when she was struck by an arrow that ripped open her womb. Four eggs fell out and fell to the ground. The ground was bloodsoaked, hence soft. The eggs did not break. The bell of a war-elephant fell on top of them and protected them through the battle. When they were discovered after the war, the Rishis realized the birds had heard much during the war and knew more than most humans. Their perspective and insights would be unique. So they were given the gift of human speech. Thus blessed, these birds were able to talk and clarify Jaimini's doubts. They also told Jaimini many stories that no one else knew.

As Vyasa's tale moved from one storyteller to another, new tales were added, tales of ancestors and descendants, of teachers and students, of friends and foes. The story grew from a tiny sapling into a vast tree with many branches. At first it was about an idea. Then the idea changed and it came to be known as Vijaya. Before long it became not about any idea but about people. It was retitled Bharata, the story of the Bharata clan and the land they ruled.

The expansion continued. Detailed conversations on genealogy, history, geography, astrology, politics, economics, philosophy and metaphysics were included. The Bharata came to have eighteen chapters and over a hundred thousand verses. Even the story of Krishna's early years, the Harivamsa, was added as an appendix. That is how the Bharata came to be the Mahabharata, the 'great' epic of the Indian people.

Over the centuries, the Mahabharata has been retold a hundred thousand times, in temple courtyards and village fairs, in various languages, in different forms, by dancers, singers, painters, wandering minstrels and learned scholars. As the epic spread from Nepal in the north to Indonesia in the south, old plots were changed and new characters emerged. There was Arjuna's son, Iravan, also known as Iravat or Aravan, who was worshipped by the transgender Alis or Aravanis of Tamil Nadu and Bhima's son, Barbareek, who was worshipped in Rajasthan as Khatu Shyamji. In the Mahabharata of Bengal, there surfaced a tale of Draupadi leading an army of women and routing the Kauravas after the death of Abhimanyu. Theyyam performers of Kerala sang of how the Kauravas compelled a sorcerer to perform occult rites against the Pandavas, and how this was reversed by the sorcerer's wife.

In the 20th century, the epic cast its spell on the modern mind. Long essays were written to make rational sense of its moral ambiguity, while its plots were used by novelists, playwrights and film-makers as potent vehicles to comment on numerous political and social issues—from feminism to caste to war. Its wisdom has often been overshadowed by its entertainment value, its complexities oversimplified by well-meaning narrators, leading to ruptures in the traditional discourse.

With so many retellings and so widespread a popularity, some argue that the Mahabharata actually means the tale of the greatness of India, and not the great epic of India, for it contains all that has made Indians what they are—a tolerant people who value inner wisdom over outer achievement.

This book is yet another retelling of the great epic. Inspired by both the Sanskrit classic as well as its regional and folk variants, it is firmly placed in the context of the Puranic worldview. No attempt has been made to rationalize it. Some tales in the epic are sexually explicit, and need to be read by children only under parental guidance. The exile in the forest (Vana Parva), the song of Krishna (Bhagavad Gita) and Bhishma's discourse (Shanti Parva and Anushasan Parva) have had to be summarized, so they remain true to the original only in spirit. The Ashwamedha Parva is based on Jaimini's retelling, hence focuses more on the doctrine of devotion rather than the military campaign.

Shaped by my own prejudices as well as the demands of the modern reader, restructured for the sake of coherence and brevity, this retelling remains firmly rooted in my belief that:

Within infinite myths lies the Eternal Truth
Who sees it all?
Varuna has but a thousand eyes
Indra, a hundred
And I, only two

- Most people believe that the epic was inspired by a real war that was fought amongst nomadic herdsmen, who followed the Vedic way of life and grazed their cattle in the north of modern-day Delhi, probably in what is now the town of Kuru-kshetra in the state of Haryana.
- According to the Aihole inscription of the famous Chalukya king, Pulakesin II, 3735 years had passed since the Mahabharata war. The inscription is dated to 635 CE (Common Era, formerly known as AD), suggesting that the war was believed by ancient Indians to have taken place in 3102 BCE (before Common Era, formerly known as BC).
- Based on astronomical data found in the epic—that two eclipses separated by thirteen days took place around the war—some have dated the events of the Mahabharata to around 3000 BCE. Others have dated it to around 1500 BCE. There is no consensus among scholars in this matter.
- The fourteen-year drought, the drying of the river Saraswati and the loss of Veda is a recurring theme in the scriptures. This is perhaps a real event that led to the collapse of the Indus Valley civilization in 1500 BCE, as indicated by some geological studies, or maybe it is a metaphysical event, when the core of Vedic thought was lost and all that remained were customs and rituals bereft of wisdom.
- Around the time the Mahabharata reached its final form, Bhasa wrote plays on the Mahabharata in Sanskrit which have plots that are often quite different from those in the epic.
- The 16th century Mughal Emperor, Akbar, got the Mahabharata translated into Persian and his court painters illustrated the tales. It is called the Razmnama or the Book of War.
- The Sanskrit Mahabharata makes no reference to the Rashi or Zodiac, the twelve solar houses of astrology. It refers only to Nakshatra, the twenty-seven lunar houses of astrology. Scholars conclude that Nakshatra is native to India while Rashi came from the West, perhaps Babylon. Rashi became part of Indian astrology only after 300 CE, confirming that the Sanskrit text reached its final form latest by 300 CE after centuries of oral transmission.

Who narrated the epic?	Who heard the epic?
Vyasa	Ganesha, Jaimini, Vaisampayana, Suka
Vaisampayana	Janamejaya, Romaharshana
Romaharshana	Ugrashrava (Sauti)
Ugrashrava (Sauti)	Shonak
Suka	Parikshit
Four birds	Jaimini

Vyasa's family line

Brahma
↓
Vasishtha
↓
Shaktri
↓
Parasara
↓
Vyasa
↓
Dhritarashtra
↓
Duryodhana
↓
Lakshman

Structure of Vyasa's Epic

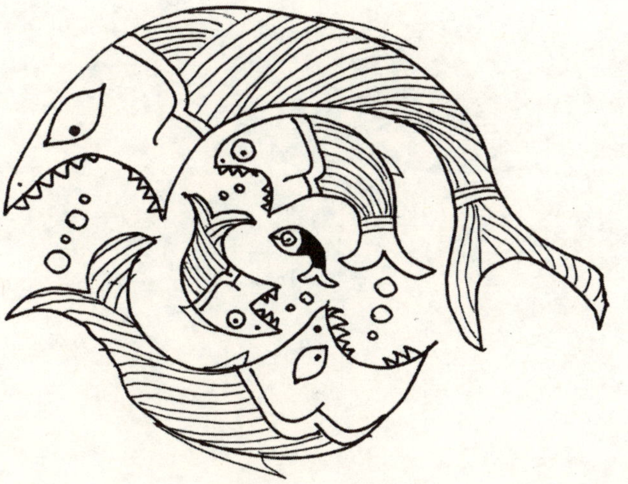

Chapter or Parva	Original Title	Number of Verses	Meaning of the Title	Original Content
1	Adi	9984	Primal	Introducing the characters and tales right up to the rise of the Pandava kingdom of Indra-prastha.
2	Sabha	4311	Assembly	Gambling match in which the Pandavas lose their fortune.
3	Vana	13,664	Forest	Twelve years of forest exile.
4	Virata	3500	King of Matsya	Final year in hiding in Matsya.
5	Udyoga	6998	Effort	Negotiations for peace.
6	Bhishma	5884	First Kaurava commander	First ten days of battle including Bhagavad Gita.
7	Drona	10,919	Second Kaurava commander	Next five days of battle.
8	Karna	4900	Third Kaurava commander	Next two days of battle.
9	Shalya	3220	Fourth Kaurava commander	Eighteenth day of battle.
10	Sauptika	2870	Slumber	The ambush on the eighteenth night.
11	Stree	1775	Women	Wailing of widows.
12	Shanti	14,525	Peace	Discourse on peace.
13	Anushasan	12,000	Discipline	Discourse on organization.
14	Ashwamedha	4420	Conquest	Pandavas establish their dominion.

15	Ashrama	1106	Retirement	The elders retire.
16	Mausala	300	Mace	End of Krishna's clan.
17	Mahapras-thanika	120	Renunciation	Pandavas retire.
18	Swarga-rohanika	200	Ascent to heaven	Yudhishtira's challenge when he reaches Indra's paradise.
Appendix	Harivamsa	16,423	Hari's family	The early life of Hari (Krishna).

- The Mahabharata is actually the consequence of a complaint made by the earth in the form of a cow to her cowherd, Govinda, who is Vishnu, the guardian of earth. So says the Vishnu Purana. Thus the epic is part of a greater narrative. It cannot be seen in isolation.
- The Mahabharata in its current form has eighteen sections, of which the first section establishes the context of the rivalry between the Pandavas and the Kauravas. The next three build up to the war. Then come six sections describing the war in detail, followed by eight sections describing the emotional, material and spiritual consequences of the war.
- The Hebrew word for life has a numerical value of 18. Thus the tradition has arisen in Jewish circles to give monetary gifts in multiples of 18 as an expression of blessings for a long life. In the Chinese tradition, the sound of the number 18 resembles the sound of the word meaning prosperity. Consequently, building floors numbered 18 tend to be very expensive as they come with the promise of fortune.
- The epic is made of one hundred thousand verses, making it an epic longer than the Greek epics Iliad and Odyssey put together.
- A third of the verses are devoted to the war. The verses before the war are devoted to tales of romance, sex, childbearing and other worldly issues, while the verses after the war dwell on the meaning of it all and tilt towards spirituality.
- In the Hindu tradition, purushartha or the validation of human existence has four aspects, dharma, artha, kama and moksha, that is, social conduct, economic activities, pleasurable pursuits and spiritual activities. Through the tales of the Mahabharata, Vyasa draws equal attention to all four aspects of human existence, making it a complete epic.

PROLOGUE

The Start of the Snake Sacrifice

The king of Hastina-puri, Parikshit, scion of the Kuru clan, had locked himself in a tall tower that rose in the centre of his great kingdom. He had isolated himself from his wives, and his children, and his subjects. He was terrified. He paced night and day, unable to eat or sleep. Bards were sent to tell him tales that would soothe his soul, but nothing could allay his fear.

There were whispers on the streets, 'Our king's grandfather was the great Arjuna, who defeated the Kauravas in Kuru-kshetra. His father was Abhimanyu who single-handedly broke the Chakra-vyuha, most complex of battle formations. With such an illustrious lineage, he should be afraid of nothing. Yet he cowers in his tower. Why?'

'I am cursed to die in seven days of snakebite,' the king finally revealed. 'Keep them away. Let not one slithering Naga come close to me. I don't want to die.' Guards kept watch on every door and every window of the tower, ready to strike down any serpent who even dared turn in the direction of the king. Everything that entered the tower was searched; Nagas could hide anywhere.

Six nights later, on the seventh day, a famished Parikshit bit into a fruit; hidden within was a worm that instantly transformed into a fearsome serpent. It was the Naga Takshaka!

Takshaka sprang forward and sank his deadly fangs into Parikshit's flesh. The venom spread rapidly; Parikshit cried out in agony but before any of the guards could come to his aid, he was dead and the Naga had slithered away.

Parikshit's son, Janamejaya, was furious. 'I will avenge the killing of my innocent father,' he said. He ordered all the Brahmans of his kingdom to perform the Sarpa Sattra, a sacrificial ritual with the power to destroy all the snakes on earth.

Soon a fire blazed in the centre of Hastina-puri and a plume of black smoke rose to the sky. Around the altar sat hundreds of priests pouring spoonfuls of ghee to stoke the flames. They chanted strange magical hymns and invoked invisible forces that dragged the Nagas out of their subterranean homes into the pit of fire. Hastina-puri saw swarms of wriggling serpents in the skies being drawn towards the sacrificial hall. The air was filled with the heart-wrenching cries of snakes being roasted alive. Some people were filled with pity, and cried, 'This is a mindless massacre.' Others screamed in righteous indignation, 'Serves them right for killing our king.'

Then, from the horizon a youth shouted, 'Stop, king! This is adharma.'

'How dare you accuse me of adharma,' roared Janamejaya. 'Who are you?'

'I am Astika, nephew of Vasuki, king of the Nagas.'

'No wonder you want to save the Nagas. You are one of them!' said the king, his tone accusative.

'My father was the Rishi Jaratkaru, a Manava like you. My mother was a Naga. I am you and your enemy, human and serpent. I take no sides. Listen to what I have to say, otherwise you will deny peace to all your descendants.'

'Speak,' said the king.

'Seven days before he died,' said Astika, 'your father was out on a hunt when he experienced great thirst. He saw a sage sitting under a banyan tree and asked him for some water. But the sage was deep in meditation and did not respond to the royal request. Annoyed, Parikshit picked up a dead snake and placed it round the Rishi's neck. The Rishi's student, who saw this from afar, could not bear his teacher being insulted so. He cursed Parikshit that he would die within seven days of snakebite. Thus you see, Janamejaya, your father brought his death upon himself.'

'And Takshaka? Why did he bite my father?'

Astika responded with another tale. 'Long ago, Arjuna, your great grandfather, set aflame a forest called Khandava-prastha to clear land for the city of Indra-prastha. That forest was the home of many Nagas. Its burning left Takshaka and many like him homeless and orphaned. Takshaka swore to make Arjuna, or one of his descendants, pay. The killing of your father was his revenge. Now the Nagas burn once more in your sacrificial hall. More orphans will be created. More vengeance will be wreaked. You do what your ancestors did. And you too, like them, will suffer as they suffered. Blood will flow and widows will weep, as they once did in Kuru-kshetra. Is that what you want, Janamejaya?'

Astika's question boomed across the sacrificial hall. The chanting stopped. The fire stilled. Silence descended as curious eyes fell on the king.

Janamejaya pulled back his shoulders and replied with conviction, 'I do this for justice.'

Astika retorted passionately, 'Takshaka killed your father for justice. You kill the Nagas for justice. The orphans you create by this yagna will also crave for justice.

Who decides what justice is? How does one end this unending spiral of revenge where everyone believes they are right and their opponents are wrong?'

Janamejaya was silent. He pondered over what Astika had said. Then he asked, with a little hesitation, 'Did the Pandavas not fight the Kauravas for justice?'

Astika replied, 'No, my king. That war was about dharma. And dharma is not about justice; it is about empathy and wisdom. Dharma is not about defeating others, it is about conquering ourselves. Everybody wins in dharma. When the war at Kuru-kshetra concluded even the Kauravas went to paradise.'

'What!'

'Yes. The Kauravas, reviled as villains by you and your forefathers, went to Swarga, that abode of pleasure where the gods reside.'

'And the Pandavas?' asked the king, disturbed by this revelation.

'They went to Naraka, that realm of pain.'

'I never knew this.'

'There is so much you don't know, my king. You may have inherited the kingdom of the Pandavas but not their wisdom. You do not even know the true meaning of dharma that was revealed to Arjuna by God himself.'

'God?'

'Yes, God. Krishna!'

'Tell me more.'

'Send for Vaisampayana,' said Astika, 'Ask him to narrate the tale that was composed by his teacher, Vyasa, and written down by Ganesha. It is the tale of your forefathers, and all those kings who came before them.'

Messengers were sent to fetch Vaisampayana, guardian of Vyasa's great tale. When Vaisampayana finally arrived, he saw in the sacrificial hall thousands of serpents suspended above a sacrificial fire, hundreds of priests around the altar impatient to complete their ritual, and a king curious about his ancestry.

The storyteller-sage was made to sit on a deer skin. A garland of flowers was placed around his neck, a pot of water and a basket of fruits were placed before him. Pleased with this hospitality, Vaisampayana began his tale of the Pandavas and the Kauravas and of all the kings who ruled the land known as Bharata. This was the Jaya, later to be known as the Mahabharata.

'Listen to the tale carefully, Janamejaya,' Astika whispered in the king's ear, 'Do not be distracted by the plots. Within the maze of stories flows the river of wisdom. That is your true inheritance.'

- In the Vedic age that thrived around 1000 BCE, yagna was the dominant ritual that bound society. It was performed by specially trained priests who chanted hymns and made offerings into fire in a bid to invoke cosmic forces and make them do man's bidding. A Sattra was a yagna performed on a grand scale with hundreds of priests over several years.
- While rituals helped man cope with the many material challenges of the world, they did not offer man any spiritual explanations about life. For that stories were needed. And so, during yagnas, and between them, bards were called to entertain and enlighten the priests and their patrons with tales. In due course, the tales were given more value than the yagna. In fact, by 500 CE, the yagna was almost abandoned. Sacred tales of gods, kings and sages became the foundation of Hindu thought.
- The Mahabharata is populated not only by Manavas or humans but also by a variety of beings such as Devas who live in the sky, Asuras who live under the earth, Apsaras or nymphs who live in rivers, hooded serpents who talk called Nagas, forest spirits called Yakshas, warrior-musicians of the woods called Gandharvas and brute barbarians called Rakshasas. Some like Asuras and Rakshasas

were hostile to humans and hence deemed demons, while others like Devas and Gandharvas were friendly hence worshipped as gods and demi-gods. The Nagas had an ambiguous status, sometimes feared and sometimes worshipped. Rationalists speculate that these various non-human races were perhaps non-Vedic tribes that were gradually assimilated into the Vedic fold.

- It is said that the chief priest, Uttanaka, who was conducting the Sarpa Sattra had his own grouse against the Nagas. As part of his tuition fee, his teacher had asked him to give his wife the jewelled earrings of a queen. With great difficulty, Uttanaka had managed to get such earrings but these were stolen by the Nagas. To avenge that theft, Uttanaka wanted to perform the Sarpa Sattra. But he did not have the wherewithal to conduct it. King Janamejaya, in his quest to avenge his father's death, inadvertently provided him with the opportunity. Thus while Janamejaya thought his was the only reason for the sacrifice, he was mistaken. There were many besides him who wanted to destroy the Nagas.

Janamejaya's family line

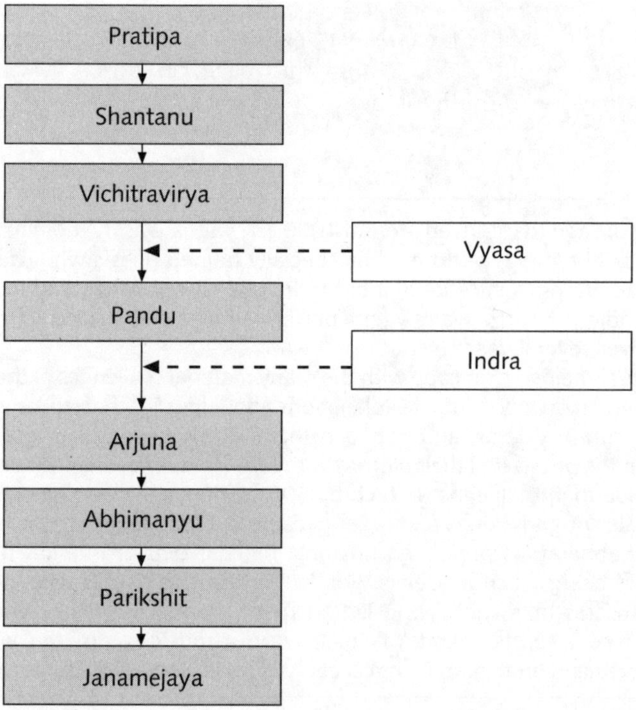

BOOK ONE

Ancestors

'Janamejaya, what happened before repeated itself again and again in your family history.'

Chandra's son

When a man dies, he can, if he has earned enough merit, enter the paradise of the gods located high above the clouds. Humans call this realm Swarga. Its residents, the Devas, know it as the city of Amravati. Here there is no pain or suffering; all dreams are fulfilled and all wishes are granted.

To sustain this delight, the Devas have to at regular intervals defeat their eternal enemies, the Asuras, who live under the earth. Their victory depends on the power of yagna. Brihaspati, god of the planet Jupiter, performs the yagna for the Devas. For the ritual to be successful, Brihaspati needs his wife, Tara, goddess of the stars, to sit by his side.

But one day, Tara left Brihaspati's side and eloped with the moon-god, Chandra. Tara had grown tired of her analytical husband, who was more interested in ritual than her. She had fallen in love with the passionate Chandra who adored her.

'Bring my wife back if you want the yagna to succeed,' said Brihaspati to Indra, king of the Devas.

The Devas were divided: should they force Tara to return to her husband, who saw her merely as an instrument of ritual, or should she be allowed to stay with her lover, who made her feel alive? After much debate, pragmatism prevailed. The yagna of the Devas was more important than the happiness of Tara; without the power of yagna, the Devas would be unable to shower the earth with light and rain. Without yagna, there would be darkness and drought on earth. No, Tara had to return to Brihaspati. This was Indra's final decision.

Tara returned reluctantly. When she came, it was clear she was with child. Both Chandra and Brihaspati claimed to be the father. Tara remained silent, stubbornly refusing to give out the identity of the man who had made her pregnant. Then, to everyone's astonishment, the unborn child cried out, 'Tell me mother, of which seed am I fruit? I deserve to know.'

Everyone assembled was impressed by the unborn child's desire to know the truth. They declared this child would be the lord of Buddhi, the intellect, that part of the mind which enables one to distinguish truth from falsehood and thereby make choices. He would be called Budh.

Compelled by her child, Tara lowered her eyes and said, 'You spring from Chandra's seed.'

Hearing this, Brihaspati lost control over his dispassionate disposition and lashed out in rage, 'May this love-child of my unfaithful wife be of neuter gender, neither male nor female.'

The gods were horrified by this cruel curse. Indra intervened in his capacity as king. 'The child you so contemptuously cursed, Brihaspati, will henceforth be known as your son, not Chandra's. It does not matter who sowed the seed in the field; what matters more is who the master of the field is. As Tara's lawfully wedded husband, you are the master, the father of all of her children, those born after marriage or before, by you or by anyone else.'

So it came to pass, Tara gave birth to Budh, lord of planet Mercury, a shape-shifting liminal being, neither male nor female. Biologically, he descended from the emotional Chandra but as per Indra's decree, he was raised in the house of the logical Brihaspati.

Since that day, law took precedence over natural phenomena in heaven and on earth; fatherhood was defined by marriage. That is why Janamejaya's great grandfather, Arjuna, would be called a son of Pandu even though Pandu was incapable of fathering children.

- For humans, the Amravati of the Devas is the paradise of pleasure that one can go to if one lives a meritorious life.
- Muthuswami Dikshitar, the 18th century doyen of Carnatic music, in his kriti dedicated to the Nava-grahas, or nine celestial bodies of astrology, refers to Mercury as being neuter. In many images of Nava-grahas, Budh is sometimes shown as male and sometimes as female, suggesting his nature is mercurial.
- The Devas are sky-gods, the enemies of Asuras who live under the earth. Their fights are endless. Their alternating victory and defeat ensure the rhythmic change of seasons.
- In art, Budh rides a Yali, a mythical creature that has the head of an elephant but the body of a lion, a reminder of his liminal nature.

A wife for Budh

As Budh grew up he wondered if he would find anyone to share his life, for he was neither man nor woman. 'We will get you married,' Tara said with confidence.

'To whom, mother, a husband or a wife?' asked Budh.

'Whatever fate considers appropriate,' said Tara. 'Everything in this world happens for a purpose. Your father's curse must have a reason. It will all work out. Have faith.'

Sure enough, one day Budh saw a woman called Ila, and fell in love.

But Ila was no woman; she was once a man, a prince called Sudyumna, son of Manu, the first king of humans.

One day Sudyumna had ridden into a forest over which the great hermit Shiva had cast a spell that turned all male creatures into females. Lions of the forest had turned into lionesses and peacocks into peahens. Shiva had done this to please his consort, Shakti, who did not want any male, animal or human, to disturb her when she was in the company of her lord. When Sudyumna realized that he had lost his manhood in the forest, he begged the goddess to restore it. 'I cannot undo Shiva's spell,' she said, 'but I will modify it so that you will be a woman only when the moon wanes and a man when the moon waxes.'

Budh who was neither male nor female found a perfect spouse in Ila who was both male and female. Together they had many sons. They were called the Ailas, the descendants of Ila. They were also called the Chandra-vamsis, descendants of the moon, a title that did not quite please either Brihaspati or the Devas. This is why perhaps logical reasoning often eluded the passionate kings of this lineage.

In time, the Chandra-vamsis would forget the gender ambiguity of both Budh and Ila. They would mock it when it would become manifest in Arjuna's brother-in-law, Shikhandi. They would stop him from entering the battlefield. Such is the nature of man-made laws: ignorant of the past and insensitive to the present.

- The Mahabharata tells the stories of the Chandra-vamsis, descendants of the moon, or rather Budh-vamsis, descendants of Mercury, who were infamous for their moral ambiguity, and quite different in character from the upright Surya-vamsis, descendants of the sun, whose tales are told in the Ramayana.
- Boons and curses are an integral part of Hindu mythology. They are rooted in the concept of karma that states that all actions have reactions that one is obliged to experience in this life or the next. Actions that yield positive results are punya; in narratives they take the shape of boons. Actions that yield negative results are paap; in narratives they take the form of curses. Punya is spiritual merit that generates fortune and paap is spiritual demerit that generates misfortune. The concept of paap and punya is meant to explain why bad and good things happen in the world.
- The story of Ila being both male and female is found in the Mahabharata and in many Puranas. In some retellings, Ila is called the daughter of Manu. While performing a yagna for a son, Manu mispronounced the magic formula and ended up with a daughter instead.
- Manu was the son of Surya, the sun-god. Besides Ila, Manu had another son called Ikshavaku whose descendants came to be known as Surya-vamsis, or the solar line of kings. This line included Ram, prince of Ayodhya, whose tale is told in the Ramayana.
- The story of the star-goddess' tryst with the moon-god attempts to explain the behaviour of lunar kings through Jyotish-shastra, or Vedic astrology. Moon is associated with emotions, Jupiter with rationality and Mercury with clarity, communication and cunning. The story suggests that the Chandra-vamsis were by nature rather emotional, a trait that needed to be contained by logic.

Pururava's obsession

Pururava, a Chandra-vamsi, once saw Urvashi bathing in a river. Urvashi was an Apsara, a river-nymph, who lived with the gods and only occasionally stepped on earth. She was so beautiful that when she walked, all the animals stopped to gaze at her; every tree, every bush, every blade of grass reached out to touch her. Pururava fell in love with her. 'Marry me,' he said. 'Be my queen and live in my palace.'

In a spirit of play, the nymph indulged the king and said, 'Only if you promise to take care of my pet goats and never let anyone but I see you naked.' To her great surprise the mortal Pururava agreed, leaving her no choice but to become his wife.

It was a new experience for Urvashi and she enjoyed it. She bore her human husband many sons.

It is said that the lifetime of man is just a blink of Indra's eye. And yet, Indra could not bear this momentary separation from Urvashi. He ordered the celestial musicians known as Gandharvas to bring her back.

The Gandharvas stole Urvashi's pet goats from under her bed while Pururava was busy making love to her. Urvashi saw this from the corner of her eye and

cried in a stricken voice, 'My goats! Someone is stealing my goats! Keep your promise, husband, and bring them back.'

Pururava immediately jumped off the bed and ran to catch the thieves without bothering to cover himself. As he ran out of the palace behind the thieves, Indra hurled a thunderbolt across the sky. In the flash of the lightning, everyone in the city saw Pururava naked. The condition that kept Urvashi on earth, away from the gods, was as a result broken. It was time for her to return to Amravati.

Without Urvashi, a heartbroken Pururava became mad and could not rule. Such is the power of passion. The Rishis were forced to replace him with one of his more disciplined sons, one more fit to rule.

Some say, Pururava still weeps in the forest and scours the riverbanks in search of Urvashi. Others say, she has turned him into a Gandharva and he follows her wherever she goes as music maker to her dance.

The obsessive passion of Pururava for Urvashi that led to his downfall would become manifest generations later in Shantanu, not once but twice, first in his love for Ganga and then his love for Satyavati, with the same disastrous consequences. Because human memory is short, and history always repeats itself.

- Apsa means water and so Apsara means a water-nymph. Water comes to earth from the heavens in the form of rain and returns after a brief stay. This water sustains life on earth. Thus the story symbolically refers to the craving of man (Pururava) for water (Urvashi) that comes from, and eventually returns to, the sky (Indra).
- Urvashi lays down conditions that have to be met before she accepts any man as husband. It suggests a pre-patriarchal society where women were mistresses of their own sexuality. In Vedic society, women were considered extremely valuable because only through them could a man father a child, repay his debt to his ancestors and keep rotating the cycle of rebirths.
- Pururava's yearning for the elusive and ethereal Urvashi forms a dialogue that is recorded in the Rig Veda, the oldest Vedic text, dated conservatively to 1500 BCE. In Kalidasa's play, *Vikramorvasiyam*, written in 500 CE, two thousand years later, Pururava is a dashing king who does not chase the nymph. It is she who chases him; the gods allow her to stay with him provided he never sees the child she bears him. Urvashi therefore secretly delivers the child while he is away attending a yagna, and requests the sage Chyavana to raise him in secret. Years later, the inevitable happens: the father sees the son and the nymph returns to the abode of the gods. After a long period of separation, Indra lets Urvashi return to Pururava because he needs Pururava's help in his battles against the Asuras.

- According to the Kalpasutra, Pururava's first son by Urvashi, Ayu, established the kingdom of Kuru-panchala in the east while their second son, Amavasu, established the kingdom of Gandhara in the west. These kingdoms set the stage for the great war at Kuru-kshetra.

Shakuntala's innocence

A king called Kaushika, a Surya-vamsi or descendant of the sun, wanted to become a Rishi. So he gave up his material possessions, took the vow of celibacy and started performing ascetic practices known as tapasya. If successful, he would become more powerful than any man, or god.

Fearing that Kaushika intended to displace him, Indra sent an Apsara called Menaka to distract Kaushika. Of all the damsels in Amravati, Menaka was the most beautiful. Kaushika lost all control of his senses when she danced before him. He abandoned his tapasya, forgot his vow of celibacy, and surrendered to passion. From that union of hermit and nymph was born a girl.

The child was abandoned on the forest floor by both her parents; by her father because she represented his monumental failure and by her mother because she was nothing more than proof of her success.

A Rishi called Kanva found the abandoned girl under the wings of a flock of Shakun birds who had surrounded her. So he named her Shakuntala, she who was found sheltered by birds. Kanva raised Shakuntala as his own daughter in his hermitage in the forest, and she grew up to be a very beautiful and cultured woman.

One day, Dushyanta, descendant of Pururava, arrived at Kanva's hermitage. He was hunting in the forest and wanted to pay his respects to the sage, and maybe rest for a few days in the hermitage. Unfortunately, Kanva was away on a pilgrimage; he found himself being welcomed by Shakuntala. Dushyanta fell in love with Shakuntala instantly.

'Marry me,' he said, unable to control his desire.

'Ask my father,' said a coy Shakuntala.

'If you wish, we can marry as the Gandharvas do with the trees as our witness. This is allowed by tradition,' said Dushyanta. The innocent Shakuntala, smitten by the handsome king, agreed.

So the two got married with the trees as their witness and spent days in the hermitage making love. Finally, it was time for Dushyanta to return home. Kanva had still not returned and Dushyanta could not wait any longer. 'It is not right to take you with me while he is away. I will return when he is back,' he promised.

Many weeks later Kanva returned. No sooner did he enter his hermitage than he realized his daughter was in love, and that she was carrying her beloved's child. He was overjoyed. Both celebrated the event and waited for Dushyanta to return. Days turned into weeks. Weeks turned into months. There was no sign of Dushyanta.

In due course, Shakuntala gave birth to a son who was named Bharata. Bharata grew up in the care of Kanva and Shakuntala. Father and daughter forgot all about Dushyanta's promise until Bharata one day asked, 'Who is my father?'

'He needs to know,' said Kanva.

Rather than wait for Dushyanta to send an invitation, Kanva felt it was best that Shakuntala go to Dushyanta on her own and introduce the boy to his father. Shakuntala agreed and, with her son by her side, ventured out of the forest for the first time. As she left, the trees gifted her with cloth and flowers and fragrances so that she looked beautiful when she met her beloved again.

But when Shakuntala stood before Dushyanta and introduced herself and her son, Dushyanta showed no sign of recognizing her. 'Are there any witnesses of our alleged marriage?' he asked caustically.

'The trees,' she said.

Everyone including Dushyanta laughed. Shakuntala, a simple woman of the forest, uncontaminated by the politics of kings and kingdoms, was indignant. 'I came here not seeking a husband but to show my son his father. I have done so. I have raised him as a mother should. Now, I request you to raise him as a father should.' So saying, Shakuntala turned her back to Dushyanta and proceeded for the forest.

Suddenly, a voice boomed from the sky admonishing Dushyanta for doubting Shakuntala. She was indeed his wife and Bharata was indeed his son. Dushyanta apologized for his behaviour and blamed it all on his fear of social disapproval. He then declared Shakuntala his queen and Bharata his heir.

Bharata was one of those unique kings who descended from the solar line of kings through his mother, Shakuntala, and from the lunar line of kings through his father, Dushyanta. Since his descendants ruled all of Jambudvipa, the rose-apple continent of India, the land itself was named Bharata-varsha, or simply Bharata, after him.

- Tapa means spiritual fire that is generated through ascetic practices known as tapasya. The conflict between a Tapasvin or fire-churning hermit and an Apsara or water-nymph is a recurring theme in the scriptures. It is the conflict between spirituality and sensuality. Spirituality earns merit and gives one access to the pleasures of the world, but indulgence in sensual pleasures causes loss of merit. Hence, there is constantly a conflict between the hermit and the nymph.
- Shakuntala's story in the Mahabharata is quite different from Kalidasa's very popular Sanskrit play written around 500 CE. In Kalidasa's play, Shakuntala is brought to Dushyanta as soon as her father discovers she is pregnant but due to a Rishi's curse Dushyanta is unable to recollect her. In Vyasa's epic, Shakuntala comes to Dushyanta years later when her son enquires who his father is—Dushyanta pretends not to recognize her to protect his reputation. Kalidasa's Shakuntala seeks her husband while Mahabharata's Shakuntala seeks her son's father. Kalidasa's Shakuntala is very conscious of social stigma while Mahabharata's Shakuntala is indifferent to it. This perhaps is a reflection of change in social values over time.

Bharata's heir

Bharata grew up to be a great king. He had three wives. Every time they presented a son to him, he would say, 'He does not look like me,' or 'He does not behave like me,' perhaps suggesting his wives were unfaithful to him or that the children were unworthy. In fear, Bharata's wives abandoned these children.

A time came when Bharata was old and had no heirs. So he performed a yagna. At the end of the yagna, the Devas gave him a son called Vitatha.

Vitatha was conceived when Brihaspati, in an uncharacteristic moment of lust, had forced himself on his sister-in-law, Mamata, wife of Utathya.

Both Brihaspati and Mamata rejected this child, Brihaspati because the child reminded him of his moment of weakness and Mamata because this child was forced upon her. Vitatha was thus, like Shakuntala, a child abandoned by his parents. He was accepted by the Devas who passed him on to Bharata.

Vitatha grew up to be an extremely capable ruler and so despite being adopted, was crowned king by Bharata.

For Bharata the criteria for kingship rested in worthiness, not bloodline. This made Bharata the noblest of kings in the eyes of the people. This was, perhaps, another reason why the rose-apple continent of Jambudvipa came to be known as Bharata-varsha, or simply Bharat, the land that was once ruled by one such as Bharata.

Later kings did not follow in Bharata's footsteps. Dhritarashtra preferred his son, Duryodhana, over his nephew, Yudhishtira, even though the latter was clearly more worthy.

- The epic states that when Brihaspati came to Mamata she turned him away not because she was married to another man, his brother Utathya, but because she was already pregnant. This perhaps reveals an ancient practice of sharing wives between brothers.
- The child in Mamata's womb is cursed that he will be born blind. So is born a sage called Dirghatamas. Dirghatamas has a wife called Pradweshi who tired of taking care of her blind husband has her sons throw him into the river. Dirghatamas survives by clinging to a tree trunk and is found by a childless king, Vali, who requests Dirghatamas to go to his wife Sudeshna and make her pregnant. So are born the kings who rule the eastern kingdoms of Anga, Vanga and Kalinga.
- The story of Vitatha, which comes from a slip of a verse in the scriptures, draws attention to a question that bothered Vyasa: Who should be king? The son of a king or any worthy man? This theme recurs through the epic.

Yayati's demand

Sarmishtha was the daughter of Vishaparva, king of the Asuras and Devayani was the daughter of Shukra, guru of the Asuras. They were both the best of friends. But one day they had a fight.

After a swim in a pond, while dressing up hurriedly, Devayani wore Sarmishtha's robes by mistake. A livid Sarmishtha called Devayani a thief and her father a beggar. She then pushed Devayani into a well and walked away in a royal huff.

When Devayani returned home late in the evening, she related the events to her father and raised a storm of tears and wailing until her father promised he would teach the Asura princess a lesson. 'Until the king apologizes for his daughter's behaviour, I will not perform any yagna for them,' said Shukra.

Vishaparva begged Shukra to change his mind and restart the yagnas; without them he was powerless against his eternal enemies, the Devas. 'I will,' said Shukra, 'but only if you punish your venom-tongued daughter. Make Sarmishtha my daughter's maid and I will return to your sacrificial hall.'

Vishaparva had no choice but to agree. The princess Sarmishtha was thus made to serve Devayani as her lady-in-waiting. This humiliation, however, turned out to be a blessing in disguise.

It so happened that the man who had rescued Devayani from the well she had been pushed into by Sarmishtha was Yayati, a Chandra-vamsi. During the rescue, Yayati had held Devayani by her hand. 'As you have held me, a virgin, by my hand, you are obliged to take me as your wife,' said Devayani to Yayati, quoting the scriptures.

'So be it,' said Yayati, who was equally well informed about the scriptures. He came to Shukra's hermitage, and with his blessings took Devayani to his kingdom as his lawfully wedded wife.

'Let my maid accompany me,' said Devayani, eager to continue the humiliation of Sarmishtha.

'As you wish, my queen,' said Yayati. Sarmishtha had no choice but to accompany Devayani to her husband's house as a maid.

One day, Sarmishtha caught the eye of Yayati. It was love at first sight. Unlike Devayani, who had priestly blood in her veins, Sarmishtha had royal blood in her veins, and spirit to match. And this pleased Yayati greatly. The two got married secretly and even had children.

Devayani had no knowledge of this; Sarmishtha managed to convince her that her lover was a palace guard. But one day, Devayani heard Sarmishtha's son refer to Yayati as father. Realizing she had been duped both by her husband and her maid, an enraged Devayani left the palace and ran back to her father and once again, at her behest, Shukra promised to teach her husband a lesson.

Shukra cursed Yayati, 'You will become old and impotent.' The curse took immediate effect. But it was soon clear that the one most to suffer from the curse was Devayani herself. An old and weak husband is of no value to anyone! Shukra, however, could not reverse his curse. All he could do was modify it. 'You will regain your youth and your potency, Yayati, if one of your sons accepts the curse on your behalf.'

Yayati immediately sent for his sons. Yadu, the eldest son, born of Devayani, refused to suffer on his father's behalf. 'Is it not against dharma to reverse the march of time, make the son renounce the world when it is time for the father to do so?' he asked.

Yayati then turned to Puru, his youngest son, born of Sarmishtha. Puru agreed.

So it came to pass that Puru suffered old age while his father enjoyed his youth. He coughed and stammered and stooped on a stick while Yayati embraced his wives and went on hunts and fought wars.

Years later, realizing that youth and virility do not bring contentment, Yayati relieved Puru from the effects of his curse.

When the time came to announce a successor, Yayati declared Puru, though youngest, as his heir. 'Because he suffered for me,' explained Yayati. Yadu, though eldest, was not only denied the throne but also cursed, 'Since you refused to suffer for your father, neither you nor your descendants will ever be kings.'

An indignant Yadu left Yayati's kingdom and travelled south to Mathura, the kingdom of the Naga people. There his beauty and mannerisms impressed a Naga called Dhumravarna. 'Marry my daughters. Be my son-in-law. Make Mathura your home,' he said. Yadu agreed because the Nagas of Mathura had no king; they were ruled by a council of elders through the system of consensus. This suited him well. Cursed, he could not be king. Still, in Mathura, he could be ruler. Yadu married Dhumravarna's daughters and they bore him children from whom descended various tribes such as the Andhakas, the Bhojakas and the Vrishnis. Collectively, these descendants of Yadu were called the Yadavas.

Krishna would be born in the Yadava clan. Like other Yadavas, he would never be king, only a kingmaker.

Puru became the patriarch of the illustrious Kuru clan. From him descended the Kauravas and the Pandavas.

The curse of Yayati sowed the seeds of the war that would take place much later in Kuru-kshetra: for it gave greater value to a son's obedience than to the natural march of generations. Inspired by this event, Bhishma would sacrifice his own conjugal life to enable his old father to remarry.

- The alternating fortunes of Devayani and Sarmishtha draw attention to the nature of karma—what seems like bad luck (Devayani being pushed into a well, Sarmishtha being reduced to a maid) ends up as good luck (Devayani finds a husband, Sarmishtha finds love). Even Shukra's curse does not have the desired effect—it punishes the daughter more than the son-in-law. Thus no one on earth can foretell the consequences of any action, however wise he may be.
- The psychoanalyst Freud proposed the theory of the Oedipus complex based on Greek myths to explain the human need to compete with the father for the mother's affections. The son always triumphs over the father and is consequently consumed by guilt. Indian psychoanalysts believe that this concept is inadequate in the Indian context, where the tendency is for the son to submit to the father and be revered for it. They have proposed the theory of the Yayati complex instead where the father demands and secures a sacrifice from the son. In the Greek worldview, dominated by the Oedipus complex, it is the next generation which inherits society, while in the Indian worldview, dominated by the Yayati complex, it is the older generation which always dominates society, explaining the stranglehold of tradition over modernity in Indian society.

- Though the Chandra-vamsis originally sprang from Devas, Yayati's marriage to the daughters of an Asura king and an Asura priest, and the marriage of Yadu to Naga women, indicate the mingling of races and tribes. Janamejaya, who performed a sacrifice to kill the Nagas, was actually killing a race of people related to his ancestors by marriage.
- In Vedic times, men were allowed to marry women who belonged to their station in life or to those who belonged to lower stations. Yayati's marriage to Devayani is a departure; she is the daughter of a priest hence of higher station. This was a pratiloma marriage—inappropriate according to the scriptures. His association with Sarmishtha, a princess-maid, was an anuloma marriage and was deemed more appropriate as it was with a woman of inferior rank. Puru, the child of Sarmishtha, is therefore projected as a more suitable son than Yadu, son of Devayani.
- Historians believe that the ruling council of Mathura indicates that the Nagas were a tribe that followed an early form of democracy. Perhaps they were descendants of or related to Indo-Greeks who settled in India following the invasion of Alexander.
- The story of the descendants of Yadu through Naga women comes from Karavir Mahatmya that narrates the local legends of Kolhapur, the temple town of Maharashtra. It is narrated to Krishna by a Yadava elder called Vikadru.

Madhavi's forgiveness

Yayati had a daughter called Madhavi who was destined to be the mother of four kings. One day, a sage called Galava came to Yayati and asked for eight hundred white horses with one black ear, which he wished to give to his guru, Vishwamitra.

Yayati did not have these horses. Not wanting to turn the sage away empty-handed, he offered the sage his daughter, Madhavi. 'Offer her to four men who want to be the father of a king and ask them for two hundred such horses in exchange,' said Yayati.

Accordingly, Galava offered Madhavi to the kings of the earth. Three kings accepted the offer: they begat sons on

Madhavi, enabling Galava to obtain six hundred horses. Finally, he went to his teacher and said, 'Here are six hundred of the eight hundred horses that you wanted. You can beget a son on this maiden, Madhavi, daughter of Yayati, and that will be equal to the remaining two hundred horses.' Vishwamitra accepted the horses and the maiden and fathered a son on her. Thus was Galava's fee repaid.

After bearing four sons, Madhavi returned to her father. He offered to get her married. But she chose to become an ascetic.

After passing on the crown to Puru, Yayati renounced the world and ascended to Swarga. He enjoyed the pleasures of paradise for a very short while. Then the gods cast him out. When he asked for an explanation, the gods said, 'Because you Yayati have exhausted all your merits.'

Yayati fell on earth in a forest where his daughter, Madhavi, was performing tapasya. Feeling sorry for her father, she went to her four sons, who were now illustrious kings, and requested them to give a quarter of their merits to their grandfather. At first the sons refused. 'How can you ask us to give our merits to the man who treated you like a commodity, passing you from king to king so that he could benefit from the trade?'

And Madhavi replied, 'Because he is my father and you are my sons. Nothing will change what he did. And because I realize the futility of rage and know the power of forgiveness.' Enlightened by their mother's words, the four sons of Madhavi did as their mother requested. They gave their grandfather a portion of their merits.

Yayati, once again the bearer of merit, thanked his daughter and returned to the paradise of the gods.

The wisdom of Madhavi was forgotten as the years passed. And neither the Pandavas nor the Kauravas learnt the value of forgiveness, something that ultimately cost the Kuru clan dearly.

- Yayati's tale elaborates the concept of karma. Merit and demerit can pass through generations. A father's paap can be passed on to his sons and so Yayati's curse is endured by Yadu and his descendants. Likewise, a father can benefit from the punya of his children. And so, Madhavi's sons are able to restore their grandfather back to heaven.
- Yayati exploits his sons and daughters. Puru suffers his father's curse while Madhavi is effectively prostituted by Galava. Puru benefits from his suffering; he becomes king. Madhavi, however, retires to the forest and is able to shed her rage over time. She even forgives her father and helps him ascend to heaven. The theme of asceticism as a practice to rid oneself of rage is a recurring theme in the Mahabharata.

BOOK TWO

Parents

'Janamejaya, in your family, a son suffered for the sake of the father.'

Mahabhisha becomes Shantanu

For merits earned during his lifetime, a king called Mahabhisha was granted entry into Swarga. There he enjoyed the dance of the Apsaras and the music of the Gandharvas in the company of the Devas. He was allowed to drink Sura, the drink which fills one with joy. He was even given access to the tree called Kalpataru, to the cow called Kamadhenu and to the gem called Chintamani, each of which had the power to fulfil any wish and grant every desire.

One day, the river-nymph Ganga paid a visit to Indra's sabha. While she was there, a gentle breeze caused her upper garment to fall exposing her breasts. The assembled Devas lowered their eyes out of respect but Mahabhisha, spellbound by Ganga's beauty, kept staring unashamedly. This display of unbridled passion so angered Indra that he cursed Mahabhisha to return to the earth.

Ganga who had enjoyed Mahabhisha's shameless attention was also instructed by Indra to leave Amravati and return only after breaking Mahabhisha's heart.

Mahabhisha was reborn as Pratipa's son Shantanu in the city of Hastina-puri.

Pratipa, a descendant of Puru, renounced the world as soon as he felt his children were old enough to rule the kingdom in his stead. The crown should have gone to his eldest son, Devapi, but Devapi had a skin disease, and the law clearly stated that a man with a physical defect could not be king. So Shantanu, the younger son, became king instead. Devapi chose to become a mendicant, refusing to live in Shantanu's shadow.

One day, while Pratipa was meditating on a river bank, Ganga came and sat on his right lap. 'Beautiful woman, you sit on my right lap. Had you sat on my left, it would mean you want to be my wife. That you sit on my right means you wish to be my daughter. What is it that you desire?'

'I want to marry your son, Shantanu,' said Ganga.

'So it will be,' said Pratipa.

A few days later when Shantanu came to pay his respects to his father on the river bank, Pratipa told him, 'One day a beautiful woman called Ganga will approach you and wish to be your wife. Fulfil her desire. That is my wish.'

Shortly thereafter, Shantanu saw Ganga gliding on a dolphin. He fell in love with her instantly. 'Be my wife,' he said.

'I will,' said Ganga, 'provided you promise never to question my actions.' Driven both by lust and his promise to his father, Shantanu agreed and Ganga followed him home.

Soon, Ganga gave birth to Shantanu's first son. But there was little to cheer for as soon as the child slipped out of her womb, Ganga took the newborn to the river and drowned him. Though horrified by her action, Shantanu said nothing. He did not want to lose his beautiful wife.

A year later, Ganga gave birth to Shantanu's second son. She drowned him too. Even this time Shantanu did not voice his protest. In this way Ganga gave birth to, and drowned, seven children. Each time Shantanu said nothing.

But when Ganga was about to drown Shantanu's eighth child, Shantanu cried, 'Stop, you pitiless woman. Let him live.'

Ganga stopped and smiled. 'Husband, you have broken your word,' she said, 'So it is time for me to leave you as Urvashi once left Pururava. The children who I killed were seven of the eight gods known as Vasus who were cursed to be reborn as mortals for the crime of stealing Vasishtha's cow. On their request, I became their mother and tried to keep their stay on earth as brief as possible to spare them the misery of earthly existence. But alas, I could not save the last one. This eighth Vasu, who you have saved, Shantanu, will live. But a terrible life it shall be! Though man, he will neither marry nor inherit your throne. He will have no family, yet will be obliged to live as a householder. And finally, he will die a death of shame at the hands of a man who will actually be a woman.'

'It will not be so, I will not let that happen,' Shantanu argued passionately.

'I shall take your son and raise him as a perfect warrior. He shall be trained by the martial sage, Parashurama. I shall send him to you when he is ready to marry and be king. Then we shall see.' So saying Ganga disappeared with her son leaving Shantanu all alone.

- The Mahabharata gives great importance to the law of karma. According to this law, nothing in this world is spontaneous. Everything is a reaction to the past. Shantanu falls in love with Ganga and has his heart broken because of events in his past life. Ganga kills her own children because of events in their past life. By interfering with the course of karma, as Shantanu does when he stops Ganga from killing his eighth son, one ends up causing more harm than good. The epic constantly reminds us that what is apparently a good deed need not really be a good deed, for every moment is governed by factors that are often beyond human comprehension.
- The eight Vasus are ancient Vedic deities associated with the elements. For the paap of stealing Vasishtha's cow, they had to be reborn as mortals. The leader of the eight, Prabhas, who stole it for his wife, suffers more than the other seven and lives a longer and more miserable life as Devavrata.
- Vyasa draws attention to the dangers of lust and blind obedience to the father when Shantanu agrees to the conditions laid down by Ganga. At the root of all human tragedy is human folly.
- Hastina-puri, or the city of elephants, is named after Hastin, a little-known ancestor of the Pandavas. Some say Hastin was another name for Puru. Scholars speculate that the city name suggests that in the era of the Mahabharata, herds of elephants roamed in and around what is now known as Punjab and Haryana.
- In Jain chronicles, Hastina-puri was an ancient city, built by the gods themselves. Three of the twenty-four great Tirthankaras of Jainism—Shanti-nath, Kuntha-nath and Ara-nath—were born in this city.

Bhishma's sacrifice

Devavrata grew up to be a handsome prince and a skilled warrior. When his mother sent him back to his father, the people of Hastina-puri loved him and looked forward to the day when he would be king. But this never happened.

Shantanu had fallen in love again. And the object of his desire was Satyavati, a fisherwoman, who ferried men across the Ganga. He longed to make her his wife. But, like Ganga, Satyavati had a condition before she accepted Shantanu's offer of marriage: she wanted to be sure that only her children would be his heirs. Shantanu did not know how to satisfy this condition for Devavrata was already the crown prince of Hastina-puri.

When Devavrata learnt the cause of his father's misery, he went to Satyavati and said, 'So that my father can marry you, I renounce my claim to the throne.'

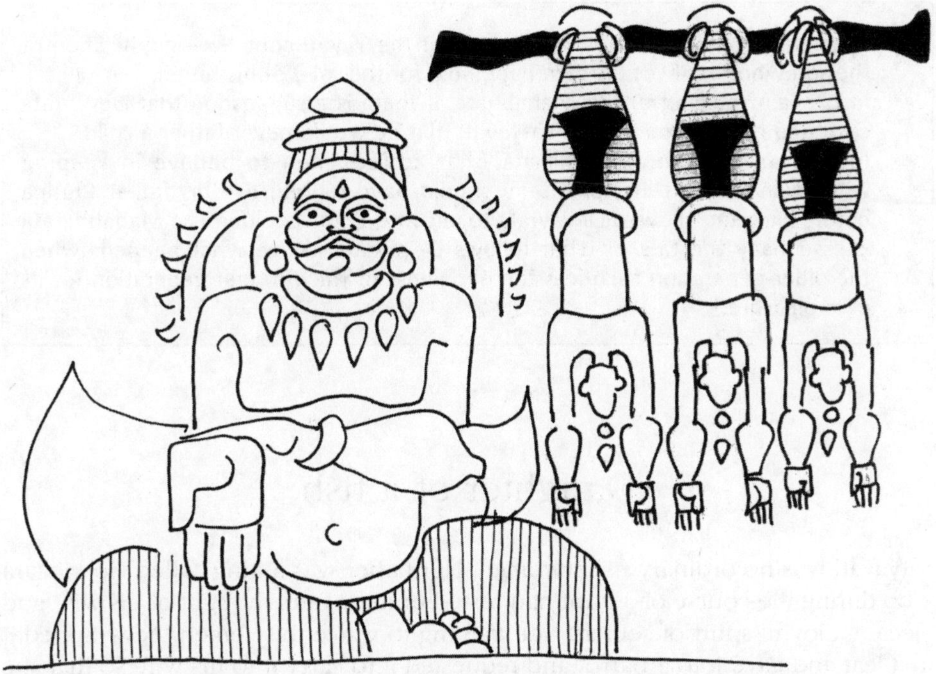

Though impressed by Devavrata's decision, Satyavati's father, chief of the fisherfolk, was not satisfied. He said, 'But your children will surely fight with my daughter's children over the throne. How will you ensure that this does not happen?'

Devavrata smiled and without remorse or regret took a decision that would change the course of his family history. 'I shall never marry. I shall never be with a woman. I shall never father children.'

Devavrata's vow stunned all the creatures of the cosmos. So impressed were the Devas that they descended from the skies and showered him with flowers. They gave him a new name, Bhishma, the one who took the most terrible of vows. For a terrible vow it was. Since Devavrata would father no children, there would be no one left on earth after his death to facilitate his rebirth. He would be doomed to live forever in the land of the dead across the river Vaitarni. The Devas in fact felt so sorry for Devavrata that they decreed Bhishma would have the power to choose the time of his own death.

With Devavrata taking the vow of celibacy, there was nothing to stop Shantanu from marrying Satyavati.

- Bhishma's vow is yet another example of the Yayati complex—glorification of the son who sacrifices his own happiness for the sake of his father.
- In the Jain retelling of the Mahabharata, there is a suggestion that Devavrata castrated himself to reassure Satyavati that he would never father a child.
- Ideally, as per ashrama-dharma, that advises men to behave in keeping with their stage in life, Shantanu should have retired, like his father Pratipa before him, and allowed Devavrata to become a householder. The Mahabharata is essentially the tale of what follows Devavrata's vow, what happens when the older generation sacrifices the happiness of the younger generation for its own pleasure.

Daughter of a fish

Satyavati was no ordinary fisherwoman. Her father was a king called Uparichara who during the course of a hunt had rested under a tree, thought of his wife and ejected a joyful spurt of semen. Not wanting to waste this semen, he wrapped it in a leaf and gave it to a parrot and requested it to carry it to his wife so that she could bear a child with it.

On its way, the parrot was attacked by a falcon and the packet containing the semen fell into a river where it was eaten by a fish. This fish was once an Apsara called Girika, cursed by Brahma to be a fish until she gave birth to human children.

A few days later, some fishermen caught this fish and found in its belly twin children: a boy and a girl. They presented the twins to Uparichara, who accepted the male child but let the female child be raised by the fisherfolk. The chief of the fisherfolk adopted the girl and raised her as his own daughter. She was called Satyavati but teased as Matsya-gandha for she smelt dreadfully of fish.

Matsya-gandha ferried people across the river Ganga. One day, she found herself ferrying a sage called Parasara. Midstream, near a river island, the sage expressed his desire to make love to Matsya-gandha and have a child by her. 'No one will marry me if you do this,' she said.

'Don't worry,' said the sage, drawing a curtain of mist over the ferry, 'With my magical powers I will ensure you will bear a child instantly and regain your virginity. And you will never ever smell of fish again. Your body will give out a fragrance that men will find irresistible.'

Before the ferry reached the other shore, Matsya-gandha had become a lover then a mother then a virgin and finally a fragrant woman. The child born of this union was raised by Parasara. He was named Krishna Dwaipayana, the dark child delivered on a river island. Eventually, he became known as Vyasa, he who compiled the sacred scriptures.

Matsya-gandha's new fragrant body got her the attention of Shantanu and made her the queen of Hastina-puri.

- The story of Uparichara's 'joyful spurt of semen' in the forest and its consumption by a fish is perhaps an elaborate tale to cover a king's indiscretion with a fisherwoman.
- One wonders if Satyavati's insistence that her children be kings stems from her resentment at being rejected by her royal father, Uparichara, who chose only her brother and let her be raised by fisherfolk. As the story continues, Vyasa draws attention to the desperate and sometimes brutal steps taken by Satyavati to change her destiny.
- The tale of Parasara and Matsya-gandha can be seen as a tale of sexual exploitation of a young girl by a powerful elderly sage, or it can be seen as a tale of sex hospitality that was prevalent in the epic age when fathers and husbands offered their daughters and wives to guests, sages and kings. Or it can be seen as an attempt by Matsya-gandha to manipulate a sage by offering him sexual favours.

The three princesses

In due course, Satyavati gave Shantanu two sons: Chitrangada and Vichitravirya. Soon after, Shantanu died leaving his wife and her sons in the care of Bhishma.

Satyavati wanted her sons to grow up fast, marry and produce children for she was determined to be the mother of a great line of kings.

Unfortunately, Chitrangada died before marriage. An arrogant man, he was challenged to a duel by a Gandharva of the same name who killed him after a prolonged fight.

Vichitravirya was a weakling, unable to find a wife for himself. So it was left to Bhishma to find a wife for him.

The king of Kashi had organized a swayamvara where his three daughters—Amba, Ambika and Ambalika—could select a husband from among the guests. No invitation had been extended to Vichitravirya. Some said this was because it was known that Vichitravirya was an unfit groom for any woman. Others said this was to get back at Bhishma who, while taking the vow of celibacy, conveniently overlooked the consequences of his decision on the woman he was engaged to marry, the sister of the king of Kashi.

Bhishma took the absence of an invitation as an affront to the dignity of his household. He rode into Kashi and abducted the three princesses. The assembled guests tried but failed to stop him. Bhishma then gave the three princesses to his younger brother.

Amba, eldest daughter of the king of Kashi, was in love with Shalva and she had planned to select him as a groom from among those invited by her father to her swayamvara. 'Let me go to the man I love,' she begged, 'You have two wives. Why do you need three?' Feeling sorry for her, both Vichitravirya and Bhishma let her go to the man she loved.

But Shalva refused to take Amba back. 'How can I take back as queen a woman abducted by another man and then returned as charity,' he said.

A mortified Amba returned to Vichitravirya only to be told, rather imperiously, 'What is once given away is never taken back.'

Amba then went to Bhishma and demanded that he take her as his wife. 'You are the cause of all this. If you had not abducted me, I would not be in this situation. I am therefore your responsibility. Besides, by taking us on your chariot you, and not your half-brother, are our true husband.'

Bhishma would hear none of this. He dismissed her with a wave of his hand. 'I have taken a vow that prevents me from being with any woman. Since neither Shalva nor Vichitravirya shall accept you, you are free to go wherever you wish.'

'You have ruined my life,' cried Amba. 'If your vow prevented you from marrying, what right did you have to abduct me? Now I am nobody's wife.'

Amba went around the world seeking a warrior who would avenge her humiliation. But all Kshatriyas feared Bhishma. So she took the help of Parashurama, who was Bhishma's teacher.

Parashurama was a Brahman who feared no Kshatriya. In fact he hated them. Kshatriyas had killed his father and stolen his cows. To teach them a lesson, he had picked up an axe and massacred five great Kshatriya clans, filling five lakes with their blood. These five lakes were known as Samanta Panchaka and were located at Kuru-kshetra. Every Kshatriya trembled on hearing Parashurama's name. He had sworn to kill any Kshatriya who crossed his path.

Parashurama was so shocked to hear Amba's story that he immediately challenged his student to a duel. A terrible fight ensued which lasted for several days. Finally, Parashurama gave up. 'No one can defeat Bhishma. And no one can kill him unless he wants to die. If this fight continues, both of us will release weapons that will destroy the world. So it has to stop,' he said.

In despair, Amba then took a vow. She would not eat or sleep until the Devas revealed to her the means of killing Bhishma.

She stood on one foot on top of a hill for days until Shiva, the destructive form of God, appeared before her. 'You will be the cause of Bhishma's death,' said Shiva, 'But only in your next life.' Determined to hasten Bhishma's death, Amba killed herself by leaping into a pit of fire. She would be reborn in the household of Drupada, king of Panchala, as Shikhandi, and fulfil her destiny as Bhishma's nemesis.

- In the 15th century, Kabi Sanjay wrote the Mahabharata in Bengali in which Chitrangada dies of tuberculosis and Vichitravirya is killed by Bhishma's pet elephant when he, despite express instructions not to do so, enters Bhishma's palace while Bhishma is away.
- The name Vichitravirya is derived from 'vichitra' meaning odd and 'virya' meaning masculinity, suggesting that Vichitravirya was either a weakling or impotent or sterile, or perhaps asexual or homosexual, lacking manliness, unable or unwilling to get a bride for himself.
- Amba's tale draws attention to the gradual deterioration in the status of women in Vedic society. Unlike Urvashi, Ganga and Satyavati who could make demands of the men who sought to marry them, Amba and her sisters were chattels—to be claimed as trophies in tournaments. Iravati Karve's collection of essays, *Yuganta*, elaborates on the changing times reflected in the epic.

Birth of Vichitravirya's children

Vichitravirya died before he could father any children.

Satyavati's dream of being the mother of kings was shattered.

Then she went to Bhishma and told him to make his widowed daughters-in-law pregnant. 'By the law of niyoga, prescribed in the books of dharma, any child they bear belongs to their deceased husband. I request you to do what my sons could not do.'

'That may be the law, mother,' said Bhishma, 'but I will not break my vow of celibacy, even for you, the one for whose pleasure this vow was taken.'

A desperate Satyavati then sent for her first son, Krishna Dwaipayana, who lived with his father Parasara. By then everyone referred to him as Vyasa, the compiler, because he had successfully organized the Veda into four books. 'Make the two wives of my son pregnant,' she said.

'I will,' said Vyasa, 'if so is your wish. But give me a year to prepare myself. For fourteen years I have lived in the forest as an ascetic. My hair is matted and my skin coarse. My gaunt features will scare the two women.'

But Satyavati was impatient. 'Go now, as you are. They will welcome you. And I cannot wait.'

Not wanting to disobey his mother, Vyasa went first to Ambika. She was so disgusted by his looks that she shut her eyes when he touched her. The child that Vyasa conceived in her womb was therefore born blind. He was named Dhritarashtra.

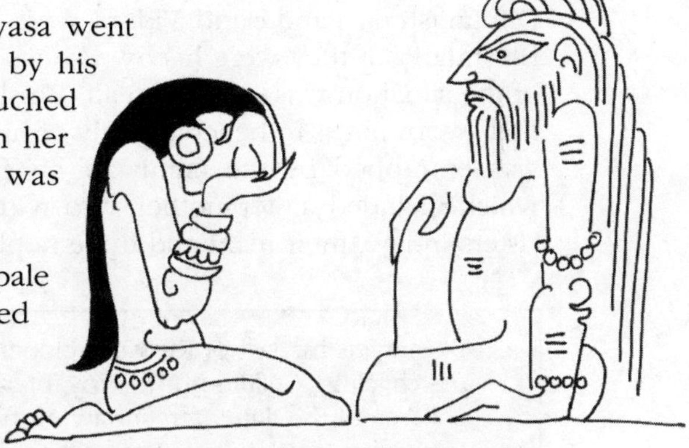

Next, Vyasa went to Ambalika. She grew pale on seeing Vyasa. The child thus conceived in her womb would be a pale weakling called Pandu.

'Go to Ambika again. This time she will not shut her eyes,' said Satyavati, disappointed by the birth of imperfect grandsons.

Vyasa did as he was told. But on the bed lay not Ambika but her maid who made love to him fearlessly. The child she conceived would be healthy and wise. He would be named Vidura. Though fit to be king, he would never be allowed to wear the crown as he was born of a maid.

Vidura was none other than Yama, the god of death, living out a curse. This is how it happened.

Once, a group of thieves took refuge in the hermitage of sage Mandavya who was at that time lost in meditation, totally unaware of their presence. When they were discovered by the king's guards, Mandavya was accused of aiding them and as punishment was tortured and impaled. When he appeared before Yama, ruler of the dead, he demanded an explanation for his suffering for he had hurt no living creature in his life. 'Yes, you have. When you were a child, you took delight in impaling tiny insects on a straw,' said Yama. 'Your suffering was repayment for the karmic debt incurred then.' Mandavya protested that being punished for crimes committed in childhood, when one is innocent, was not fair. 'That is the law of karma,' replied a dispassionate Yama. A furious Mandavya then cursed Yama that he would take birth as a man and suffer the fate of never being a king despite having all the qualities of the perfect ruler. And so was born Vidura.

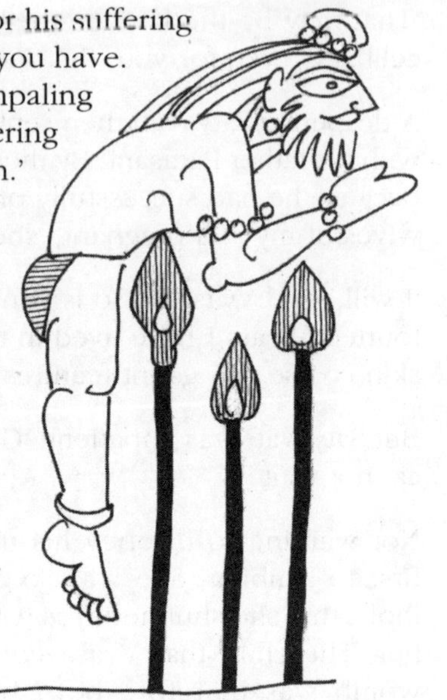

Dhritarashtra, Pandu and Vidura were raised by Bhishma as if they were his own sons. The irony of the situation was evident to all. Bhishma, who had sworn never to beget a family of his own, was entrapped by the family of his father, which included a stepmother, two widowed sisters-in-law, their maid and three nephews.

- Bhishma is the last of the Kuru bloodline. The sons his father bears on Satyavati die childless. Children of the royal family thereafter are not true Kurus; they are children of the daughters-in-law of the household by other men.
- Vyasa draws attention to the frailties of human laws that try to correct what nature has ordained. Satyavati's son dies childless but by the law of niyoga he can still be a father. Thus Dhritarashtra and Pandu become the 'sons' of Vichitravirya even though their mothers were made pregnant by Vyasa.
- The laws say that only children of the lawfully wedded wife are the true sons, not the children of concubines. Thus only Pandu and Dhritarashtra can be kings, not Vidura, even though Vidura is the most worthy.
- The story of Vidura's past life is an attempt to explain why bad things happen to good people. In a further elaboration of the law of karma, it informs that even acts performed in ignorance or innocence have repercussions that one is obliged to experience either in this life or the next.
- Yama, god of death, is also known as Dharma, god of order. A dispassionate god who oversees death and destiny, he ensures that the law of karma is followed meticulously.

BOOK THREE

Birth

'Janamejaya, in your family, sterile men became fathers by asking gods to visit their wives.'

Satyavati's grand-daughters-in-law

South of Hastina-puri, on the banks of the river Yamuna, the Yadava council ruled the prosperous city of Mathura. One of the members of the Yadava council, Surasena, had a daughter called Pritha who was adopted by his cousin, Kuntibhoja, who renamed her Kunti.

When Kunti was of marriageable age, a swayamvara was organized where, from among the assembled guests, she chose Pandu as her husband.

Around the same time, the princess of Gandhara, Gandhari, was brought to Hastina-puri and given in marriage to Dhritarashtra. She did not know at the time of her wedding that she was marrying a blind man. When she learnt this, she decided to blindfold herself to share her husband's suffering.

For reasons never clarified, though many suspect it was because of Pandu's inability to father a child on Kunti, a second wife was purchased for Pandu. She was Madri, sister of Shalya, king of Madra. Second wives were usually purchased when the first wife was suspected of being infertile. But Kunti had proof of fertility: she had secretly borne a child before marriage. Perhaps rumours of her premarital liaisons stained her reputation and provided reason enough for getting a second wife.

Though elder, since Dhritarashtra was born blind, he was forbidden from sitting on the throne. Pandu was made king instead, superseding Dhritarashtra just as

Shantanu had superseded Devapi. This decision caused great heartburn in the blind prince, but he never voiced his protest for he was well versed with the quirks of laws. While some laws made him the legitimate son of Vichitravirya, there were others which prevented him from becoming king. At night, in bed, the blind prince whispered to his wife, 'Let us make a son quickly, Gandhari, before Pandu makes one, so that he can reclaim what should rightfully be mine.'

- Vedic literature classifies eight different ways in which man and woman come together. 1. If a woman is given away as charity to help a needy man, as Gandhari is, it is the way of Prajapati, father of all creatures. 2. If a bride is accepted more for her dowry than for herself, it is the way of Brahma, the creator who is entrapped by his own creation. 3. If a daughter is given as a fee for services rendered to the father, it is the way of the Deva, the sky-gods. 4. If a daughter is given for ritual purposes along with a cow and a bull, it is the way of the Rishi. 5. If a woman chooses her husband freely, as Shakuntala and Kunti do, it is the way of the Gandharva, the celestial musicians. 6. If a woman is purchased, as Madri is, it is the way of the Asura, the subterranean hoarders of wealth. 7. If a woman is abducted, as Ambika and Ambalika are, it is the way of the Rakshasa, the forest-dwelling barbarians. 8. If a woman is raped, it is the way of the Pisachas or vampires.

- By blindfolding herself to share her husband's blindness, Gandhari attains the status of 'sati' or the perfect wife. Later in the epic, her sacrifice grants her magical powers. Playwrights suggest that Gandhari blindfolded herself in outrage to protest against her marriage to a blind man. Rather than being exploited, she disables herself.
- In the Bhil Bharata of the Doongri Bhils of Gujarat, there is a story connecting Kunti and Gandhari to the mother-goddess, Shakti. Once seven sages were busy performing tapasya. Intrigued, Shiva and Shakti paid them a visit in the form of eagles. But pushed by the winds, the female eagle got impaled on the trident of the sages. When the sages saw this, they were so upset that they decided to use their magical powers to bring life into the dead bird. Two women emerged from the dead bird: Gandhari from the skeletons and Kunti from the flesh.
- The laws say that only a physically fit man can be king. So Dhritarashtra who is blind is bypassed and his younger brother, Pandu, is made king. Ironically, even Pandu is physically unfit; his disability (sterility or impotency) is not as evident as blindness.

Birth of Kunti's children

One day, not long after his second marriage, Pandu went on a hunt, perhaps to vent his frustration at being unable to give even the highly fertile Madri a child. Would he die, like his father, leaving two childless widows behind?

Pandu's arrow struck an antelope. When Pandu came closer, he realized he had killed the antelope while he was mating with a doe. To make matters worse, the antelope turned out to be a sage called Kindama and the doe turned out to be his wife. They had used magical powers to turn themselves into animals so that they could make love freely in the open.

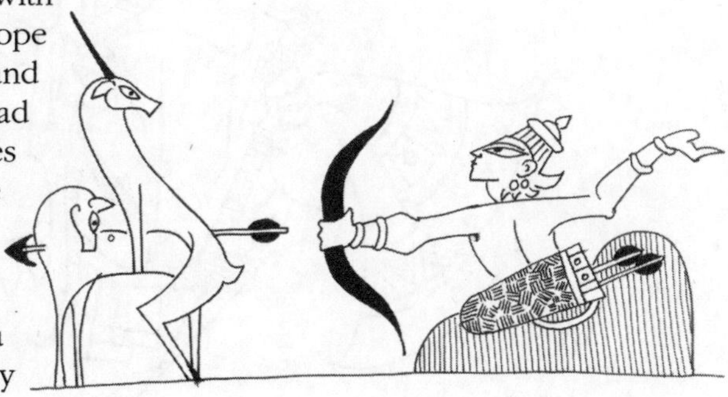

Before dying, Kindama cursed Pandu, 'You, who have so violently stopped a man from making love to a woman, may you never know the pleasure of lovemaking. If you ever touch a woman, you will die instantly.'

A distraught Pandu felt that a man who cannot father a child is unfit to be king. So he refused to return to Hastina-puri. He decided to live the life of a hermit in the forest of Satasringa along with the Rishis there.

When news of Pandu's decision to become a hermit reached Hastina-puri, his wives rushed to be with him. They found him living in the forest, wearing clothes of bark, having abandoned his royal robes, with Rishis for company.

'Go back,' said Pandu to Kunti and Madri, 'I can never be a husband to you.' But the two women insisted on staying with him. For it is the dharma of wives to follow husbands, both in joy and in sorrow.

In the absence of Pandu, Bhishma had no choice but to pass on the crown of Hastina-puri to the blind Dhritarashtra. It was perhaps in the destiny of Hastina-puri to be ruled by a blind king and his blindfolded queen.

A few months later, news reached Pandu that Dhritarashtra's wife, Gandhari, was pregnant with child. The news depressed him. Not only had fate taken the crown from him, it also left him in a state whereby he could never father kings.

Kunti consoled her husband, 'There was a time when women were free to go to any man they pleased. This alarmed the sage Shvetaketu who saw his father, Uddalaka, unfazed by his mother's association with other sages. Shvetaketu then introduced the law of marriage so that women were bound to husbands, enabling all men to know who their fathers were. They could only have children by their husbands and if their husbands were unable to give them children, they could go to men chosen by their husbands. Children borne by the wife belonged to the husband whether he fathered them or not. So it is that the father of the planet Mercury is the planet Jupiter even though it was the moon who conceived him in the womb of the stars. So it is that you are the son of Vichitravirya even though he never made your mother pregnant.'

Pandu decided to take advantage of this rule. He decided to ask a sage to come to his wives. 'Why a Rishi when I can call upon a Deva?' asked Kunti. Pandu looked at her quizzically. Kunti explained, 'When I was young, the Rishi Durvasa visited by father's house. My father asked me to take care of all his needs. Pleased with my devotion and service, he gave me a magic formula by which I could call upon any sky-god and have a child with him instantly. Perhaps, in his foresight, he realized I would have need of such a formula in my life. So, if you wish, I can use this formula, and have a child by any god of your choice.'

What Kunti did not tell her husband was that in her curiosity she had used the magic formula to invoke Surya, the sun-god, and that she had a child by him. To protect her reputation, she had put the child in a basket and abandoned it to a river's whim soon after. It was an act of shame that weighed heavy on her heart.

Pleased with Kunti's solution to his situation, Pandu said, 'Call Yama, who is the lord of dharma, and the model for all kings.' Kunti used the magic formula, invoked Yama and had a child with him. He was named Yudhishtira. He would be the most honest of men.

Later, Pandu asked Kunti to invoke Vayu, the god of the wind. 'Because he is father of the mightiest of all gods, Hanuman.' The child thus conceived was named Bhima. He would be the strongest of men.

Kunti then called upon Indra, king of the Devas and ruler of the sky. By him she had a son called Arjuna. He would be the most skilled archer in the world, capable of using the bow with both his right and left hand. Since Kunti had invoked Indra of her own volition and not because her husband had told her to, the son of Indra, Arjuna, became her favourite child. Only he was referred by all as Partha, the son of Pritha.

'Call another Deva,' said Pandu after the birth of Arjuna.

'No, I have been with four men,' said Kunti. 'If I call another, I will be known as a whore. So it is decreed in the books of dharma.' Pandu thought the four men Kunti was referring to were the three gods and himself. Kunti, however, was referring to the three gods who had given her three sons after marriage, and the one god who had given her one son before marriage—a secret that she shared with no one.

- The accidental killing of Kindama seems like an elaborate afterthought to explain or cover up the sterility and/or impotency of Pandu.
- Shvetaketu is believed to be the fountainhead of patriarchy. Before he introduced the law of marriage, women had full sexual freedom. In fact, a woman could go to any man and a man who refused her was deemed a eunuch. This freedom was allowed because childbirth was considered of prime importance to facilitate the re-entry of forefathers into the land of the living. Shvetaketu insisted on fidelity from women so that all children knew who their biological fathers were. If a man could not father children because he was impotent, sterile or dead, the woman was allowed to go to other men, with the permission of her husband or his family.
- The number of men a woman was allowed to go to if her husband could not give her children was restricted to three. Including the husband, a woman thus could be with up to four men in her life. If she went to a fifth man, she was deemed a whore. This law gains significance later in the epic when Kunti lets Draupadi marry all five of her sons.
- As per some Vedic marriage rites, a woman is first given in marriage to the romantic moon-god, Chandra, then to the highly sensual Gandharva named Vishwavasu, then to the fire-god, Agni, who cleanses and purifies all things, and finally to her human husband. Thus, the 'four men' quota is exhausted. Clearly this was an attempt of society to prevent Hindu women from remarrying.
- In the Oriya Mahabharata by Sarala Das, at the time of Bhima's birth, a tiger roars. Kunti runs away in fear, abandoning her newborn but Bhima is so strong that he kicks the tiger on his head and pushes him away. With another kick he breaks a mountain. Apologizing to the mountain, Kunti transforms each broken piece of the mountain into a local deity.

Birth of Gandhari's children

Gandhari was angry on learning that Kunti had become a mother before her. She had conceived much earlier but mysteriously her pregnancy continued for two years. She could wait no more and so she took a terrible decision: to force the child out of her womb.

Gandhari ordered her maids to get an iron bar. 'Now strike me on my belly with it,' she ordered. The maids hesitated. 'Do it,' shouted Gandhari. With great reluctance, the maids did as they were told, and struck the queen on her belly. 'Again. Strike me again. Again and again,' said Gandhari. The maids kept striking her until Gandhari's womb quivered and pushed out a ball of flesh, cold as iron.

'Does it cry? Is it a boy or girl?' asked Gandhari. When told what she had delivered, Gandhari wailed. Fate was indeed cruel.

She sent for the sage Vyasa. 'You told me that I would be the mother of a hundred sons. Where are they?' she asked. Feeling sorry for Gandhari, Vyasa instructed Gandhari's maid to break the ball of flesh into a hundred pieces and put them in jars full of ghee. They would incubate over a year and transform into sons, he told Gandhari.

'Can I have a daughter too?' asked Gandhari, softly. Vyasa smiled and told the maids to divide the ball of flesh into a hundred and one pieces.

Thus were born the hundred sons and the one daughter of Gandhari and Dhritarashtra. Collectively, the sons were called the Kauravas.

The first among them was Duryodhana. When his pot was broken, on the day when Kunti gave birth to Bhima, the palace dogs wailed. 'He will bring misfortune,' advised Vidura to Dhritarashtra, 'Let us be rid of him, brother.'

'I don't care,' said Gandhari clinging firmly to the newborn. 'No one will harm this son of mine. He is my firstborn, my favourite.'

Her second son was called Dusshasana.

The daughter was called Dusshala. She was given in marriage to Jayadhrata, king of Sindhu.

During his wife's long pregnancy, Dhritarashtra had taken for his pleasure a maid. She bore him a son called Yuyutsu. Like Vidura, he was an extremely capable man but disqualified from ever sitting on the throne.

- Contrary to popular projection, both Gandhari and Kunti are viewed by Vyasa as ambitious women who knew the value of sons in a royal household.
- The traditional Hindu blessing for brides has always been, 'May you be the mother of a hundred sons.' Gandhari holds Vyasa to that blessing. But she wants a daughter too. Thus the Kuru household had a hundred and five sons (hundred Kauravas and five Pandavas) and one daughter, Dusshala, who was so indulged by the entire household that her husband, Jayadhrata, was forgiven repeatedly despite his immoral behaviour.
- Scholars wonder if the story of the miraculous birth of Gandhari's children is a record of occult secrets known to ancient sages. Maybe they could transform the remnants of a miscarriage into live children by incubating them in magically charged pots of ghee. Or maybe it is all a poet's imagination. The latter is suggested when the Rishi called upon to create Gandhari's hundred children is none other than Vyasa, the poet of the epic.
- Rationalists believe Gandhari had only two sons, Duryodhana and Dusshasana, who are the only two of the hundred to play a significant role in the epic. They were probably twins, the 'two-year' pregnancy probably meaning 'twin' pregnancy.

Birth of Madri's children

'Since you cannot go to other men,' said Pandu to Kunti, 'invoke a Deva for Madri. Let her be mother too. And let me be father of more sons.'

Kunti obeyed. 'Who shall I invoke?' she asked Madri.

'The Ashwini twins,' said Madri. Instantly the two gods, lords of the morning and evening star, appeared and gave Madri twin sons: Nakula, the handsomest man in the world and Sahadeva, the most knowledgeable man in the world.

'Madri can go to another god,' said Pandu. 'Invoke another Deva,' he told Kunti.

But Kunti refused. With one invocation, Madri had cleverly called twin gods and become mother of two sons. She feared with another invocation, Madri could call another set of gods, a male collective, and have as many as three, four, five, why even seven sons. And with the following one, she would be mother of more sons. She could not allow that. She would not let the junior wife have more sons, hence more power than her.

The five sons of Pandu, three by Kunti and two by Madri, became known as the Pandavas. Collectively, the five sons had the five qualities of the perfect king—honesty, strength, skill, beauty and wisdom.

- Were the 'gods' who made Kunti and Madri pregnant actually Devas or simply priests performing a ritual role to compensate for the inadequacies of Pandu? This has been elaborated in Bhyrappa's Kannada novel, *Parva*. Some scholars believe that even the tale of Kunti's premarital tryst with Surya is an attempt to hide the truth, that she was asked by her father to satisfy all the needs of the sage Durvasa in keeping with the laws of hospitality. The Mahabharata has at least two tales that refer to sex hospitality, according to which a guest was allowed access to the host's wife or daughter for pleasure. Even Satyavati's tryst with Parasara on the boat is interpreted sometimes as a case of sex hospitality. This practice, once glorified, came to be frowned upon with the passage of time.

- Kunti restricts access of Madri to the gods for fear that she will end up bearing more children and so yield greater influence than her. Through this little episode Vyasa makes us aware that the desire for power is not restricted to men alone. In the entire epic, the children of Madri are overshadowed by the children of Kunti. This is often overlooked in modern retellings of the Mahabharata which prefer portraying Kunti as a kind, selfless and helpless widow when in fact she is a woman very conscious of palace politics, never sharing her premarital secret with anyone, quoting laws that enable her husband to father children, and later, doing everything she can to keep her sons and the sons of Madri united, even when Madri's brother sides with the Kauravas.
- The gods invoked by the two wives of Pandu are early Vedic gods known as Devas: Yama, Indra, Vayu and the Ashwini twins. Neither Kunti nor Madri invokes Shiva or Vishnu or Brahma who are forms of Bhagavan or God. The notion of an all-powerful God is a later development in Hindu thought. This clearly indicates that the epic first took shape in Vedic times which were dominated by belief in elemental spirits. Later, with the rise of bhakti or path of passionate devotion to the almighty, the ideas of God and Shiva and Vishnu and Krishna were added to the tale.

Death of Pandu

Pandu lived a happy life in the forest with his two wives and five sons in the company of many sages. But he was a young man and there were times when he sorely missed intimacy with his wives.

One day, he saw sunlight streaming through the sheer fabric that Madri had draped round her body. He realized how beautiful she was. He could not resist touching her. No sooner did he do that than Kindama's curse was realized and he died.

A heartbroken Madri leapt into Pandu's funeral pyre leaving her two sons in the care of Kunti.

The Rishis in the forest then took Pandu's widow and his five sons to Hastina-puri so that they could be raised as princes should be in the royal household of the Kurus.

Unknown to all, Pandu had a premonition of his death and had told his sons a secret. 'Years of celibacy and meditation in the forest have given me great knowledge. It is embedded in my body. When I die, eat my flesh and you will be blessed with great knowledge. That shall be your true inheritance.'

After Pandu died, his body was cremated. The children could not do what their father had asked them to do. But Sahadeva noticed ants carrying a tiny piece of their father's body. He put that piece in his mouth. Instantly, he knew everything about the world—what had happened in the past and what would happen in the future.

He ran to tell his mother and brothers about it when a stranger stopped him and said, 'Do you want God as your friend?'

'Yes,' said Sahadeva.

'Then never tell what you know to anyone voluntarily. And when a question is asked, reply with a question.' Sahadeva divined the stranger was none other than Krishna, God on earth. Sahadeva had no choice but to keep quiet, knowing all but never being able to tell people what he knew or do anything to avert the inevitable.

He realized the future that he knew could be deciphered if one observed nature carefully. And so he put together various occult sciences that helped man predict the future.

As for himself, Sahadeva waited for people to ask him the right question. They asked him many questions—but never the right one. Hence, he was always wistful and forlorn, the youngest of Kunti's five fatherless sons.

- The Mahabharata does refer to Sati or the practice of widows burning themselves on their husbands' funeral pyres. But in all cases, it is voluntary; nobody forces the women to submit to this violent practice. Vedic funeral rites refer to the practice of the widow being asked to lie next to her husband's corpse, but then she is asked to stand up and return to the land of the living. She was allowed to remarry or at least cohabit with other male members of her husband's family, usually the younger brother. Greek chroniclers who accompanied Alexander the Great to India did report the practice of Sati in North India. Around 500 CE the practice of Sati became part of liturgical manuals and a common theme in folklore as well as worship.
- In South India, Sahadeva is renowned as the master of astrology, face reading and all other forms of divination. Even today, a secretive man who never reveals anything despite having full knowledge of a situation is colloquially described as a 'Sahadeva'.

BOOK FOUR

Education

'Janamejaya, your ancestors turned a teacher into a trader and a priest into a warrior when they paid half a kingdom as tuition fee.'

Kripa and Kripi

Shantanu had found a pair of twins—a boy and a girl—abandoned in the forest. They had been placed on a tiger skin and next to them were a trident and a pot, indicating they were the children of a sage. They were the children of sage Sharadwana and an Apsara called Janpadi. Shantanu named them Kripa and Kripi and raised them in the palace.

Kripa grew up to be a teacher. Bhishma appointed him tutor to the five sons of Pandu and the hundred sons of Dhritarashtra who were now under his care.

Kripi was given in marriage to Drona. Drona was the son of sage Bharadvaja. He was born in a pot into which his father had spilt semen at the sight of a beautiful Apsara called Ghrutachi. In time, Kripi gave birth to a son, Ashwatthama.

Drona was extremely poor, so poor that he did not have a cow in his house. Ashwatthama grew up without ever having tasted milk. He could not even distinguish milk from rice water.

Unable to bear the poverty, Kripi finally convinced Drona to go to his childhood friend, Drupada, king of Panchala, and ask him for a cow. 'When we were children, we were such good friends that he promised to share all his wealth with me,' Drona told his wifc.

Unfortunately, Drupada burst out laughing when Drona reminded him of the childhood promise. 'Friendship exists among equals. We were friends then. Now I am a rich king and you are a poor priest. We cannot be friends. Do not claim cows in the name of friendship; ask for alms and I shall give you a cow in charity.'

Hurt and humiliated by Drupada's words, Drona stormed out of Panchala, determined to one day become Drupada's equal.

- Kripa, Kripi and Drona are illegitimate children born after nymphs seduce ascetics and make them break their vows of celibacy. This is a recurring theme in the Mahabharata which values the householder's life over that of the hermit's. The epic age was one of tension between those who believed the purpose of life was to enjoy material pleasures and those who believed the purpose of life was to renounce the same.

- In the epic age, kings were supposed to take care of Rishis either by daan or charity or by dakshina or fee paid for services rendered. Drupada treats Drona as the son of a Rishi and offers him daan. Drona is angry because he is not treated as a friend and equal. Drupada is thus the dispassionate follower of the code of civilized conduct (dharma) while Drona yearns for human affection and respect that transcends social stratification. The conflict between Drupada and Drona is thus the conflict between head and heart. Through Drona, Vyasa draws attention to the disruptive power of desire (kama).
- Drupada's treatment of Drona needs to be contrasted with the tale of Krishna and Sudama. Like Drupada and Drona, they were the best of friends, one a rich nobleman and the other an impoverished priest. Unlike Drupada, however, Krishna shares all his wealth with his friend. For Krishna, there can be no dharma without the spirit of generosity. Without genuine love, laws and rules are worthless.

Drona, the teacher

Drona went to Parashurama and learnt from the great warrior-priest the art of war. 'Never share my knowledge with Kshatriyas,' said Parashurama. Drona promised never to do so.

But as soon as he left Parashurama's hermitage, Drona forgot all about this promise. He made his way to Hastina-puri, intent on making the Kuru princes his students and using them against Drupada.

When Drona reached Hastina-puri, he found the Kuru princes trying to retrieve a ball from a well. Drona decided to help the princes. He picked up a blade of grass and threw it with such force into the well that it pierced the ball like a pin. Then he threw another blade of grass which pinned itself to the free end of the grass pinned to the ball. Then he threw a third blade of grass which pinned itself to the far end of the second blade of grass. Soon he had a whole chain of grass that could be pulled up along with the ball.

Drona then dropped his ring into the well. He raised a bow and shot an arrow which pierced into the waters and ricocheted back along with the ring.

The children, astonished by what they had seen, ran into the palace and told Bhishma about this strange priest-warrior near the well. 'Let us make him the royal tutor,' said Bhishma to Kripa.

Kripa was more than happy to give employment to his brother-in-law. But Drona had a condition. 'As fee, I want my students to use their knowledge to capture Drupada, king of Panchala, alive.'

'So be it,' said the Kuru princes.

Drona accepted the hundred Kauravas and the five Pandavas as his students. Soon, Yudhishtira became skilled with the spear, Arjuna with the bow, Bhima, Duryodhana and Dusshasana with the mace, Nakula and Sahadeva with the sword.

In due course, the Kauravas and Pandavas were well versed in the art of war. It was time to pay Drona's fee. They rode into Panchala, herded away Drupada's cows by force, and challenged Drupada to war.

When Drupada emerged from his city with his army to save the cows, Arjuna said, 'Our teacher wants us to capture Drupada alive. We must not lose focus by fighting his army. It will wear us down.' The Pandavas saw sense in what Arjuna said but Duryodhana, who never agreed with the Pandavas even when what they said made sense, ordered his hundred brothers to take Drupada's army head-on. They rushed forward but the Pandavas stayed back.

While the Kauravas were busy fighting the army of Panchala, Arjuna climbed a war-chariot and told Yudhishtira, 'You go to our teacher. We four shall meet you there after capturing the king of Panchala.' With Bhima leading the way, swinging his mace like a wild elephant, and Nakula and Sahadeva protecting the wheels of his chariot, Arjuna raced through the ranks of the Panchala soldiers straight towards Drupada. Drupada, distracted by the Kauravas, was caught by surprise. Before he could defend himself, Arjuna pounced on him and pinned him to the ground. Bhima got a rope and bound him. Then placing him on their chariot they took him straight to Drona.

'My students will let you go only if you part with one half of your kingdom,' said Drona to a humiliated Drupada, who nodded his assent. Then, said Drona, 'My students claim the half of Panchala north of the Ganga. Your rule is now restricted to the southern half.'

The Kuru princes gave the conquered Panchala lands as dakshina to their teacher which Drona accepted with joy. Then the royal tutor turned to Drupada and said, 'I am now master of one half of Panchala and you are master of the other half. We are equals. Can we be friends now?'

'Yes,' said Drupada, taking care not to reveal the desire for vengeance that burned in his heart.

- Rishis were supposed to focus only on spiritual pursuits and stay away from society. This spiritual pursuit gave them many magical powers. Over time, unable to resist material desires, Rishis became members of society. They split into world-renouncing ascetics known as Tapasvins or Yogis and world-affirming scholars, priests and teachers known as Brahmans. Parasara and Bharadvaja belonged to the former category while Kripa and Drona belonged to the latter.
- Some sages like Parashurama gave up spiritual practices and took up arms in revolt against the excesses of the warrior community. In contrast, some warriors like Kaushika, father of Shakuntala, became Rishis when they realized true power lay in spiritual practices and not in weapons. The epic age was a time of flux.
- Education involved not just the study of Vedic hymns, rituals and philosophy, but also the study of the Upavedas which included the study of warfare (Dhanur-veda), health (Ayur-veda), theatre (Gandharva-veda), time (Jyotish-shastra), space (Vastu-shastra) and polity (Artha-shastra).
- At the end of education, students were expected to pay their teacher's fee before moving out of the teacher's house. This was called guru-dakshina, a transaction fee, after which all obligations to the teacher were severed. Ideally, a teacher was

supposed to take only that which he needed for sustenance. But Drona takes much more.

- Wealth in Vedic times took three forms: livestock which included cows, horses and elephants, land which was turned into pastures, fields and orchards and finally gold and gems. Most Vedic warfare was over livestock and pasture lands.

Arjuna, the greatest archer

There were skills that Drona was reluctant to teach the Kuru princes. These he reserved for his son, Ashwatthama. Arjuna noticed this. So he followed Drona wherever he went, determined to learn all that Drona had to teach, never leaving father and son alone, making it impossible for Drona to pass on any teaching to Ashwatthama exclusively. Eventually, there were lessons that were exclusive to Arjuna and Ashwatthama, secret lessons that no other student of Drona was given access to.

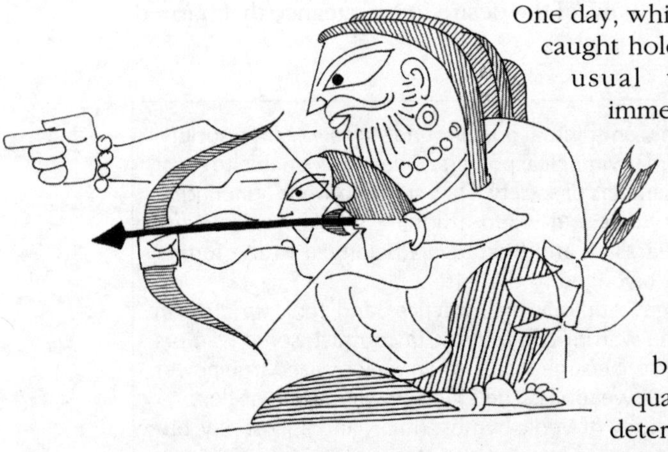

One day, while bathing in the river, a crocodile caught hold of Drona's foot. Arjuna, who as usual was following his teacher, immediately raised his bow, released an arrow, struck down the crocodile and rescued his master. Drona, until then irritated by Arjuna's persistence, came to admire it. He declared that he would make Arjuna the greatest archer in the world, not out of gratitude, but because Arjuna possessed all the qualities of a good student: persistence, determination, hard work and focus.

One night, the wind blew out all the lamps in Drona's academy. Still Arjuna found that his fingers carrying food could find their way to his mouth. 'If this is the case, then surely in the darkness my arrow can find its way to the target,' he realized. He started practising archery at night blindfolded and, to the amazement of his teacher, developed the skill of shooting arrows at the target without depending on his sight. Because of this he became renowned as Gudakesha, he who has conquered sleep.

Arjuna also was able to shoot his bow using either his left or his right hand. Hence, he came to be known as Sabyasachi.

In an archery test, Drona asked his students to point their arrows at the eye of a stuffed parrot placed high on the wall. 'What do you see?' he asked them.

Yudhishtira said, 'I see a parrot.'

Duryodhana, determined to outdo Yudhishtira, said, 'I see a stuffed parrot placed on top of a wall.'

To outdo Duryodhana, Bhima said, 'I see a stuffed parrot placed on top of a wall under a cloudy sky.'

Arjuna, however, was focused, 'I see an eye. Only an eye.'

'Release the arrow,' said Drona to Arjuna. The arrow was released and sure enough, it hit the mark.

- India is the home of the guru–shishya tradition where pupils stay in the house of the teacher. The teacher is supposed to treat his students as his own sons. This tradition is prevalent even today especially in the fields of music and dance. But as many art lovers have discovered, many teachers are blinded by their love for their children and give them priority over students at the cost of true talent. Vyasa perhaps experienced this in his lifetime too. Had it not been for Arjuna's dogged determination and sheer talent, Drona would have kept reserved the best of his secrets for his dear son, Ashwatthama.
- Arjuna is considered to be the greatest archer in Indian epics, second only to Ram, the protagonist of the Ramayana. More than talent, Vyasa portrays him as one with grit and determination.
- The bow is the symbol of poise and balance. The third of the five Pandavas is an archer, suggesting his role in balancing his brothers. His two elder brothers represent royal authority (Yudhishtira) and force (Bhima), while his two younger brothers represent royal splendour (Nakula) and wisdom (Sahadeva). He is neither as aggressive as his elder brothers nor as passive as his younger brothers.

Ekalavya

Ekalavya was a Nishadha or forest dweller who wanted to be an archer and had learnt that Drona was the best teacher in the land. But when he approached Drona, Drona turned him away on the grounds that he was too busy to take more students.

'How do I learn then?' asked the young tribesman.

'If you have faith in me, you can teach yourself,' said Drona without giving his words any thought.

Ekalavya took Drona's words seriously. In a clearing in the woods, not far from Hastina-puri, Ekalavya created an effigy of Drona, and taught himself archery under its watchful gaze.

A few weeks later, he was disturbed by the sound of a barking dog. He shot several arrows in the direction of the dog. The arrows entered the mouth of the dog such that, without harming him in any way, they kept his jaws pried open making it impossible for him to bark.

The dog turned out to be the hunting hound of the Pandavas. Arjuna was surprised to find his dog gagged thus. He presented it to Drona and said rather enviously, 'You said you would make me the greatest archer in the world, but whoever did this unbelievable feat is surely greater.'

Drona decided to investigate and found himself face to face with his own effigy in a clearing in the woods. Ekalavya, who stood before it with a bow in hand, rushed towards him and fell at his feet. 'Welcome,' he said.

'Who taught you this?' asked Drona grumpily.

'You did, not in person of course, but by blessing and inspiring me to teach myself,' replied Ekalavya, his eyes full of earnest excitement.

Drona looked at Arjuna and remembered his promise to make Arjuna the greatest archer in the land. 'You must pay me a fee for what you have learnt because of me,' said Drona craftily.

'Whatever you wish is yours,' said Ekalavya bowing humbly.

'The thumb of your right hand. Give me your thumb,' said Drona, his voice cold and unfeeling. Without a moment's hesitation, Ekalavya pulled out a knife, sliced his right thumb and placed it at his guru's feet.

Arjuna returned to Hastina-puri shaken by the cruelty of his teacher, for without the right thumb Ekalavya would never be able to wield the bow. 'This was necessary for the sake of social stability—we cannot allow everyone to become archers. Now, there is no one greater than you in archery,' said Drona softly. Arjuna did not comment.

- Vyasa portrays Arjuna as a highly insecure and competitive youth. Ekalavya's cut thumb mocks his position as the greatest archer in the world. Through the tale Vyasa demonstrates how greatness need not be achieved by being better than others; it can also be achieved by pulling down others who are better.
- As per varna-dharma, a son is supposed to follow in his father's footsteps. Drona therefore was supposed to be a priest like his father, or a sage, but he chooses to become a warrior, as does his son, Ashwatthama. While he breaks the varna-dharma code himself, his argument against Ekalavya bearing the bow, that encouraging lower castes to become archers would destroy the varna system of society, seems rather hypocritical.
- The Mahabharata does not refer to the classical four-tiered Vedic society of Brahmans (priests), Kshatriyas (warriors), Vaishyas (merchants) and Shudras (servants). Instead, it refers to a three-tiered society where Rajanyas or Kshatriyas (warriors-kings-rulers) provided for Rishis or Brahmans (priests-teachers-magicians) and ruled over commoners—cowherds, farmers, fisherfolk, charioteers, potters, carpenters. Outside this society were the Nishadhas, or forest-dwellers, who were treated with disdain. There are clear signs of prejudice against those outside or at the bottom of society. They were forbidden from learning archery, for example.
- The bow was the supreme weapon of the Vedic civilization. It represented poise and balance. It also represented desire, aspiration and ambition. When a king was crowned, he was made to hold the bow. Winners of archery contests were given women as trophies. All the gods held bows in their hands.

The graduation ceremony

Drona organized a tournament to showcase before the people of Hastina-puri the skills of his students.

The star pupil was none other than Arjuna who could use his bow to shoot multiple arrows and who never missed a target. Everyone cheered for the royal archer and this filled Kunti with great pride. The Kauravas were envious for Arjuna outshone everyone and was clearly the favourite of the people.

Suddenly, there entered in the tournament another archer. On his chest dazzled a brilliant armour and on his ears were radiant jewels. Identifying himself as Karna, he declared, 'I can do all that Arjuna can and more.'

Drona asked him to prove it. Karna performed all of Arjuna's feats and surpassed in each one of them, earning the adulation of the crowds. 'He is as great as Arjuna,' they said, 'perhaps greater.' The Pandavas, who until then were the centre of attention, now felt small and neglected.

Suddenly Adiratha, the chief of the royal stables, ran into the arena and hugged Karna. 'My son, my son, you have done me proud,' he said beaming.

'What! This man is the son of a charioteer. How dare he challenge Kshatriyas in an archery tournament?' shouted Bhima.

Karna did not know what to say. The cruel words of Bhima stung him like a swarm of bees. Was his skill not good enough? Why should his birth matter?

It was then that Duryodhana came to Karna's rescue. 'Surely merit matters more than birth,' he said. 'I think Karna is a Kshatriya by merit. Let us treat him as one.'

'No,' said Yudhishtira, standing up. 'Dharma states that a man should be what his father is. Karna's father is a charioteer. He cannot therefore be a Kshatriya.'

Karna wanted to say that he was only raised by a

charioteer. But then people would ask who his father truly was and he would have no answer, for he was a foundling, abandoned at birth by his mother, found by Adiratha floating on the river in a basket.

Karna swallowed his pride and kept quiet. Duryodhana placed his hand around Karna and said, 'This man is a great archer. I will not let him be insulted. I take him as my friend, closer to my heart than my brothers. He who insults him insults me.' Turning to his father, he said, 'Father, if you declare him warlord, no one will insult him again.' Dhritarashtra who could never deny his son anything, agreed to make Karna a warlord, the king of Anga.

Karna felt a lump in his throat. No one had ever come to his defence thus. He was eternally obliged to Duryodhana. He swore that he would be the friend of the Kauravas till the day he died.

The Pandavas protested quoting the dharma-shastras. The Kauravas argued, realizing that with Karna on their side they were as powerful as the Pandavas, if not more.

Bhishma sensed the family feud was becoming a public spectacle. On one side were the five Pandavas and on the other side were the hundred Kauravas and their new friend Karna. He was embarrassed as his grand-nephews abused each other over Karna. They were about to come to blows when suddenly, in the pavillion reserved for the royal women, they heard a cry. Kunti had fainted. Everyone rushed to her side. Taking advantage of this moment, Bhishma declared the tournament to be formally closed and ordered the princes to return to the palace.

Watching her great grandsons snarl at each other like street dogs, Satyavati took a decision. 'I see this family I worked so hard to create will soon destroy itself. I cannot bear to see it. I will therefore go to the forest.' Ambika and Ambalika decided to join their mother-in-law. The tensions between Kunti and Gandhari and their sons were becoming unbearable. It was clearly time to leave.

- With Karna, Duryodhana becomes as powerful as Yudhishtira. While Yudhishtira has Arjuna, Duryodhana has no archer on his side. This deficiency is made up when he accepts Karna as an equal. Vyasa never clarifies if Duryodhana is using Karna or genuinely admiring him.
- Arjuna is the son of Indra, god of the sky and rain. Karna is the son of Surya, god of the sun. Indra and Surya were ancient rivals, each claiming supremacy in the Vedic pantheon. In the epic Ramayana, this rivalry takes the form of a conflict between Vali, who is the son of Indra and Sugriva, who is the son of Surya. God in

the form of Ram sides with Sugriva over Vali. In the Mahabharata, God changes allies and prefers the son of Indra, Arjuna, over the son of Surya, Karna. Thus the balance is achieved between the two gods over two lifetimes.

- Karna embodies a man who refuses to submit to the social station imposed upon him by society.

Karna's story

Kunti fainted during the tournament because she recognized the youth with armour and earrings as her first son. He was born before marriage, hence abandoned to save her reputation.

Pleased with her services, the sage Durvasa had given Kunti a magic formula by which she could call upon any Deva she wished and have a child by him. This happened when she was still a girl at her father's house. Curious to test the mantra out, without realizing the consequences of such an action, she had invoked Surya, the sun-god. Surya appeared before her and gave her a son. He was born with a pair of earrings attached to his ears and a golden armour that clung to his chest. A terrified Kunti put the child in a basket and left it to a river's whim.

This basket was found by Adiratha who served the Kuru clan as a charioteer. He and his wife, Radha, had no children and so they raised the foundling as their own.

As the years passed, Karna had this great desire to be a warrior. He even approached Drona but Drona refused to teach him the art of war. 'Stick to learning your father's trade,' he was told. But his mother, Radha, encouraged him to follow his own heart.

Determined to learn archery, Karna went to Drona's teacher, Parashurama, disguised as a Brahman because Parashurama was ever willing to teach Brahmans the use of weapons to stand up against the Kshatriyas. Parashurama accepted Karna as a student and was pleased with his eagerness to learn. Soon, Karna became Parashurama's best student, well versed in all the martial arts.

One day, Parashurama took a nap resting his head on Karna's lap. When he woke up, he found Karna's thigh soaked in blood. A worm had eaten into his flesh. 'The agony must have been unbearable. Why did you not shout or move to pull the worm away?' asked Parashurama.

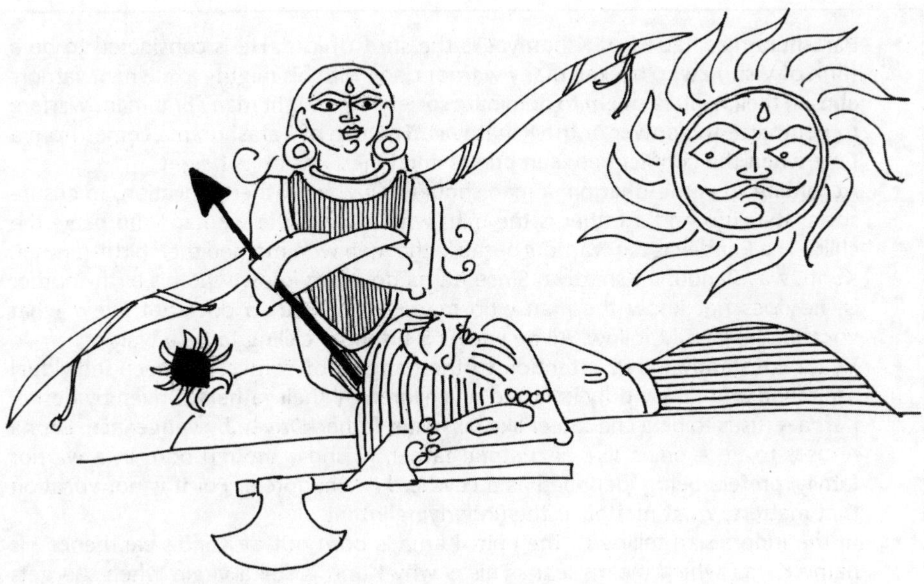

'I did not want to disturb you as you slept. So I suffered the pain silently without movement,' said Karna, hoping to earn his teacher's admiration.

Instead of being impressed, Parashurama lost his temper. His eyes widened in realization. 'You cannot possibly be the Brahman you claim to be. Only a Kshatriya is strong and stupid enough to suffer such pain silently. Tell me truly who you are.'

Realizing there was no fooling his teacher, Karna fell at Parashurama's feet and revealed, 'I was raised by a charioteer but I do not know my true origins.'

'You lie. You are the child of a warrior. You are a Kshatriya and that is why you have been able to display such strength. Because you duped me into teaching you, you will forget what I taught you the day you need it most.' Having uttered this curse, Parashurama drove Karna away.

- There are those who speculate that Karna was a love-child, a product of a pre-marital liaison with a prince of the solar dynasty, hence the reference to the sun-god. This story is narrated to warn women against the dangers of submitting to passion before marriage.

- Parashurama's hatred of Kshatriyas is the stuff of lore. He is considered to be a form of Vishnu who hacked many warrior clans with his mighty axe when warriors abused their military might to dominate society. He taught many Brahmans warfare to neutralize the power of the Kshatriyas. The tale of Parashurama comes from a time when the conflict between priests and kings was at its height.
- According to varna-dharma, a man should follow his father's vocation, to ensure social stability. And a father is the man who marries the woman who bears the child. The Pandavas are warriors because the man who married their birth-mother, Kunti, was Pandu, a Kshatriya. Since Karna does not know who his birth-mother is, he does not know the man who married her, and so does not know what vocation he should follow. All he knows is his inner calling to be a warrior.
- Vyasa constantly draws attention to the dangers of conflict between individual aspiration and family duty imposed on children by their fathers. Driven by desire, Karna refuses to be a charioteer like his foster father. Driven by vengeance, Drona refuses to be a priest like his natural father. Krishna, though born in a warrior family, prefers being identified as a cowherd or charioteer. For it is not vocation that matters; what matters is the underlying intent.
- In the Indonesian telling of the epic, Karna is born out of Kunti's ear, hence his name Karna which means 'ear'. This is why Kunti is still a virgin when she gets married to Pandu.

BOOK FIVE

Castaway

'Janamejaya, Rakshasas and Nagas and Gandharvas helped your family survive.'

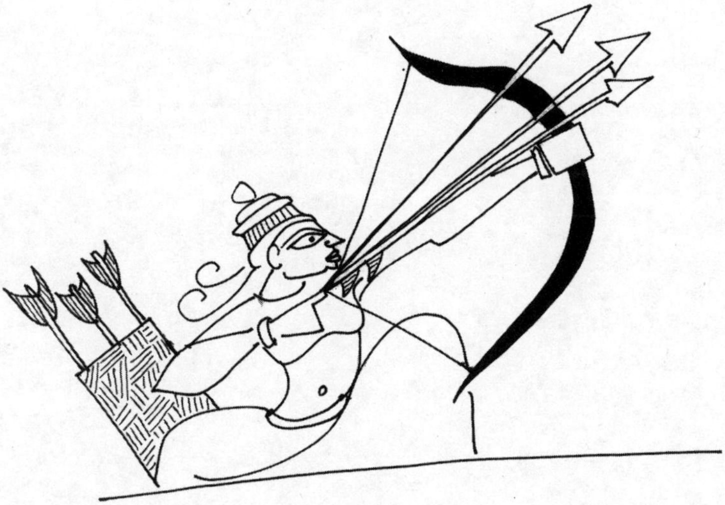

Bhima and the Nagas

Ever since Kunti returned to Hastina-puri with her five sons, the hundred sons of Gandhari feared they would have to share their inheritance with their cousins.

'But they are not the true sons of Pandu. They were conceived by the law of niyoga through other men. Truly, ours is the royal bloodline,' said Duryodhana to Vidura one day.

And Vidura said, 'No. The blood of Pratipa and Shantanu flows only in Bhishma. Neither Pandu nor Dhritarashtra belong to the original bloodline. They are sprouts of Vyasa's seed nurtured in the wombs of the princesses of Kashi. So your argument has little weight. Besides, Pandu was crowned king before your father.'

'But my father is elder,' protested Duryodhana.

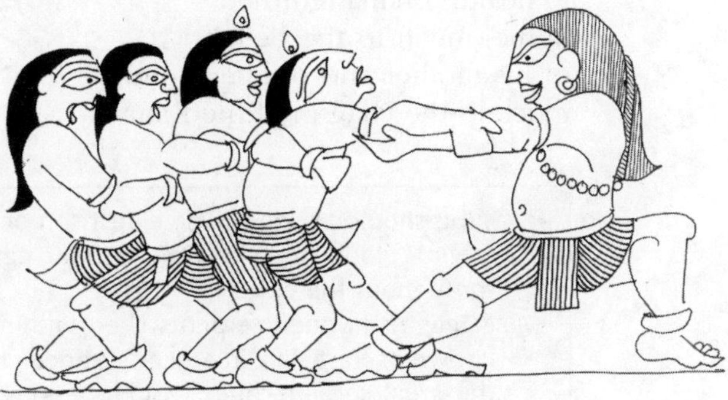

'By that logic, Yudhishtira should be the next king, as he is the eldest grandchild of Vichitravirya.'

Duryodhana was thus silenced but that did not stop him from hating his cousins. The hatred was mutual.

The Pandavas feared the Kauravas as they had no real power in the court; their mother was a widow and their father dead. They all lived in the shadow of the blind king and his blindfolded wife.

Bhima often bullied the Kauravas, picking them up and throwing them to the ground, or shaking trees that they had climbed on until they fell down like nuts.

One day, tired of Bhima's bullying, the Kauravas decided to poison him. They offered him sweets laced with poison. When he had lost consciousness, they tied his limbs and threw him into a river.

Bhima would surely have drowned. But in the river lived Nagas. Their leader, Aryaka, rescued Bhima and asked his Nagas to draw the poison out of him. Aryaka then took Bhima to Bhogavati, the city of the Nagas, and presented him to the Naga king, Vasuki.

Vasuki welcomed Bhima, 'Your mother, Kunti, is a descendant of Yadu and Yadu was the son-in-law of Dhumravarna, a great Naga. Thus the blood of Nagas flows in your veins. You are one of us.' The Nagas danced for Bhima and hosted a banquet in his honour. They also made him drink a potion that would forever protect him from any poison in the world.

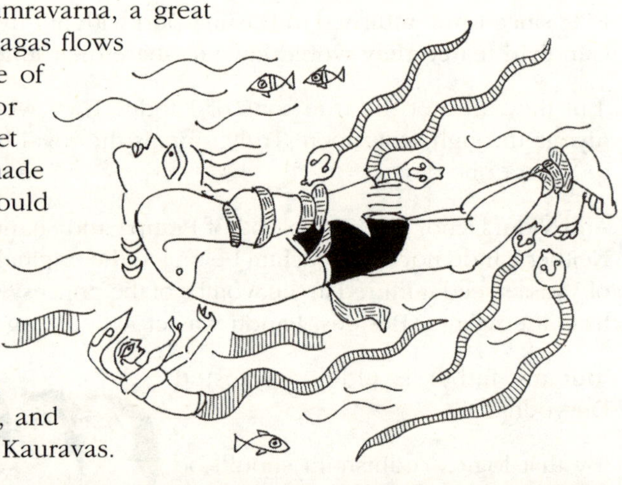

Thus revived and restored to health, Bhima returned home, much to the delight of his mother and brothers, and much to the chagrin of the Kauravas.

- Who should be king? The eldest son or the fittest son? A child belonging to the original bloodline, or anyone with the right capability? Vyasa ponders on this point throughout the epic.
- Nagas or hooded serpents lived within rivers, beneath the earth, in the realm known as Rasa-tala in a gem-studded city known as Bhogavati that was ruled by the great serpent-king, Vasuki. Besides being highly venomous, they were also guardians of gems that fulfilled all wishes, cured all ailments, resurrected the dead, restored fertility, granted children and brought good fortune.

- Anthropologists believe that the Nagas referred to in the epic were actually settled agricultural communities who worshipped serpents who they regarded as guardians of fertility. Even today serpents are worshipped for children as well as for a good harvest.
- A folktale from Tamil Nadu informs us that the entire Kuru household assumed that Bhima had drowned and that his body had been washed away. So they mourned his death and even organized a funeral feast a fortnight later to mark the end of the period of mourning. On that day, after all the vegetables had been cut and spices prepared, Bhima emerged from the river to the great relief of his mother and his brothers. Not wanting the vegetables and spices to be wasted, Bhima offered to cook a special meal, something different to indicate his new life. He mixed all the vegetables and spices, added coconut milk, and prepared the famed Tamil dish known as 'aviyal' or the mixture. This was quite different from a typical Vedic dish where mixing of vegetables was prohibited.
- During his stay with the Nagas, some folk versions of the epic state that Bhima was given a wife. From that Naga wife he bore a son who participated in the war at Kuru-kshetra. This son's name was Bilalsen in retellings from Orissa and Barbareek in retellings from Rajasthan.

A house of lac

The Kuru household was clearly divided into two rival camps: the Pandavas and the Kauravas. Each one believed they were the rightful heirs to the throne.

Yudhishtira was the eldest son of the consecrated king, the first of Vichitravirya's grandsons. As far as the Pandavas were concerned, their uncle was only a regent. But the Kauravas believed that their father had been wronged and that he was, as the eldest son of Vichitravirya, the rightful heir to the throne.

Despite having ninety-nine brothers, Duryodhana felt weaker than the Pandavas. Yudhishtira had beside him an archer in Arjuna, a strongman in Bhima and an adviser in Sahadeva. Who did he have besides Dusshasana? Things changed when Karna became his friend; Karna was as great an archer as Arjuna. And for advice, he had Shakuni, his mother's brother.

The smallest of things would lead to quarrels in the palace between the cousins. Kunti and Gandhari advised their sons to show restraint but their words were left unheeded. Sometimes, even the mothers submitted to the rivalry.

Once, Kunti decided to perform a ceremony that involved worshipping elephants for the well-being of her sons. She ordered the potters of the city to make for her elephant dolls using clay. When Gandhari learnt of her plans, she also decided to perform a similar ceremony for her sons, but to upstage Kunti, she ordered the metal smiths of the city to make for her elephant dolls of gold. This made Kunti acutely aware of her low status in the palace. She was the dependant widow of the former king. To bring a smile back on his mother's face, Arjuna said, 'I shall ask my father, Indra, to send down the celestial elephant, Airavat, for your ceremony.' Indra agreed, but drew Arjuna's attention to a problem: how would an elephant that lived in the sky descend to the earth? Arjuna simply raised his bow and shot many arrows to create a bridge connecting the sky and the earth. The world watched in astonishment as Airavat descended to Hastina-puri for Kunti's puja.

The people were not sure who should be king. At first, they sided with Yudhishtira who was honest, nice and noble. Supporting him were four brothers, one strong, one skilled, one beautiful and one wise. What more did a kingdom want? But they also felt sorry for Duryodhana, son of a blind father and a blindfolded mother, whose friend Karna, treated so harshly by the Pandavas, was not only strong but also generous.

'When they get married and women from other lands start entering this household, it will make matters worse,' said Vidura to Dhritarashtra. 'It makes sense therefore to build a separate house for the wife and sons of Pandu.' Dhritarashtra agreed and ordered a palace to be built for Kunti and her sons in Varanavata.

When Vidura visited this palace, he was horrified to discover that the house was made of lac and all kinds of inflammable material.

Vidura went to Kunti and said, 'My brother wishes to kill you and your sons. He will gift you a house—a gift you cannot refuse. Once you move in, he plans to burn it down. But fear not, you shall be safe. Below the house I have built a tunnel which leads to the forest. Accept the gift of the house to avoid suspicion and then escape through the tunnel. When you return, you will have a moral high ground that will go a long way in getting your children their rightful inheritance.'

Sure enough, the palace was given to the Pandavas and their mother and as soon as they moved in, on the first night itself it was set afire. The Pandavas escaped unhurt with their mother but they were shaken by the events. The family feud had suddenly taken a very serious turn.

When the flames died out, the charred remains of a woman and five young men were discovered. Everyone assumed these were the remains of Kunti and her sons. Dhritarashtra wept for them, Gandhari wept for them, Duryodhana and Dusshasana also wept for them. Bhishma and Drona were inconsolable in their grief.

Vidura pretended to mourn, for he knew the bodies were those of six people who had been drugged and left in the palace to burn in place of Kunti and her children. He kept wondering who in the household knew of this horrific plot. Whose tears were true and whose were false?

- The story of rivalry over the elephants comes from an elephant festival in Karnataka. It shows that the rivalry was not limited to the sons; both Kunti and Gandhari were fiercely competitive and sought glory for their sons.
- Much has been said about Kunti's relationship with Vidura. Vidura is seen as a form of Yama, the first god called upon by Pandu to make Kunti pregnant. Yudhishtira thus is the son of Yama and finds a father figure in Vidura. Rationalists believe that Vidura perhaps, in his role as a younger brother, was the first one invited by Pandu to make his wife pregnant. This explains his soft corner for Kunti and her sons.

- The story of the lac palace marks the Kauravas and their blind father as the villains of the epic. By this one shameful action, they lose all sympathy.
- Barnawa, located in Meerut district, close to Hastina-puri, is identified as Varanavata, where the palace of wax was built for the Pandavas.

Killing Baka

'Except Vidura, no one in the palace cares for us. Bhishma and Drona try not to take sides and Vidura cannot support us openly. We have to fend for ourselves. Let us not show ourselves till we have powerful allies of our own,' said Kunti. The Pandavas agreed.

So, pretending to be impoverished Brahmans, the widow and her five sons took refuge in the forest, never stopping in any one place for long, wandering through the wilderness wondering what life had in store for them. Was this the life they were meant to live? Homeless, rootless, children of the gods. The Pandavas often found their mother sobbing. They wondered how they could bring a smile back to her face.

Sometimes, when walking became too tiresome for all, Bhima would carry his entire family in his arms: his mother on his back, Nakula and Sahadeva on his shoulders and Yudhishtira and Arjuna on his arms or hips. Passers-by who saw this were astonished not merely by his strength but also by his devotion to his family.

When wandering in the forest became unbearable, the Pandavas took shelter in villages but they never stayed there for long as they did not want to attract any unnecessary attention. Fear of discovery and death haunted them every moment.

The Pandavas foraged for food all day long while in the forest. In villages, they would go from house to house seeking alms. The food collected would be divided in the evening. Kunti would give half to Bhima and divide the rest equally among the rest. She ate the leftovers.

In the village of Ekachakra, Kunti and her sons were given shelter by a young Brahman couple. One night, they overheard the wife cry, 'I know it is our turn to feed that monster. But if you go, he will surely eat you and I will be left a widow, with no means of supporting either myself or our daughter, left to the mercy of the world.'

Feeling sorry for her kind hosts, Kunti asked the Brahman what the problem was. She learnt that the village lived in the shadow of fear. A Rakshasa called Baka lived nearby and every time he was hungry he would raid the village, destroy property and kill all those who came in his path. To minimize the damage, the villagers came to an agreement with the Rakshasa: instead of him raiding the village randomly and spreading mayhem, they would every fortnight, send him a cartload of food. He could eat the food as well as the bullocks as well as the man, or woman, who delivered the food. Every family in the village had to take turns providing the Rakshasa his fortnightly food. Thus the suffering was distributed equally among all the villagers. It was now the turn of the Brahman couple.

'Fear not,' said Kunti to the Brahman couple, 'This house has given us shelter. The least we can do is save this household. One of my sons shall go in place of your husband. I have five sons; I can afford to sacrifice one.'

The Brahman couple protested, 'But you are our guests.' But Kunti's mind was made up. She ordered Bhima to deliver the cartload of food to Baka. The Brahman couple were touched by Kunti's sacrifice. As Kunti bid Bhima farewell, the other Pandavas smiled. Their mother had, in one masterly stroke, taken steps to rid the village of the Rakshasa menace while ensuring her hungry son had ample to eat, after days of frugal meals.

No sooner did Bhima enter the forest than he stopped the cart and began eating the food meant for the Rakshasa. When Baka heard the sound of slurping and burping, he was furious. He approached the cart and saw what Bhima was up to. Furious, he attacked Bhima but Bhima caught him by his neck and pinned him to the cart with one hand while continuing to eat with the other. When he finished his meal, Bhima smiled with satisfaction and then turned his attention to Baka.

The two fought like wild bulls. The earth shook and the trees trembled as they showered blows on each other. After a prolonged fight, Bhima managed to break Baka's neck.

The next day, the villagers saw the cart carrying Baka's body entering the village. There was no sign of the widow's son. In fact, there was no trace of the widow and her other sons. The villagers thanked the mysterious strangers for delivering them from their misery. 'They must be Kshatriyas in disguise. For is it not the dharma of warriors to protect the weak without seeking either reward or recognition?'

- In the rural hinterland of India, in tribal communities and even in South East Asia where the Mahabharata plays a central cultural role, the mace-wielding Bhima is the most popular Pandava. He is the great warrior who defeated many Rakshasa warriors and made the world a safer place. Perhaps the village folk were drawn by his straightforwardness. He was a passionate simpleton who could be provoked easily. He loved his food and enjoyed fighting demons. He was a hero of commoners, unlike the focused and highly insecure Arjuna who was the hero of the bow-wielding elite.
- Among many tribes of Orissa and Madhya Pradesh, such as the Konds, Bhima is seen as the one who brought civilization to earth. He is worshipped as a deity under a tree that is considered to be his wife, a tribal princess.
- Baka uses his might to subdue the weak villagers. He represents matsya nyaya or the law of the fishes, which is an Indian metaphor for the law of the jungle. In the jungle, might is right. Such laws are unacceptable in civilized society. That is why Baka is a barbarian in the eyes of Vedic scholars. For them, he who helps the helpless is a true Arya or noble being. That is why they extol the virtues of Bhima.

Hidimba and Hidimbi

Back in the forest after killing Baka, the Pandavas and their mother decided to rest in a clearing in the woods. There they were attacked by a Rakshasa called Hidimba, brother of Baka, who recognized Bhima as the killer of his brother.

After a fierce duel, Bhima managed to overpower and kill Hidimba. Hiding in the bushes was Hidimba's sister, Hidimbi. She saw her brother being killed but rather than getting angry, she was drawn by Bhima's strength and power. She decided to make Bhima her husband. Using her magical powers, she took Bhima's mother and brothers to a wonderful place and provided them with food, clothing and shelter. Impressed by this hospitality, Kunti accepted Hidimbi as her daughter-in-law.

In due course, Hidimbi gave birth to Bhima's son, Ghatotkacha.

Kunti watched her second son enjoying the company of his wife and child. She feared this attachment would distance him from his brothers. So, one day, she summoned Bhima and said, 'Our destiny lies elsewhere. Not with Rakshasas. It is time to go,' she said.

Bhima nodded his head and with a heavy heart bid farewell to his wife and son. As they were leaving, Hidimbi's son, though an infant, spoke like a grown man, 'Should you ever need my help, father, just think of me and I shall come.' Bhima smiled, touched his son's cheek one last time, gave a tender look at his wife, and then followed his mother and brothers out of the Rakshasa settlement.

- In Himachal Pradesh there is a village goddess identified as Hidimbi, suggesting that the Rakshasas were probably forest tribes who did not follow the Vedic way, hence were looked down upon as barbarians. They were also considered barbarians because they lived by brute force and admired strength over intelligence or wit. By becoming the wife of Bhima, Hidimbi perhaps gave up her Rakshasa ways and became worthy of worship.
- Although the words Rakshasa and Asura are used interchangeably, they need to be distinguished. Rakshasas reside in the forest while Asuras reside under the ground. In mythology, the Asuras fight the Devas while the Rakshasas harass humans.
- That Hidimbi accepts her brother's killer as her husband indicates that the Rakshasas respected the law of the jungle that might is right.
- Kunti is uncomfortable with Bhima's relationship with the Rakshasa woman. She tolerates it to a point but then encourages her son to move on as his destiny lay in the palace, not in the forest. She fears Bhima's domestication by Hidimbi will not be good for the family.

A Gandharva called Angaraparna

One day, while collecting water from a lake, the Pandavas were attacked by a Gandharva called Angaraparna. He claimed the lake belonged to him. A fierce fight followed during which Arjuna was forced to release his arrow charged with the power of Agni, the fire-god. The arrow set the Gandharva's chariot aflame. Before long, Angaraparna was unconscious and Arjuna's captive.

The Gandharva's wife, Kumbhinasi, begged Arjuna to release him. 'Let him go,' said Yudhishtira. Arjuna obeyed.

In gratitude, the Gandharva gifted the Pandavas a hundred horses. He also told them many stories.

One of the stories told was that of Shaktri, son of Rishi Vasishtha. One day, Shaktri found his way on a narrow bridge blocked by a king called Kalmashpada. Angry because the king refused to give him right of passage, he cursed the king to turn into a Rakshasa. The curse came into effect instantly, but it ended up hurting Shaktri the most. As a Rakshasa, Kalmashpada developed an appetite for human flesh. He pounced on Shaktri and devoured him. On learning of his son's death, Vasishtha was so overwhelmed by grief that he tried to kill himself by jumping into fire, off a cliff and into a river. But neither the fire nor the hard ground nor the waters were willing to harm Vasishtha. 'Live,' said the elements to the sage. 'Live for your grandson who lies unborn in his mother's womb.' In due course, Vasishtha's widowed daughter-in-law gave birth to Parasara, who became Vasishtha's reason for living. When Parasara grew up, he decided to perform a yagna which would destroy all the man-eating Rakshasas of the world, including his father's killer, Kalmashpada. 'Stop,' said Vasishtha. 'Forgive. Your father's outrage made him curse a king and that curse ended up hurting none other than your father the most. In the same way, your act of vengeance will achieve nothing but create a spiral of vendetta. Find it in your heart to forgive. Let the Rakshasas be at peace. And may you find peace too.'

Parasara saw sense in these words of his grandfather and abandoned his ritual that sought to destroy the Rakshasas. This Parasara was the father of Vyasa, who was the father of Pandu.

The Pandavas realized that the Gandharva had told them this story because he sensed rage in their hearts against their cousins.

'We are the Pandavas,' they revealed to the Gandharva, 'much wronged by the Kauravas.' They told the Gandharva everything from their father's death to their uncle's treachery. 'It is difficult to forgive when one has suffered so.'

'Shed anger. Make your own fortune instead,' said the Gandharva. 'You have now my horses. Now get yourself a priest. And a wife. Then land. Establish your own kingdom. Make yourselves kings.'

- The Gandharvas, like the Rakshasas, are forest-dwelling creatures. But they seem to be more sophisticated, travelling in flying chariots and using bows. Perhaps the non-Vedic tribes were classified into gods or demigods if they were found admirable, and demons if they were found to be abhorrent.
- In the epic, Angaraparna says that the main reason why he was able to attack the Pandavas is because the Pandavas had completed one stage of life, that of being students, but had not yet entered the next stage of life, that of being a husband and householder. Thus Vyasa draws attention to the importance of marriage. In Vedic times, as per ashrama-dharma, a man's student days came to an end with marriage while his householder days came to an end when his son bore a child.
- The story of Vasishtha and Parasara is consciously placed at this juncture. The Gandharva knows and does not approve of the Pandavas' anger, howsoever justified, against the Kauravas. This anger will yield nothing but more pain and suffering.
- The motif of two men on a narrow bridge and who will give the right of passage to whom provides a setting to explain the generosity that is the essence of dharma and the stubbornness which is the essence of adharma.
- The horse is not a native animal of the Indian subcontinent. That the Gandharva gives horses to the Pandavas suggests they took refuge in the North West Frontier through which traders brought stallions of Central Asia and Arabia to India.

BOOK SIX

Marriage

'Janamejaya, in your family, a mother asked her sons to share a wife.'

Children from Shiva

Directed by the Gandharva, the Pandavas went to the forest outside Panchala where they came upon a sage called Dhaumya, who on learning of their identity was more than happy to serve them as guru.

'The household of Kunti is incomplete without a daughter-in-law,' was Dhaumya's first advice. 'Let us find one. Let us go to the court of Drupada where an archery contest is being held. The prize is his daughter, Draupadi.'

Dhaumya then proceeded to tell how Drupada came to be the father of Draupadi.

Burning with humiliation after his defeat by the students of Drona, Drupada invoked Shiva, the destructive form of God, and sought a way to destroy not just Drona but also his patrons, the Kuru clan. 'A son to kill Drona. A son to kill Bhishma. A daughter who will marry into the Kuru household and divide it,' he cried.

'So be it,' said Shiva.

In due course, Drupada's wife gave birth to a daughter. The oracles said she would acquire a male body in due course. 'It will be a gender transformation like that of Manu's son, Sudyumna, who became the woman, Ila. Thus will she be the cause of Bhishma's death,' said the oracles, who also divined that Drupada's daughter was Amba reborn.

Drupada was not satisfied with this child. So he sought the help of the Rishis, Yaja and Upayaja, who knew the secret art of creating a magic potion which when consumed could give women children. The two sages performed a great yagna. But when it was time to give the magic potion to Drupada's queen, she was busy bathing. Yaja and Upayaja refused to wait for her and threw the magic potion into the fire-pit.

From the flames emerged two children: a man called Dhrishtadyumna who would kill Drona and a woman called Draupadi who would marry into the Kuru household and divide it.

Shiva thus gave Drupada three children. A daughter who would become a son, followed by twins, a son who was all man and a daughter who was all woman. The first was destined to kill Bhishma, the second was destined to kill Drona and the third was destined to cause a rift in the Kuru household.

Drupada wanted to give his daughter to Arjuna, the greatest archer in the world, but since everyone believed that Arjuna along with his brothers and his mother had all been killed in a palace fire, Drupada had no choice but to hold an archery contest and find the next best archer for his daughter.

- In Vedic times, all kings were expected to have by their side a sage who advised them on ritual, spiritual, occult as well as political matters. This was the raj-guru or royal tutor. Jupiter or Brihaspati served as the guru to Indra, king of the Devas. Venus or Shukra served as guru to Bali, king of the Asuras. Since the Pandavas were destined to be kings, they are advised to keep by their side a guru. This could be seen as an early form of alliance between state and religion.
- The Mahabharata is a Vaishnava epic, that is it focuses on the virtues of Vishnu, the world-affirming form of God. Shiva, the world-renouncing form of God, appears repeatedly in the epic as the deity invoked by characters burning with vengeance such as Amba, Drupada, and later, Arjuna.
- Shiva is considered Ardha-nareshwara, a god who is half woman. The children born through his grace possess both male and female qualities. Drupada's first daughter, Shikhandi, transforms into a son later in life. The next time, the magic potion splits creating two children—one totally male and the other totally female. Dhrishtadyumna is visualized as a highly violent man while his twin sister, Draupadi, is visualized as a highly sensuous woman.
- It is significant to note that Hidimbi, the Rakshasa woman, is not considered as a daughter-in-law either by Kunti or Dhaumya. It suggests a racist stance.

Draupadi's swayamvara

'Go to the swayamvara of Drupada's daughter disguised as priests and see what happens,' advised Dhaumya. 'If she was created to be Arjuna's bride, then nothing in the world can stop that from happening.'

The Pandavas followed Dhaumya into Drupada's court. Since they presented themselves as Brahmans, they could not participate. They sat in the pavillion meant for Rishis, Tapasvins and Brahmans and watched the Kshatriyas compete.

All participants were asked to string a bow and shoot the eye of a fish rotating on a wheel suspended from the roof of the hall while looking at its reflection in a vat of oil. A difficult feat, one that everyone agreed could have been done by Arjuna had he been alive.

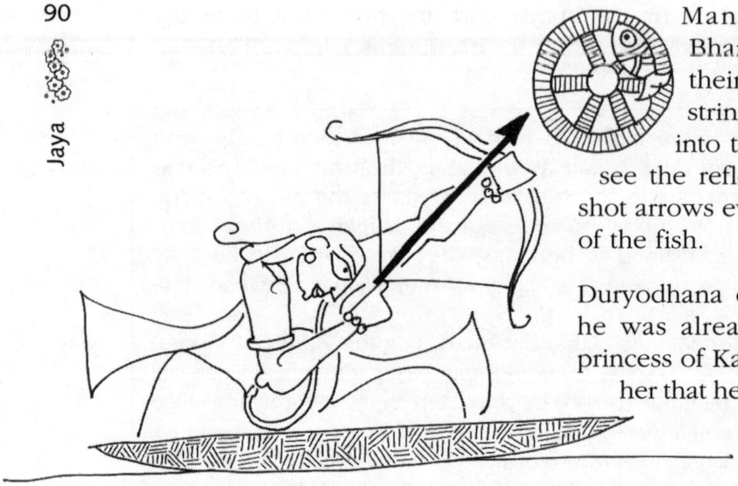

Many archers from around Bharata-varsha came and tried their luck. Some could not even string the great bow. Others fell into the vat of oil while trying to see the reflection of the fish. The rest shot arrows everywhere except at the eye of the fish.

Duryodhana did not participate because he was already married to Bhanumati, princess of Kalinga, and he had promised her that he would never marry another. So in his place, he sent his friend, Karna.

When Karna was about to try, Draupadi stood up and said, 'No, the son of a charioteer cannot contend for my hand in marriage.' Thus humiliated publicly, Karna withdrew.

When all the Kshatriyas had tried and failed, Drupada invited the Brahmans to participate. Arjuna immediately rose, picked up the bow, looked at the reflection of the eye of the rotating fish and released the arrow. The arrow hit its mark and the audience cheered. Every one was dumbfounded that a Brahman could do what Kshatriyas could not.

Some of the assembled warriors tried to stop Arjuna from claiming Draupadi as his prize, but they stepped back on finding out that the bow-wielding priest had the protection of his four very strong brothers.

- Ideally, during a swayamvara, a woman was supposed to choose a husband from among the assembled men. But as time passed, this right was taken away from women. The swayamvara became an archery contest. The bride was the winner's trophy. But the woman concerned had the right to disqualify men from the tournament as Draupadi disqualifies Karna.
- A folktale from Gujarat says that Jarasandha, the emperor of Magadha, wanted to participate in the swayamvara of Draupadi. But he did not go when he overheard people on the street saying, 'If he loses, everyone will make fun of him, for humiliating himself so publicly. If he wins, everyone will still make fun of him, for getting himself so young a wife.' Thus, in life, there are situations that you cannot win, no matter what happens.

- Draupadi rejects Karna on grounds of his apparent social status when unknown to all, he is actually a warrior. When no warrior is able to strike the target, Drupada compromises and allows priests to participate. Draupadi accepts her father's compromise, and marries a priest who turns out to be a warrior in disguise. Thus Vyasa draws attention to the folly of being driven more by external apparent truths rather than by underlying actual truths.

The common wife

'Look what I won at the tournament, mother,' said Arjuna.

Without turning around, Kunti said, 'Whatever it is, share it equally with your brothers.'

'But it is a woman,' said Arjuna.

Kunti turned around and found the beautiful Draupadi next to Arjuna. She also noticed that all her sons were attracted to her. Fearing that a woman would disrupt the unity of her sons, she said, 'What I have said must be done if you are truly my sons, provided dharma allows it.'

Dharma did allow it. Yudhishtira narrated the story of Vidula who according to the ancient chronicles had married the ten Prachetas brothers. With this reference, there was nothing to stop Draupadi from becoming the common wife of the five Pandavas.

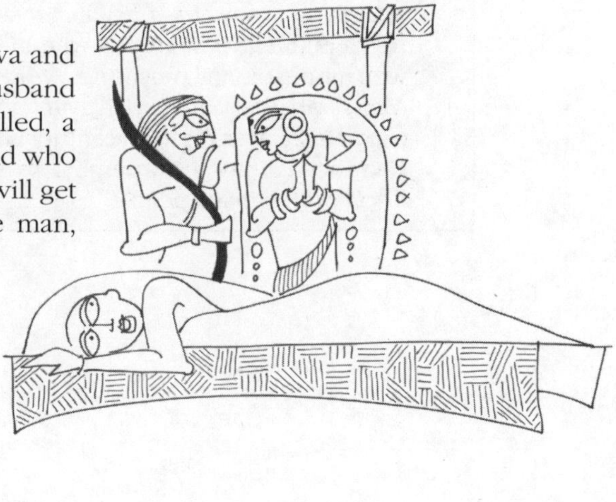

In her past life, Draupadi had invoked Shiva and asked for a husband who was honest, a husband who was strong, a husband who was skilled, a husband who was handsome and a husband who was knowledgeable. Shiva had said, 'You will get all five men that you want for no single man, except God, can have all those qualities.'

In another past life, Draupadi was Nalayani, the wife of a Rishi called Maudgalya. He had a terrible disease that made him cough and spit all day and covered his skin with scales and rashes. Still Nalayani served him as a devoted wife. Pleased with her unstinting service, the sage offered her a boon. Nalayani requested that he use his ascetic powers to indulge all her sexual desires. Accordingly, Maudgalya took the forms of many different men, some human, some divine, all handsome, and made love to her in many different ways. After indulging in sexual pleasures for many years, Maudgalya decided it was time to renounce the world. But Nalayani was not satisfied. 'Who will make love to me after you are gone?' she asked. Disgusted by her insatiable lust, the Rishi cursed her that in her next life she would be the wife of many men.

In their previous lives, all the Pandavas had served as Indras and single-handedly protected their queen, Sachi, and their celestial city of Amravati. But in their current life, they would, even collectively, be unable to protect their queen or their kingdom. For this was the twilight of the Dvapara yuga, the third quarter of the world's lifespan.

- Vyasa never clarifies why Kunti does not retract her statement when she realizes that what Arjuna is referring to is a woman and not a thing. Kunti knows that the only strength she has is the unity of her sons. She insists they marry the same woman because she fears if Draupadi marries only Arjuna, sexual jealousy will cause a rift between the brothers.
- There are a few tribes in India such as the Todas in the south and the hill tribes of Uttaranchal where polyandry is followed to prevent division of property. The household always has one kitchen and one daughter-in-law. The sons have the freedom to either share the wife or become ascetics or find pleasure elsewhere with mistresses and prostitutes, who have no legal right over the family property.
- Many variations of the Nalayani story are found in Malayalam literature, for example, such as the 16th century Bharatam Pattu and the 18th century Nalayani Charitram. They are attempts to explain Draupadi's polyandry that clearly discomforted many people.

BOOK SEVEN

Friendship

'Janamejaya, God, who walked this earth as Krishna, gave up his beloved and his music, so that he could take care of your family.'

Krishna enters

Just as Draupadi's hand was given in marriage to the five Pandavas, a stranger walked into Kunti's house. He was a dark and extremely handsome man with bright charming eyes and a disarming smile. He was dressed in a bright yellow dhoti. He had a garland of fragrant forest flowers round his neck and a peacock feather stuck out from the topknot on his head.

Falling at Kunti's feet, the stranger said in a soft melodious voice that touched everyone's heart, 'I am Krishna, son of your brother, Vasudeva. Your father, Surasena, who gave you in adoption to Kuntibhoja, is my grandfather. The blood of Yadu and the Nagas flow in both our veins. Your sons are my cousins.'

Krishna was born during turbulent times in Mathura, the city of Kunti's birth. Shortly after Surasena had given Kunti away in adoption, Surasena's nephew, a youth called Kansa, son of Ugrasena, audaciously disbanded the Yadava ruling council and declared himself dictator of Mathura with the support of his father-in-law, Jarasandha, the powerful king of Magadha. All those who protested were either killed or imprisoned.

Kansa's younger sister, Devaki, had married Kunti's elder brother, Vasudeva. On the wedding day, oracles foretold that the eighth child born of this union would be the killer of Kansa. A terrified Kansa wanted to kill his sister then and there, but was persuaded to let her live on condition that Vasudeva would present to him their eighth child as soon as it was born.

When Devaki bore her first child, Kansa became nervous. What if the child Vasudeva finally presented to him was not his eighth? So he decided to kill all of Devaki's children as soon as they were born. He stormed into her chambers, grabbed her firstborn by the ankles and smashed its head against the stony floor.

Devaki was beside herself. She did not want to bear any more children knowing what fate awaited them but Vasudeva persuaded her to change her mind. 'The sacrifice of seven children is necessary so that the eighth one can save Mathura from the excesses of Kansa.'

And so it came to pass, Devaki kept producing children and Kansa kept killing them as soon as they were born.

Thus were killed six children of Devaki and Vasudeva. The Rishis revealed, 'Your children suffer the pain of dying at birth because in their past life they angered sages with their misbehaviour. And you suffer the pain of watching them die at birth because in your past you angered sages by stealing cows for your yagna. All suffering has its roots in karma. But fear not, the seventh and eighth child will bring you joy. The seventh will be the herald of God. The eighth will be God himself.'

Sure enough, things changed when Devaki conceived the seventh child. A goddess called Yogamaya magically transported the unborn child into the womb of Vasudeva's other wife, Rohini, who lived with her brother, Nanda, in the village of cowherds, Gokul, across the river Yamuna. The child thus conceived in one womb and delivered by another was Balarama, fair as the moon, strong as a herd of elephants. Kansa was told that fear had caused Devaki to miscarry and lose her seventh child.

Balarama was an incarnation of Adi-Ananta-Sesha, the serpent with a thousand hoods in whose coils rested Vishnu, God who sustains the rhythms of the cosmos. Some said he was Vishnu himself, born when God plucked a white hair from his chest and placed it in Devaki's womb.

God also plucked a dark hair from his chest and placed it in Devaki's womb. Thus was conceived her eighth child.

He slipped out of his mother's womb nine months later on a dark and stormy night, the eighth night of the waning moon, when the wind blew out all the lights in Mathura. He was as dark as the darkest night and as charming as the sun is to a lotus flower.

Yogamaya caused the whole city to sleep and advised Vasudeva to place the child in a basket and take it out of the city, across the river, to Gokul. Ignoring the piteous pleas of Devaki, Vasudeva did as he was told.

At Gokul, in the cattle sheds, he found Yashoda, Nanda's wife, sleeping with a newborn girl beside her. Instructed by Yogamaya, Vasudeva exchanged the babies and returned to Mathura with Yashoda's daughter.

The next day, Kansa strode into Devaki's chamber, and after a moment of surprise on finding a girl in her arms, picked up the eighth child of Devaki intent on dashing her head to the ground. But the child slipped out of his hands, flew into the sky, and transformed into a resplendent goddess with eight arms, each one bearing magnificent weapons and announced that the killer of Kansa was still alive. And that Kansa would die as foretold.

- Krishna is no ordinary character. He is God to the Hindus, Vishnu, who descends from Vaikuntha to establish dharma. He does so as Parashurama and Ram before him takes the form of Krishna.
- Krishna's entry into the Mahabharata at the time of Draupadi's swayamvara is significant; she embodies the world he is meant to protect. Krishna comes only after Draupadi rejects Karna and chooses instead a Brahman who turns out to be a Kshatriya in disguise. She ends up marrying not only this fraud, but also his four brothers. Krishna knows the consequences of her decision. These husbands will end up gambling her away. He therefore becomes a part of her life to protect her from a distance.
- The story of Krishna's life was first narrated by Vyasa's son, Suka, to Parikshit, seven days prior to Parikshit's death. This narration helped Parikshit come to terms with his life. It is retold by Ugrashrava, the narrator of the Mahabharata, in the Naimisha forest. This narration is called the Harivamsa, or the tale of the clan of Hari, Hari being another name for Vishnu and Krishna.
- Kansa struggles to overpower what fate has in store for him. According to one tradition, Kansa was a child of rape; his father was a Gandharva and not of true Yadu bloodline. By the law of Shvetaketu that made the Pandavas the son of Pandu, Kansa should have been treated as a Yadava. But he was not. He was considered illegitimate and ostracized by the people of Mathura and he ended up hating them. Since he was not treated as a Yadava, he refused to submit to the ancient Yadava tradition of never wearing the crown. His hatred for the Yadavas fuelled his ambition to be dictator of Mathura.
- In some traditions, Yashoda's daughter who Kansa tries to kill is reborn later as Devaki's youngest child, Subhadra. In other traditions, she is reborn as Draupadi.

> Both Subhadra and Draupadi marry Arjuna. Arjuna and Krishna are said to be Nara and Narayana, two ancient Rishis, both incarnations of Vishnu. Both Subhadra and Draupadi are thus in some way connected to the Goddess.

The cowherd of Gokul

Krishna meanwhile grew up among gopas and gopis, the cowherds and milkmaids of Gokul. Few suspected his origins although many wondered why the fair Nanda and Yashoda had given birth to a dark child. Perhaps it had something to do with Yashoda being childless for many years.

The arrival of Krishna changed everything in Gokul. His life, right from his birth, was full of adventures.

Kansa sent Putana, a wet-nurse who had poison in her breasts, to kill all the newborns around Mathura, his nemesis among them. But when Krishna suckled on her breasts, he sucked out not only the poison but also Putana's life.

A demon called Trinavarta took the form of a gust of wind and tried to overturn the cradle in which Krishna slept. Krishna caught him by the neck and choked him so tight that the gust turned into a gentle breeze that lulled him to sleep.

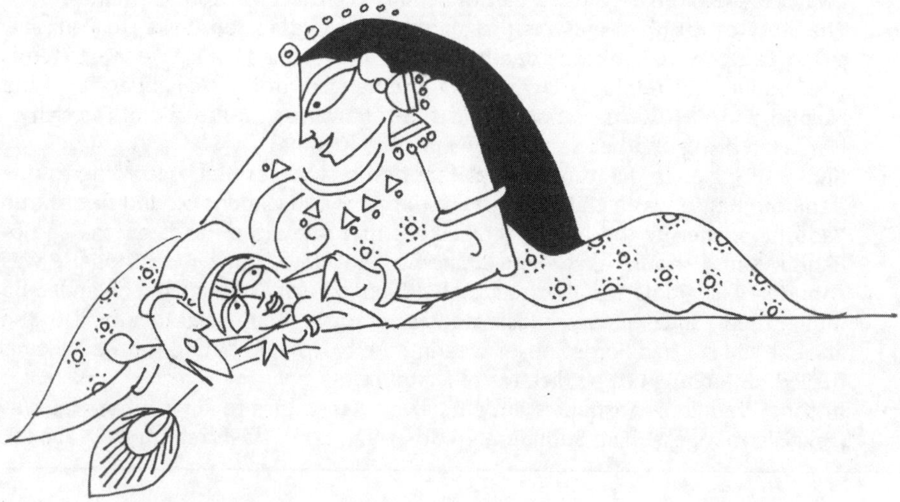

Another demon took the form of a loose cartwheel and tried to run Krishna over but Krishna kicked him with his tiny feet and smashed him to smithereens.

The incidents with the wet-nurse, the wind and the cartwheel so frightened Yashoda that she insisted that the entire village move from Gokul to a more auspicious location downstream, on the banks of the river Yamuna, next to a forest of Tulsi plants, at the base of the Govardhan hill.

This new settlement of cowherds came to be known as Vrindavan. Here Krishna grew up with a fondness for butter. A mischievous prankster, nothing gave him greater pleasure than raiding the dairies of milkmaids and stealing all that had been churned and stored in pots hanging from the rafters. The exasperated milkmaids tried to stop him and get him punished, but he always gave them the slip.

As Krishna grew up, he was given the responsibility of taking the cows to graze. He went to the pastures with his brother and the other gopas. There he entertained all with his flute and protected the cows from many threats including a forest fire, a giant heron, a wild bull, a hungry python and even a five-headed serpent called Kaliya who had poisoned the waters in a bend of the river Yamuna.

Krishna's brother, Balarama, watched over the orchards and protected the toddy palm trees there from monkeys. With his plough, he even dragged the Yamuna and made canals so that the waters flowed into the fields and the village.

As the years passed, Krishna opposed the blind rituals of the Rishis; he preferred acts of charity and devotion. This would eventually bring him into confrontation with Kansa.

Every year, Kansa performed a great yagna where ghee was poured into fire to please Indra, the rain-god. Krishna opposed this practice. 'Why worship Indra? Let us instead worship Govardhan, the mountain who stops the rain clouds and brings rain,' he said. When the villagers decided not to send ghee from the village for the yagna and instead began worshipping the hill, Indra got angry and caused torrential rain to fall flooding the village.

It was then that Krishna picked up the Govardhan mountain with his little finger and raised it, turning it into a giant parasol that protected the whole village from the downpour. This sight was enough to tell Indra that Krishna was no ordinary lad. He was God on earth. News of this event was enough to make Kansa nervous. Krishna was no ordinary child of cowherds. He was the lost son of his sister—his prophesied killer.

- Krishna's life in the village of cowherds is described in the Harivamsa, the appendix to the Mahabharata and later elaborated in the Bhagavata Purana and the later Brahmavaivarta Purana, written in the 5th, 10th and 15th centuries respectively.
- The cow is the most sacred symbol in Hinduism. This may be taken literally as a legacy of the Vedic past when cows were the only means of livelihood. Or it may be taken symbolically to mean the earth. In Vishnu Purana, which narrates tales of Vishnu, the earth comes before God in the form of a cow, Go-mata, and seeks protection. He promises to be the cowherd of the earth, Go-pal. To ensure harmony between earth and human culture, Vishnu establishes the code of civilization known as dharma. Each time this code is broken, Vishnu descends on the earth as an avatar. The scriptures say that the greatest of these descents is that of Krishna. Krishna loves the cowherds and milkmaids and protects them from all calamities. The world he creates is how the world should be, full of affection, love and security.
- That the plough-yielding Balarama is also said to be an incarnation of Adi-Sesha, the serpent of Time, on which Vishnu reclines, further reiterates the close association between serpent-worshipping tribes and agriculture.
- Krishna's entry clearly marks a shift in the Vedic mindset from the yagna-rituals aimed at pleasing distant sky-gods to puja-rituals aimed at pleasing earth-bound deities.
- Krishna is a cowherd-god while Balarama is a farmer-god. Krishna holds a cartwheel that is pulled by oxen and horses. Balarama holds a plough. In time, the cartwheel becomes the famous Sudarshan Chakra or discus of Vishnu and the plough becomes Vishnu's club or gada known as Kaumodaki.

Return to Mathura

Every night, outside the village, in the forest, on the banks of the Yamuna, in a meadow known as Madhuvan that was full of fragrant flowers, Krishna would stand and play the flute. All the milkmaids would leave their homes while the rest of the family slept, and come to this meadow to dance around Krishna. This was their secret pleasure. Neither the darkness of the night nor the creatures of the forest frightened them. They felt secure and loved in the company of Krishna.

Krishna had once stolen their clothes when they were bathing and had forced them to come out of the water naked. They had done so with great embarrassment but then, in his eyes, they saw no lust, only affection, a complete appreciation of who they were, not their external forms, not their flesh or their ornaments or their looks or their clothes, but their hearts. He loved them with all their imperfections. It was a feeling the gopis had never experienced before.

In Madhuvan, Krishna danced with all of them. If they became possessive and demanded exclusive attention, he disappeared completely, filling them with great misery and longing. They realized that bliss comes when love is shared with all.

This wonderful relationship of Krishna with the milkmaids came to an end when Kansa sent a chariot to Vrindavan ordering Krishna to come to Mathura and participate in a wrestling competition. Nanda had no choice but to let Krishna go. But he insisted Balarama accompany him.

The gopis and gopas of Vrindavan beat their chests in grief. They wept and threw themselves on the path of the chariot, trying to stop the boys from leaving, for they knew that life in the village without their beloved Krishna would never be the same again.

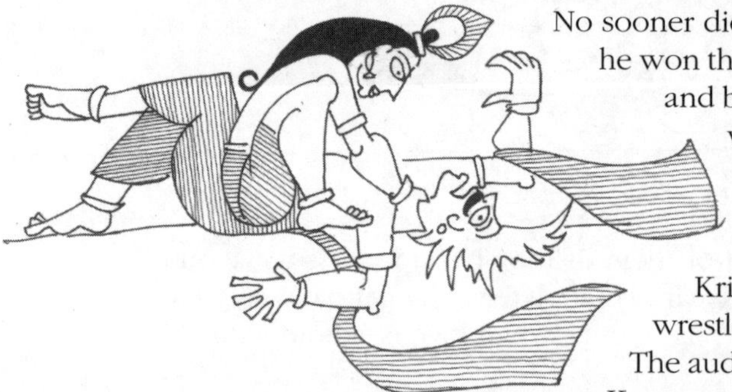

No sooner did Krishna enter the city of Mathura than he won the hearts of the Yadavas with his strength and beauty. Fearlessly, Krishna killed Kansa's washerman who had showered abuse on him. He then broke the royal bow on display and subdued the royal elephant who tried to block his path to the arena. Krishna and Balarama then defeated all the wrestlers of Mathura, including the champions. The audience cheered the two cowherds making Kansa angrier than ever. Kansa ordered that Krishna and all those who had cheered him be killed. In response, Krishna pounced on Kansa and smote him to death.

- That Krishna had a dark complexion and an opposition to Vedic yagnas has led to speculation that he was perhaps a deity of non-Vedic animal-herding communities.
- Metaphysically, Krishna's dark complexion aligns with his world-affirming nature (he absorbs all colours) while Balarama's fair complexion aligns with his world-renouncing nature (reflects all colours back). Between them is their little sister, Subhadra, born to Devaki after Krishna, who like Draupadi, is considered a form of the earth-goddess.
- The story of Krishna stealing clothes of women needs to be compared and contrasted with the disrobing of Draupadi which occurs later in the epic. In both, women are deprived of clothes but while there is romance and joyousness in Krishna's teasing of the gopis, there is humiliation and horror in Draupadi's tale. Ultimately, it is not about behaviour alone; it is about intent.
- In the temple folklore of Puri, Orissa, it is said that the daughter of Yashoda who had been sacrificed to save Krishna was reborn through the pit of fire in Drupada's palace. This made Draupadi Krishna's sister. Krishna left his village to rescue her. He had promised to return after destroying Kansa but then he had to destroy the Kauravas. He is still destroying the unrighteous rulers of the earth, unable to keep

> his promise to the gopis. Each year, at the height of summer, devotees celebrate the chariot-festival in Puri where images of Krishna, his brother Balarama and his sister Subhadra are taken out in a grand procession to remind God to return to his beloved Radha who waits for him in Madhuvan.
>
> - Of all the milkmaids who were dear to Krishna, there was one Radha who was dearer to him than most. Her name is not found in the early Puranas such as the Bhagavata, but is found in later Puranas like the Brahmavaivarta. In Jayadeva's Sanskrit ballad, written in the 12th century CE, Gita Govinda, the relationship of Radha and Krishna that takes place in secret, at night, outside the village, is at once clandestine, erotic and spiritually sublime. In time, Radha became a goddess in her own right, the symbol of sacrifice, surrender and unconditional love.

Migration to Dwaraka

Having killed Kansa, Krishna was hailed as the liberator of the Yadavas. His true identity as the son of Vasudeva and Devaki was revealed. This marked the end of Krishna's days as a cowherd. He was recognized as a Kshatriya, a descendant of Yadu.

After being educated in the ways of warriors by Sandipani, Krishna was accepted as a member of the ruling Yadava council which had been restored soon after Kansa's death.

Not every one accepted Krishna as a true Yadava though. When a Yadava called Prasenajit got killed while hunting and the jewel called Syamantaka that he wore round his neck went missing, many accused Krishna of stealing it. For was he not known as the thief of butter and the thief of hearts by the gopas and gopis of Vrindavan?

Krishna managed to prove that Prasenajit had been killed by a lion and that the jewel had been stolen by a bear. To make amends, Prasenajit's brother, Surajit, gave his daughter, Satyabhama, in marriage to Krishna, a marriage that consolidated Krishna's position in the Yadava council.

But all was not well.

Jarasandha, king of Magadha, was incensed that rather than punishing the cowherd who had murdered his son-in-law, the Yadavas had accepted him into their fold by giving him one of their daughters. He ordered his army to launch an attack on Mathura and raze it to the ground. Jarasandha's army attacked Mathura seventeen times. Each time, Krishna and Balarama defended the city valiantly and led the Yadavas to victory.

But the eighteenth time, Jarasandha's army was led by one Kalayavan who was destined to destroy the city of Mathura.

Realizing that discretion is the better part of valour, Krishna organized for all the Yadavas, including himself, to slip out of Mathura while the city was set ablaze by Jarasandha's soldiers. This act of withdrawal earned Krishna the title of Ran-chor-rai, the deserter.

Krishna and the Yadavas moved west, away from the river-fed plains, across the desert and mountains, towards the sea. They finally reached the island of Dwaraka.

Dwaraka was ruled by one Revata. Long ago, he had gone to the abode of Brahma, father of all living creatures, to find out who would be a suitable groom for his daughter, Revati. Unfortunately, he had not realized that a day with Brahma is equal to a thousand years on earth. When he returned with his daughter, all human beings had shrunk in size and no man was ready to marry his giant of a daughter.

Krishna's brother, Balarama, hooked his plough to Revati's shoulder and forced her to bend so that he could have a better look at her face. No sooner did he do that than she reduced in size. A much pleased Revata requested Balarama to marry his daughter. Balarama agreed and in gratitude, Revata allowed the Yadavas to settle on his island.

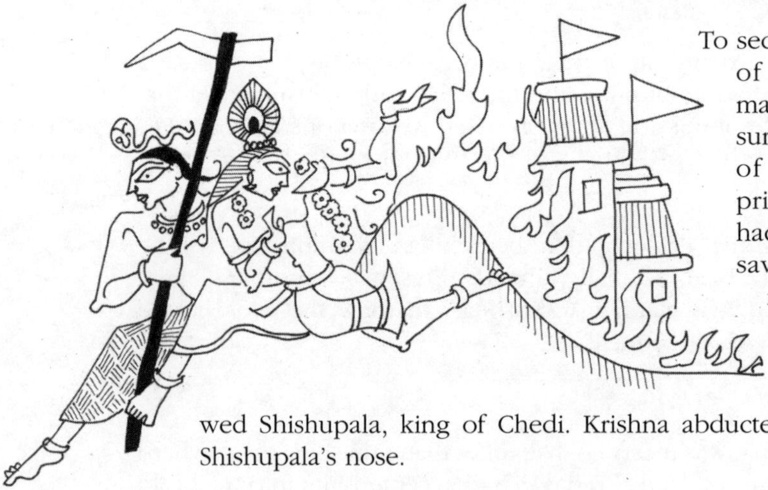

To secure this new island-home of the Yadavas, Krishna married many women from surrounding kingdoms. One of them was Rukmini, princess of Vidarbha, who had appealed to Krishna to save her from the loveless marriage that her brother was forcing her into. Rukmini's brother, Rukmi, had arranged for her to wed Shishupala, king of Chedi. Krishna abductedher right from under Shishupala's nose.

Shishupala happened to be an ally of Jarasandha, just like Kansa. He immediately informed the king of Magadha that while Mathura had been razed to the ground, Krishna was very much alive and safely ensconced with the Yadavas on the island of Dwaraka. Jarasandha could do nothing but fume in frustration.

Krishna then went on to marry many more princesses including the princesses of Avanti, Kosala, Madra and Kekaya. It was this desire to forge political alliances through marriage that brought Krishna to the court of Drupada where he met for the first time the Pandavas, sons of his father's sister, given up for dead after the fire at Varanavata.

- The name Kalayavan means 'the black Greek' suggesting Indo-Greek roots. Following the invasion of Alexander of Macedonia, the Indo-Greeks played an important role in the history of North India, from 300 BCE to 300 CE, about the same time that the Mahabharata was reaching its final form. Krishna lore is closely associated with many things Greek. Like a Greek hero, Krishna escapes death as a child and comes back as a youth to avenge the wrong done to his family. Mathura, with its ruling council, and aversion for monarchy, was clearly influenced by the Greek political system. Megasthenes, the Greek ambassador in the court of Chandragupta Maurya, identified Krishna with the Greek hero Heracles.

- The migration of the Yadavas from Mathura in the Gangetic plains to the island in the Arabian Sea following the destruction of their city, suggests a period of great turmoil. Through marriages, both Krishna and Balarama strengthen the political position of their tribe and restore their glory.
- The city of Dwaraka was also known as Dwaravati. The Yadavas gain rights over the island by getting Balarama to marry the local princess, Revati.

Krishna's family line

Yadu
↓
Ahuka
↓
Surasena
↓
Vasudev
↓
Krishna
↓
Pradyumna
↓
Aniruddha
↓
Vajranabhi

BOOK EIGHT

Division

'Janamejaya, your family destroyed a forest, killing countless birds and beasts, to establish their city.'

The division of Kuru lands

The Pandavas, who had seen Krishna at the swayamvara of Drupada's daughter, were a little wary. 'Why did you not participate in the tournament?' they asked. Krishna did not reply. He just smiled.

Kunti hugged Krishna and wept, enveloped by waves of memories: her childhood with the Yadavas, her adoption by Kuntibhoja, her tryst with Durvasa and Surya, her marriage to Pandu, the birth of her children through the intervention of the gods, her widowhood, her return to Hastina-puri with her children and finally, the attempt on her life and that of her sons. Krishna comforted his aunt, 'You have faced your destiny fearlessly and triumphed over it with your decisions.'

'Yes, I did,' said Kunti, her smile restored once again by the soft, comforting voice of Krishna. This was the life she was supposed to live. And it was the very same life that had brought her strange, delightful nephew to her. But why?

As if reading her mind, he said, 'Now you can return to Hastina-puri and tell them that you are alive. They will dare not harm you again for now your sons are married to the daughter of the mighty Drupada. They will go out of their way to make peace with you.'

'Will they give my sons the throne of Hastina-puri?' asked Kunti.

'I don't think so,' replied Krishna, 'But there is another way.'

The whole city rejoiced when they learnt that the Pandavas had survived the terrible fire and that they had returned more powerful than ever before as the sons-in-law of Drupada.

Dhritarashtra, Gandhari, Bhishma, Drona, Vidura and the Kauravas received them with great love and affection.

The Pandavas kept wondering who among them had hatched the plot to kill them. Duryodhana? Dusshasana? Or could it be Bhishma, ever willing to make a great sacrifice to end the family feud? Or Drona or his son, Ashwatthama, ever eager to please Duryodhana? Or was it Karna, who never forgave the Pandavas for humiliating him? Or was it Dhritarashtra, blind to the misdeeds of his sons?

Vidura advised Dhritarashtra that to crush all gossip and to show the world that he loved his brother's sons, he should renounce the throne and pass it on to Yudhishtira. Dhritarashtra, however, was unwilling. 'What will happen to my sons then? They will never serve the Pandavas. Maybe we should ask the Pandavas to let Duryodhana be king, for the sake of peace.'

Knowing that the Pandavas would never agree, Krishna suggested to Vidura that the only way to keep peace was to divide the kingdom. Bhishma protested at first but relented later realizing that there was no other way out.

In a public ceremony, Dhritarashtra gave the Pandavas the forest of Khandava-prastha. 'Make your home there. Go in peace,' said the elders of the Kuru clan blessing the Pandavas.

- With Draupadi by their side, the Pandavas are able to reclaim their destiny. Draupadi's entry also marks the division of the Kuru lands. Her footfall thus brings fortune but also breaks a household.
- The practice of using marriage to forge political alliances was common in Vedic times. The Pandavas had no power until Draupadi came into their lives. With the powerful Drupada as their father-in-law, they were in a position to negotiate. Krishna makes them aware of this.
- Since the Mahabharata talks about cousins who divide the family property between themselves, it is never read inside a traditional Hindu household. In fact, it is considered inauspicious. People prefer the Ramayana where brothers selflessly surrender their inheritance to each other.
- Vyasa never explains why Krishna chose not to participate in Draupadi's swayamvara. Draupadi is undoubtedly the embodiment of the world that God has descended to save, just as Sita was the embodiment of the world when God took the form of Ram. Krishna's decision not to be her husband must therefore have a reason. Draupadi had forbidden the very capable Karna from participating in her swayamvara on grounds that he was raised by charioteers. Through this display of caste prejudice, she inadvertently rejected Krishna who was raised by lowly cowherds. Draupadi embodies a world full of prejudice. This world may turn away from God and therefore suffer, as Draupadi inadvertently does, but God will never turn away from the world.
- A folktale from Gujarat says that Bhishma found the idea of the division of Kuru lands unbearable. He went around talking to the people of Hastina-puri, asking them if they were for or against it. The elders of the city told him, 'You never consulted us when you took the vow of celibacy for your father. Why do you consult us now when the consequences of that stupid vow are finally taking shape? Take responsibility for the mess you yourself created.'

Burning of Khandava-prastha

Khandava-prastha was a great forest full of birds and beasts. It was home of the Nagas as well as the Rakshasas. 'Burn it to the ground,' advised Krishna.

'Is there no other way?' wondered Yudhishtira.

'Can anyone establish a field or an orchard or a garden or a city without destroying a forest?' asked Krishna.

Agni, the fire-god, came to the Pandavas in the form of a fat priest and said, 'All the ghee that has been poured in me has made me ill. Burning something raw will restore my lustre, of that I am sure.'

Agni's timely arrival gave the Pandavas an excuse to set Khandava-prastha aflame. All things started to burn. The trees, the herbs, the shrubs, every tiny blade of grass. The birds and beasts cried out and tried to escape the flames. 'Kill them all,' said Krishna.

'Why?' asked Arjuna.

'So that no one returns to claim the land you claim to be yours. Know the price of ownership. Bear the burden of civilization.'

'When should we stop?'

'When your needs are met and before you fall prey to greed. Knowing when to stop is the hallmark of a good king,' said Krishna.

A great slaughter followed. Arjuna and Krishna and all the Pandavas went around the burning forest on their chariots shooting down everything that tried to escape:

deer, lion, monkeys, serpents, turtles, pigeons, parrots, even a swarm of bees and a line of ants, and all the resident Nagas and Rakshasas. Everything.

The Nagas cried out to their friend, Indra, who hurled his thunder and made the clouds shed rain. Krishna saw the rain fall and instructed Arjuna to create a great parasol of arrows so that not a drop touched the ground. Thus, under the parasol of arrows, the forest continued to burn.

After days of burning, Agni had his fill of the forest and regained his lost lustre. In gratitude, he gave Arjuna a mighty bow called Gandiva and Krishna a discus called Sudarshan. 'With these weapons, institute and maintain dharma on earth,' said Agni before returning to his celestial abode.

Nothing had survived the great conflagration expect one demon. His name was Maya. He had slipped between the walls of fire and begged the Pandavas to show him mercy. 'Spare my life and I will build you a great city, for I am the architect of the demons,' he said. The Pandavas looked at Krishna, who nodded

his assent. And so, on the land cleared by burning the forest, Maya proceeded to build a great city for the Pandavas. The Pandavas named it Indra-prastha, the city of Indra, determined to make it a paradise on earth. For sparing his life, Maya gave Arjuna a personal gift: the conch-shell trumpet called Devdutt.

Before long, Indra-prastha became the envy of all Bharata-varsha, for it was a prosperous city with fields and orchards and pastures and markets and river-ports. Priests, warriors, farmers, herdsmen and artisans from all over came to make this their new home. Yudhishtira with the help of his brothers instituted and maintained the code of dharma in this city. All men were supposed to do their duties determined by the role of their father in society and by their stage in life. All women were supposed to take care of their fathers, brothers, husbands and sons and help them fulfil their duty.

Advising the Pandavas was their guru, Dhaumya, who had witnessed their rise in fortune from their days in abject poverty in the forests of Ekachakra.

- It is interesting that Indra, a Deva, which is conventionally translated to mean god, opposes the Pandavas while Maya, an Asura, conventionally translated to mean demon, supports the Pandavas. While Indra, king of the Devas and god of rain, who resides in the sky, tries to save the Nagas whose habitat is being destroyed, Agni, another Deva, god of fire, who sits on the ground, consumes the Nagas and their habitat. Thus the relationship of humans, Devas, Asuras and Nagas is quite complex.
- Devas and Asuras had great architects who built vast citadels based on the principles of Vastu-shastra. Devas had Vishwakarma while Asuras had Maya. That Pandavas take the help of Maya indicates that the Asuras, though feared as demons, were also seen as allies under suitable conditions. Maya means magician, suggesting that the techniques he used to build the palace for the Pandavas were considered magical.
- Since weapons were so integral to warriors in Vedic times, they were given names and treated with respect. Arjuna's bow is called Gandiva while Krishna's discus is called Sudarshan. Krishna has other weapons too—a sword called Nandaka, a mace called Kaumodaki and a bow called Saranga. Balarama called his pestle Sunanda.
- Indra-prastha is believed to have been located on the banks of the Yamuna not far from modern Delhi. Hastina-puri was located further north on the banks of the Ganga. Kuru-kshetra is a barren stretch of land in what is now the state of Haryana.
- For helping him regain his lustre, Agni, the fire-god, gifts Arjuna many weapons including the famed bow Gandiva and a chariot drawn by four horses: Saibya, Sugriva, Meghapuspa and Balahaka.

Sharing Draupadi

All the five Pandavas loved Draupadi equally. This was a recipe for disaster for it was a question of time before they experienced jealousy and possessiveness.

Krishna told the Pandavas the story of Tilotamma, an Apsara who was sent by the Devas to create discord and eventually destroy the two Asura brothers, Sunda and Upasunda. No sooner did the two brothers see her than both desired her hand in marriage. 'I will marry the one who is the stronger of you two,' said Tilotamma smiling slyly. The brothers decided to fight for her. And since both were equally matched, they ended up killing each other in the fight.

'If you don't want to end up killing each other as Sunda and Upasunda did, you must agree to allow Draupadi to be exclusive to one brother for a year at a time. Once the year is over, you must let her go to your other brothers and return to her only four years later. The brother who enters Draupadi's chamber out of turn will go into exile for a year,' said Krishna to the Pandavas.

The Pandavas agreed. Each brother had exclusive access to Draupadi's chamber for a year at a time and she served each one dutifully. It was said that before moving on to the next husband she would walk through fire and regain her virginity.

Draupadi enjoyed Yudhishtira's honesty, Bhima's strength, Arjuna's skill, Nakula's beauty and Sahadeva's knowledge. She bore each one of her husbands a son. Thus she became mother of five sons.

The Pandavas were allowed to marry other women to take away their loneliness in the four years they were deprived of Draupadi's company. But none of these other wives were allowed to stay in Indra-prastha. This was Draupadi's demand and the Pandavas agreed to it.

One day, the cows of the Pandavas were being herded away by thieves. The cowherds sought the help of Arjuna who rushed to the palace to collect his bow. He looked everywhere but could not find it. Finally, he decided to look for his bow in the one place he had not searched: Draupadi's bedchamber. When he entered, he found her in the arms of Yudhishtira.

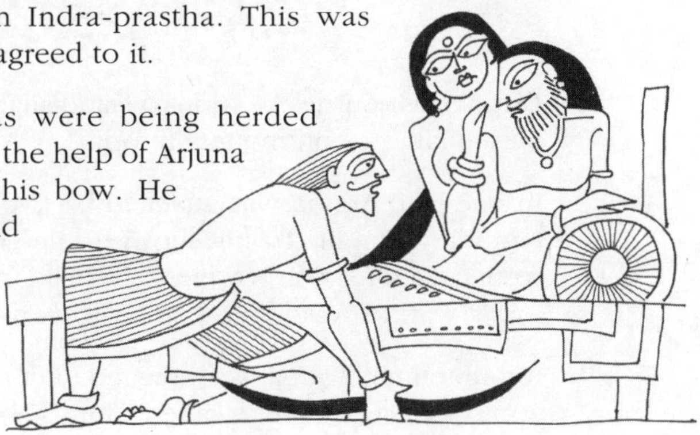

Since he had entered the bedchamber out of turn, Arjuna had to go into exile for a year as punishment. He decided to go on a pilgrimage.

- Draupadi bore the Pandavas five sons. They were: Prativindhya, son of Yudhishtira; Satsoma, son of Bhima; Shurtakirti, son of Arjuna; Shatanika, son of Nakula; and Shrutasena, son of Sahadeva.
- Besides Draupadi, each Pandava had other wives. Yudhishtira married Devika, the daughter of Govasana of the Saivya tribe, and begat upon her a son called Yaudheya. Bhima married Valandhara, the daughter of the king of Kashi, and begat upon her a son named Sarvaga. Nakula married Karenumati, the princess of Chedi, and begat upon her a son named Niramitra. Sahadeva obtained Vijaya, the daughter of Dyutimat, the king of Madra, and begat upon her a son named Suhotra.
- There is a Punjabi folklore connecting Draupadi's conjugal arrangements with the reason why dogs copulate in public. A Pandava would always leave his footwear outside Draupadi's chamber to let the other brothers know of his presence. A dog stole Yudhishtira's footwear and so Arjuna assumed Draupadi was alone when he entered her chamber in search of his bow. Draupadi, embarrassed, cursed the dog that since its actions caused her intimate moments to be known to another, all dogs in the future would copulate only in full view of the public, stripped of all shame.
- In the Oriya Mahabharata, Agni, the god of fire, demands that he be allowed to see Yudhishtira. Unfortunately, at that time, the king is busy in the chambers of Draupadi. Agni threatens to destroy the city of Indra-prastha if the king does not meet him immediately. Arjuna therefore is forced to enter Draupadi's chamber, out of turn, resulting in his long exile.

Ulupi and Chitrangada

During his journeys, Arjuna visited many holy shrines located on riverbanks, beside lakes or on mountain tops.

In one lake Arjuna was attacked by five crocodiles, but he managed to wrestle and kill them all. To his surprise, the crocodiles turned into five nymphs. 'We were cursed to be crocodiles by a Rishi whose meditation we disturbed. We were told a warrior would liberate us. That warrior is you. Thank you.'

Another time, Arjuna was dragged under the river where he found himself in the arms of a Naga woman called Ulupi. 'I have no husband. Make me yours. Make love to me,' she requested. Arjuna refused. 'It is against dharma to reject a woman who comes to you willingly and full of desire,' she said, quoting the scriptures. Arjuna had then no choice but to spend a night with her. Then he went on his way, forgetting the strange encounter.

From his union with Ulupi, Arjuna would become the father of a young warrior called Iravan who would, years later, play a crucial role in the great war at Kuru-kshetra.

Arjuna then came to the kingdom of Manipur whose princess, he had heard, was a great warrior woman called Chitrangada.

Chitrangada had heard many great things about Arjuna, and had fallen in love with him without even seeing him. She feared that Arjuna would be repelled by her rather masculine bearing. So she invoked Shiva and begged him to make her more feminine. Shiva answered her prayers and she transformed into a coy young girl. When she approached Arjuna in her new form, he paid her no attention for he had seen many such women. His eyes searched for that great warrior woman with manly gait called Chitrangada. When Chitrangada learnt what Arjuna sought, she begged Shiva to restore her to her original form. Arjuna took one look at Chitrangada as she really was and fell in love with her.

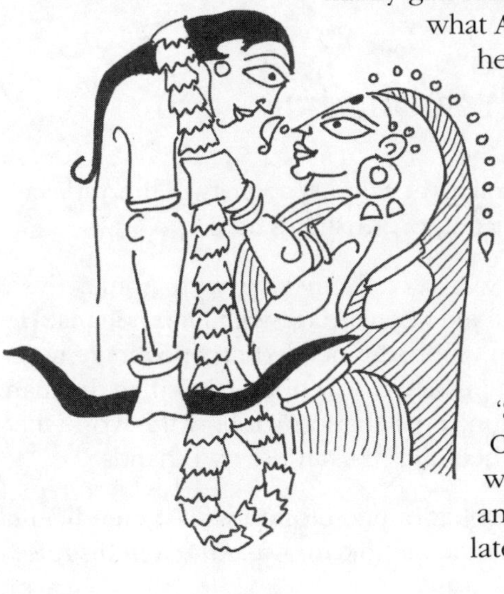

'May I marry your daughter?' Arjuna asked the king of Manipur.

'Yes, you may,' replied the king, 'provided you let me adopt the son she bears.'

'So it shall be,' said Arjuna. In due course, Chitrangada gave birth to Arjuna's son who was named Babruvahana. He would play an important role in his father's life years later, after the war at Kuru-kshetra.

- During his exile, Arjuna fell in love with many women and many women fell in love with him. Some he married and some he did not. Vyasa refers only to three of these women: Ulupi, Chitrangada and Subhadra. In Tamil lore, there are tales of his romantic liaisons with the daughters of Devas and Asuras.
- One of Arjuna's many wives was an amazon queen called Ayli, who he seduced while she slept, taking the form of a serpent and slipping into her bed. There is a Tamil folktale of how Krishna took the form of a snake charmer and Arjuna the form of a snake in the latter's quest to seduce Ayli.
- Rabindranath Tagore's Chitrangada in the dance drama of the same name written in the 19th century is different from the princess of Manipur of the Mahabharata. She is a learned and capable woman who yearns for love. She proclaims, 'The flower of my desire shall never drop into the dust before it has ripened to fruit.' So, when the ungainly warrior princess is rejected by Arjuna, she unashamedly conspires with Madana, the god of love, to bring Arjuna to heel, by disguising herself as a bewitching beauty. In time, Arjuna tires of mere beauty and hearing tales about the valour of princess Chitrangada, he seeks her out. The princess then reveals her true self to Arjuna. Her words are one of the most beautiful declarations of the angst of a woman, 'I am not beautifully perfect as the flowers with which I worship. I have many flaws and blemishes. I am a traveller in the great world-path, my garments are dirty, and my feet are bleeding with thorns. Where should I achieve flower-beauty, the unsullied loveliness of a moment's life? The gift that I proudly bring you is the heart of a woman. Here have all pains and joys gathered, the hopes and fears and shames of a daughter of the dust; here love springs up struggling towards immortal life. Herein lies an imperfection which yet is noble and grand.'

Eloping with Subhadra

Arjuna finally arrived in Dwaravati or Dwaraka, the famous port city of the Yadavas. He entered the city disguised as a mendicant, on Krishna's advice.

Krishna knew that his sister, Subhadra, was secretly in love with Arjuna even though their elder brother, Balarama, had fixed her marriage with Duryodhana. He encouraged Arjuna to elope with his sister. Subhadra needed no encouragement. As soon as she realized that the mendicant in the city was none other than the man she loved, she rode out of the city with Arjuna on a chariot. To show the world that she was leaving of her own volition, she held the reins in her own hands.

Balarama was furious on learning that Subhadra had eloped with a mendicant, and even more furious when he learnt that the mendicant was Arjuna in disguise.

'I shall follow them and bring her back,' shouted Balarama.

'Why?' asked Krishna, 'Can't you see she is in love with him? She is not being forced. Look, how she smiles as she holds the reins of the chariot that takes them out of the city.'

Balarama admitted reluctantly that ultimately it was her decision who she wanted to spend the rest of her life with.

Arjuna was in a fix when he reached the gates of Indra-prastha along with Subhadra. Draupadi had made it clear that no other Pandava wife would be allowed to stay in her city. Where could Subhadra go? She could not return to Dwaraka. Not knowing what to do, the newlyweds sought Krishna's advice.

Advised by Krishna, Subhadra entered Draupadi's chambers disguised as a milkmaid and begged shelter for herself and her husband. 'I have eloped with him and am afraid his senior wife may not allow me to stay with him,' she said without disclosing her identity.

'Don't worry, you can stay with me,' said Draupadi affectionately. 'You will be like a sister to me.'

'I am like a sister to you. I am Krishna's sister. And my husband is Arjuna,' disclosed Subhadra shyly, nervous at how Draupadi would react.

Draupadi realized she had been tricked but she forgave Subhadra and let her stay in Indra-prastha, allowing her to give company to Arjuna in the four years when he was not with her. In due course, Arjuna and Subhadra gave birth to a son. His name was Abhimanyu.

- In Indonesia, Arjuna is said to have married seven women besides Draupadi. The most important among them were Sumbadra, sister of Krishna, who is subservient and gentle and Srikandi (Shikhandi?), sister of Draupadi, a saucy and skilled archer, who later participates in the battle at Kuru-kshetra and is responsible for killing Bhishma. The woman who later became Duryodhana's wife was also in love with him but Arjuna felt it would be inappropriate for him to marry the woman already promised to his cousin brother, a side of Arjuna not seen in the Sanskrit Mahabharata where Arjuna gets pleasure in claiming what Duryodhana hopes will be his.
- In a strange tale that is unique to the Oriya Mahabharata, Krishna decides to play a trick on Arjuna while he is in the forest. He approaches him in the form of a monster, the Nabagunjara, a creature that is a composite of nine animals—serpent, horse, bull, tiger, elephant, horse, peacock, rooster and man. Instead of getting frightened, Arjuna sees the lotus flower in the human hand of the creature and recognizes Krishna. The story brings out an important Hindu philosophy: what cannot be understood by the human intellect need not be feared because it ultimately comes from God.
- Balarama teaches the art of mace warfare to both Duryodhana and Bhima but he always favours the former. The reason for this is never explained. Was it sibling rivalry, for Krishna always preferred the Pandavas?
- In Tamil tradition, Draupadi is a goddess and one Muttal Ravuttan is her royal guard and gatekeeper. He is said to be a king whose daughter married Yudhishtira. It was known that Draupadi would not let any of her five husbands' other wives stay in the palace. So that she makes an exception to his daughter, Muttal offers to become Draupadi's servant for all eternity.

Beheading Gaya

Gaya, a Gandharva, but some say he was an Asura, was once flying over Dwaraka when he spat on the ground. His spit fell on Krishna's head. Furious, Krishna swore to behead the creature who showed him such disrespect. He picked up his weapons, mounted his chariot and set out in chase of Gaya.

A terrified Gaya ran to Indra-prastha and fell at Subhadra's feet trembling. 'Save me, noble lady, from the mad warrior who seeks to behead me for a crime committed accidentally.'

Feeling sorry for Gaya, Subhadra said, 'Do not be afraid. My husband, Arjuna, is the greatest warrior in the land. He will offer you protection.' Gaya smiled. He was safe.

Shortly thereafter, an angry Krishna came to the gates of Indra-prastha, ordering Gaya, who he had seen entering the city, to come out. Subhadra realized that the mad warrior threatening to behead Gaya was none other than her own brother, but she could not go back on her word. 'Arjuna has sworn to protect him; you cannot harm him,' she said.

'I have sworn to kill him. Nothing will come in my way,' said Krishna.

Before long, Krishna and Arjuna stood face to face. Arjuna held the Gandiva in his hand while the dreaded Sudarshan Chakra whirred around Krishna's finger. Gaya lay quivering at Subhadra's feet. The situation was tense. Neither would give way for each one had given his word. 'To keep one's word is the fundamental principle of dharma,' said the two warriors. If Arjuna struck Krishna then the world would cease to be, and if Krishna struck Arjuna then that would mean the end of the Pandavas, which would mean the end of all hope for the world.

The Devas watching from Swarga were so alarmed that they begged Brahma, the creator of the world, and Shiva, the destroyer of the world, to intervene. Creator and destroyer both appeared between the battling Krishna and Arjuna. 'Stop,' they said. 'Your battle threatens the whole world.'

Turning to Arjuna, Brahma said, 'Let Krishna behead Gaya and do what he swore to do. Then I myself will restore Gaya to life so that you are able to do what you swore to do. Thus both of you will be able to keep your word.' Realizing the gravity of the situation, Arjuna lowered his bow and let Krishna behead Gaya; Brahma then resurrected Gaya.

Gaya thanked Arjuna and apologized to Krishna for having caused such cosmic disruption.

- The story of Gaya who creates conflict between Arjuna and Krishna is performed by the Yakshagana folk theatre in Karnataka. It was written by Halemakki Rama in the 17th century. It is not part of the classical Sanskrit narrative.
- The story shows how even good intentions can disrupt the bonds of friendship and how people can exploit friendship to their own advantage.

Nara and Narayana

One day, while walking by the river, Arjuna said, 'I have heard that Ram of Ayodhya was a great archer. With my arrows I have been able to build bridges that enabled elephants of Indra to descend to earth. Surely Ram could have built a bridge of arrows across the sea to rescue his wife, Sita, abducted by the Rakshasa-king, Ravana. Why did he not? Was he not as good an archer as I?'

Hanuman, the monkey, servant and devotee of Ram, overheard Arjuna speak so. He did not like Arjuna's boast. Leaping down from a tree, he told Arjuna, 'A bridge of arrows would never support the weight of monkeys. That is why he had to build a bridge of stones. You try building a bridge of arrows across this river and see if it can withstand the weight of one monkey.'

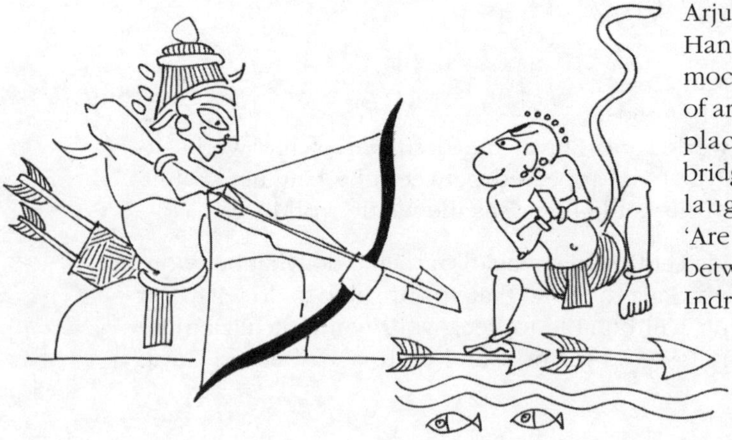

Arjuna, who did not recognize Hanuman, felt the monkey was mocking him. So he built a bridge of arrows over the river. Hanuman placed his paw on it and the bridge broke instantly. Hanuman laughed and mocked Arjuna, 'Are you sure you built a bridge between paradise and earth for Indra's elephants?'

Arjuna felt so humiliated that he contemplated killing himself. A sage who was passing by said, 'Build a bridge of arrows once again. Only this time chant "Ram-Krishna-Hari" each time you shoot an arrow, and see the difference.'

Arjuna did as told. This time, the bridge held firm when the monkey stepped on it. Hanuman then revealed his true form and danced on the bridge—it stood firm! Hanuman then increased his size, growing as tall as a mountain, but the bridge did not break despite the gigantic pressure.

The sage said, 'It is the name of Ram that ensured the bridge of stones to Lanka did not crack under the weight of the monkeys. Likewise, it is the name of Krishna that ensures this bridge of arrows withstands Hanuman's weight. Strength alone is not enough in this world; divine grace is needed. Krishna is Ram and both are Hari or Vishnu. Never forget that. Without Krishna you are nothing. You are Nara and he is Narayana.'

Arjuna bowed to the sage and then fell at Hanuman's feet, apologizing for his arrogance. He then asked Hanuman, 'What does it mean—I am Nara and Krishna is Narayana?'

Hanuman replied, 'This secret will be revealed to you shortly.'

A few days later, a Brahman appealed to Arjuna to save his children. 'They disappear as soon as they are born. Now my wife is pregnant again and due for delivery. I fear I shall lose this child too.'

Arjuna assured the priest that with his mighty bow, the Gandiva, he would save his children even if it meant fighting Yama, the god of death. Krishna joined him in this adventure. 'If I don't succeed,' said Arjuna, 'I will burn myself alive.'

When the Brahman's wife went into labour, Arjuna sealed the Brahman's hut with a barricade of arrows and then stood guard at the door. 'Now let me see who enters and takes the child away.'

A few minutes later, the child was born. Arjuna and Krishna heard the child cry. Then the crying stopped. 'The baby has disappeared,' screamed the Brahman. 'Oh Arjuna, you failed!'

How could this happen? No one entered the hut? Neither god nor demon nor man? A distraught Arjuna decided to end his life then and there. But Krishna stopped him. 'Before you take such a drastic step,' he said, 'there is something you must see.'

Arjuna mounted a chariot and Krishna took hold of the reins. Together they set out towards the horizon. It was a long journey. Arjuna realized that the chariot no longer touched the earth. It flew in the sky and they had left the mountains and rivers far behind. Soon the chariot was crossing the sea. Everything was a blur. The sky whizzed past as the speed increased. Krishna looked straight ahead. The sky became so dark that even the stars could not be seen. Krishna released his Sudarshan Chakra and it whirred in front of the chariot illuminating its path. Arjuna realized they had crossed the ocean of salt water. They were over another ocean of fresh water full of serpents, gigantic fish and strange magical creatures. Then they passed an ocean of fire writhing with fiery reptiles, then an ocean of treacle and finally the sea of milk.

There at the centre of the sea of milk, Arjuna saw a magnificent sight. He saw a majestic being reclining on the coils of a vast serpent with a thousand hoods. This being had a gentle smile and four arms in which he held a conch-shell, a discus, a mace and a lotus. It was Vishnu. The serpent was Adi-Ananta-Sesha, the serpent of time. At Vishnu's feet sat Lakshmi, the goddess of wealth and fortune. On his tongue sat Saraswati, the goddess of wisdom. This was God. The God who sustains the rhythm of the cosmos. The God who can fold time and space and do the impossible—even make babies disappear without a trace after they leave their mother's womb.

Overwhelmed by the divine sight, Arjuna prostrated himself. When he arose, he found Vishnu holding many babies in his arms. 'These are the Brahman's children. I brought them here so that you follow them and learn the true purpose of your existence.'

Arjuna did not understand. Krishna smiled and explained, 'Once you were Nara and I was Narayana. Together we fought many demons and won many battles. Now we are Arjuna and Krishna. We have been created to restore dharma on earth.'

Vishnu told Arjuna, 'Krishna is wisdom. You are action. One without another is useless. All your battles you will win only when you are together.'

- These stories come from the Bhagavata and other Puranas that identify Krishna as God.
- The notion of an all-powerful God enters quite late in the history of Hinduism. Early Vedic scriptures are best described as agnostic. There are numerous references to natural spirits and cosmic forces that can be invoked through rituals but there is no clear mention of God. At best, the Upanishads associate God with the soul (atma). With the rise of atheistic monastic orders such as Buddhism, ideas such as samsara (cycle of rebirths), karma (influence of past actions) and moksha (liberation) gain popularity. As a counter to them, the idea of God, first propagated by the Bhagavata cult, becomes increasingly acceptable to the mainstream. The people find great solace in the idea of a personal God whose grace, obtained through devotion, can overpower the shackles of karma and samsara. The Mahabharata is

among the earliest Hindu texts to endorse the idea of a very personal anthropomorphic God who is very responsive to the human condition. It is the presence of Krishna who is Viṣhnu on earth that transforms the Mahabharata into a sacred scripture.

- In popular belief, men have vestigial nipples as a mark of the feminine within them. Arjuna had only one nipple, not two, because he was more man than others. Krishna had no nipples because he was a purna-purusha, a full man.
- Nara and Narayana were two inseparable sages. They lived in the Himalayas under the Badari or berry tree. Their name repeatedly recurs in the epic as the former incarnations of Arjuna and Krishna. Visualized as warrior-ascetics, they are believed to be the earliest worshippers of Vishnu, who later came to be identified with Vishnu. Metaphysically speaking, Nara means human while Narayana is God. The relationship of Arjuna and Krishna is that of man and God, inseparable.
- By associating Arjuna and Krishna to Nara and Narayana, Vyasa makes them creatures of destiny. Their birth is not random; they are born for a reason.

BOOK NINE

Coronation

'Janamejaya, kings were killed before and during the coronation of your forefather.'

Death of Jarasandha

Shortly after Arjuna's return from his pilgrimage, Yudhishtira expressed his desire to be king. 'I want to perform the Rajasuya yagna,' he said.

But for that he needed other kings of the land to participate in the ceremony, a symbolic acknowledgement of his sovereignty.

Krishna said, 'You have to first prove you are worthy to wear the crown. And the best way to demonstrate your power, so that your claim to kingship is uncontested, is to overpower Jarasandha.'

'The king of Magadha, destroyer of Mathura!' exclaimed Yudhishtira, suddenly unsure, for Jarasandha was greatly feared in Bharata-varsha. It was said that he had imprisoned a hundred kings and planned to conduct a human sacrifice. 'My army is no match for his.'

Krishna smiled and said, 'Mighty brawn is no match for a nimble brain. Let us go to his city disguised as priests. In keeping with the laws of hospitality, he will offer us anything we desire. We shall ask him for a duel. A hand-to-hand combat to the death.'

The Pandavas were impressed with Krishna's plan. They knew that Krishna and Jarasandha were old enemies. This plan would benefit both, the Yadavas and the Pandavas. The Yadavas would be rid of the man who destroyed Mathura and the

Pandavas would be able to declare themselves kings and repay their debt to Krishna who had done so much for them.

Predictably, Jarasandha welcomed the three Brahmans who had come down from Hastina-puri and in keeping with the code of hospitality, offered to fulfil any of their wishes. 'Ask and it shall be yours,' he said.

'We wish a hand-to-hand combat with you, to the death,' said the three Brahmans.

Jarasandha immediately realized these were no Brahmans but Kshatriyas in disguise. He had been duped but he was too proud to go back on his word. 'I suspect one of you is Krishna, the coward who ran away to Dwaraka when I burnt down his city of Mathura. And the other two must be the Pandavas with whom he has forged a powerful alliance.' Looking at Arjuna, he said, 'You are lean and thin, unworthy in a hand-to-hand combat. Besides the marks on your arms indicate you are an archer. You must be Arjuna.' He then turned to Bhima and said, 'You are big and strong. A worthy opponent. I suspect you are Bhima.' Then he turned to Krishna. 'You are dark and your eyes radiate mischief. You must be the boy who killed my son-in-law. I will deal with you after I have dealt with Bhima here.'

As Bhima was about to enter the wrestling arena, Krishna picked up a leaf, tore it into two along the spine, and said, 'The only way to kill Jarasandha is to tear his body into two vertical halves as I do this leaf. His childless father divided the magic potion meant to give him a child equally between his two wives. As a result, each wife bore him half a child. These two halves were fused together by a demoness called Jara who protects Jarasandha and makes him invincible. He cannot be killed by any weapon. Only if he is split into two can he die.'

Bhima realized soon enough that Jarasandha was indeed an invincible opponent. The powerful punches with which he had killed demons like Baka and Hidimba had no effect on the king of Magadha. They fought like wild elephants for hours. Finally, Bhima pinned Jarasandha to the ground, caught hold of his leg and with all his might tore his body into two. A cheer rose from the spectators.

But then all fell silent. To everyone's astonishment, the left half of the body magically moved towards and fused with the right half of the body and Jarasandha stood up unhurt. Bhima looked at Krishna quizzically. Krishna immediately picked up another leaf, split it into two along its spine, but this time threw the left half of the leaf on the right side and the right half of the leaf on the left side. Bhima understood the message.

The fighting resumed. A terrible fight that caused the pillars of the wrestling arena to tremble and the Devas to gather along the horizon and cheer Bhima. After many hours, Bhima was finally able to pin Jarasandha to the ground. Holding one leg, he tore Jarasandha into two as he had done last time. He then threw the left side of the body to the right side of the arena and the right side of the body to the left side of the arena.

Thus was Jarasandha killed. With this, Krishna was finally rid of the man who had destroyed the Yadava city of Mathura. No king now remained in Bharata-varsha who would challenge Yudhishtira's bid to be king. Thus did Indra-prastha, a city established by the Pandavas, become a sovereign kingdom.

- A Rajasuya yagna granted kingdoms their sovereignty. To achieve this status, the ruler of the kingdom had to prove his military might so that other kings of the land accepted him as an equal. By performing a Rajasuya, Yudhishtira was formally breaking all ties with his uncle and telling the world that his kingdom was autonomous.
- While helping the Pandavas, Krishna also uses them to defeat his enemy, Jarasandha. Krishna's running away when Jarasandha's army destroyed Mathura, earned him the rather derogatory title of Ran-chor-rai, he who withdrew from battle.
- In Jain traditions, every world cycle witnesses sixty-three great heroes known as the Salaka-purushas. They include twenty-four hermits or Tirthankaras, twelve kings or Chakra-vartis and nine sets of three warriors comprising the righteous and peaceful Baladeva, the righteous but violent Vasudeva and the unrighteous Prativasudeva. Krishna and Jarasandha are considered to be Vasudeva and Prativasudeva, fated to fight. Krishna's elder brother, Balarama, is the gentle Baladeva who prefers peace to war. In the next world cycle, say the Jain scriptures, Balarama will be reborn as a Tirthankara much earlier than Krishna because of his preference for the Jain principle of ahimsa or non-violence.

Duryodhana falls into a pond

The coronation of Yudhishtira was a grand affair attended by kings from all over the land. Among the guests were Rakshasas, Devas, Asuras, Yakshas, Nagas and Gandharvas. There were also Duryodhana and Shishupala.

Duryodhana went around the great city built by the demon Maya. He saw the grandeur of the palaces, the organization of the streets, the beauty of the gardens and the orchards. He realized the main palace was built such that a breeze moved gently through all its corridors and sunlight bounced off all its walls. Poets equated the great palace of the Pandavas to the sabha of Indra, the city to Amravati and the kingdom to Swarga. Duryodhana was filled with envy.

As Duryodhana walked along the corridors staring at the painted roof, he slipped and fell into a pond.

Draupadi who was walking past, rather thoughtlessly, let out a peal of laughter and said, 'The blind son of blind parents.'

Duryodhana was certainly not amused. He swore that day that one day he would take pleasure in Draupadi's humiliation as she had taken in his.

- In many narrations, Draupadi's insensitive comments about Duryodhana's parents is presented as the reason why she was humiliated later in life. This event is narrated as a warning to people not to make fun of disabilities.
- Indra-prastha's magical palace is the envy of all the kings who come there. Duryodhana is especially disturbed. He realizes that his cousins have created something magnificent out of nothing while he had never created anything in his life. His jealousy reaches its acme at Yudhishtira's coronation.
- Vibhishana, king of Lanka and leader of the Rakshasas, refused to bow to Yudhishtira stating that he bowed to none but Ram, king of Ayodhya, who had defeated his brother, Ravana, and was Vishnu on earth. Krishna, who was also Vishnu on earth, fell at Yudhishtira's feet stating that any king who upholds dharma on earth is like Ram of Ayodhya. Seeing this, Vibhishana changed his mind and fell at Yudhishtira's feet.

Death of Shishupala

The Brahmans poured water and milk and honey on Yudhishtira in the presence of all the kings of Bharata-varsha. He was thus declared king. Around him stood his four brothers and on his left lap sat their common wife, the queen of Indra-prastha. Some guests like their father-in-law, Drupada, and their uncle, Shalya, and their cousins, Krishna and Balarama, were happy for the Pandavas. Others like Duryodhana and Karna, Shalva and Shishupala, were rather jealous.

During the ceremony, the priests asked the Pandavas to select from all the assembled guests a guest of honour. The Pandavas selected Krishna for without him they would not have been able to achieve what they had achieved. Krishna was placed on the seat of honour and offered many gifts by the five brothers and their wife.

Suddenly, Shishupala, king of Chedi, stood up and protested, 'A hundred kings are gathered here and the Pandavas choose to honour Krishna, a Yadava, whose

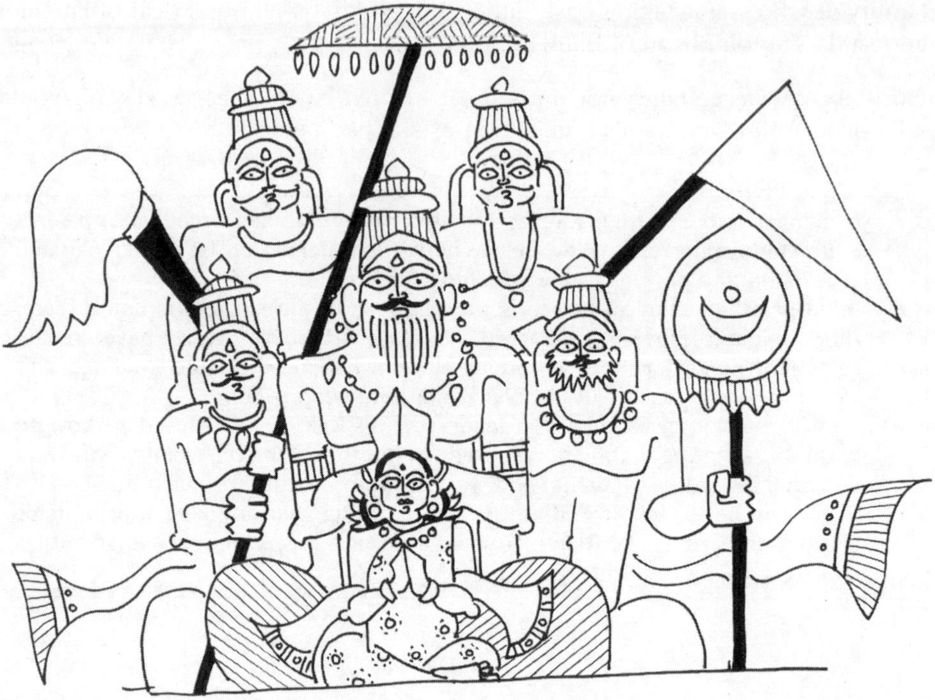

ancestor Yadu was rejected by his father, who can never be king, who was raised by common cowherds, who spent his entire childhood killing animals and dancing with milkmaids, who killed his own mother's brother, who ran away like a coward and let his city be burned down by Jarasandha, who eloped and abducted princesses as a defence against further attacks . . .'

Shishupala's tirade so annoyed the Pandavas that they raised their weapons to stop Shishupala. The assembled kings also raised their weapons to protect Shishupala, for nothing Shishupala said was false. The royal hall of Yudhishtira was in real danger of turning into a battlefield. In this tense situation, Krishna said, 'This is between Shishupala and me. Let him say what he wants to say. He is my cousin, son of my father's sister, just like the Pandavas.'

Krishna did not tell the assembled guests that at the time of Shishupala's birth, oracles had foretold that Krishna would kill Shishupala. To save Shishupala, his mother had begged Krishna to forgive all her son's misdemeanours. 'I will forgive him a hundred times. No more,' Krishna had promised.

Shishupala's tirade continued. He kept insulting Krishna. Krishna forgave each insult hurled at him.

At the hundredth insult, Krishna stood up and raised his hand. 'Enough, cousin. You have insulted me a hundred times. And as promised to your mother, I have forgiven you each time. But no more. If you insult me again, I will kill you.'

Shishupala did not care. He hated Krishna. Krishna was a common cowherd and he was king of Chedi, yet Krishna was more respected and more popular in all of Bharata-varsha. It was Krishna who had abducted and married Rukmini, the woman he loved, right from under his nose. It was Krishna who had killed Jarasandha, who had been like a father to him. And it was Krishna who had been chosen by the Pandavas to be the guest of honour. Full of bitterness and jealousy, Shishupala insulted Krishna once again. The hundred and first insult.

Before anyone in the great hall could even blink, Krishna hurled his discus, the Sudarshan Chakra, and severed Shishupala's neck. As the head fell to the ground, there was an uproar among the kings. 'Is this how the Pandavas treat their guests? Let a common cowherd kill a king. Let us leave. Yudhishtira may be king, but he

does not deserve our respect.' So saying, many kings of Bharata-varsha stormed out of the sabha. The great coronation ceremony of Yudhishtira thus ended on an extremely inauspicious note.

Among the kings who stormed out were Shalva and Dantavakra, who were friends of Shishupala and allies of Jarasandha. They decided to teach Krishna a lesson. They raised armies and launched an attack on the island of Dwaraka, forcing Krishna to leave Indra-prastha and rush to the defence of his city.

- According to the Bhagavata Purana, in their previous life, Shishupala and Dantavakra were Jaya and Vijaya, the doorkeepers of Vishnu who prevented the four sages, the Sanat Kumars, from entering Vaikuntha. The sages cursed them that they would take birth three times away from God. Each time they were born, Jaya and Vijaya performed terrible deeds that forced Vishnu himself to descend on earth and kill them. The first time, they were born as the Asura brothers, Hiranayaksha and Hiranyakashipu, who were killed by Vishnu taking the form of a boar and a man-lion. The next time, they were born as Rakshasa brothers, Ravana and Kumbhakarna, and were killed by Vishnu who descended as Ram. The third time they were born as Shishupala and Dantavakra (some say Kansa and Shishupala), and were killed by Vishnu who descended as Krishna. Thus the death of Shishupala was preordained.
- To protect her son, Shishupala's mother gets from Krishna a boon that he will forgive a hundred crimes of her son. But she does not bother to warn her son never to commit a crime. Thus Vyasa draws attention to a peculiar human trait of trying to solve a problem through external means without bringing about any internal transformation.
- According to one folktale, Krishna cut his hand when he hurled the Sudarshan Chakra at Shishupala. Draupadi immediately tore her upper garment and tied it around Krishna's wound to stop the bleeding. Since she gave him cloth, Krishna promised that the day she needs cloth, he will provide it, which he does later in the epic when the Kauravas try to disrobe Draupadi in public.
- Yudhishtira's coronation is surrounded by inauspicious events. It is preceded by the death of a king, Jarasandha; it witnesses the humiliation of another king, Duryodhana; and finally the ceremony itself is followed by the killing of yet another king, Shishupala, leading to an uproar among all Kshatriyas.

BOOK TEN

Gambling

'Janamejaya, your ancestors treated their kingdom and their wife as property to be gambled away in a game of dice.'

Shakuni's plan

Duryodhana returned from Indra-prastha a broken man, consumed by envy. 'The Pandavas had nothing. And now they are kings. Their kingdom is wealthier than mine and their reputation far greater.' He felt inferior once again to his cousins.

Gandhari's brother, Shakuni, then came up with a plan that brought cheer back into Duryodhana's heart. 'Yudhishtira may be great, but he has one weakness: he loves to gamble. Invite him to a game of dice. Even though he is a terrible gambler, he will come. He will not be able to say no. Let me play in your stead. You know of my skill with the dice. I can make the dice fall the way I want it to. I will win. And with each victory, we will take all that the Pandavas possess. By the end of the game, you will be the lord of Indra-prastha and the Pandavas will be nothing but beggars.'

Duryodhana was overjoyed to hear this, but he did not realize that his uncle was playing a devious game to destroy the Kuru household.

Years ago, when the Pandavas and Kauravas were children, they were playing a game which ended, as usual, in a fight. The Kauravas abused the Pandavas, 'You are children of a whore,' pointing to the widely known fact that the Pandavas were not children of their mother's husband.

The Pandavas retorted by saying, 'And you are children of a widow!'

The Kauravas were surprised to hear this. Surely their mother was no widow. They went crying to Bhishma and narrated the entire incident to him. Bhishma decided to investigate and sent out spies to the kingdom of Gandhara to find out the truth.

The spies found out that when Gandhari was born, astrologers had foretold that while her first husband would have a short life, her second husband would have a long life. Her father, Suvala, then decided to get his daughter 'married' to a goat and that goat was sacrificed soon after 'marriage'. Technically, that made Gandhari a widow.

Bhishma was very furious when astrologers revealed that the Kauravas were actually the children that the goat would have fathered had he not been sacrificed. 'I have been duped by Suvala. A widow entered my noble household as a daughter-in-law. If the world learns of this, I will be the laughing stock of all Bharata-varsha. I will kill Suvala's entire family and let this terrible secret die with them.'

Bhishma locked Suvala and his sons in a dungeon. Every day, only a fistful of rice was given to them. Suvala told his sons, 'Bhishma knows it is adharma to kill family. So he has found a way to kill us without breaking the code of dharma. He feeds us every day but the quantity of food is so less that we are bound to starve and die. There is nothing we can do about it, for it is adharma to ask for more food. And it is adharma to run away from the daughter's house when food is still being served.'

As the days passed, things got worse. The brothers of Gandhari began fighting over the food being served. A starving and suffering Suvala came up with an idea, 'Let only one of us eat: the most intelligent one among us. Let only he survive and remember this great wrong done to us by Bhishma. Let him live to take vengeance.'

Shakuni, the youngest, was the chosen one and alone he ate the food being served while the rest of his family starved before his eyes.

Before dying, Suvala struck Shakuni's foot with a staff and cracked his ankle. 'Now you shall limp every time you walk. And every time you limp, remember the crime of the Kauravas against your family. Never forgive them.'

Suvala had noticed Shakuni's fondness for the game of dice. He told his son, with his dying breath, 'When I die, take my finger bones and turn them into dice. They will be filled with my rage and will turn whichever way you want them to. That way you will always win the game of dice.'

Shortly thereafter, Suvala and his sons died. Shakuni survived and he lived in Hastina-puri along with the Kauravas under the care of Bhishma. He pretended to be the friend of the Kauravas, but all the while he plotted the downfall of Bhishma's household just as Bhishma had destroyed his own.

- Duryodhana's envy of the Pandava fortune is the root cause of the tragedy that is the Mahabharata. It is not that he has less but that his cousins have more that makes him suffer.
- The story of Shakuni's family is part of many folk traditions. In some variants, Duryodhana, not Bhishma, is responsible for killing Shakuni's father and brothers. The aim of his narrative is to remind all not to judge people without knowing their story. Even the worst of villains has a story that perhaps explains their actions, without condoning them.
- In other versions of the story, Suvala is put in prison along with his sons for refusing to let Gandhari marry a blind man. Thus Gandhari, like Ambika and Ambalika, is a captive and so is Shakuni.
- The story of Gandhari and the goat comes from the Jain retellings of the Mahabharata.
- In epic times, it seems that the mother's family played a prominent role in family politics. Shakuni is the maternal uncle of the Kauravas while Krishna is the maternal cousin of the Pandavas.
- The Mahabharata attributes all downfall to greed. In a story that is further elaborated in the Vishnu Purana, Vishnu descends on earth in the form of a tiny fish and asks Manu, the first man, to save him from the big fish. The notion of big fish feeding on small fish is known as 'matsya nyaya' and denotes the law of the jungle. By promising to save the small fish, Manu, in effect, establishes the code of civilization or 'dharma' where even the weak can thrive. Manu puts the small fish in a pot. But as the days pass the fish grows in size and becomes too big for the pot. So Manu moves him to a pond. The fish in due course becomes too big for the pond. Manu moves him to a river. As the days pass, even the river proves inadequate for the fish. The fish is then moved to the sea. It grows too big even for the sea. So the skies burst and torrential rains fall which end up submerging the whole earth. This, the fish declares ominously, is Pralaya, the end of the world. The story ends with the giant fish, identified as Vishnu himself, towing a boat with Manu and his family through the devastating flood to safety. The latter part of the story is similar to Noah's ark and establishes Vishnu as the saviour. The earlier part explains the rise and fall of civilization. Civilization comes into being when the small fish is rescued from the big fish; civilization comes to an end when the fish keeps growing bigger than its pond.

Gambling match

The Pandavas received an invitation from the Kauravas to come to Hastina-puri and play a game of dice. Yudhishtira accepted, saying it would be considered rude not to do so. What he did not say was that he loved to play dice.

Krishna had no idea either of the Kaurava invitation or of the Pandava decision to participate in the game of dice. He was busy fighting Shalva and Dantavakra, friends of Shishupala, who had laid siege to Dwaraka.

On the day of the game, Draupadi was menstruating and so, in keeping with tradition, isolated herself in a room in the far corner of the women's quarters.

Without waiting to hear from Krishna or for Draupadi to sit beside them, the Pandavas entered the gambling hall.

Yudhishtira played on behalf of the Pandavas and Shakuni on behalf of the Kauravas. The game was based on the throw of dice and the movement of coins on a game board. A mixture of luck and skill. To make the game interesting, wagers were decided at the beginning of each game.

At first the stakes were small, an umbrella or a necklace. Each time, Shakuni would roll his dice and say, 'Lo, I have won.' Defeat fuelled Yudhishtira's desire to win back all he lost. So with each passing game, the value of his wager increased. And each time, Shakuni would roll his dice and say, 'Lo, I have won.'

Yudhishtira staked his chariots of gold. Shakuni rolled the dice and said, 'Lo, I have won!'

Yudhishtira staked all the jewels in his treasury. Shakuni rolled the dice and said, 'Lo, I have won!'

Yudhishtira staked his servant girls. Shakuni rolled the dice and said, 'Lo, I have won!'

Yudhishtira staked his servant boys. Shakuni rolled the dice and said, 'Lo, I have won!'

Yudhishtira staked his elephants, then his horses, then his cows, then his goats and sheep. Each time, Shakuni rolled the dice and said, 'Lo, I have won!'

As the losses continued, the Pandava brothers suspected Shakuni's dice was loaded. But they could not prove it. As the day progressed, they were stripped of all their possessions: their gold and grain, their livestock and land, even the jewels on their body. 'Stop,' begged the Pandava brothers, 'there is no shame in withdrawal. Even Krishna withdrew after trying to save Mathura seventeen times.' But Yudhishtira refused. He was convinced that with the next game he would win all that he had lost. The Kauravas encouraged this belief, smirking silently.

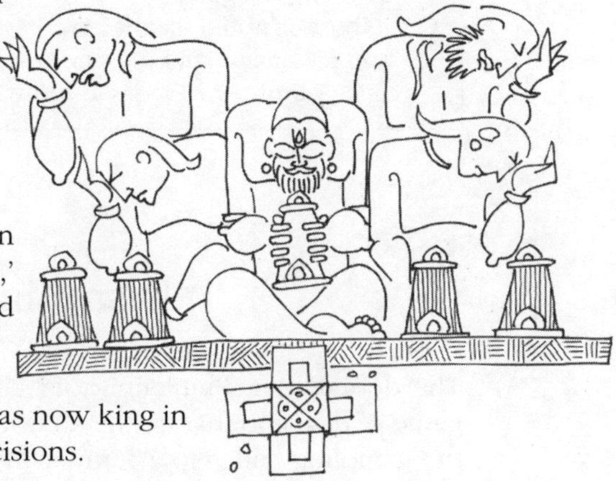

Bhishma, Vidura, Drona and Kripa watched in silence. 'Maybe we should stop this madness,' said Vidura. The blind Dhritarashtra said no. He could not stop his sons who were winning and it would not be appropriate for him to stop Yudhishtira, as Yudhishtira was now king in his own right capable of taking his own decisions.

After the eleventh game, with all his wealth gone, Yudhishtira did the unthinkable. He began staking his own brothers, one by one. First the beautiful Nakula, then the learned Sahadeva, then the strong Bhima and finally the archer Arjuna. He lost all of them. He staked himself too, and lost. Still he refused to give up.

'I stake our wife,' he said. Everyone in the gambling hall gasped. Duryodhana smiled and accepted the wager. Shakuni rolled the dice the seventeenth time and said, 'Lo, I have won!'

- In Vedic times, gambling with dice was considered a sacred ritual. Just as no king could ignore a challenge to a duel or a call to a battle, no king could turn down an invitation to a gambling match. Gambling showed if a king was blessed with intelligence and luck. Krishna embodies intelligence and Draupadi luck. The Pandavas enter the gambling hall with neither.
- This is the only time in the epic when the Pandavas take decisions alone—without mother, without friend, without wife. And they fail miserably.
- The throw of dice in a gambling match indicates fate while the movement of coins on the board indicates free will. Thus the Vedic game of dice was not just a game but a representation of life controlled by fate and free will. It was a part of fertility rituals. It was said that in the game of life, Yama, god of death and destiny, threw the dice while humans guided by Kama, god of life and desire, had the power to move the coins.
- India is the home of all kinds of board games: those that are totally dependent on luck such as snakes and ladders, those that are a mixture of luck and skill such as the dice game or chausar and those that are based totally on skill such as chess.
- Hindus consider life to be a game or leela based on man-made rules. These rules create winners and losers. Winning makes us happy and losing makes us sad. By making a game of dice the cornerstone of his tale, Vyasa reminds us that ultimately all of life is a game.
- It must be noted that here Yudhishtira first gambles away his stepbrothers, Nakula and Sahadeva, and then his own brothers. Did he differentiate between his two sets of brothers? One is left to wonder.

Disrobing of Draupadi

The doorkeeper, Pratikami, told Draupadi that her husbands had lost her in a game of dice and that her new masters, the Kauravas, demanded her presence in the gambling hall. 'Go ask my gambler husband if he staked himself first or me.

For if he staked himself first and lost himself first, how can he still have any rights over me?'

Draupadi's question irked Duryodhana. He felt it was beneath him to be answerable to any woman, even Draupadi.

They sent the doorkeeper to fetch her once again. This time Draupadi said, 'Ask the elders if it is morally appropriate for a woman, the royal daughter-in-law at that, to be staked and lost so in a game of dice?'

Draupadi's questions further annoyed Duryodhana. 'She speaks too much,' he said. Turning to Dusshasana, he said, 'Go and fetch her, by force, if necessary.'

The ever-obedient Dusshasana went into the women's quarters where Draupadi sat with hair unbound dressed in a single cloth stained with blood. Draupadi was startled by his audacity but before she could protest, Dusshasana grabbed her by her hair and dragged her through the palace corridors into the gambling hall. Draupadi kicked and tried to hold on to the pillars, but to no avail. She was no match for Dusshasana's brute force. She screamed but the women in the palace corridors withdrew into the shadows, too terrified to help.

The gambling hall saw what could not be imagined—Draupadi, barely covered, hair unbound, pushed to the floor at Duryodhana's feet. Not one of the assembled men came to Draupadi's rescue. The elders maintained a stony silence while the Pandavas hung their heads in shame. 'For shame, stop! I am the daughter of the king of Panchala, your sister-in-law, the king's daughter-in-law,' cried Draupadi. No one responded.

Duryodhana who could never stand Draupadi's haughtiness said, 'Your husbands are useless. They cannot protect you. They have staked and lost their kingdom, their weapons, themselves and even you. So come to me. Sit on my thigh. I will take care of you.' He then exposed his left thigh and mocked Draupadi with a lascivious look. Draupadi was disgusted by Duryodhana's vulgarity. And horrified that not one among the assembled Kshatriyas protested. Everyone stared and watched the fun.

'Is this dharma,' she asked, 'to treat a woman so?'

Vikarna, the youngest of the Kauravas, said, 'Yudhishtira staked himself first and lost. He had therefore no right over anyone, hence could not stake Draupadi.'

To this Karna retorted, 'Young prince, where is your allegiance? Your brothers have broken no law. When a man loses himself in gambling, his master becomes the master of all his possessions including his wife. Thus Draupadi became the slave of the Kauravas the moment her husbands became slaves. Yet, out of consideration, she was allowed to be staked independently, when there was no need for it. In your immaturity you let emotions cloud your judgement.' Turning to Draupadi, who had disqualified him from participating in her swayamvara, he said, 'Ancient law allows a woman to go to only four men with the permission of her husband. You have been with five husbands. That makes you a whore, public property, to be treated as your master's will.'

'Yes, we can do anything we want with you,' said Duryodhana arrogantly. 'I want my slaves, all six of them, to be stripped of their clothes.' The Pandavas lowered their heads and did as told, removing their upper and their lower garments. Draupadi wailed at their misfortune. 'Her too,' said Duryodhana pointing to Draupadi, 'Strip her naked, Dusshasana. Let the world see the legendary beauty of our new slave.'

Everyone was shocked by Duryodhana's instructions, yet not one spoke up: the Pandavas because they were not in a position to do so and the elders because they felt Duryodhana was behaving within the confines of dharma. Yuyutsu, Dhritarashtra's son by a maid, tried to protest. But he was silenced and so lowered his eyes in shame. Dhritarashtra, the king, said nothing because he loved his sons too much and could never find fault with them. Bhishma and Drona and Kripa struggled with their

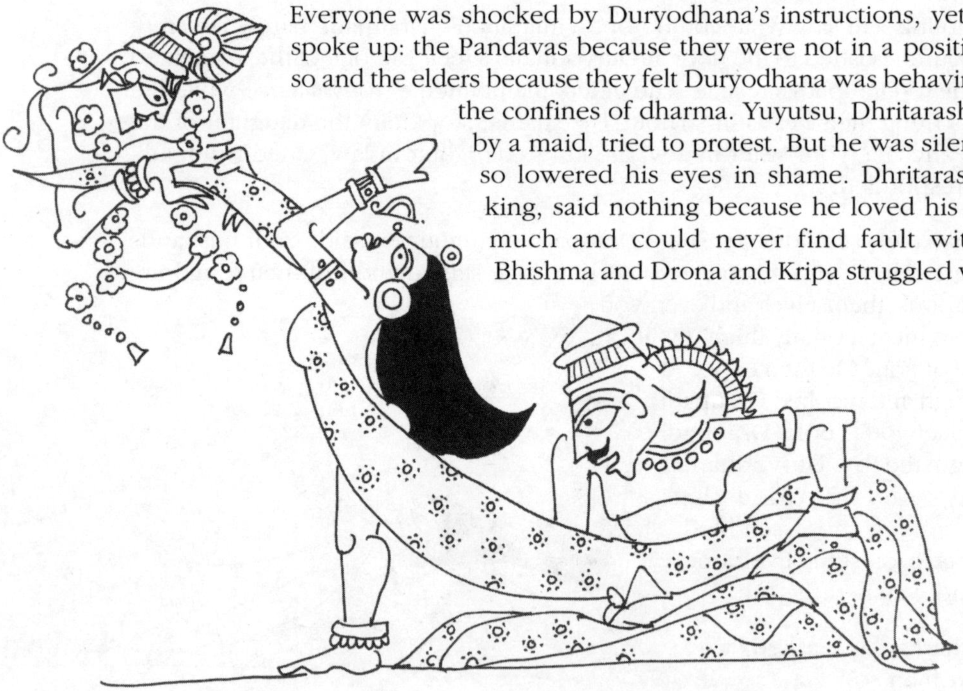

own emotions; no law had been broken, so they found it difficult to even register a protest.

Draupadi realized she was all alone and helpless. As Dusshasana grabbed her robe and started to yank it, she raised her arms towards the heavens and cried, 'Save me, God, there is none but you who I can turn to.'

Her wail reached the heavens. The pillars of the gambling hall began to weep. The skies turned dark. The sun hid in shame. Then, something happened—something truly incredible!

Every time Dusshasana pulled away Draupadi's sari, he found her covered with another sari. When he pulled that away, he found her still covered with yet another sari. He pulled several reams of fabric off Draupadi's body but she remained covered, her honour intact.

This was unbelievable. This was without doubt a miracle, an act of God defying the laws of logic, space and time. God was on the side of Draupadi and against the Kauravas. God had stood up when man had not.

- Naked, the Goddess is Kali, bloodthirsty and wild as the undomesticated forest. Clothed, she is Gauri, gentle as a domesticated orchard or field. The unclothing of Draupadi is not merely the unclothing of a woman; it represents the collapse of civilization, the move from field to forest, from Gauri to Kali, when dharma is abandoned and matsya nyaya reigns supreme, so that might dominates the meek.
- Hair-splitting arguments regarding whether a man can gamble his wife after losing himself take attention away from the fact that a woman is being gambled away like chattel and one is seeking legal justifications for it. That is the tragedy of the situation.
- According to one folk narrative, once Krishna was bathing in the river with the Pandava brothers when his lower garment got pulled away by the current. Draupadi immediately gave him her upper garment so that he could cover himself. Krishna repaid that act of generosity by coming to Draupadi's rescue and covering her with cloth when the Kauravas tried to disrobe her.

The last game

Draupadi's eyes flashed fire. 'I shall never forgive the Kauravas for doing what they have done to me. I shall not tie my hair until I wash it in Dusshasana's blood.'

Bhima could not keep quiet any more. 'And I will kill each and every Kaurava, drink Dusshasana's blood and break Duryodhana's thigh with which he insulted my wife.' His voice boomed across the hall with such force that the dice trembled and the game board burst into flames.

Outside, the dogs began to wail. Donkeys began to bray. Cats whimpered. Fear crept into Dhritarashtra's heart. Vidura told his brother, 'The gods frown upon you and your sons. Stop this madness before it gets further out of hand.'

The blind king shouted, 'Stop, Draupadi. Don't utter that curse that sits on your tongue.' He then hobbled towards her and said, 'Shame on me, that I let things go so far. Shame on me, that I tolerated this stupid game. Shame on me, that I enjoyed it too. I am old and blind, and foolish. Forgive them for my sake. I offer you three boons. Take them and leave in peace.'

Draupadi stopped sobbing and said, 'First, I want freedom for my husbands and second, I want their possessions to be restored to them.'

'And the third boon? Something for yourself?'

'Nothing,' said Draupadi. 'Greed is unbecoming of a warrior's wife.'

As the Pandavas were leaving with their weapons and their wife, Karna chuckled and shouted, 'Draupadi is the raft that saved the drowning Pandavas. Have they no shame? Saved by a woman. What they lost in a game, they accept in charity instead of earning it back.'

'Come back and play a final game, Yudhishtira. One game. Just one and win all that you have lost. Especially your honour,' cried the Kauravas.

'And if I lose?' asked Yudhishtira, indicating his willingness to play to the dismay of his brothers. 'Twelve years of exile in the forest, taking with you nothing but what you carry on your persons, with no claim on Indra-prastha for that period, followed by a final thirteenth year living in hiding. Should you be discovered during this final year, you shall go back into exile for another twelve years.'

Yudhishtira accepted the terms of the game and made his way to the gambling table. His brothers protested. His wife begged him to stop. But Yudhishtira refused to listen. 'I will surely win this last game.'

The dice was rolled once again. And once again Shakuni said, 'Lo, I have won!'

The Pandavas were now obliged to leave their city and move into the forest for thirteen long years. Without uttering a word, Yudhishtira bowed to the king and

bid farewell to all the members of the royal family and set out with his wife and brothers, carrying nothing but the clothes and weapons on their person.

Dhritarashtra was told by his charioteer, Sanjay, that while leaving the palace, Yudhishtira covered his face with a cloth, lest his angry eyes destroy Hastina-puri; Bhima flexed his arms that were restless to break the bones of each and every Kaurava; Arjuna picked up a fistful of sand and let it trail behind him, indicating the shower of a million arrows that would soon fall upon those who had wronged his family; Nakula covered himself with mud so that no beautiful woman was tempted to follow him into the forest; Sahadeva painted his face black in shame; and Draupadi let her unbound hair streak across her face, terrifying the women of the city of their eventual fate.

As they were leaving, Kunti ran after her sons. Vidura ran behind her. Yudhishtira stopped and hugged his mother but requested her to stay back. 'Whatever be his feelings for me, Duryodhana will not treat you with disrespect. Stay here with my uncles and their wives and your nephews. Wait for us till we come back from exile.'

With a heavy heart, Kunti let her sons go. 'Take care of my sons,' she told Draupadi as she bid a tearful farewell to her daughter-in-law. 'Pay special attention to Sahadeva. He is sensitive and may not be able to bear the pressure of his calamity too well.'

Then Kunti and Vidura watched all six pass through the gates of the city and walk towards the southern horizon. Many from the city followed them. They watched them bathe in the Ganga and bid them farewell from the other side of the river. Beyond lay the forests that would be their home for a long, long time.

- Why does Dhritarashtra finally intervene? Is it because good sense finally prevailed? Is it because he suddenly notices bad omens all around and realizes he must protect his sons from the consequences of their megalomania? Is it because, as many folk versions suggest, the palace women including Gandhari and the wives of the Kauravas rise up in protest? Vyasa leaves the reader guessing.
- In South India, Draupadi is worshipped as the fierce virgin-goddess who is let down by her five husbands. In festivals that last up to eighteen days, the whole Mahabharata is re-enacted at the end of which young men walk on fire. This ritual is believed to represent an act of collective expiation by the men for letting down the goddess. In Bangalore, during the Karaga festival, a man dresses up like a woman and travels through the city surrounded by brave men carrying swords, known as Veerakumaras. The man is supposed to represent Yudhishtira, the eldest Pandava, undergoing ritual humiliation as he asks his wife, the goddess, to forgive him and bestow her grace upon his people.
- A solar eclipse is supposed to have occurred when the Pandavas went into exile. This is described by Vidura in the Sabha Parva.
- In the Bhil Bharata, a version of the Mahabharata from the Dungri Bhil community in the northern parts of the Gujarat state, who claim descent from Rajputs, there is a tale of the Pandavas being asked to find 'a man who is sold by a woman' before they can proceed with a particularly powerful yagna. Bhima offers to find such a man. He wanders the earth but finds no such man as all the women he meets say that the men who belong to them are their husbands. They inform Bhima that a husband is like a jewel that makes a woman beautiful and therefore cannot be given away like cattle. Finally, Bhima is directed to a courtesan who has many customers. They all chase her but she does not care for them. She willingly sells a man to Bhima so that the Pandavas can perform their yagna. This tale compiled by Dr Bhagwandas Patel seems like an expression of folk outrage on the gambling of Draupadi by the men who were supposed to protect her. They treated her as chattel, not as wife.

BOOK ELEVEN

Exile

'Janamejaya, in the forest, your once prosperous ancestors lived in poverty and were repeatedly humiliated and humbled.'

Krishna visits the Pandavas

While the gambling match was taking place in Hastina-puri, and while the Pandavas were losing all their fortune, Krishna was away at Dwaraka defending his city from attacks by Shishupala's friends, Shalva and Dantavakra. After pushing them back, he rushed to Hastina-puri. By the time he arrived, however, the match was over and the Pandavas had lost everything.

Krishna found his cousins and their queen outside the city, near a cluster of caves in the forest of Kamyaka, looking despondent, surrounded by sages who were trying to comfort them and make sense of all that had happened. Royalty just a few days earlier, surrounded by grain and gold, cows and horses, they had nothing now.

Draupadi was the first to see Krishna approach. Tears, held back until now, burst forth in a gush as she ran to hug him, unmindful of the men around. The Pandavas followed her and hugged Krishna too. Somehow, seeing Krishna, it seemed all wrongs would be made right.

'We still have our weapons. Let us march to Hastina-puri right now and destroy the Kauravas,' said a determined Bhima.

'Did you not agree to spend thirteen years in exile if you lost the match?' asked Krishna.

'Yes,' said Yudhishtira.

'Then, keep your word.'

'They tricked us,' shouted Arjuna. 'Shakuni used loaded dice. Exile or no exile, Duryodhana will never let go of Indra-prastha.'

'That should be a concern only thirteen years later,' said a calm Krishna, sensing the bubbling rage in the brothers.

'Yudhishtira played the game of dice,' reasoned Bhima. 'Not us. Let the rest of us fight and reclaim what is ours.'

Krishna looked at Bhima sternly. 'Don't blame him for this situation. You allowed him to play on your behalf. You are as much responsible for this situation as he is. No one forced any of you to accept the invitation to the game of dice and nobody forced you to wager your wife. Your pride prevented you from withdrawing. You continued, abandoning all good sense. All five of you lost. All five of you must keep your word and suffer exile quietly. To keep your word is dharma.'

Hearing Krishna speak so, Draupadi started sobbing uncontrollably. Her unbound hair reached her feet like an unfurled banner seeking vengeance. 'Surely I am not responsible for what happened to me,' she said.

Krishna looked at Draupadi, his eyes full of empathy. 'God does not hate you, Draupadi. But you are responsible for rejecting Karna on the grounds of caste. A great warrior, he would never have gambled you in a game of dice. You chose a priest instead, who turned out to be a prince, who shared you with his four brothers, but who could not protect you. And so here you are—helpless, humiliated, and alone, in a situation that you inadvertently helped create. Take responsibility for it.'

Draupadi was shattered on hearing Krishna's grating truth. Krishna hugged her and wept with her and wept for her. He then consoled her. 'Those who tormented you, Draupadi, had the option of not doing so. Those around could have helped you. But they chose to abuse you. The elders could have protested, but they hid behind rule books. Each one of them, the criminals as well as the silent witnesses of the crime, will pay a price, Draupadi. As you weep now, so shall their widows. Be assured of that.'

Sensing Draupadi's concern for her children, Krishna said, 'Do not fear for them. I will give them, Subhadra and Subhadra's son shelter in Dwaraka. There they will be raised as my own sons by my wives.'

- In both the great Indian epics, the Mahabharata and the Ramayana, the forest is both a physical reality as well as a metaphor for the unknown, untamed realms of the mind. The Rishis are the first to explore both these spaces, creating trails connecting caves and water bodies that offer refuge to travellers. Warriors accompany them or follow them, protecting them from beasts and demons. Thus the Vedic way reaches the unexplored realms of the world; the forests become tame, a safe place for mankind, where even the weakest can thrive. Politically, this can be seen as the tales of the so-called Aryan invasion, how the followers of the Veda established their supremacy in India. Metaphysically, it can be seen as the tales of gradual domestication of the mind.
- As in the Ramayana, the forest exile in the Mahabharata begins as a tragedy and ends as a great learning experience that transforms the Pandavas into better human beings and hence better kings.
- The Pandavas were born in the forest. After the burning of the lac palace, they took refuge in the forest. When they lost the game of dice, they again go into forest exile. By contrast, the Kauravas spend their entire life in the palace. This shows that the Kauravas have luck on their side while the Pandavas have none. The Pandavas have to rely on their intelligence, strength and unity to make their fortune.

Draupadi's vessel

Dhaumya, the chief priest of the Pandavas, followed them to the forest. Accompanying him were hundreds of Brahmans from Hastina-puri who were disgusted by the behaviour of the Kauravas. 'You may not have a kingdom,' they told Yudhishtira, 'but you are our king. Let us perform yagnas for you as we always did. Let us invoke the Devas and wipe away your misfortune.'

Watching the Brahmans sit around her husbands, Draupadi was overwhelmed with despair. 'When they came to my house in Indra-prastha, they never left unfed. Now, I have nothing to offer them. Oh, what shame!' she wailed.

Krishna noticed that among the priests who surrounded the Pandavas there were many who had come there on Duryodhana's express instructions. The sole reason for their presence there, Krishna divined, was to make the Pandavas feel miserable over their inability to feed guests, and thereby win favour with the Kauravas. And the Pandavas were undoubtedly miserable. The five brothers scoured the forest for berries and fruit, but there was never enough to go around.

Krishna asked Draupadi, 'I have travelled so far to see you. Will you not feed me, Draupadi? What has happened to your famed hospitality?' Draupadi felt Krishna was mocking her misfortune. Tears rolled down her cheeks. Krishna held her chin, raised her head, looked into her eyes and with an encouraging smile said, 'Surely there is something.'

Draupadi wiped her tears. She realized her friend was up to something. She started thinking. 'Half a berry,' she said. 'That's what I have. I was eating it when you arrived.'

'That will do,' said Krishna. Draupadi's face lit up. She untied a knot in her garment where she had kept the berry, and offered it to Krishna. Krishna ate it with relish and even burped in satisfaction making Draupadi laugh.

No sooner did Krishna burp than all the Brahmans felt as if they had eaten a vast meal. Their stomachs were so full that they could barely sit. All of them stood up and kept burping in satisfaction. 'We have not eaten yet our stomachs are full,' they said. They realized the blessings of the gods were with the Pandavas; even though they had no food, no one left their doorstep hungry. They blessed the Pandavas and Draupadi.

Krishna then advised Yudhishtira to pray to the sun-god to save him from such embarrassing situations. In response, Surya gave him a magic vessel. 'Give this to Draupadi. It will be always full of food until all your guests have been fed and you have been fed and Draupadi has had her meal,' said the Deva.

The arrival of the vessel was a welcome relief for Draupadi. She bowed to Surya and thanked Krishna. Having thus provided for his cousins, Krishna took leave and returned to Dwaraka.

- For Kshatriyas, it was a matter of great pride that whoever visited their houses left after being refreshed and well fed. This was the law of hospitality. This is why, even today, many households in India insist that whosoever enters their house must not leave without having at least a glass of water or a cup of tea or a small snack.
- Draupadi's vessel is like Lakshmi's Akshay Patra and the Greek cornucopia which are always full of food. Across India, the term 'Draupadi's vessel' means a kitchen that is overflowing with the best of foods that is offered to all guests, servants and members of the household. Such a kitchen is an indicator of a good housewife.
- Even though Draupadi had humiliated his son, Karna, on grounds of caste, the sun-god helps Draupadi by providing her with the magic vessel of food, yet another instance of forgiveness in the epic.

Kauravas gloat

Duryodhana was not content with the exile of the Pandavas. 'They have gone into the forest. But they will come back. Let us go into the forest and hunt down the Pandavas instead like wild beasts. That will secure my position forever.'

Dusshasana, Shakuni and Karna agreed with Duryodhana. But before they could act, Vyasa stormed into Hastina-puri and admonished the blind king and his blindfolded wife, 'Stop your sons. Have they not brought enough shame to the good name of Kuru? Now they plan a dastardly hunting expedition against your nephews!'

'This is truly shameful,' agreed Vidura. 'Brother,' he told Dhritarashtra, 'You are the king and you let this happen to your own nephews. You can still salvage the situation. Call them back. Say it was a big mistake. Punish your sons for their wickedness. Save the household from doom.'

'If you are so concerned about the Pandavas, then why don't you go to them? Why are you sitting here with me?' snapped Dhritarashtra, tired of being criticized by his brother.

'I will,' said Vidura. He got up, left the palace and the city, and went straight to the Kamyaka forest, not turning back once to look at his brother.

No sooner did Vidura leave than Dhritarashtra regretted his harshness. 'What have I done? How could I have been so rude to my brother who thinks only of my welfare?' He immediately dispatched a servant after Vidura. 'Do not return until he agrees to come back.'

The servant found Vidura with the Pandavas. They were seated under a huge Banyan tree on the banks of the Ganga. 'Please come back. The king regrets his harsh words,' said the servant. But Vidura refused to budge.

Yudhishtira knew how much the two brothers loved each other. 'Uncle, please go back,' he told Vidura. 'You are the one voice of reason in the palace. He needs your support in this horrible time. You may not agree with his politics but please do not abandon him at such a time. Stand by him. He needs you more than we need you.'

Vidura started to cry thinking of his weak and blind brother. Then he blessed his nephews and Draupadi and returned to the palace.

Rishi Maitreya accompanied Vidura. When the Kauravas came to greet him, the sage said, 'Beware, sons of the blind king. Beware the power of the sons of Pandu. You have driven them away from civilization but even in the forest they earn glory for themselves, glory that the Kauravas can only aspire for.'

Maitreya proceeded to tell Dhritarashtra and his hundred sons how when the Pandavas entered the Kamyaka woods, their path was blocked by a Rakshasa

called Kirmira. Instead of being afraid, despite the burden of calamities on their shoulders, the Pandavas faced him unafraid. Bhima struck him with a mace and pinned him to the ground as a cowherd pins down an errant calf. He then snapped Kirmira's neck. News of Kirmira's death spread through the forest and the Rishis, long troubled by Kirmira, rushed to meet the Pandavas, to thank them, and to shower them with blessings.

'No one can hide the radiance of the sun. No one can hide the glory of the Pandavas. Let them live their days in exile in peace,' said Maitreya.

On hearing this, Duryodhana decided to abort his hunting expedition. He justified his decision by saying, 'Vidura must have told them of our plans. The element of surprise is lost. We must do this later when they are not on their guard.'

After the sage Maitreya left, Karna crept up towards Duryodhana and said, 'Now that you are the master of all that the Pandavas once possessed, why not travel across your vast kingdom and count all the cows you have? And on the way, we can pass the woods where the Pandavas are now residing to see how they are faring. I know you have promised not to hunt them down, but surely you are allowed to feel sorry for them.'

'Are you suggesting we go to the forest and gloat?' asked Duryodhana. Karna grinned. So did Dusshasana and Shakuni. Duryodhana laughed. What joy it would be to laugh at Draupadi, who once laughed at him. What joy it would be to see Bhima live as a beggar. It did not take long to convince Dhritarashtra.

So a great procession was organized of horses and elephants and palanquins with wives, attendants, musicians, dancers, cooks and slaves, to go around Hastina-puri and Indra-prastha and count the cows that now belonged to the Kuru clan. This was the Ghoshayatra.

Since the unspoken intention was to make fun of the Pandavas, the great Kaurava procession stopped not far from the forest where the Pandavas had taken refuge, and made a lot of noise as the tents were set up, food was cooked and musicians got ready to entertain the revellers.

Bhima, who was sent to investigate the sudden commotion in the forest, saw all this and went to Yudhishtira fuming, 'They have camped upwind of us and are cooking in large pots so that I can smell all my favourite dishes. This is a cruel exercise to mock us in our misfortune, brother,' he said.

'I think they plan to go on a hunt. And we are the prey!' said Arjuna sombrely as he watched Karna string his bow.

'Hold your thoughts and be still,' said Yudhishtira. 'They can tempt us but we don't have to be tempted. We have fallen prey to their traps before. We shall not do so again.'

Suddenly, a cry arose from the Kaurava camp. All the sounds of chattering and dancing stopped. The air was filled with the sound of hundreds of arrows descending from the sky. Nakula and Sahadeva were sent as scouts to find out what was happening.

'The Gandharvas have attacked the Kauravas and taken them hostage,' they said on their return. 'The very same Gandharvas we encountered after the palace fire at Varanavata. They have bound and gagged all the Kauravas as well as Karna and Shakuni and all their servants. I think they plan to kill them all.'

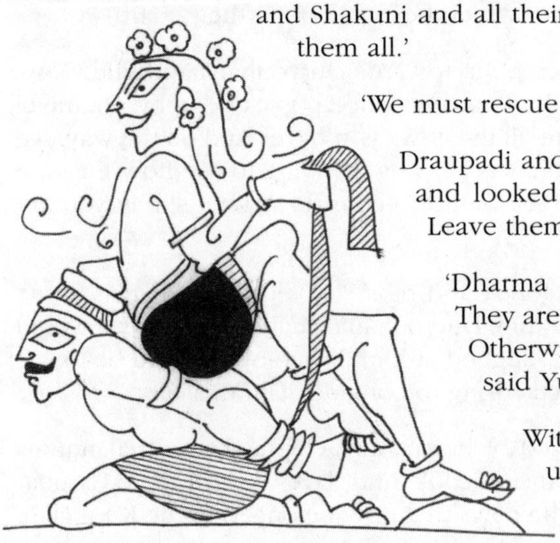

'We must rescue them,' said Yudhishtira.

Draupadi and Bhima and Arjuna turned around and looked at Yudhishtira in disbelief. 'Why? Leave them to their fate.'

'Dharma is all about helping the helpless. They are helpless now. We must help them. Otherwise, we are no different from them,' said Yudhishtira.

With great reluctance, Bhima picked up his mace and Arjuna his bow and followed Yudhishtira's instructions. They went to the Kaurava camp and challenged the Gandharvas. After a little skirmish, the Gandharvas ran away allowing the Pandavas to set the Kauravas free.

The Kauravas returned to Hastina-puri shamed by the nobility of the Pandavas. Karna felt especially humiliated because he saw Arjuna defeat the very same Gandharvas who had defeated him. Duryodhana decided that he would leave the Pandavas alone in the forest. 'We will find them in the thirteenth year of their exile and force them once again to return to the forest.'

In the forest meanwhile, the Gandharvas hugged the Pandavas with great affection and revealed that they were sent to teach the Kauravas a lesson by Indra, king of the Devas.

- For rescuing his life, Duryodhana is indebted to the Pandavas. Krishna advises Duryodhana to repay this debt by giving him five golden arrows that are in Bhishma's possession. Duryodhana steals these golden arrows and gives them to Krishna, not realizing these arrows had the power to kill the five Pandavas. This is a folklore to explain how Krishna protected the Pandavas from the mighty Bhishma.
- The Theyyam dancers of Kerala tell the story of black magic used by the Kauravas to destroy the Pandavas while they are in the forest. Each of their attempts is foiled either because of the grace of Krishna or the power of Draupadi.
- There is a Kathakali dance drama from Kerala that informs us that Kirmira had a sister called Simhika who, on learning of Kirmira's death at the hands of Bhima, decided to kill Draupadi. Taking the form of a maiden, she befriended the wife of the Pandavas in the forest and offered to take her to a secret Durga temple. Simhika planned to offer Draupadi as a sacrifice to Durga, but Draupadi recognized her in time and called out to her husbands who cut the nose of Simhika and drove her away.
- Some say that Lakshmi, the goddess of fortune, sat on Duryodhana's shoulder all the time. That is why he was always surrounded by wealth. When Lakshmi made her way into the lives of the Pandavas in the form of Draupadi, they gambled her away.
- The ceremonial counting of cows suggests that the society described in the Mahabharata depended on livestock for its sustenance. The cities were mainly established to protect cows and pasture lands. Perhaps the Vedic city was like the Kraal of the South African Zulu tribes where houses were built around cattle sheds. At dawn, the cows were let out and at dusk they returned, attended to by cowherds and protected by warriors. The cattle raid was the chief cause of war. In times of peace, men gambled over cows and bulls.
- While the Pandavas were in the forest, Karna encouraged Duryodhana to conduct an Ashwamedha yagna and get all the kings of the earth under his control so that should ever a war break out against the Pandavas, everyone would side with the Kauravas.
- The Hindi phrase 'chandal chaukdi', or menacing foursome, comes from the villainous quartet of the Mahabharata: Duryodhana, Dusshasana, Shakuni and Karna.

Jayadhrata

A few days later, while the Pandavas were away in the forest, Draupadi found to her surprise Jayadhrata at the mouth of the cave which now served as her home. He was the king of Sindhu and married to Dusshala, the only sister of the Kauravas.

Draupadi offered him a seat and served him water and some fruits, and wondered what brought him to the forest. Perhaps he came to express his sympathy and solidarity. Perhaps he wanted to clarify he did not appreciate the actions of the Kauravas, or perhaps he came here just to gloat? 'My husbands will be back soon,' she said.

'I hope not,' he said, a lusty glint in his eyes, 'I came to see you.' Draupadi suddenly felt uncomfortable. Jayadhrata placed before her a box. In it were fine fabrics, exquisite jewels and cosmetics. 'For you,' he said. 'And there is more, if you come with me to Sindhu.'

Draupadi was shocked and disgusted by the audacity of the man. 'I am the queen of Indra-prastha and the wife of the Pandavas. And you speak to me like this? How dare you?'

Jayadhrata laughed, 'You have no kingdom and hence are queen of nothing. You are a beggar. Nothing but a whore of five brothers, disrobed in public by the Kauravas. I offer you a better life, as a concubine in my palace.' So saying, the king of Sindhu grabbed Draupadi by her hand and dragged her towards his chariot.

'My husbands will kill you,' screamed Draupadi. Jayadhrata just picked her up, bundled her into his chariot and sped away.

The Rishis nearby who saw this ran to Bhima and Arjuna and told them what had happened. The two brothers immediately followed the trail left by the chariot. They caught up with the abductor of their wife in no time. With his arrows, Arjuna broke the chariot wheels. Bhima then pounced on Jayadhrata and hit him furiously, injuring him seriously.

Jayadhrata would surely have been killed had Yudhishtira not arrived on the scene. 'No, don't kill him. He is the husband of the only sister we have. Let her not suffer widowhood for his misdemeanours.'

The Pandavas and Draupadi realized Yudhishtira was right. And though they were furious, and yearned for revenge, they forgave Jayadhrata and let him go.

As Jayadhrata was leaving, Bhima caught hold of him and pulled out his hair, all except five tufts, to remind him that he was spared by the five Pandavas.

- The dark unspoken aspects of family life were not unknown to Vyasa. Even though Draupadi is abused by Jayadhrata, she is forced to forgive him as he is the husband of her sister-in-law, Dusshala.
- Vyasa keeps asking what makes a woman a wife. It emerges that it is civilized society with its laws of marital fidelity that makes a woman a wife. But in the forest, there are no rules. Can a woman still be a wife? It is evident through the story of Jayadhrata that neither society nor forest can make a woman a wife; it is only the desire and the discipline of man that can do so.
- Draupadi's effect on men is a recurring theme in the Mahabharata. Besides Jayadhrata, there are other men who lust after her. Later in the epic, she has to fend off the unwarranted attention of Kichaka, brother-in-law of Virata, king of Matsya.

The story of Ram

Tired of being troubled by the Kauravas and their relatives, the Pandavas decided to go deeper into the forest. They withdrew from the Kamyaka woods into the dense forests known as Dwaita-vana. They made their home in caves but decided not to stay in one place too long.

As the days passed, there was nothing to do but talk. Bhima kept fretting and fuming. The idea of spending thirteen years doing nothing did not appeal to him. 'I still think we must fight and claim what is rightfully ours.' Draupadi moaned her fate and cursed her husbands. But all through, Yudhishtira kept his cool. He urged patience and serenity.

'Are you not angry? Are you not humiliated? Are you not irritated? With the Kauravas, with fate, with God?' asked Bhima.

'No, why blame external factors when the root cause is our passion,' said Yudhishtira. 'Henceforth, let us not be swayed by passion. Let us be governed by what is right. Let us be governed by dharma.'

Despite his logic, Yudhishtira could sense the fury and frustration brewing inside his brothers and his wife. All this filled him with great shame and guilt.

One day, feeling sorry for being the cause of his family's downfall, he wailed, 'Surely there has never been a man who has suffered as much as me.'

Rishi Markandeya, who heard Yudhishtira say this, responded, 'No. That is not true. There was one called Ram, who suffered much more. You are exiled for thirteen years, he was exiled for fourteen. While you brought this misery upon yourself, he suffered because dharma states a good son must obey his father.' Glancing towards Draupadi and Bhima, he said, 'And while your brothers endure this exile because they have little choice, Ram's brother, Lakshman, suffered voluntarily out of love and affection for him.'

Rishi Markandeya then proceeded to tell Yudhishtira the Ramopakhyan, the story of Ram, prince of Ayodhya.

Dasharatha, king of Ayodhya, had three wives and four sons. Ram was the eldest. On the eve of Ram's coronation, Dasharatha's second queen, Kaikeyi, reminded Dasharatha of a boon he had offered her long time ago, when she had saved his life in battle. 'Let Ram live as a hermit in the forest for fourteen years and let my son, Bharata, be made king of Ayodhya instead.'

Since he had given his word, Dasharatha had no choice but to ask Ram to leave Ayodhya and give the crown to Bharata. Ram, the dutiful son, obeyed without protest; he shed his royal robes and left for the forest dressed in clothes of bark, armed with his bow. His wife, Sita, and his younger brother, Lakshman, followed him because they were committed to sharing his burden of misfortunes.

In Ayodhya, meanwhile, Bharata refused to be king of a kingdom obtained through deceit. He served as regent and waited for Ram to return and reclaim his kingdom.

In the forest, Ram suffered great hardships along with his wife and his brother for thirteen long years. They travelled through untamed land battling demons, taking shelter in caves, occasionally meeting sages and hearing tales of encouragement and wisdom.

In the final year of exile, a Rakshasa woman called Surpanakha was so smitten by the beauty of Ram and Lakshman that she solicited them repeatedly. When they refused to respond, she assumed it was because they had the company of Sita. So she tried to kill Sita. Ram and Lakshman stopped her in time. To teach her a lesson she would never forget, Lakshman then cut off her nose and breasts and drove her away.

A mutilated Surpanakha ran to her brother, Ravana, king of the Rakshasas, and demanded that he avenge her humiliation. Accordingly, Ravana abducted Sita while the two brothers were away hunting a golden deer. He took her to his island-kingdom of Lanka intending to make her queen by force.

A heartbroken Ram raised an army in the forest comprising monkeys, bears and vultures. He built a bridge across the sea and launched an attack on Lanka. After a war that lasted for days, Ram was finally able to kill Ravana and liberate Sita.

Ram then returned to Ayodhya along with Lakshman where he was crowned king by Bharata; Sita sat by his side as queen.

- Ram's story is part of the Mahabharata but the poet Valmiki made it an epic in its own right. Known as the Ramayana, the story of Ram speaks of a model king and his model reign. The Mahabharata, by contrast, is more about imperfect kings and their imperfect reigns. In the Ramayana, Vishnu upholds rules as Ram, while in the Mahabharata, Vishnu changes rules as Krishna. In the Ramayana, God is king, while in the Mahabharata, God is kingmaker.

- Through the story of Ram, Vyasa is trying to explain that while we believe our problems are the greatest and our misfortunes the worst, there is always someone out there who has suffered more. And just as they survived and triumphed over their suffering, we must too.
- Together, the Ramayana and the Mahabharata are known as Itihasa; they need to be distinguished from the Veda and the Purana. Itihasa is about the struggle of man to uphold dharma in his pursuit of perfection and divinity. The Veda, by contrast, lists rather abstractly the principles governing life while the Puranas embody these principles in various divine beings and tell stories of how God cyclically creates and destroys the world.

Shiva humbles Arjuna

Arjuna knew in his heart that there would be a fight thirteen years later. Just as Ram had fought Ravana, the Pandavas would have to fight the Kauravas. He felt there was more merit in preparing for that fight than spending time in the forest cursing fate like Draupadi or being angry like Bhima.

'Let me invoke Shiva, the God of destruction, and obtain weapons such as the Pashupat, which contains the strength of all birds and beasts, which I can use against the Kauravas,' he said. He took leave of his brothers and travelled north towards the snow-clad mountains whose peaks reached up to the sky.

At the base of the mountains was a dense forest of tall pine trees. In a clearing of the forest, Arjuna fixed into the soft earth a smooth oval stone collected from a river bed. 'I shall look upon this formless stone as a linga, the symbol of Shiva, God without form,' he said. He offered it flowers and then sat before it withholding his senses and his breath, his mind focused on Shiva.

Days passed. Those who saw the still and immobile Arjuna were impressed by his concentration.

Suddenly, a wild boar rushed towards Arjuna and interrupted his meditation. Arjuna opened his eyes, picked up his bow, shot one arrow that hit the boar and killed him instantly.

As Arjuna approached the boar, he noticed that he had been hit by another arrow. He looked up and found a Kirat or hunter standing next to the dead animal. Beside him was his beautiful wife. 'My husband killed the boar,' she said, beaming with pride.

'No, I killed the boar,' said Arjuna.

'No, my husband did,' insisted the hunter's wife.

'My wife is right. It was my arrow that killed the boar. You shot a dead boar,' said the hunter.

'Do you know who you are talking to?' asked Arjuna, unused to being dismissed in this fashion.

'A boy who always wants to win,' said the hunter, making a face to mock Arjuna.

An incensed Arjuna said, 'I am Arjuna, student of Drona, and the greatest archer in the world.'

The hunter smiled, 'Greatest? By whose measuring scale?'

His wife said, 'This is the forest. Your city rules don't apply here, boy. You may be a prince somewhere else. But here you are a common dog who must make way for the lion.'

Arjuna was furious. He would not allow this uncouth tribal couple to humiliate him so. 'Let us fight then. He who wins is surely the better warrior and the true hunter of the boar,' he said. The hunter accepted the challenge with a mocking look in his eyes, further annoying Arjuna.

Arjuna picked up his bow and shot arrows at the hunter. The hunter responded calmly by shooting arrows that struck Arjuna's arrows midair. Arjuna grudgingly had to accept that the hunter was indeed a skilled archer. When his quiver got empty, he picked up a sword and started fighting with the hunter. When the sword broke, a hand-to-hand combat followed. Arjuna found that the hunter was not only skilled but also very strong; he overpowered Arjuna effortlessly.

Angry, desperate, stripped of all confidence, Arjuna went back to the linga of Shiva and offered it flowers. When he opened his eyes, he found the hunter sitting in front of him, smiling tenderly, covered with the same flowers that he had just offered the linga.

It dawned on Arjuna that the hunter was none other than God himself. 'I wanted to see how determined you are for the weapons. You don't give up, do you?' said Shiva, his voice booming across the forest. Arjuna realized the hunter's wife was the goddess Shakti. The boar with the two arrows was actually their sacred bull, Nandi, pretending to be dead.

Arjuna prostrated himself before God. 'Here,' said Shiva, 'take the Pashupat. Use it wisely.'

Arjuna then had a vision of Shiva's true form. His hair was matted and his body smeared with ash. He had wrapped himself in the hide of a lion and a tiger and he held in his hand a trident, a rattle-drum and a skull as a begging bowl. Round his neck was a string of Rudraksha beads and a hooded serpent. He sat on a great white bull with his wife beside him. She was dressed in the sixteen love-charms of marriage—a red sari, flowers in her hair, betel leaf in her mouth, bangles, armlets, anklets, bracelets, toe rings, rings on her nose and ears, necklaces and bejewelled belts around her waist. The divine couple, embodiments of the soul and the flesh, raised their hands and blessed Arjuna.

- Arjuna performs a puja, a ritual quite different from the yagna, the primary ritual prescribed in Vedic scriptures. Puja involves adoration of a deity represented by an image with offerings of flower, food, perfumes and water. Pu means flowers in Tamil—an ancient language with roots different from those of the Vedic Sanskrit, suggesting that puja was a ritual of non-Vedic tribes, a people who were probably less nomadic and more rooted to the earth.
- The notion of the measuring scale is critical in Hindu thought. The value of an object depends on the scale being followed. And since all scales are man-made, all values are artificial. Thus all opinions ultimately are delusions, based on man-made measuring scales. According to one scale followed by Arjuna, a prince is superior to a forest dweller. According to another, followed by the Kirat, he who wins in a duel is superior. The world that is perceived through any measuring scale is called maya.
- Arjuna's tryst with Shiva is not just about obtaining the Pashupat; it is also about learning a lesson in humility. Arjuna cannot bear the thought of being trounced by a forest dweller, who he considers socially inferior.
- Vyasa portrays Arjuna as an arrogant prince with a fierce competitive spirit. While competition is a powerful tool to excel, Vyasa warns us not to make it an exercise to dominate others. Domination through display of prowess is the way of the beast, not the way of the civilized man.

- In Garhwal region is found the Pandava Leela that retells the legend of Kalia Lohar, the blacksmith who helped forge weapons for the Pandavas in exile. Some say that the blacksmith was a form of Shiva, hence is worshipped locally as a deity.

Arjuna in Amravati

Arjuna then climbed the snow-clad mountains known as the Himalayas. On the way, he saw the sky was overcast with dark clouds. Then he saw a flash of thunderbolts. It was his father, Indra, god of the sky, making his presence felt.

Arjuna saw a chariot descend from the skies. It was Indra's chariot. The charioteer, Matali, invited Arjuna to come to Swarga and join his father. 'Why does my father call me?'

'He needs your help. He is troubled by Asuras and feels you can defeat them more easily than any Deva, with your knowledge of Pashupat.'

Arjuna beamed at this recognition of his skills. 'I shall surely help my father. I shall raise my bow and defeat the Asuras who trouble him.'

Arjuna fought alongside the Devas and defeated many Asuras including the ones known as Kalakeyas and Nivatakavachas. Indra hugged his son and welcomed him to Swarga. 'Enjoy the pleasures of paradise, my son. All that you wish will be yours.'

Arjuna indulged in the joys of paradise, sorely missing his brothers and his wife. He took special interest in learning dancing from the Gandharvas. As his warrior body moved to the tunes of the flute, the Apsaras realized how beautiful his human body, covered with sweat, was.

One day, the Apsara known as Urvashi approached Arjuna dressed in her finest garments, and said, 'I want you to be my lover.'

'How is that possible?' said Arjuna, 'You were wife of my ancestor, Pururava. You are therefore like a mother to me.'

'Rules of mortals do not apply to immortals.'

'But they apply to me. I cannot touch you. Or even think of you in the way you want me to.'

'You reject me, you mortal! You reject me?' said Urvashi furiously. 'You are nothing but a eunuch. May you lose your manhood instantly.'

'But . . .'

Urvashi walked away in a huff. Arjuna ran to his father hoping he could get rid of the curse but Indra could only modify it, 'You will have to lose your manhood but only for a year. You choose which year it shall be.'

'I am so unfortunate,' moaned Arjuna.

'Turn this curse into an opportunity,' said the king of the Devas. 'Use it in the thirteenth year of your exile when you are expected to live in hiding.'

- The Devas ride on vimanas or flying chariots. This has led to speculation that Mahabharata refers to flying saucers. There are many who believe that in Vedic times, people had the knowledge of aerodynamics and had actually built planes. Rationalists, however, consider reference to flying chariots of the gods as poetic flights of fancy.
- Urvashi's values are different from Arjuna's. She is nature; in nature, desire is not contained by morality and ethics. He is, however, a creature of human society where desire is contained by morality and ethics. Unlike Shantanu and Yayati before him who could not contain their desire, this episode shows Arjuna triumphing over his desires. The exile has made him a stronger man.
- The lifespan of an Apsara and a Deva is different from the lifespan of a Manava. Their values are different too. What is mere passion and pleasure for Urvashi is incest for Arjuna. Vyasa thus shows how confrontation and conflict does not necessarily happen when one is right and the other is wrong; it can happen simply because two people follow different value systems.
- The Mahabharata identifies the Himalayas as the stairway to the paradise of the gods because their peaks touch the sky.

A journey full of tales

While Arjuna was enjoying the comforts of Amravati, he was worried about his wife and brothers. So Indra sent the Rishi Lomasha to earth to inquire about their well-being and to direct them to the hermitage of Nara and Narayana atop the snow-clad peaks of the Himalayan range. 'Tell them that Arjuna will meet them there after he has spent time with his father,' said Indra.

When Lomasha met the Pandavas, he found they sorely missed Arjuna and were eager to hear of his well-being. 'He enjoys the company of his father. Indra advises you to spend your days in exile travelling, visiting places on river banks, atop hills, in caves, scattered across the rose-apple continent of Jambudvipa. Spend time with sages, hear stories, learn new skills and gain wisdom. Twelve years is less than a blink of Indra's eyes; it shall pass quickly. When you return, you will be better rulers of the earth.'

And so began the great pilgrimage of the Pandavas. Accompanied by many sages including Dhaumya, Narada, Parvata and Lomasha, they went south, then

east, then west. They bathed in the confluence of holy rivers and dipped in lakes guarded by ancient deities. They meditated in caves and saw the sun rise from sacred mountain tops. The journey gave them a fresh perspective on life.

During this journey, they also met many great Rishis such as Vrihadashwa and Arshitsena who told them many stories and discussed many philosophies. All this greatly enriched Yudhishtira. He did not have material wealth but certainly he had no dearth of spiritual wealth.

The Rishis told Yudhishtira the importance of balancing spiritual pursuits with material needs. They equated extreme monasticism with sterility. 'Once, there was a sage called Vibhandaka who refused to teach his son, Rishyashringa, anything about women. As a result, the region where Rishyashringa dwelt suffered from a long spell of drought. The drought ended and rains came only when Shanta, daughter of the local king, Lompada, succeeded in seducing Rishyashringa and teaching him the pleasures of the flesh.'

They told him the value of marriage. 'Rishi Agastya was tormented by his ancestors who appeared in his dreams. They hung upside down over a bottomless pit and moaned that they would never be able to escape their miserable fate unless they were reborn. And the only way they could be reborn was if their descendant married and produced children. In deference to the wishes of his ancestors, Agastya married Lopamudra, a princess, and had children by her. Thus did he repay his debt to his ancestors and facilitated their rebirth.'

They told him the value of sons. 'Once, a man called Kahoda was incensed when his understanding of the Veda was corrected by his own unborn son. He cursed the child that he would suffer from eight physical defects at birth. Later, this very same son, born with eight defects, hence called Ashtavakra, defeated a scholar called Bandi in an intellectual debate. Bandi had earlier humiliated Kahoda in a gathering of Rishis. Thus the son, though cursed by the father, ended up avenging his father's insult.'

They told him the importance of keeping one's word. 'King Sala borrowed the swift Vami horses belonging to Vamadeva for a month, but then refused to return them incurring the wrath of Vamadeva who by his austerities had the king killed by invoking demons. Sala's brother, Dala, also refused to part with the horses; he raised an arrow at Vamadeva but the arrow ended up striking his own son. Dala's queen then begged Vamadeva to forgive her husband and forced Dala to return the horses that rightfully belonged to the sage.'

They told the king tales that showed the importance of worldly responsibilities. 'Kaushika abandoned his old parents to become a hermit, undergo spiritual practices and accumulate magical powers. But while these powers enabled him to kill a bird with the mere glance of his eyes, it did not give him any peace of mind. From a housewife and then from a butcher, he learnt that peace of mind does not come from renouncing worldly life; it comes from knowledge of the soul and a true understanding of the world as it is. With this knowledge in one's heart, one can carry on doing one's worldly duties. One must accept that one's life is the result of past karmas and that one has the power to choose one's response to every situation. Realizing that the truth resides not in the forest but in one's heart, Kaushika returned home and took care of his old parents. More than magical powers, it was a true insight into the workings of the world that gave Kaushika peace of mind.'

They told him tales of greed. 'King Somaka was punished by the gods for killing his only son, Jantu, with the intention of having a hundred more sons like him.'

They also told him tales of forgiveness. 'A Rishi called Raibhya found his daughter-in-law in the arms of a youth called Yavakri. Enraged, he killed Yavakri. Yavakri's father, Bharadvaj, cursed Raibhya that he would die at the hands of Paravasu, the son whose wife, he claimed, had seduced Yavakri. The curse realized itself a few days later. Paravasu killed Raibhya mistaking him for a wild animal. To save himself, Paravasu accused his younger brother, Aravasu, of the crime. Aravasu protested his innocence but nobody believed him. In disgust and anger, Aravasu went to the forest and performed terrible austerities intent on gaining occult powers with which he could teach his elder brother a lesson and clear his soiled reputation. As the days passed, Aravasu's mind was illuminated by the spiritual fire known as tapa. In its light and warmth he was filled with wisdom. Wisdom took away all desire for vengeance and filled him with peace. Instead of punishing his brother, he realized there was greater joy in forgiving him.'

They also told Yudhishtira tales of leaving behind a legacy through generosity. 'After spending centuries in the paradise of Indra, Indradyumna was cast out and told to return only if people on earth still remembered his meritorious deeds. Indradyumna first went to Markandeya, the sage who had lived longer than most humans. Markandeya, however, did not remember him and took him to meet an owl who had lived longer than him. The owl did not remember him either. He directed Indradyumna to a stork. Unfortunately, even the stork did not remember Indradyumna. The stork directed the old king to Akupara, a turtle. The turtle who lived longer than most animals remembered Indradyumna as the king who had built the lake in which he lived. But Indradyumna did not remember ever building a lake. The turtle explained that Indradyumna did not plan to build a lake, but it happened as a result of his generosity. The king gave away so many cows that the cows he gave away kicked up enough dust while leaving their sheds to create a depression that turned into a lake following the rains. That lake later became home to many fishes and turtles and serpents and birds. Thus Indradyumna could never be forgotten—there were many on earth that benefited either directly or indirectly from his good deeds. This knowledge enabled Indradyumna to rise to Swarga and take residence beside the gods once again.'

The Rishis also told Yudhishtira of his great ancestor Kuru, after whom the land around Hastina-puri came to be known as Kuru-kshetra. 'Kuru kept tilling the earth using his flesh as seed and blood as water until an exasperated Indra asked him what he sought. Kuru wanted nothing for himself. His only wish was that those who die on the land tilled by him would ascend to paradise instantly. Indra agreed but on one condition. It was not enough to die in Kuru-kshetra; the manner of death mattered too: either death by renunciation or death in war.'

- In the twelve-year exile the Pandavas and their wife were never alone. They were constantly accompanied by their family priest Dhaumya and many Rishis who took them to holy spots and told them sacred stories. Both travelling to holy spots and listening to sacred stories are believed to reduce the burden of karmic debts and increase the load of karmic equity. The unlucky Pandavas thus use their long period of exile to clean up their fate.
- Pilgrimage is an important part of Hindu spiritual practice. The Mahabharata uses every occasion to list the sacred spots of India and the stories connected with each one. These narrations fired the imagination of settled communities, inspiring them

to go on a pilgrimage sometime in life. Travel, realized the wise men, was an important way to widen the outlook of otherwise inward-looking communities.

- In Hindu tradition, telling and listening to stories are critical as they are vehicles of profound truths; they shape a person's understanding of the world.

Tryst with Rakshasas

Eleven years passed. After visiting holy spots associated with various gods and goddesses, the Pandavas finally decided to move north, in the direction of the Pole Star towards the snow-clad Himalayas. Rishi Lomasha had informed them that Arjuna would meet them there after descending from Amravati.

Among the many Rishis who accompanied the Pandavas on their journey to the Himalayas, there was one who was no Rishi but a Rakshasa in disguise. His name was Jata.

One day, while the entire group was resting and Bhima was away hunting and the Rishis were busy collecting flowers, Jata revealed his true form. Turning into a giant, he caught hold of Yudhishtira, Nakula, Sahadeva and Draupadi in his two hands and began running into the woods. He wanted to eat the three Pandavas and ravish their wife.

'Help, help,' cried Sahadeva, alerting Bhima, who immediately turned around and ran in the direction of the sound.

Yudhishtira meanwhile told Jata, 'You fool. This action of yours will earn you no merit. What hope you have of being reborn as a human or even a god is lost because of the demerit earned by killing us and ravishing our wife. You are making matters worse for yourself. You, who have hope of becoming a higher being, may turn into an animal, or vegetable, or worse, a stone, in your next life.'

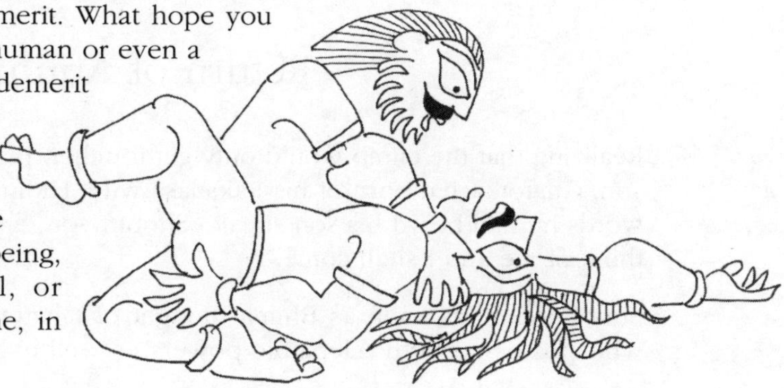

Yudhishtira's words set Jata thinking. As he thought, he slowed down. He started walking rather than running. Bhima was able to catch up with him and strike him down with a mace. Yudhishtira, Nakula, Sahadeva and Draupadi escaped and Bhima punched him on his face repeatedly till he was dead.

After their encounter with Jata, the Pandavas continued on their journey north. While the sight of the slopes and the view from the many peaks of the Himalayas was breathtaking, the climb was steep and dangerous. Sometimes, the wind blew violently and pushed the Pandavas back. Sometimes, the chill caused their joints to freeze forcing them to stop and rest in a cave. Yudhishtira soon found himself breathless and Draupadi fainted, unable to bear the strain. Nakula and Sahadeva rushed to her side, rubbed her limbs and comforted her with soothing words.

They had to continue climbing. On top, they would finally be reunited with Arjuna.

- The days spent by the Pandavas in the Himalayas had a profound impact on the local people. Rivers, passes, mountain peaks and caves are associated with various events and characters mentioned in the epic. Even today, the Pandava Leela recounting the heroic deeds of the Pandavas is an integral part of the culture of the Garhwal region.
- Every time the Pandavas enter the forest, they have violent encounters with many Rakshasa warriors such as Hidimba, Baka, Kirmira and Jata. These were perhaps hostile non-Vedic tribes, some of whom like Ghatotkacha who finally did befriend the Pandavas.
- The Newar community of Nepal worships Bhima as Bhairava, the violent form of Shiva, and offers him blood sacrifices.

Return of Arjuna

Realizing that the climb would only get tougher, Bhima decided to summon his son, Ghatotkacha, born of his Rakshasa wife, Hidimbi. He remembered the last words he had heard his son speak, 'Should you ever need my help, father, just think of me and I shall come.'

Sure enough, as soon as Bhima thought of Ghatotkacha, the Rakshasa youth, who possessed both telepathic powers as well as the power of flight, arrived instantly. He came with many other Rakshasas. They carried all the Pandavas and their wife on their shoulders and helped them reach the highest peaks of the mountains.

The Pandavas reached Alakapuri, the city of the Yakshas, where they were entertained by Kubera, king of the Yakshas. Both Yakshas and Rakshasas had a common ancestor, Pulastya's son, Vaishrava. While the Yakshas lived in the north atop mountains, the Rakshasas lived south in forests. Yakshas were guardians of treasures and were extremely fond of riddles. Kubera had a mongoose that spat jewels every time he opened his mouth.

The Pandavas also visited Badari, the cave where Nara and Narayana once meditated. The sages Lomasha and Dhaumya who accompanied the Pandavas said that Nara and Narayana were destined to walk the earth once more. It was whispered that they had taken birth as Arjuna and Krishna.

Shortly thereafter, Arjuna descended from Amravati on a glittering flying chariot. Draupadi rushed to greet him. The Rishis welcomed him with garlands. His brothers requested him to show the divine weapons he had acquired from the gods.

No sooner did he unwrap the weapons than the earth began to tremble, the wind stilled and the sun paled. All creatures from all the four quarters cried out, 'Beware, beware. These are powerful weapons. They can destroy all life. Do not treat them with such disrespect.' Arjuna immediately withdrew these weapons and wrapped them in celestial cloth, so that no mortal eyes could lay eyes on them.

- The Himalayan region is full of folktales associated with the Pandavas. Once, they saw a herd of cattle grazing and recognized among them Shiva who had taken the form of the most ferocious bull. Bhima tried to catch the bull but it disappeared; the hump remained above the ground and was worshipped as Kedarnath. Another time, Arjuna was defeated by a warrior who unknown to him was his own son Nagarjuna, born of a local Naga princess. This tale is similar to that of Babruvahan found later in the Sanskrit telling. Another tale refers to the hunt of a rhinoceros by Arjuna who wanted to present it as an offering to his dead father.
- In Bhasa's play, *Madyamavyayogam*, dated 100 CE, Bhima rescues a Brahman boy from being devoured by a Rakshasa who turns out to be Ghatotkacha.
- In the Ramayana, Rakshasas are projected as a sophisticated race, related to the Yakshas. They live in golden cities and possess flying chariots. In the Mahabharata, they are projected as barbaric brutes lacking in sophistication.

Daughters of Balarama and Duryodhana

It was time for Ghatotkacha to leave. Before parting, Ghatotkacha decided to tell his father's family all that was happening in Dwaraka and in Hastina-puri, between the Yadavas and the Kauravas.

Ghatotkacha said, 'The children of Draupadi have grown up to be fine young men. And Subhadra's son, Abhimanyu, has become a warrior of repute. They all live happily in the company of Krishna's children. Balarama's daughter, Vatsala, fell in love with Abhimanyu. Unfortunately for her, Balarama had fixed her marriage with Duryodhana's son, Lakshman. As the wedding day approached, an unhappy Vatsala sought Krishna's advice and Krishna sent for me. He ordered me to carry Vatsala on my shoulders and fly to the hills outside Dwaraka where Abhimanyu could marry her according to the rites of the Gandharvas, with the trees as witness. He then told me to take the form of Vatsala

and pretend to be the bride. During the wedding, I squeezed Lakshman's hand with such force that he fainted. With my identity revealed, there was chaos in Dwaraka. The Kauravas accused the Yadavas of duping them.'

'Duryodhana would have been furious,' said Bhima, unable to hold back his smile, 'He wanted to marry Balarama's sister, Subhadra, but she married Arjuna instead. He wanted his son to marry Balarama's daughter, Vatsala, but she married Arjuna's son instead.'

'Duryodhana did not take this insult kindly,' said Ghatotkacha. 'To teach the Yadavas a lesson, he declared that his daughter, Lakshmani, would not marry Krishna's son, Samba, as planned. Samba, not one to take this lying down, secretly slipped into Hastina-puri and tried to abduct Lakshmani, determined to marry her. But he was caught in the act and put in a dungeon. When Balarama learnt of this, he went to Hastina-puri alone and demanded Samba be released and allowed to return to Dwaraka along with the woman he loved. Duryodhana not only refused, he started insulting the Yadavas who never kept their word. He mocked their ancestor Yadu, whose descendants could never be kings

because he did not suffer for his father. Duryodhana's tirade so incensed Balarama that, in rage, he became a giant, his head reaching the sky. He swung his plough and hooked it on the foundations of Hastina-puri and started dragging the great city of the Kurus towards the sea. Duryodhana realized that Balarama was no ordinary Manava. He had known Balarama long as an expert in mace warfare, as a teacher and as a friend. Unlike Krishna who always favoured the Pandavas, Balarama had always treated him with extra affection. Now he had angered Balarama and had seen a side that he had never before imagined. He fell at Balarama's feet and begged forgiveness. As you know, Balarama is quick to anger but also easily pacified. He forgave the Kauravas and returned to Dwaraka with Krishna's son and his new wife.'

The Pandavas imagined Balarama's giant form. Who was he, truly, they wondered. And the Rishis revealed, 'He is Sesha, the remainder. He who exists even when God is asleep and the world is dissolved. He is Adi, that which exists before the beginning, and Ananta, after the end. He is the great serpent in whose coils reclines God in the form of Vishnu.'

All these tales once again reinforced what the Pandavas always suspected; Balarama and his younger brother, Krishna, were not quite what they appeared to be.

- Duryodhana was Balarama's favourite. He wanted his sister to marry Duryodhana and his daughter to marry Duryodhana's son. Both attempts were foiled by Krishna who got the women married to Arjuna and Arjuna's son.
- It has been speculated that Balarama is a form of Shiva, the ascetic, guileless in nature, hence blinded in love and unable to see the flaws of the Kauravas.
- The story of Balarama's daughter, known variously as Vatsala and Shasirekha, is part of many folk literatures. Illustrations of this tale in the Chitrakathi style have been found in 19th century manuscripts in Maharashtra.
- The story of the marriage of Krishna's son and Duryodhana's daughter comes from the Bhagavata Purana.
- The tales of the two marriages, one of a Yadava woman, Vatsala, and one of a Kaurava woman, Lakshmani, can be seen politically. As the family of Abhimanyu's wife, the Yadavas are forced to side with the Pandavas and as the family of Samba's wife, the Kauravas are forced to side with the Yadavas. Thus the marriages turn enemies into members of the same extended family, making it difficult to take sides.
- At a philosophical level, one can see the conflict between arranged marriages governed by the intellect and love marriages governed by emotions. What is appropriate conduct? Krishna clearly favours the heart over the head in matters of marriage. Or does he? For the marriages do impact political alliances, something that Krishna is well aware of.

Hanuman humbles Bhima

One day, the wind carried with it a golden lotus with a thousand petals and a heavenly fragrance. 'Can I have more of these?' said Draupadi, her voice full of excitement.

It had been a long time since Bhima had seen his wife so happy. 'Yes, of course,' he said, and set out in the direction from which the wind had carried the flower.

Bhima walked straight, taking no turns, his strides long, forceful, impatient and full of determination. He smashed all that came in his way. Boulders, mountains, trees. Birds and beasts fled as they saw him approach. He was a man on a mission, determined to get his wife, who had suffered so much, those flowers that brought her so much joy.

Finally, Bhima entered a thick plantain grove, so thick that sunlight did not reach the floor. He found there an old, frail monkey lying on the floor blocking his path. 'Move aside,' growled Bhima impatiently.

'I am too old to move,' said the monkey in a feeble voice. 'Push my tail aside and be on your way.'

'If you say so,' said Bhima and proceeded to sweep the old monkey's tail aside. To his surprise, the tail was heavy and immoveable. Despite all his strength, he could not kick it away. Bhima put down his mace and tried to pull it up with both his hands. He grunted as he used all his might but the tail remained where it was.

Bhima stood up and looked at the old monkey curiously. This was no ordinary monkey. It was too strong. Suddenly, it dawned on Bhima that this monkey was none other than Hanuman, the commander of the monkey forces that helped Ram rescue Sita from the clutches of Ravana. It was said that Hanuman was destined never to die. Like him, Hanuman was the son of Vayu, the wind-god. That made Hanuman his brother.

'Yes, I am he who you think I am. Your brother,' said the old monkey sitting up, his

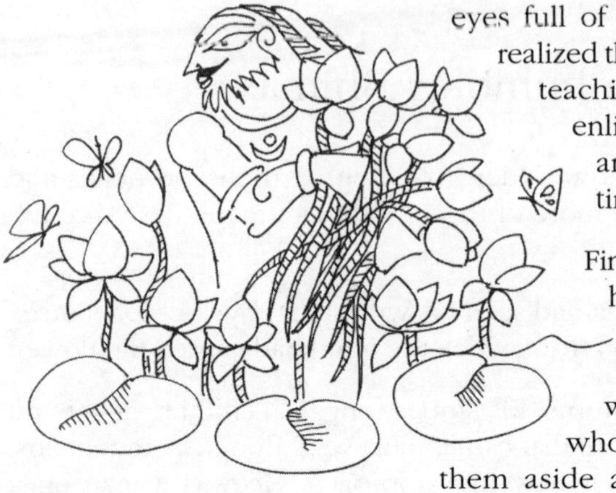

eyes full of wisdom and compassion. Bhima realized that through Hanuman, Krishna was teaching him a lesson in humility. Thus enlightened, he bowed to Hanuman and proceeded on his journey, this time his steps a little less haughty.

Finally, Bhima reached the lake where he found hundreds of fragrant golden lotuses. As he began plucking them for Draupadi, he was attacked by the Gandharvas who guarded the lake. Bhima swatted them aside as if they were mosquitoes and continued collecting the flowers. He then returned to where his brothers were with a huge bunch of flowers that Draupadi was delighted to receive.

- Just as Shiva teaches Arjuna, Hanuman teaches Bhima a lesson in humility. The forest transforms the Pandavas, makes them better kings. The tragedy of exile thus seems very much part of a divine plan to help men be better rulers.
- Once, Bhima pretended to have fever and requested Draupadi to massage his feet. He took large fruits and covered them with a bedsheet. Without removing the bedsheet, Draupadi massaged what she thought were the firm limbs of Bhima while her husbands watched from afar. When the truth was revealed, she was so angry that she cursed the fruits. In future, they would not be smooth; they would be covered with spikes. That is why the jackfruit skin is covered with spikes.
- The people of the Himalayas possessed different features from the people of the plains. That is why rationalists say they were described as demons and goblins, or Rakshasas and Yakshas, by the Aryas.
- The romance of Bhima and Draupadi is the stuff of many folk legends. In the horse dance of Tanjore, the riders of the dummy horses represent Bhima and Draupadi.

Draupadi admits a secret

Memories of Draupadi's humiliation plagued Bhima. He longed to make her happy but realized that he never could. She was always melancholy. Even physically, he who could satisfy a thousand women could never fully satisfy Draupadi. Why, he wondered?

As the twelve years drew to a close, the Pandavas realized they were not what they were before the exile. Yudhishtira had cultivated the spirit of restraint. Both Arjuna and Bhima had learnt lessons in humility. But Draupadi, had she learnt anything?

One day, while wandering through the woods, Draupadi came upon a rose-apple or Jambu tree on which she saw a low-hanging, fine-looking fruit which made her mouth water. No sooner did she pluck it than she heard the tree speak, 'What have you done? This fruit has been hanging here for twelve years. On the other side of this tree sits a Rishi who has been performing tapasya for twelve long years. Later today, he will finally open his eyes and eat this fruit, his first meal in twelve years. But now you have contaminated the fruit with your touch. He will go hungry. And the demerit of making him go hungry will all be yours.'

A terrified Draupadi fetched her husbands and begged them to do something. 'You are strong, Bhima. Can you fix the fruit to the tree?' Bhima shook his head helplessly. 'What about you Arjuna? Can your arrows fix it?' Arjuna also said no. There were many things strength and skill could do, but reattaching a plucked fruit was not one of them.

The tree boomed, 'If you were truly chaste, Draupadi, you could have done it with the power of your chastity.'

'But I am chaste. Although I have five husbands, I am always faithful to the one brother who is allowed to come to my bed for a year.'

'You lie, Draupadi. There is someone that you love more.'

'I love Krishna, but as a friend, not as a husband or a lover,' said Draupadi, embarrassed by this public discussion of her most intimate thoughts.

'There is someone else you love. Someone else. Tell the truth, Draupadi.'

Draupadi broke down. She did not want her secret to be the cause of a Rishi going hungry. She revealed the truth, 'I love Karna. I regret not marrying him on account of his caste. If I had married him, I would not have been gambled away. I would not have been publicly humiliated. I would not have been called a whore.'

The revelations came as a shock to the Pandavas. They were not sure whether to be angry with Draupadi or be ashamed of themselves. They realized they had failed her individually and collectively.

Having revealed the truth of her heart, Draupadi had been cleansed. She was now able to attach the Jambu fruit to the Jambu tree. That evening, the Rishi opened his eyes after twelve years of tapasya. He took a dip in a nearby river, ate the Jambu fruit and blessed the Pandavas and their chaste wife, Draupadi.

Both Bhima and Arjuna found it difficult to accept that their wife cared for Karna. One night, they saw Yudhishtira touching Draupadi's feet. They demanded an explanation. In response, Yudhishtira asked them not to sleep that night. At midnight, the three brothers saw a vermilion-red Banyan tree rise outside their cave. Under it were nine lakh deities who invoked the Goddess. In response, Draupadi presented herself before them. They made her sit on a golden throne and showered her with flowers. Bhima and Arjuna realized that their wife was no ordinary woman; she was a form of the Goddess herself. Not only had they failed to protect her, they had even dared to judge her character.

- The story of the Jambu fruit comes from a folk play from Maharashtra called *Jambul-akhyan*. It is said that the Jambu fruit stains the tongue purple to remind us of all the secrets that we keep from the world. Folk narratives, in contrast to classical Sanskrit narratives, tend to be cruder and raw. They celebrate the imperfections of the human condition.
- In many folk epics, such as the Bhil Mahabharata, Draupadi is identified with the Goddess.
- In the Tamil Mahabharata, Draupadi is worshipped as Virapanchali. In various adventures, she helps her husbands find sacred objects such as a bell, a drum and a box of turmeric that will empower them to avenge her humiliation. One night,

the Pandavas watch her run naked in the forest, hunt elephants and buffaloes and quench her thirst with their blood.

- According to one South Indian folktale, in order to satisfy his wife sexually, Bhima requests Krishna to enter his body and give him more power. Draupadi realizes this immediately and admonishes both her husband and her friend for attempting this mischief.
- The Goddess is the earth itself. Her relationship with Vishnu, the world-affirming form of God, expresses the changing relationship of man with the earth over time. As the first quarter of the world cycle drew to a close, marking the end of the world's innocence, the Goddess was Renuka, mother of Vishnu who descended on the earth as Parashurama. As the second quarter of the world drew to a close, marking the end of the world's youth, the Goddess was Sita, wife of Vishnu who descended on the earth as Ram. As the third quarter of the world drew to a close, marking the end of the world's maturity, the Goddess was Draupadi, who God in the form of Krishna treated as a sister and a friend.

Savitri and Satyavan

Tired of her terrible situation, Draupadi one day asked the sages, 'Is man fettered to his destiny? Can one change one's fate?'

In response, the sages told her the story of Savitri, a woman who overpowered death itself through love, determination and intelligence.

Savitri, the only child of king Ashwapati, fell in love with a woodcutter called Satyavan and insisted on marrying him even after learning that he was in fact the son of a man who had lost his kingdom and that he was doomed to die in a year's time. With great reluctance, Ashwapati gave his consent to the marriage, and Savitri happily gave up all royal comforts to live in the forest with her impoverished husband.

A year later, Satyavan died and Savitri saw Yama take his life away before her very eyes. Rather than cremate her husband's body, she decided to follow the god of death. Yama noticed the woman following him as he made his way south towards the land of the dead. The journey was long and Yama was sure Savitri would stop when she grew tired. But Savitri showed no signs of exhaustion. Her pursuit was relentless.

'Stop following me,' yelled Yama, but Savitri was determined to be wherever her husband was. 'Accept your fate. Go back and cremate your husband's body,' said Yama, but Savitri cared more for her husband's life breath that lay in Yama's hands than her husband's corpse that lay on the forest floor.

Exasperated, Yama said, 'I give you three boons, anything but the life of your husband. Take them and go.' Savitri bowed her head respectfully and for her first boon asked that her father-in-law should regain his lost kingdom. As her second boon she asked that her father be blessed with a son. As her third boon she asked that she be the mother of Satyavan's sons.

Yama gave Savitri all three boons and continued on his journey to the land of the dead. Just when he reached the banks of the river Vaitarni which separates the land of the living from the land of the dead, Yama found Savitri still following him. 'I told you to take your three boons and not follow me.'

Savitri once again bowed her head respectfully and said, 'The first boon has come true. My father-in-law has regained his lost kingdom. The second boon has come true. My father has a son now. But the third boon. How will it be fulfilled? How can I be the mother of my husband's sons when he lies dead on the forest floor? I came to ask you that.'

Yama smiled for he realized Savitri had outwitted him. The only way his third boon could be realized was by letting Satyavan live once again. He had no choice but to let Satyavan live.

Thus Savitri was able to rewrite not only her own future but the futures of her father-in-law and father.

- The story of Savitri is unique as it challenges the traditional notion of Indians being fatalistic. It clearly shows that since Vedic times, Indians have been grappling with the conflict between fate and free will, destiny and desire. The Veda states that desire is the root of creation. Thus desire plays an important role in shaping the future as does destiny. In the Upanishads, Yagnavalkya says that life's chariot has two wheels—desire and destiny. One can depend on one or both. Savitri changes her destiny through intense desire manifesting as unshakeable will. Herein lies the root of the rituals known as 'vrata' observed by Hindu women. Through fasting and all-night vigils they express their desire and determination and thereby hope to influence the destinies of their households.

Trapped by Nahusha

One day, while hunting in the forest, Bhima was caught in the coils of a giant python. This was no ordinary snake; he spoke. 'I was once Nahusha, descendant of Pururava,' said the python. 'I was so great a king that I was made temporary ruler of Amravati by the Devas while their king, Indra, was away, meditating to cleanse himself of a crime he had committed. While in paradise, I got to sit on Indra's elephant and wield his thunderbolt. This newfound power so corrupted me that I felt that I should have access to Indra's queen, Sachi, too. The queen was naturally not amused by my proposition. To teach me a lesson, she said she would allow me to come to her bed only if I came to her palace on a palanquin borne by the Sapta Rishis, the seven celestial guardians of the Veda. I foolishly agreed and forced the venerable sages to serve as my palanquin bearers. I was in such a hurry to reach Sachi's palace that I kicked Rishi Agastya on his head because he was walking too slowly. Agastya was so infuriated with my open display of lust and disrespect, that he said I was unbecoming of the position bestowed upon me by the gods. He cursed me to fall from the skies and return to earth not as a king, or even a human, but as a python, forever moving on my stomach, waiting for food to come to me. I will be released from this wretched body the day my descendant called Yudhishtira teaches me the true meaning of Brahman.'

Bhima tried to tell the python that he was Yudhishtira's brother but the python did not believe him. He opened his jaws intent on swallowing Bhima. 'Help, brother, help,' shouted Bhima. Hearing Bhima's cry, the Pandava brothers rushed to his rescue. 'Stop, don't eat my brother,' said Yudhishtira. 'Eat me, instead. I am Yudhishtira, son of Pandu.'

Hearing this name, the serpent stopped. Loosening his grip around Bhima, he said, 'If you are who you claim to be, answer my question and you will release not just your brother but also me from this terrible situation. Tell me: who is a Brahman?'

To this Yudhishtira, enlightened by years of discussions with Rishis, said, 'He is not the son of a Brahman as most people believe. He is one who by mastering his senses and by disciplining his mind has attained Brahma-vidya, knowledge of the eternal, infinite and boundless soul. This makes him content and gentle and generous, for he is one with the truth.'

Hearing this answer, the serpent was filled with joy. He released Bhima and was himself released from his body. Acquiring a celestial form, he blessed Bhima and Yudhishtira and rose to Swarga.

The brothers returned to their camp and were received by all who were worried about their long disappearance.

- Sachi, the wife of Indra, is considered to be a form of Lakshmi. She is the goddess of fortune. It is said that any one can become an Indra by earning more merit than the previous Indra. On becoming an Indra, one has access to Sachi. Sachi is faithful to the rank of Indra, not to the person who is Indra. Nahusha is not yet Indra; he is a temporary replacement, a lesser being. Though not worthy, he dares desire Sachi and thus pays for it. The tale is less about morality (do not desire the wife of another man) and more about prudence (do not aspire for things until you are worthy).
- Scriptures state that the five Pandavas were Indras in their previous lives and that their common wife, Draupadi, was Sachi.
- As in the dialogue between Yudhishtira and Nahusha, the Mahabharata repeatedly states that one becomes a Brahman not by birth but by effort. Thus the epic challenges the traditional understanding of caste.

The Yaksha's questions

Yudhishtira, one day, had a dream. He saw a deer weeping, begging him to leave the forest and return to where he came from. 'In all these years, you and your brothers have hunted down so many of us that our numbers have dwindled. Please go back. Your days in exile are almost over. Go home. Leave Dwaita-vana.'

Yudhishtira immediately decided to make his way out of Dwaita-vana. He returned to Kamyaka woods.

There a Rishi came to the Pandavas for help. 'The sticks

that I use to produce fire for my rituals were hanging on the branches of a tree. They got entangled in the horns of an antelope. Can you bring them back for me? I am no hunter. But I know the pond where the antelope goes to drink water every evening.'

Since it was a simple mission, Yudhishtira ordered Nakula to hunt down the deer. Nakula soon caught sight of the deer next to a pond, but it ran away as fast as the wind. Suddenly thirsty, Nakula decided to drink some water from the pond before pursuing the deer. As he was about to take a sip, he heard a voice, 'I am the Yaksha, lord of this lake. You may drink after answering my questions.' Nakula looked all round and saw no one. Without heeding the words he had heard, he drank the water cupped in his hands. He fell down dead at once.

Yudhishtira sent his other brothers one after another, to look for those who had not come back and to bring water; but the same fate befell all of them.

Finally, Yudhishtira hurried to the spot. He was taken aback to see his brothers lying dead on the ground. There was no one anywhere nearby! Nor was there any sign of wild animals! And none of his brothers were hurt. As he too was fatigued by thirst, as his brothers were when they reached the pond, he decided to drink some water before investigating further. Like his brothers before him, he heard a voice, 'I am the Yaksha, lord of this lake. You may drink after answering my questions.'

Yudhishtira immediately let go of the water he had cupped in his hands. 'Are you the one who has hurt my brothers?'

'Yes,' said the voice. 'They disregarded my warning.' The Yaksha then appeared before Yudhishtira.

'I shall answer your questions as best as I can,' said Yudhishtira.

'Who makes the sun rise?' asked the Yaksha.
'God,' replied Yudhishtira.

'And set?'
'The sun's natural duty, its dharma.'

'In whom is the sun established?'
'In truth.'

'Where is truth captured?'
'In the Veda.'

'What makes a Brahman?'

'Understanding of the Veda.'

'What makes Brahmans worthy of worship?'

'Ability to control their mind.'

'What makes Kshatriyas powerful?'

'Their weapons.'

'What makes them noble?'

'Their charity.'

'When is a man who is alive considered to be dead?'

'When he does not share his wealth with gods, guests, servants, animals and ancestors.'

'What is faster than the wind?'

'The mind.'

'More numerous than grass?'

'Thoughts.'

'What is more valuable than gold?'

'Knowledge.'

'More desirable than wealth?'

'Health.'

'Most desired form of happiness?'

'Contentment.'

'What is the greatest deed?'

'Non-violence.'

'What measures a man?'

'Conduct.'

'What is forgiveness?'

'Enduring the worst of enemies.'

'What is mercy?'

'Wishing happiness to all.'

'What is simplicity?'
'Equanimity.'

'What is the only thing man can conquer?'
'His own mind.'

'What when renounced makes one agreeable?'
'Pride.'

'What when renounced makes one wealthy?'
'Desire.'

'Who is man's most dreaded enemy?'
'Anger.'

'What is the worst disease?'
'Greed.'

'What is charity?'
'Helping the helpless.'

'What is the most amazing thing about the world?'
'Every day creatures die, yet the rest live as if immortal.'

'How does one know the true path?'
'Not through arguments—they never reach a conclusion; not from teachers—they can only give their opinions; to know the true path one must, in silence and solitude, reflect on one's own life.'

The Yaksha proceeded to ask many more questions, on the nature of the world, society and the soul. Yudhishtira's answers impressed him greatly. Finally, he said, 'I shall let one of your brothers live. Who shall it be?'

Without a moment's hesitation, Yudhishtira said, 'Nakula.'

'Why him? A stepbrother? Why not Bhima or Arjuna, who are powerful warriors critical to protect your kingship?'

Yudhishtira replied, 'My father had two wives. I, the son of Kunti, am alive. Surely a son of Madri must be kept alive too.'

Impressed by Yudhishtira's sense of fair play, the Yaksha revealed his true identity. He was Yama, also known as Dharma, Yudhishtira's father. He restored all the four Pandavas to life.

The Pandavas, reborn and refreshed, then hunted down the deer, untangled the fire sticks from its horns and returned them to the Rishi who performed a yagna to thank the Pandavas.

- That the Yaksha takes the form of a heron, or a goose, is significant because heron and geese are associated with Saraswati, goddess of knowledge. They represent the power of the mind to discriminate. Just as the mythical heron and goose can separate milk from water, so can the discriminating mind separate truth from falsehood.
- Yudhishtira's brothers disregard the Yaksha and drink the water before answering questions. In other words, they do not think before acting. Yudhishtira, who did not think before gambling away his brothers and wife, has clearly been transformed by the exile. He answers the questions before drinking the water.
- Traditionally, in India, all things in nature—trees, caves, lakes, ponds—have guardian and resident spirits. Hence, before occupying a piece of land or plucking a fruit or drinking water, one must make offerings to the guardian deity. They are commonly known as Yakshas, visualized as misshapen, short and corpulent beings.
- During the gambling match, Yudhishtira first gambled away his stepbrothers, the sons of Madri, before gambling his own brothers, the sons of Kunti. In this episode with the Yaksha, he rescues his stepbrother first, thereby undoing the wrong he committed in the gambling hall. This indicates Yudhishtira has changed.
- In the forest, the sons of Kunti encounter the three gods who made their mother pregnant. Yudhishtira meets Yama, Arjuna meets Indra, and Bhima meets Hanuman, his brother, the other son of Vayu, god of the wind. These three meetings have a major transformatory effect. All three are humbled and enlightened by their divine fathers. The exile is clearly a time when the Pandavas are transformed through stories and adventures.

BOOK TWELVE

Hiding

'Janamejaya, once kings and gamblers, your ancestors were reduced to servants, stripped of all identity and respect.'

Nala and Damayanti

As the twelfth year of the exile drew to a close, Yudhishtira met Rishi Vrihadashwa who taught him the secret of playing dice. While learning this art, Yudhishtira complained, 'We have to spend all of next year hiding ourselves. Should we be discovered, we have to stay in the forest for another twelve years. Such a miserable fate, all because of a game of dice! Is there anyone who has suffered like me?'

To this Vrihadashwa replied, 'Yes, there was once a king called Nala who suffered so. He had to serve as cook and charioteer to the king of Ayodhya. And like your wife, his wife, Damayanti, followed him to the forest and served as a maid to the queen of Chedi.' He then told the Pandavas the romance of Nala and Damayanti.

The most beautiful of women, Damayanti, princess of Vidarbha, chose the most handsome of men, Nala, to be her husband, rejecting proposals of marriage that came from the gods themselves.

They lived a happy life for twelve years and had two children. Then Nala's cousin, Pushkara, paid them a visit and invited Nala to a game of dice. During the game, just like Yudhishtira, Nala wagered all that he possessed and lost it all.

Nala was asked to leave his own palace with his family. They were not allowed to carry anything except a single garment to cover their body. Damayanti had her children sent to her father's house. 'You should go with them too,' said Nala to his wife, 'I cannot show my face to my subjects. I do not want to go where I will be recognized. I have brought shame upon myself. Go, leave me, wife. Leave me to my fate.'

But Damayanti refused to leave her husband in this hour of need. 'I will follow you in misfortune as I did in fortune,' she said, 'Let us go into the forest together. No one will recognize us there.'

The forest was an unkind realm. Without weapons, Nala could not hunt an animal. And Damayanti, used to the comforts of the palace, did not know how to find fruit or water. Desperately hungry, Nala decided to use the single piece of cloth he was wearing to catch a few birds. 'Maybe we can eat them. Maybe we can sell them to travellers in exchange for food.' But the birds were strong. They rose up into the air and flew away carrying the cloth with them, leaving Nala naked. Nala fell to the ground and wailed, 'I have lost everything.'

'Not everything,' said Damayanti, 'You still have me. And I will never leave your side.'

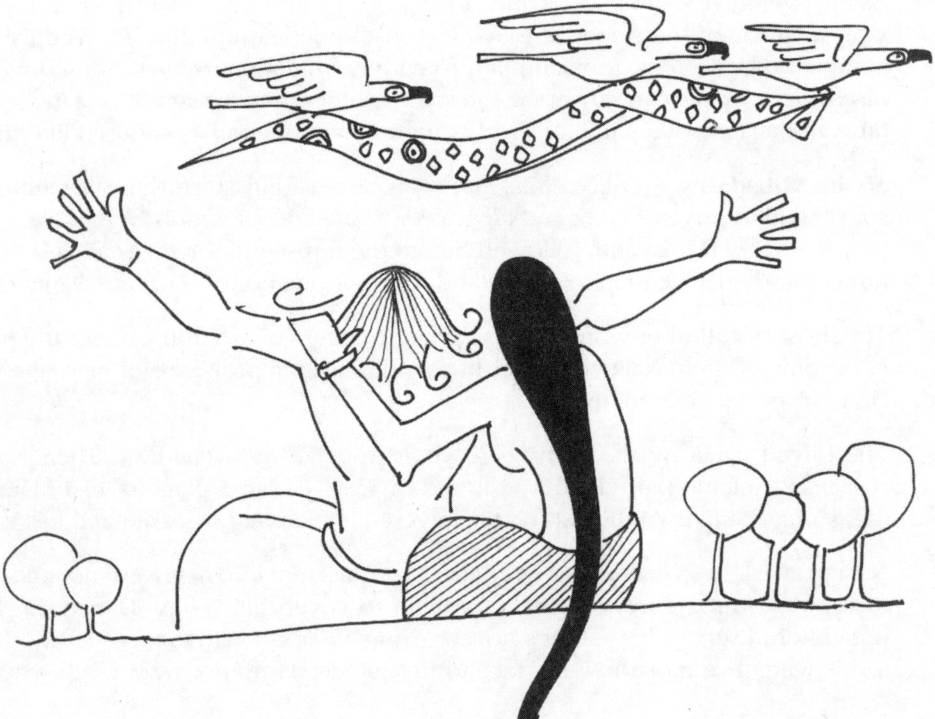

Damayanti undid the cloth she had draped her body with, ripped it in two and gave one half to her husband and used the rest to cover herself. Together, they wandered through the forest silently, he burdened by guilt, she determined to stand by him no matter what.

Nala could not bear to see Damayanti suffer so because of his foolishness. So, at night, while she slept, he got up and ran away, hoping that finding him gone, good sense would prevail and she would go to her father's house in Vidarbha.

When Damayanti woke up and discovered Nala was not by her side, her first thought was not to run to her father; it was to find her husband. She scoured the forest for Nala, shouting out his name, hoping he would hear her. As evening approached, she suddenly found a venomous serpent blocking her path, ready to strike her. Luckily, a hunter shot an arrow and rescued her from its venomous bite. She thanked the hunter profusely but soon realized that the hunter was not interested in her gratitude; he wanted to have the pleasure of her body. Damayanti was a chaste woman and no sooner did the hunter touch her than he burst into flames.

After her miraculous escape from the serpent and the hunter, Damayanti came upon a caravan of traders who invited her to join them. That very night, a herd of elephants attacked the caravan and caused much damage. The traders felt Damayanti had brought them bad luck, so they drove her away.

Alone and abandoned, Damayanti finally managed to make her way to the city of Chedi. The children there started pelting her with stones for her torn clothes, dust-laden limbs and unkempt hair which gave her the appearance of a mad woman.

As Damayanti tried to escape the mob of children, she caught the eye of the queen of Chedi. Feeling sorry for this unkempt but regal-looking woman, the queen had her brought to the palace where Damayanti became her lady-in-waiting. Damayanti did not reveal her name or identity. She called herself Sairandhri and earned her keep as a hair dresser and perfume maker.

A few days later, a priest called Sudev passed through Chedi. He recognized Damayanti and revealed her true identity to the queen. After much persuasion, Damayanti agreed to go to her father's house.

'We must find my husband,' she told her father. So her father appointed a priest called Parnada to go to each and every kingdom in Bharata-varsha looking for Nala.

'How will I recognize him?' wondered Parnada.

Damayanti said, 'Keep singing these lines as you travel: "Oh you who lost crown and kingdom in gambling, who abandoned your wife after taking one half of her clothing, where are you? Your beloved still yearns for you." Nala alone will respond to this song.'

Parnada did as told as he travelled up and down the rivers Ganga, Yamuna and Saraswati singing Damayanti's song. Everyone was intrigued by the lyrics but no one responded to it. Finally, in the kingdom of Ayodhya, ruled by Rituparna, the royal cook, an ugly dwarf called Bahuka, responded to the song with another song. 'Despair not beloved of that unlucky soul. He still cares for you. The fool who gambled away his kingdom, whose clothes were stolen by a bird, who wandered off in the middle of the night leaving you all alone in the forest.'

Parnada rushed back and informed Damayanti of this incident. 'That's Nala,' said Damayanti with a smile on her face, 'He still cares for me. That is why he responded.'

'But the man who responded is an ugly dwarf and serves as the king's cook. Not at all like the handsome Nala I remember from your marriage,' said Parnada.

'No one but Nala knows of those birds that flew away with his garment. It must be him,' said Damayanti, fully convinced.

She came up with an idea to get Nala to Vidarbha. She requested Sudev to visit Ayodhya and give the king there a message. 'Tell him that since there is no trace of Nala, the king of Vidarbha has decided to get Damayanti remarried. He has invited all the kings of the land to his city so that she chooses a husband from among them. Tell him the ceremony will take place on the day that immediately follows your arrival.'

'The next day! But how will Rituparna reach Vidarbha in one day?'

'If Nala is in his kingdom, Nala will bring him here for he is the fastest charioteer in the world. And Rituparna will want to come at any cost for he was one of my suitors before I married Nala and still desires me.'

Sudev was not sure the plan would work but he followed Damayanti's instructions. Sure enough, Rituparna offered a huge reward to whoever could take him to

Vidarbha in one night. 'I will,' said his cook. 'I will take you there provided you tell me the secret of rolling dice.'

'So be it,' said Rituparna, and the two made their way to Vidarbha, speeding through the forest like a thunderbolt on a chariot. Through the night, as they travelled, the king shared with Bahuka his secret knowledge of dice. By the time the chariot reached Vidarbha at dawn, Bahuka had become an expert in the game.

As soon as the chariot crossed the palace gates, Rituparna and Bahuka saw two children. Bahuka jumped off the chariot and hugged them and wept profusely. 'Who are these children? And why are you hugging them? And why are you crying?' asked Rituparna. Bahuka did not reply.

Damayanti observed this from afar and heaved a sigh of relief. 'That man is Nala.'

'But he does not look like Nala. He is ugly and short and deformed,' said the maid.

'I do not recognize the body but I do recognize that heart. Follow him and observe him. He may not look like Nala but he will behave like Nala. And the world around him will treat him royally for he has the soul of a king,' Damayanti said with confidence.

The maid followed Bahuka and sure enough, saw the most amazing things. 'The man has magical powers. When he passes through a gate, he does not bend; the gate rises so that he passes with head held high. When given meat to cook a meal, the meat almost cooks itself; the wood bursts forth with fire and water pours out of the ground.'

'That man is Nala for sure. He may be poor and ugly, but even the gates of the palace, the firewood and the water in the ground acknowledge his royal aura. They rise up to greet him,' explained Damayanti.

Without any consideration to those around, Damayanti ran to the stables and hugged Bahuka shouting, 'Nala, Nala.' Rituparna was shocked and her parents embarrassed. How could this ugly servant be Nala, the handsomest of men?

Bahuka then spoke up, 'Yes, I am Nala. In the forest, after I left Damayanti, I came upon Karkotaka, a dreaded Naga, who with his venomous breath transformed me into the ugliest of men. He then advised me to gain employment with the king of Ayodhya, and learn from him the art of playing dice. My ugliness and my servitude were punishments to make me see the errors of my ways.'

Rituparna found all that he was hearing too fantastic to believe. So Bahuka pulled out a magic robe given to him by the Naga Karkotaka. He wrapped it around his body and was instantly transformed to his original beautiful self. With that there was no doubt in anyone's mind: Bahuka was indeed Nala.

After thanking Rituparna for all his help, Nala hugged his wife and children. The terrible days of misfortune and separation were over. They were together once again.

A few days later, Nala visited what was once his kingdom and challenged his cousin to a game of dice. 'If I lose, you can have my beautiful wife,' he said motivating Pushkara to take up the challenge. This time, however, Nala won, thanks to the tricks Rituparna taught him.

Thus did Nala get back all that he had once lost—family and fortune.

'So it shall be with you, Yudhishtira,' said the sage Vrihadashwa, blessing the eldest Pandava.

- The Rishis explain Nala's foolish behaviour through the idea of Kali, the herald of misfortune. Kali is the ugly, misshapen carrier of bad luck who strikes those who do not observe rules of hygiene and those who touch polluted and inauspicious things. Kali is blamed for making Yudhishtira lose all good sense during gambling. This Kali needs to be distinguished from Kali, the wild goddess of the forest. Through the notion of Kali, the Rishis help Yudhishtira cope with shame and guilt: he can blame an external agency rather than himself for the Pandavas' misfortune.
- Damayanti comes across as a strong-willed woman who is unafraid of her husband's misfortunes. She never stops loving him and always stands by him. Nala, on the other hand, is consumed by shame and guilt. His ability to cope with misfortune leaves much to be desired.
- The story of Nala and Damayanti is told so that the Pandavas do not wallow in self-pity. It also gives them clues as to how they can spend their final year of exile in hiding. Like Nala, Bhima becomes a cook and Nakula becomes a stable hand while like Damayanti, Draupadi becomes a queen's maid.

- The story of Nala brings to light the concept of raj-yog or royal aura that some people possess. Even if they are poor, the cosmos acknowledges their royalty. In Nala's case, the doorway would rise so that he need not bend and food would cook itself so that he did not have to dirty his hands.
- In most retellings of Nala's tale, he is described as the best cook in the world. In some retellings, Damayanti finds him by getting to know from travellers in which country they had eaten the tastiest of foods.

Servants in Virata's court

Then came the thirteenth year.

In the dead of the night, the Pandavas hid their weapons in a bundle of cloth shaped like a corpse which they tied to the branch of a Sami tree.

Then they took various disguises.

Yudhishtira presented himself as a learned Brahman called Kanka well versed in the art of managing a kingdom. Bhima presented himself as a cook called Ballava. 'Like Nala who served Rituparna, I will be the greatest cook in the world,' he said. Arjuna wore the clothes of a woman and presented himself as an accomplished dance teacher called Brihanalla. 'I have learnt the art of dancing from the Apsaras themselves,' he said. Nakula presented himself as a groom of horses called Damagranthi and Sahadeva presented himself as a physician of cows called Tantipala. Draupadi presented herself as a beautician called Sairandhri.

All six of them went to the kingdom of Matsya and sought employment from its king, Virata.

So good were the disguises that Duryodhana's spies found no trace of them when they reached Dwaitavana. All they found in the caves last occupied by the Pandavas were Dhaumya and a few Rishis performing yagna, praying for the well-being of the Pandavas.

- Many loyal servants such as Indrasena followed the Pandavas into exile, serving them in the forest as they served them in the palace. It was these servants who acted as decoys to distract the Kaurava spies while the Pandavas made their way to the kingdom of Matsya, disguised as servants.
- The hiding of weapons in the form of a corpse tied to the branch of a tree suggests that in the period of the Mahabharata, the practice of disposing of bodies by exposing them to the elements was prevalent. Sometimes, this was done until a suitable time was found to cremate the dead.
- The final year of exile is the year in which the Pandavas learn to acknowledge and respect the servants, the vast mass of the people, who are totally ignored in the Mahabharata.
- One wonders, if the final year of exile turned out to be a blessing in disguise for the Pandava brothers who were finally able to live out their secret fantasies as a dice player, a cook, a dancer, a stable keeper and a cowherd.
- The Indonesian telling of the epic suggests that Virata was a descendant of Satyavati's twin brother. This suggestion has its roots in the name of Virata's kingdom, Matsya, which means land of the fish, suggesting a strong association with the fisherfolk.
- Bairat, located in the Jaipur district of Rajasthan, has been identified as Viratnagar or Matsya.

Kichaka

Virata had no clue that the man called Kanka who advised him on matters of dharma and often played dice with him was actually Yudhishtira, or that the man called Ballava who cooked so wonderfully in his kitchen was actually Bhima, or that the eunuch called Brihanalla who taught his daughter dance was actually Arjuna, or that the men called Damagranthi and Tantipala who took care of his horses and his cows were actually Nakula and Sahadeva. His wife, Sudeshna, did not realize that the woman called Sairandhri who made perfumes for her and styled her hair was actually Draupadi.

What the royal couple did notice was that their new servants were different: self-assured and

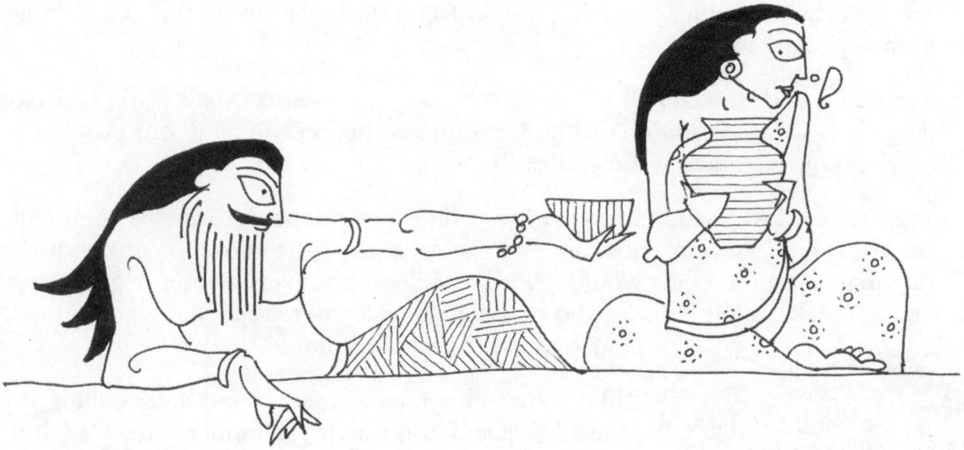

dignified. They never ate anybody's leftovers and each one had clear demands before they accepted employment. As the six never spoke to each other, neither Virata nor Sudeshna suspected they were related to each other.

Months passed without any event. Yudhishtira had to suffer watching a king who gave more value to his desires than to dharma. Bhima moaned the fact that he had to cook and serve food that he could never eat. Arjuna yearned to hold the bow but had to be content holding dancing bells. Nakula spent all day cleaning stables and Sahadeva spent all day with cows.

Then something terrible happened.

The queen's brother, Kichaka, was an oaf with a roving eye. He found Sudeshna's new maid, Sairandhri, rather attractive. Every time he saw her, he stared shamelessly making his intentions rather plain. When Sairandhri complained, the queen admonished her instead for she doted on her brother and refused to hear any criticism of him.

One day Kichaka asked his sister, 'Can you send that arrogant maid of yours to my chambers?'

Not able to say no to her brother, the queen said, 'I will surely try.' She called Sairandhri later that day and asked her to deliver a jar of wine to her brother. Sairandhri tried to wriggle out of this chore, for she knew what would happen to her if she went into Kichaka's chambers alone, but Sudeshna insisted.

Annoyed by Sudeshna's casual attitude, Sairandhri went to Kanka, 'Protect me from such harassment.'

'I cannot,' said Kanka, 'I am helpless. Please understand. None of us can risk discovery. We must endure this humiliation and do everything in our power not to reveal our identity till the end of the year.'

Tears rolled down Sairandhri's cheeks; while she understood Kanka's argument, she could not forgive his not coming to her defence. Who could she turn to now? Brihanalla and the twins would always check with Kanka and never go against his wishes. That left Ballava who was always quick to temper and who, in rage, did whatever she asked him to.

She went to the kitchens and found him cooking yet another meal for the royal family. She told him everything and he reacted predictably. His eyes turned red in fury at the thought of his wife being touched by the lout. 'I will teach him a lesson he will never forget. That I promise,' he said grimly.

That evening, when Kichaka entered his chambers, he found all the lamps had been blown out. On the bed sat a lady with anklets that looked familiar. It was Sairandhri! He was pleasantly surprised to find her so willing—he had expected her to sulk and resist. The lady in bed welcomed Kichaka with open arms. Kichaka tumbled into bed and started to grope her when he realized the arms he touched and the thighs he caressed were rather thick and muscular, certainly not those of a woman. Before he could think another thought, he found himself being crushed in a bear grip. He tried to escape but in his drunken, lustful state he was no match for his opponent. Within a few minutes, Kichaka's bones were broken, his flesh smashed and skull cracked.

The next day, the whole palace woke up to the wailing of the queen who had found her brother beaten to a pulp and literally reduced to a bundle of flesh and bones.

Sudeshna suspected that Sairandhri was somehow involved in this. When she told this to her other brothers, they decided to burn Sairandhri alive on Kichaka's funeral pyre. As they dragged her towards the flames, she screamed for help. All the Pandavas heard her cry but only Bhima came to her rescue.

Uprooting a tree, he swung it around and smashed the skulls of Kichaka's brothers. Soon, the funeral ground was strewn with the broken bodies of Sudeshna's brothers. No one saw who did it. 'I am the wife of the Gandharvas. They can appear out of thin air and protect those who harm me,' explained Sairandhri. The queen of Matsya wailed in memory of her brothers and cursed her wretched maid, and ordered her to leave the kingdom of Matsya. Virata, however, did not want to annoy the powerful, invisible Gandharvas who had protected Sairandhri. So he allowed her to stay in the palace for as long as she wished.

News of the death of Kichaka and his brothers reached Hastina-puri. This was the work of Bhima, of that Duryodhana was sure. 'Only one who has killed Baka and Hidimba and Kirmira and Jatasura could have killed Kichaka.' He smiled. He knew the hiding place of the Pandavas. He was excited by the possibility of catching them before the end of the thirteenth year, which would force them to stay in the forest for another twelve years.

- Caught in a bind whether to save his wife or keep their identity secret, Yudhishtira submits to dispassionate logic, outraging Draupadi who then seeks help from the blindly passionate Bhima.
- Though expected to treat all her husbands equally, Draupadi favours Arjuna, who unfortunately obeys only his eldest brother. Draupadi knows that Bhima does have a mind of his own and loves her passionately. She can manipulate him to do her bidding for he is a lovesick simpleton.
- Draupadi's stunning beauty makes the best of men lose all good sense and constantly draws trouble. Even though she is innocent, her beauty arouses all men who end up wanting to hurt and humiliate her because she is chaste and unavailable. Kichaka, Jayadhrata, Karna, Duryodhana are all victims of her beauty. So are the Pandavas. Fear that she could disrupt the harmony between her sons, forces Kunti to get her married to all five of them.
- In 1910, Maharashtra Natak Mandali's play *Kichaka-vadha* by Krishnaji Khadilkar was a thinly veiled political commentary where Draupadi was presented as India, Kichaka as British imperial power, Yudhishtira as the moderate parties and Bhima as the extremist leaders who were unafraid to take a tough, even violent, stand against British rule. The play was attended by leading revolutionary leaders of the time, alarming the authorities who called for its ban.

Uttara's bravery

On Duryodhana's instructions, Susarma, king of Trigarta, attacked the southern frontiers of Matsya and stole Virata's cows. Virata was at his wits' end for without Kichaka or his brothers, he had no great warrior to lead his army.

'I will help you for I am well versed with the spear,' said Kanka.

'I will help you too as I am well versed with the mace,' said Ballava.

'We are well versed with the sword,' said Damagranthi and Tantipala.

'But if we leave the city looking for the cows,' said Virata, 'who will stay back to guard the women?'

'I will, father,' said Uttara, the king's young son. 'I am well versed in archery. I will protect my mother and sisters.'

Virata beamed with pride and rushed with his four servants and other soldiers in search of the missing cows.

No sooner did they leave than the Kaurava army appeared on the northern frontier of Matsya. 'They will attack the city and raze it to the ground and drag the women away as slaves,' cried Sudeshna in fear.

'Don't worry, mother. I will ride out and drive them away single-handed,' bragged Uttara. He put on his armour, picked up his bow and arrows. But then he realized he had no charioteer for his chariot. 'What do I do now?'

'Maybe I can help?' said the eunuch Brihanalla, smiling coyly, fluttering her eyelashes, 'I was once a man and well versed in the art of charioteering.'

'You will have to,' said Uttara, sounding rather imperious, 'since there is no other.'

Soon, the Kauravas saw a chariot coming before them. The charioteer was a eunuch and the warrior a young boy. They laughed and then blew their conch-shell trumpets. The sound was deafening. Suddenly, Uttara saw before him great warriors holding every kind of weapon, seated on horses and chariots and elephants. He was filled with fear. He realized talking bravely does not make one brave. He leapt out of the chariot and started running away. Brihanalla stopped the chariot, jumped out, ran after him and carried him back to the chariot. 'I cannot fight them,' cried a totally terrified Uttara, tears in his eyes.

Brihanalla comforted him and then took the chariot out of the battlefield into the forest and stopped in front of a Sami tree. On it were dead bodies wrapped in shrouds tied to the branches. 'Climb this tree and bring that down,' said Brihanalla pointing to one of the corpses. Uttara drew back in fear. 'Don't be afraid. The dead can't hurt you,' said Brihanalla reassuringly. Uttara felt his confidence return. He noticed that the eunuch was no longer feminine. Her mannerisms were confident and manly. When the corpse was lowered, Brihanalla undid the shroud. Wrapped within were not the remains of a corpse but weapons—spears, bows, arrows, swords and maces. 'These are the weapons of the Pandavas,' explained Brihanalla.

'How do you know?' asked a wide-eyed Uttara.

'Because I am Arjuna, the third Pandava, son of Kunti.' Uttara fell to his knees as he saw Arjuna standing before him holding the bow Gandiva in his hand. 'Now we have a battle to fight and a war to win,' said Arjuna.

This time when the chariot entered the battlefield, the young prince was the charioteer and the eunuch was the warrior. Once again, the Kauravas laughed and blew their conch-shells until the eunuch raised his bow, released his arrows and brought down the flags of Duryodhana, Karna, Bhishma and Drona.

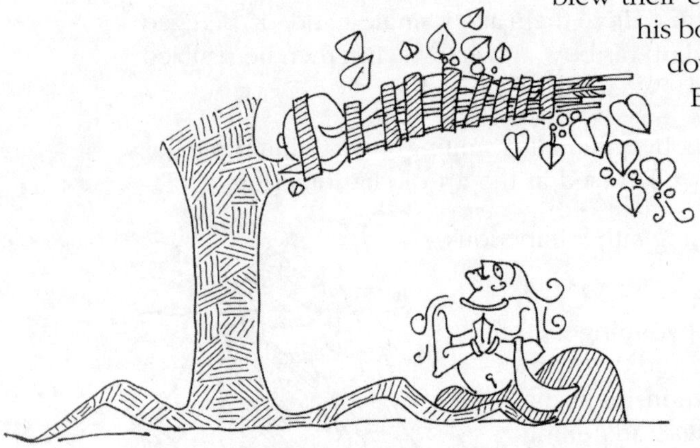

'That's not a eunuch,' said Karna. 'Look at the flag fluttering atop the chariot. It has the symbol of the monkey. And look at the bow in his hand. It looks like the Gandiva. That is without doubt Arjuna.'

Duryodhana smiled at this revelation, 'There, we have smoked them out. The thirteenth year of exile is not over and they have been discovered. They have to go back to the forest now.'

'Don't be so sure,' said Bhishma. 'The Pandavas are no fools to reveal themselves so publicly before the end of the thirteenth year. Think, Duryodhana, think. How do you calculate a year? By the movement of the sun through the twelve solar houses of the zodiac, or by the time taken for the moon to be full across twenty-seven lunar houses, or by the calendar given by astrologers? All three are different. Our astrologers add two extra months every fifth year so that their man-made calendar corresponds with the natural cycle of the sun and the moon. By that calculation, over five months have passed since the thirteenth year of the Pandava exile. Yudhishtira could have revealed himself five months earlier. But he did not want issues raised on technical grounds. So he and his brothers waited five more months to reveal themselves. So you see, they have kept their end of the agreement.'

'There is merit in what Bhishma says,' said Drona.

'You always agree with the elders of the family,' said Duryodhana. 'As per my calendar, the thirteen years are not yet over, no matter what they argue. The Pandavas must stay in exile.' Duryodhana then turned to Karna and Dusshasana and said, 'Attack. Kill Arjuna and raze Matsya to the ground.'

But before anyone could take a step forward, Arjuna released three arrows, one landed near Bhishma's feet, another at Drona's feet, indicating his reverence for the two of them, and the third one put the entire Kaurava army to sleep.

Arjuna then instructed Uttara to go and collect the upper garments of Duryodhana, Karna, Drona and Bhishma. 'When they wake up, they will know that I spared their lives. They will go away humiliated.'

- The yagna was a mobile ritual needing no permanent structure, suggesting that the followers of the Veda were primarily nomadic herdsmen. Over time, they intermingled and married people who lived more settled lives such as Naga agriculturists and Asura miners. The Mahabharata is the tale of an age when the intermingling was well on its way. But the tradition of stealing and fighting over cows had not yet waned.
- In Bhasa's play, *Pancharatra*, dated 100 CE, the cattle raid is carried out on Bhishma's instruction to teach Virata a lesson for not attending Duryodhana's yagna. Duryodhana dares his teacher, Drona, to expose the Pandavas in five days failing which he is ready to divide his kingdom. Drona fails and Duryodhana divides the kingdom and peace follows—a total departure from the classical ending.
- Stealing cows or go-harana was the easiest method to start a fight in Vedic times. The epic states that the war was fought over thousands of cows and involved hundreds of chariots, elephants and foot soldiers from Matsya, Hastinapuri and Trigarta. The scale of the war described seems rather hyperbolic, an exaggeration of a smaller skirmish with cattle thieves.
- The story of Uttara and Brihanalla riding into the battlefield adds comic relief to the otherwise serious epic. To many, the character Brihanalla proves that men were castrated in Vedic times to serve in women's quarters. There are those who dispute this, saying that this is a later interpolation and that the practice of castrating men and using them as servants came to India after the invasion of Central Asian warlords post 1000 CE.

- Ancient Indians were conversant with the complexities involved with measuring time. Attention was given to the movements of the sun and the moon across twelve solar constellations and twenty-seven lunar constellations while preparing a calendar. To align the twelve months of the lunar calendar with the six seasons and the movement of the sun and the moon, the notion of adhik-maas, or extra month, was created and used from time-to-time.

Marriage of Uttari

When Virata returned to Matsya, having successfully retrieved his cows from Trigata with the help of his adviser, cook, horse keeper and cow herder, he was told that his son had single-handedly driven back the Kaurava army which had attacked the northern frontier. Virata beamed with pride at the news. 'Can you believe it? Such a young boy and what a feat!'

'With Brihanalla by his side, Uttara was bound to succeed,' said Kanka. The king ignored this comment since it belittled his son's achievement; he decided to celebrate by playing dice.

While he was playing, he once again said beaming with pride, 'Imagine my young boy routing all those great Kuru warriors.'

'Not impossible considering Brihanalla was by his side,' said Kanka once again. This repeated reference to a eunuch, suggesting that the prince owed his success to someone, further annoyed the king. This happened a third time; this time an irritated Virata flung the die at Kanka striking his nose so hard that it began to bleed.

Sairandhri who was sitting nearby rushed with a cup so that not a single drop of Yudhishtira's blood touched the ground. 'He is an honest man,' she explained, 'if his blood touches the ground, there will be famine.'

The king did not pay much attention to what was being said, as the prince entered the court at that very moment with the upper garments of senior Kuru warriors in his hand. Brihanalla coyly stood behind him. The women of the palace rushed to greet him. He was given a hero's welcome. He tried to tell the truth but no one heard him. Nobody noticed Brihanalla walking behind the prince, smiling slyly.

The night was spent celebrating the 'success' of Virata. The next day, when the king entered his court, he was shocked to find Kanka sitting on his throne with a spear in his right hand and Sairandhri seated on his left lap. Ballava, Brihanalla, Damagranthi and Tantipala stood behind him holding fierce-looking weapons of war.

'What is the meaning of this? How dare you sit on a seat reserved for kings?'

To this Brihanalla answered, 'Because Kanka is a king. He is Yudhishtira, son of Pandu, grandson of Vichitravirya.' The Pandavas then revealed their true identities to the king.

Suddenly, everything made sense. Kanka's sense of fair play, Ballava's strength, Brihanalla's skill, Damagranthi's beauty, Tantipala's intelligence and Sairandhri's

regal bearing. Virata and Sudeshna apologized for treating them as servants. 'We were your servants,' said the Pandavas extending a hand of friendship.

'To make amends for our rudeness, committed in ignorance perhaps, I give my daughter, Uttari, to Arjuna,' said Virata.

'I spent the year teaching her dance. She is my student, like my daughter. So I accept her as a daughter-in-law. She shall marry my son, Abhimanyu.'

- Virata is so blind in his love for Uttara that he is unable to accept a truth that is evident to all. He is very much like the blind Dhritarashtra and the blindfolded Gandhari who regard Duryodhana very highly. Vyasa wonders if parents are naturally blind to shortcomings of their children like Dhritarashtra, or if they choose to be blind like Gandhari.
- There is an advice here for servants that perhaps it is wise to sometimes be quiet rather than correct. Kanka is being correct and in doing so annoying his master. Discretion here, perhaps even silence, would be more appropriate.
- In folk songs, there is a suggestion that Arjuna perhaps was secretly in love with Uttari. But since she looked upon him as a teacher, he decided to make her his daughter-in-law rather than his wife.
- The name of Virata's kingdom, Matsya, suggests that he may have been a descendant of Satyavati's brother. Matsya means fish. Both Satyavati and her brother were found inside a fish. Since Uttari's grandson eventually becomes the Pandava heir, Satyavati's dream of being the mother of kings is finally fulfilled generations later.

BOOK THIRTEEN

Gathering

'Janamejaya, those who enlisted to fight at Kuru-kshetra, were driven by many thoughts, not all noble.'

Negotiations

After thirteen years of exile, the Pandavas were ready to return to Indra-prastha.

First, a priest was sent by the Pandavas from Matsya to Hastina-puri to ask for their land. Duryodhana sent him back, claiming that while by the lunar calendar the Pandavas had completed the thirteen years of exile, they had not completed it as per the solar calendar. So they had to go back to the forest for another twelve years.

Duryodhana then sent his father's charioteer, Sanjay, as emissary to tell the Pandavas not to return for they were not welcome in Indra-prastha. All was well there and everyone had forgotten the Pandava brothers who had built the city only to gamble it away.

Sages like Sanat and Kanva rushed to Hastina-puri and tried to explain to Dhritarashtra that his son's stand was not right. It was against dharma. When the ethical and moral approach did not work, the sages warned Dhritarashtra and his sons that neither Krishna nor the Pandavas were ordinary men. Arjuna and Krishna were Nara and Narayana reborn. Krishna was Vishnu who walked the earth and no one had ever defeated Vishnu in battle.

They narrated the tale of Garuda, the king of the birds, who insisted on eating Sumukha, the serpent, who Gunakeshi, the daughter of Indra's charioteer, Matali, was betrothed to marry. Matali begged Garuda to spare the man his daughter had fallen in love with, but Garuda ignored him. Finally Matali invoked Indra, king of the Devas, who summoned Garuda. When Garuda displayed his prowess arrogantly, Indra placed his hand on Garuda. So heavy was his hand that Garuda could not stand. Humbled, he agreed to let the young Sumukha live. 'Duryodhana, do not be arrogant like Garuda. Or, you will be humbled as he was.'

When Duryodhana laughed at this story and Dhritarashtra remained silent, the sages shook their heads and went away in despair concluding that nothing now could save the Kuru household from the path of self-destruction.

Krishna then decided to travel to Hastina-puri and try and make the Kauravas see sense. As he made his way to the city, he found that all along the highway arrangements had been made by Duryodhana for his refreshment. Tents had been set up. There were men holding pots of water and baskets of food. Krishna refused all this.

In the city, he stayed in Vidura's house instead of Dhritarashtra's palace. 'I will eat food with the Kauravas only when my meeting with them is successful.' Vidura never ate in the house of the king. He and his family sustained themselves on green leafy vegetables that they grew in their own kitchen garden. This was basically to maintain their autonomy and to express their displeasure on the way the king had treated his own nephews.

When Krishna finally met the blind king and his sons, things were not pleasant. Duryodhana told Krishna, 'I will not part with Indra-prastha. I rule it well. No one wants the gamblers back.'

'A word is a word. Whether you rule well or not does not matter. You promised to return Indra-prastha after the Pandavas endured thirteen years of humiliating exile. They have kept their word. You do too,' said Krishna.

'No,' said Duryodhana.

'For the sake of peace, give them at least five villages so that they may live with dignity,' appealed Krishna.

'No.'

'Five houses in one village.'

'No. Not even a needlepoint of territory will I part with,' said Duryodhana.

'By going back on your word,' said Krishna, 'you have destroyed the foundation of dharma. By refusing to a compromise for the sake of peace, you have made yourself unfit to rule. You must therefore be destroyed.' Krishna stood up and took his decision. 'Let there be war on the plains of Kuru-kshetra between the upholders of civilized conduct and the followers of the law of the jungle. Let the earth be drenched in the blood of those who do not deserve her bounty.'

'How dare you threaten me!' shouted Duryodhana. 'Guards, seize this upstart cowherd.'

The whole court was shocked by Duryodhana's orders. Arresting Krishna! That was unthinkable. Soon, the court was filled with a dozen guards pointing their swords and spears at Krishna. Krishna smiled, 'Are you sure you want to do this?' he said. And suddenly, the court was filled with a blinding light. What followed was a vision that terrified all the Kauravas: Krishna appeared not as a man but as a being with a thousand heads breathing fire, grinding entire worlds between his teeth. His head reached beyond the skies and his feet went beyond the seas.

'What is it that everyone is seeing?' asked the blind Dhritarashtra. But everyone was too thunderstruck to reply. 'What is it? What is it? Please Krishna; let me for once see this.'

Krishna obliged. For the first time in his life, Dhritarashtra could see and what he saw brought tears to his eyes. He could see God. 'Let me not see anything more. Let me be blind once more. Eyes that have seen this must not see anything else.'

The vision was replaced by darkness. When light returned, Krishna was gone. Bliss and awe experienced for a moment in the presence of divinity was forgotten once more. War had been declared and it would be fought.

- The five villages that Krishna asked for the Pandavas during his negotiations for peace included Paniprastha (modern Panipat), Sonaprastha (modern Sonipat), Tilprastha (modern Tilpat), Vrikshprastha (modern Bagpat) and Indra-prastha (modern Delhi).
- In Bhasa's play, *Duta Vakya*, dated 100 CE, Krishna's weapons appear in human form and terrify Duryodhana, who gives up his plan to arrest Krishna. The weapons are the disc called Sudarshan, the mace called Kaumodaki, the bow called Saranga, the sword called Nandaka and the conch called Panchajanya.
- Saam, daam, dand, bhed are the four methods enumerated in the Artha-shastra, the treatise on polity, to make people do one's bidding. Saam means convincing people through talks using logic and emotion. Daam means bribing people. Dand means using force or the threat of force. Bhed means dividing and conquering the enemy. Krishna uses all four methods. He talks to the Kauravas. He is willing to settle for just five villages for the Pandavas. He narrates tales of the prowess of the Pandavas. When all this fails, he decides to divide the Kauravas.
- Just before the war, a solar eclipse is followed by a lunar eclipse. During negotiations, the sky was filled with inauspicious astrological omens. This information that comes from the Bhishma Parva has been used by astronomers to date the war.
- Before the war, following a solar eclipse, all the kings of India had gathered in Kuru-kshetra to purify themselves by bathing in the five lakes there. The Pandavas were in exile then. Krishna who was present was spellbound by the pomp and glory of the assembled royalty. He had a premonition that the next time the kings would gather in Kuru-kshetra, it would be to meet death.
- Vidura's autonomy in the midst of political intrigue is legendary. Though he lived with his brother in the palace he never ate palace food; he sustained himself on green leafy vegetables that he grew in his own garden. Vidura-saag or the green leafy vegetables of Vidura have inspired songs of devotion, for they were given to him by Krishna himself, who was pleased with Vidura's detached worldly conduct.
- After Krishna's visit, the Kauravas sent a final emissary called Uluka formally declaring war against the Pandavas.

A fierce mother and a loyal friend

Before leaving Hastina-puri, Krishna went to Kunti, mother of the Pandavas, who had stayed back with her brother-in-law. Krishna asked her if she had any advice for her sons who were rather disheartened, though not surprised, by the Kaurava refusal to return Indra-prastha after the stipulated period of exile. 'Tell my sons the story of Vidula,' said Kunti, 'Her son was similarly dispirited following his defeat by the king of Sindhu. Vidula told him, always fight for one's rights, and it is better to have a short but glorious life with head held high than a long life of mediocrity and shame. Let Vidula's advice to her sons be my advice to mine.' Krishna bowed his head and promised to deliver this message.

Krishna then decided to pay a visit to Duryodhana's friend, Karna. 'Why do you fight for the Kauravas even when you know they are wrong to cling to the land in such an unrighteous manner?' Krishna asked Karna. 'If you say you shall not fight for the Kauravas, then Duryodhana may rethink the war. The chances of a peaceful resolution will increase.'

Karna said, 'I will never abandon my friend.' He would never abandon the man who had stood by him and declared him warrior when the world rejected him as a charioteer's son. Krishna said that loyalty for a man who had gone back on his word would only breed adharma. But Karna stood his ground.

It was then that Krishna revealed to Karna the secret of his birth. 'Karna, the men that Duryodhana fights are your own brothers. You are the son of Kunti, conceived through the sun-god before her marriage. By the code of Shvetaketu, the man who married her, Pandu, is your father. That means you are a Pandava, the first Pandava, elder than Yudhishtira. And since Arjuna was asked by Kunti to share Draupadi with all his brothers, she is your wife too. Should you change sides, you will be the king of Indra-prastha and Draupadi will be your queen and the five Pandavas will serve you and Kunti will bless you.'

Karna knew that Krishna was not lying. This was indeed the truth. A lifetime of isolation and rejection crumbled away. That void in his being was finally filled. He now knew who he really was: not a rootless foundling, but a prince, with five younger brothers and a mother. He belonged to the royal arena; he did not have to scratch his way in. Visions of him hugging his mother and brothers filled his mind. He would forgive them unconditionally. He smiled as he imagined the waves of affection. Then the forlorn face of Duryodhana rose from behind his new-found family. Would he abandon that one man who had stood by him when the world rejected him? Would he abandon Duryodhana for society's sake as Kunti had abandoned him long ago? No, he would never betray his friend. Karna looked at Krishna and said, 'You flatter me with your bribes and your words. But I stand true to my word. Righteous or not, I will stand by Duryodhana and die for him, even if it means fighting my own brothers.'

Tragically though, despite his loyalty to the prince, the elders of the Kuru household did not like Karna. They always saw him as the ambitious son of a low-caste charioteer who had caste a spell on Duryodhana. Bhishma never even looked at Karna while speaking to him.

On the eve of the war, Karna said that he would single-handedly defeat the Pandavas for his dear friend. Bhishma burst out laughing and said, 'Remember how Arjuna saved Duryodhana from the Gandharvas when you could not. And remember how Arjuna single-handedly stopped us from stealing Virata's cows. You are a fool to believe you are better than him. What more can be expected from one such as you.'

Thus humiliated, a furious Karna screamed, 'Old man, you who did not have the courage to even get married, you who have achieved nothing in life, how dare you make fun of me? I will not fight in the battle as long as you are in command.'

'A good decision, Karna,' said Bhishma, 'for I would never fight with one such as you beside me. But for your venomous advice, Duryodhana would have seen sense and made peace.'

Duryodhana was shocked at the war of words between his grand-uncle and his best friend. He decided to broker peace for he needed both warriors, but neither refused to compromise. Finally he let Karna go: he did not want to annoy Bhishma. If Bhishma did not fight, Drona would not fight and if Drona did not fight, no other Kaurava would fight. Besides, it was good if Karna did not fight from the first day itself. He could rest while others fought and when he did enter the battlefield, he would be fresh and ready.

- Vidula's speech to rouse her son inspired many men to rise up against the British during the Indian freedom struggle.
- Karna's association with the sun connects him with the kings of the Surya-vamsa or the solar dynasty, such as Ram and Harishchandra, known for their charity and commitment.
- Once, Karna was playing dice with Duryodhana and Duryodhana's wife, Bhanumati. Karna saw that Bhanumati was cheating and held her hand, an act of extreme impropriety. Everyone who saw this gasped. Bhanumati herself stood up embarrassed for no man other than her husband had ever touched her. Duryodhana, however, laughed. 'So what if Karna touched my wife. I know it was innocent. I have full faith in my friend. He is pure of heart.' Such was Duryodhana's faith in Karna. Karna could never betray that faith.
- Through Karna, Vyasa presents many conflicts of life: friendship or family, personal ambition or universal good, loyalty or opportunity. This makes him the tragic figure of the Mahabharata, almost a Greek hero, striving single-handedly to create a place for himself in the world that rejects him.

Changing sides

With war being declared between the Pandavas and the Kauravas, Duryodhana sent Sanjay to Yudhishtira to remind him what he was up against. 'On this side are the great warriors Bhishma and Drona and Karna. Think again. Withdraw, for you will surely lose the war.'

Yudhishtira ignored these remarks and with his brothers sent messengers inviting kings to join his side.

Kings from across Aryavarta came with their armies. Soldiers, chariots, horses, elephants converged on Kuru-kshetra like tributaries of rivers to join either the Pandavas or the Kauravas.

Among them was Shalya, king of Madra, maternal uncle of Nakula and Sahadeva.

On the way to the battlefield, Shalya was pleasantly surprised to find arrangements made to feed his soldiers, his horses and his elephants. 'It is indeed a pleasure to fight for a commander who takes such good care of his armies,' he said, assuming that the arrangements were made by the Pandavas.

It turned out that the arrangements for his soldiers, his horses and his elephants were made by the Kauravas. Having partaken of the Kauravas' hospitality, Shalya was obliged to fight on their side against his own nephews.

'This is terrible,' he cried.

'No,' said Krishna with a smile, 'this is an opportunity. They will, for sure, ask you to serve as Karna's charioteer, to humiliate the Pandavas and to inflate Karna's ego. Do so without argument and when you ride out into the battlefield, make Karna insecure by repeatedly praising Arjuna. Insecure men make terrible warriors.'

Yudhishtira sent word to everyone on the Kaurava side that anyone who did not approve of Duryodhana's actions was allowed to fight on his side.

Two sons of Dhritarashtra did not approve of Duryodhana's actions: Vikarna, born of Gandhari, and Yuyutsu, born of a maid. Both had argued against Draupadi being staked in the game of dice. Both had lowered their eyes when Dusshasana yanked off her sari. Both were in conflict in their minds whether to side with dharma or stay faithful to the family.

Yuyutsu decided to move over to the Pandavas. Vikarna, however, stayed faithful to Duryodhana. He was among the hundred Kauravas killed by Bhima. Killing him was the most difficult.

- Some say that the king of Madra deliberately went across to the other side where the probability of victory was higher. Whatever be the case, Krishna gives Shalya a way to redeem himself by serving Pandava interests even while fighting for the Kauravas. His advice that Shalya should try and demoralize Karna is perhaps the earliest reference to psychological warfare, a case of making the enemy nervous before the fight.
- In the Mahabharata, as in the Ramayana, great stress is given on the struggle between family and righteousness. In the Ramayana, two brothers of Ravana argue

over which is the better side to fight on. Kumbhakarna feels family is foremost and fights for Ravana. Vibhishan feels righteousness is foremost; he defects and fights for Ram. In the Mahabharata, Vikarna stays loyal but Yuyutsu changes sides. At the end of the war, Yuyutsu becomes the administrator of Hastina-puri.

One or the other side

Some Yadavas who followed Kritavarma decided to side with the Kauravas, while others who followed Satyaki decided to side with the Pandavas.

Nobody was sure on which side Krishna, and the Yadavas who followed him, would fight. Both Duryodhana and Arjuna went to Dwaraka determined to get him on their side. Duryodhana was sure to get Krishna's help because his daughter, Lakshmani, had married Krishna's son, Samba. Arjuna was sure to get Krishna's help because he had married Krishna's sister, Subhadra.

Duryodhana was the first to enter Krishna's chambers in Dwaraka. He found Krishna taking a nap, so he sat at the head of Krishna's bed. Arjuna came later and sat at the foot of the bed. Krishna woke up and smiled on seeing Arjuna, 'What do you seek?' he asked.

'I came first,' shouted Duryodhana, nervous that Arjuna would get something that he wanted. 'Ask me first what I want.'

'No,' said Krishna calmly. 'You may have come first but I saw Arjuna first, so I shall ask him first.' Turning to Arjuna he asked, 'What do you want? My army or me unarmed?'

'You, Krishna, I want you, beside me, when I fight the Kauravas,' said Arjuna without a moment's hesitation.

Duryodhana heaved a sigh of relief. He wanted the battalion that Krishna led known as the Narayani. With this army, he had eleven armies fighting for the Kauravas. The Pandavas had only seven. Victory was his for sure.

Arjuna was happy because more than the might of arms he valued the power of strategy. One Krishna was more than all the armies of the Pandavas and Kauravas put together.

- The seven armies fighting on the Pandava side were led by Dhrishtadyumna, twin brother of Draupadi, who was assisted by seven commanders: Arjuna, with Krishna as his charioteer; Virata, king of Matsya; Sahadeva, king of Magadha; Drupada, king of Panchala; Satyaki, a Yadava chieftain; Dhristaketu, king of Chedi; Vrihatkshatra and his four brothers, rulers of Kekaya.
- The eleven armies fighting on the Kaurava side were led by Bhishma who was assisted by eleven commanders: Kripa, of the Gautama clan of priests; Drona, of the Bharadvaj clan of priests; Ashwatthama, son of Drona, ruler of the northern half of Panchala; Karna, king of Anga; Shakuni, king of Gandhara; Shalya, king of Madra, maternal uncle of Nakula and Sahadeva; Jayadhrata, king of Sindhu, husband of Gandhari's daughter, Dusshala; Kritavarma, a Yadava chieftain; Bhurishrava, from Bahlika, a kingdom established by Shantanu's younger brother; Sudakshina of Trigarta and his dreaded charioteers; and Srutayudha of Kalinga. Later, those who were killed were replaced by Bhagadatta of Pragjyotisha, Brihadbala of Koshala, Vinda and Anuvinda of Avanti and Nila of Haihaya.
- Krishna offers Arjuna two things: what he is and what he has. Arjuna chooses what Krishna is. Duryodhana is happy with what Krishna has. This divide between him and his, me and mine, what one is and what one has, is the difference between seeking the soul and being satisfied with matter.
- All their life, the Kauravas live in wealth but their life is full of envy and rage and bitterness. For most of their life, the Pandavas live in poverty, in forests, in exile, as dependants in the house of their uncle, but their life is full of learning. Thus, Vyasa

shows how the presence of Lakshmi, goddess of wealth, drives away wisdom. And how poverty can, if one chooses to, bring Saraswati, goddess of knowledge, into our lives which will, if allowed to, bring wisdom as well as wealth.

On neither side

Duryodhana then went to Krishna's elder brother, Balarama. 'Join me,' said Duryodhana, 'I was unable to marry your sister and my son was unable to marry your daughter. I have never had the joy of having you by my side. So please fight on my side against my wicked cousins.'

Before Balarama could reply, Bhima came before Duryodhana and said, 'It is Duryodhana who is unrighteous and wicked for it is he who clings to our lands. Join us, Balarama, fight with us, beside your brother. You know your brother is always right.'

Balarama looked at the two mighty men before him. Both were his cousins. He had taught them the art of fighting with the mace.

With eyes full of sorrow and love, he looked at the two men and said, 'Such anger, such hate, against your own family. And for what? A piece of land. Let go, Bhima. Let go, Duryodhana. Embrace and become friends. Enjoy this world together. Eat, drink and dance together. Forget this war, forget the gambling, and let bygones be bygones.' Balarama looked at the two cousins and saw the anger and rage in their hearts. Neither was willing to give up their hatred. 'Fools. Vengeance will never take away sorrow. It will breed more anger.'

Balarama then took a decision. He would fight for neither side. He would instead go on a pilgrimage. As he left he advised his students, 'If you have to fight, fight by upholding the rules of warfare that I have taught you. Never strike anyone below the waist. Never strike anyone in the back. Never strike anyone who is unarmed or helpless. Fight among equals and win by upholding the rules. Therein lies glory.'

As Arjuna was leaving Dwaraka, Krishna's brother-in-law, Rukmi, told him, 'Do not be afraid of the Kauravas. I have a great bow given to me by the gods. With me by your side, you will surely defeat them.'

Arjuna did not like Rukmi's suggestion that he was afraid of his cousins. 'I don't want you on my side. I can manage very well without you,' he snapped.

A humiliated Rukmi then went to Duryodhana who turned him away too. 'I will not accept what the Pandavas reject,' said the eldest Kaurava.

Thus two men did not fight in the war. One because he refused to side with either; the other because he was rejected by both.

- Balarama does not fight because he opposes the war on principle. Rukmi does not fight because of injured pride. Refusal to wage war is thus not always based on noble intentions.
- Balarama's refusal to fight has made him in the eyes of many scholars a form of Shiva, the ascetic, who is indifferent to worldly affairs and feels there is no value to the petty politics of human society. In Jain traditions, he is considered superior to Krishna because he refuses to fight. Hence it is foretold that in his next life he will become a Tirthankara, the supreme being who makes the bridge out of the material world. Krishna will become one much later. In some Buddhist traditions, Balarama is the Buddha, the wise but distant one, who is impatient with man's frailties, while Krishna is Bodhisattva, the wise and compassionate one, who understands and empathizes with the frailties of man.

The gathering of forces

The day of battle dawned. The Pandavas had spent the night praying to Durga, goddess of war. They then took their places in Kuru-kshetra.

Meanwhile, in the palace, Dhritarashtra's charioteer, Sanjay, was blessed with divine sight so that he could see all that was happening in the battlefield and narrate it to his blind master and his blindfolded wife.

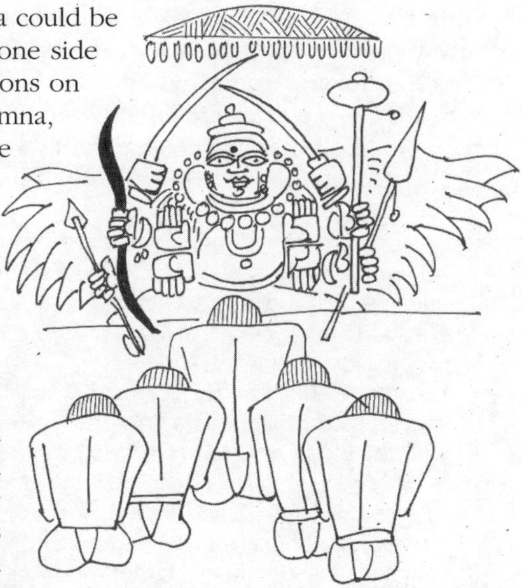

Almost all the kings of Bharata-varsha could be seen on the battlefield, standing on one side or the other. There were seven divisions on the Pandava side led by Dhrishtadyumna, Draupadi's twin brother, while there were eleven divisions on the Kauravas', led by Bhishma. Each division, known as Akshouhini, comprised chariots, elephants, horsemen and foot-soldiers. For every chariot there was one elephant, three horsemen and five foot soldiers.

Every division was led by a commander known as a Maharathi who carried a conch-shell trumpet, blowing which he demonstrated his stamina to cheer his followers and scare his enemies. Every commander also had a banner by which he could be identified. Every warrior held his own favourite weapon, either a sword, a spear, a mace or a bow.

The Pandavas stood facing the east so that when the sun rose, they shone like gold.

Before the war started, the rules of war were announced: that the fight would take place only between dawn and dusk, that no animals would be hurt unless they proved a direct threat, many warriors would not fight a single warrior, no one would fight an unarmed warrior, a woman would not enter the battlefield and if she did no one would raise weapons against her, and no one would interfere when two warriors were locked in a duel.

Then the leaders of both armies invited warriors to change sides or stay out if they wished to. Yuyutsu, son of Dhritarashtra by a maid, left the Kaurava ranks and joined the Pandavas.

Yudhishtira walked up to the Kaurava army and fell at the feet of Bhishma and Drona. 'I seek your blessings,' he said, 'so that I fight as a warrior should. And I seek your forgiveness for I will now see you as my enemy and strike you with my weapons.' Bhishma and Drona hugged the gentle son of Pandu and mourned the terrible situation they were in: they were participating in a war where father would fight sons, brother would fight brother, uncle would fight nephew, friend would fight friend. This was a war that would mark the end not just of one household but of an entire civilization.

- An Akshouhini included 21,870 chariots and chariot-riders, 21,870 elephants and riders, 65,610 horses and riders, and 109,350 foot-soldiers (in a ratio of 1:1:3:5). The combined number of warriors and soldiers in both armies was approximately four million.
- Located 150 kilometres north of Delhi, Kuru-kshetra was once marked by five ancient lakes, the Samata Panchaka. These were dug by Parashurama and filled with the blood of Kshatriyas who he killed to avenge the death of his father.
- In Haryana is a folktale as to how the land where the war was fought came to be selected. Krishna asked Bhima, a simpleton, to find a land that was beyond redemption. Bhima found a barren land where the farmer had died. Rather than cremating his son, the old father was more interested in tilling the dry land. And the widow, rather than mourning the death of her husband, was more interested in eating the share of food she had cooked for him. Such a land, Bhima concluded, was beyond redemption. Hence this land was most suitable for fighting the war of wars.
- Kshatriya warriors were identified by the mark on the banner that fluttered above their chariots.

Name of warrior	**Insignia**
Yudhishtira	Crescent moon
Bhima	Lion
Arjuna	Monkey
Nakula	Antelope
Sahadeva	Swan
Krishna	Hawk
Balarama	Palm tree
Abhimanyu	Deer
Ghatotkacha	Wheel
Ashwatthama	Lion's tail with golden rays
Bhishma	Tree with stars
Kripa	Fire altar
Drona	Pot
Karna	Elephant
Duryodhana	Snake

BOOK FOURTEEN

Perspective

'Janamejaya, only your forefather heard God reveal the goal of life and the means to achieve it.'

Song of God

The armies of the Pandavas and the Kauravas stood facing each other on the battlefield. Then suddenly, a chariot drew away from the Pandava side and came between the two armies. A banner displaying the image of a monkey fluttered above it. It was Arjuna!

Arjuna looked at the army before him. Then he looked at the army behind him. Brothers, uncles and nephews, ready to fight and kill one another—for what? A piece of land? 'I cannot do this,' he said. 'This cannot be dharma!'

To the surprise of all assembled warriors, he lowered his bow.

'Don't be such a weakling, Arjuna. Face the situation like a man!' shouted Krishna.

'I cannot,' moaned Arjuna, his shoulders drooping.

'It is your duty as a Kshatriya,' said Krishna, trying to reason with him.

'I cannot,' said Arjuna.

'They abused your wife. They encroached upon your kingdom. Fight for justice, Arjuna!' pleaded Krishna.

Arjuna remained unmoved. 'I see no sense in killing brothers and uncles and friends. This is cruelty, not nobility. I would rather have peace than vengeance.'

'Noble thoughts indeed,' said Krishna, 'but where does this nobility come from? Generosity or fear? Wisdom or ignorance? Suddenly, you are confronted by the enormity of the situation—the possibility of failure, the price of success—and you tremble. You wish it had not come to this. Rather than face the situation, you withdraw. Your decision is based on a misreading of the situation. If you knew the world as it truly is, you would be in bliss even at this moment.'

'I don't understand,' said Arjuna.

It was then that Krishna sang his song, a song that explained to Arjuna the true nature of the world. This was the Bhagavad Gita, the song of God.

'Yes, you would kill hundreds of warriors. But that would be the death only of the flesh (sharira). Within this flesh is the immortal soul (atma) that never dies. It will be reborn; it will wrap itself in a new body as fresh clothes after old ones are discarded. What is a man's true identity: the temporary flesh or the permanent soul? What do you kill, Arjuna? What can you kill?

'The flesh exists to direct you to the soul. For the flesh enables you to experience all things temporary—your thoughts, your feelings, your emotions. The world around

it is temporary. The body itself is temporary. Eventually, disappointed of all things temporary, you will seek permanence and eventually discover the soul. You grieve for the flesh, right now, Arjuna, without even realizing the reason it exists.'

'Of all living creatures, the human being is the most blessed,' Krishna continued, 'for human flesh is blessed with intellect (buddhi). Humans alone can distinguish between all that is temporary and all that is not. Humans alone can distinguish between flesh and soul. Arjuna, you and all those on this battlefield have spent their entire life losing this opportunity—focusing more on mortal things than on things immortal.

'Your flesh receives information about the external world through your five sense organs (gyan indriyas): eye, ear, nose, tongue and skin. Your flesh engages with the external material world through your five action organs (karma indriyas): hands, feet, face, anus and genitals. Between the stimulus and the response, a whole series of processes take place in your mind (manas). These processes construct your understanding of the material world. What you, Arjuna, consider as the battlefield is but a perception of your mind. And like all perceptions it is not real.

'Your intellect is not aware of the soul. It seeks meaning and validation. Why does it exist? It seeks answers in the material world and finds that everything in the material world is mortal, nothing is immortal. Awareness of death generates fear (bhaya). It makes the intellect feel invalidated and worthless. From fear is born the ego (ahamkara). The ego contaminates the mind to comfort the intellect. It focuses on events and memories and desires that validate its existence and make it feel immortal and powerful. It shuns all that makes it feel worthless and mortal. Right now, your ego controls your mind, Arjuna. It gives greater value to the finite experience of your flesh and distracts you from the infinite experience of your soul. Hence, your anxiety, fear and delusion.

'Your mind retains memory of all past stimulations—those that evoke fear and those that generate comfort. Your mind also imagines situations that frighten you and comfort you. Goaded by your ego, you suppress memories that cause pain and prefer memories that bring pleasure. Goaded by your ego, you imagine situations that the ego seeks and shuns. Right now, Arjuna, on this battlefield, nothing has happened. But a lot is occurring in your mind—memories resurface as ghosts and imagination descends like a demon. That is why you suffer.

'Your ego constructs a measuring scale to evaluate a situation. This measuring scale determines your notions of fearful or comforting, painful or pleasurable, right or wrong, appropriate or inappropriate, good or bad. It is informed by the values of the world you live in, but is always filtered by the ego before being accepted. Right now, Arjuna, what you consider right is based on your measuring scale. What Duryodhana considers right is based on his measuring scale. Which measuring scale is appropriate? Is there one free of bias?

'The world that you perceive is actually a delusion (maya) based on your chosen measuring scale. New memories and new imaginations can change this measuring scale, hence your perception of the world. Only the truly enlightened know the world as it truly is; the rest construct a reality that comforts the ego. The enlightened are therefore always at peace while the rest are constantly restless and insecure. If you were enlightened, Arjuna, you could have been in this battlefield, bow in hand, but still in peace. If you were enlightened, Arjuna, you would have fought without anger, killed without hate.

'Your ego clings to things that grant it maximum comfort. The purpose of life then becomes the pursuit of comfort-generating states, the shunning of fear-generating states. Attainment of desirable states brings joy, failure to do so becomes sorrow. The ego clings tenaciously to things and ideas that validate its existence. The ego does everything in its power to establish and retain a permanent territorial hold over all external states that give it joy. Do you realize, Arjuna, all you want is to reclaim or recreate situations that give you joy? You have attached your emotions to external events. Separate them.

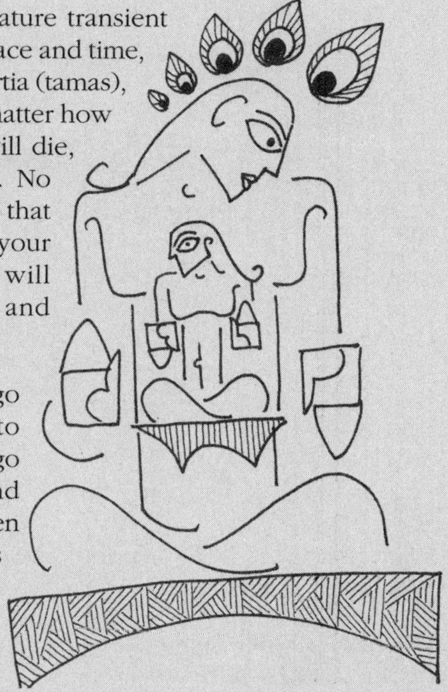

'The external world is like the flesh: by nature transient and ever-changing. Governed by laws of space and time, it fluctuates between three states (guna): inertia (tamas), agitation (rajas) and harmony (sattva). No matter how hard you try, Arjuna, the ones you love will die, either on the battlefield or in the palace. No matter how hard you try, Arjuna, all things that you shun or disapprove will come into your life, again and again. War and peace will alternate like joy and sorrow, summer and winter, flood and drought.

'Changes in external states make your ego insecure. The ego therefore struggles to prevent any change. If change gives the ego pleasure, then it will pursue change and struggle against stillness and stagnation. When unable to get its way, the ego experiences suffering and rage; it forces the body to reinstate things as they were. From this desire to make the world align to the ego's measuring scale come all pain and suffering and rage. Refusal to accept the flow of the world is the root of all misery. Thus it is with you, Arjuna. You want to control the world. You want the world to behave as you wish. It does not, hence your anger and your grief.

'Changes in the material world are not random. They are essentially reactions of past actions. No event is spontaneous; it is the result of many past events. This is karma. The events in your life are the result of your past deeds, performed in this lifetime or the ones before. You alone are responsible for it. Such is the law of karma. Unless you experience the reactions of past actions, you will continue to be reborn. If you do not wish to be reborn, you must not generate karma. Actions that generate karma are different from those that do not; in the former, the ego has a territorial hold over the action, in the latter it does not. This moment, Arjuna, is the result of past actions—yours, of those behind you, and those before you. Accept it. Don't fight it. This war is destined to happen. You cannot wish it away.

'Your intellect can choose how to react to a particular stimulation. Often, there is so much conditioning, there is little thought between stimulation and reaction. But the option exists. If the chosen reaction is meant to please the ego, the cycle of karma continues (samsara). If the chosen reaction emerges from an awareness

of the soul, the cycle of karma grinds to a halt (moksha). If you, Arjuna, fight this war in anger or righteous indignation, peace will elude you and you will be trapped in samsara; if you fight this war with empathy and wisdom, there will be liberation from samsara.

'To function with the soul as the reference point, and not the ego, you must first experience the soul. To experience the soul, you must recognize the world for what it is, and not what the measuring scale tells you. Remember, the soul is watching everything—your intellect, your ego, your measuring scale and your responses to situations. It patiently awaits discovery. Suffering and rage will continue till you discover it. When will you discover it, Arjuna? When will you find peace?'

'Peace even while fighting a war? How, Krishna, how?' asked Arjuna, overwhelmed by the wisdom of Krishna's song.

'With your head—analyse the situation and discover the roots of your emotion. Why do you feel what you feel? Are you being spurred on by your ego? Why do you wish to fight? Is it from the desire to dominate your enemies and win back your territories? Is it rage which motivates you, the desire for vengeance and justice? Or are you detached from the outcome, at peace with the act you are about to perform? If these questions don't come to your mind, Arjuna, you are not practising gyan yoga.

'With your heart—have faith in the existence of the soul. Accept that nothing happens without a reason. Accept that all experiences have a purpose. Accept that the soul does not favour either you or the Kauravas, that there is a reality greater than what you perceive. Accept that infinite occurrences of the universe cannot be fathomed by the finite human mind. Surrender unconditionally, even in the absence of evidence, to the truth of the cosmos. In humility, there is faith. When there is faith, there is no fear. Is it faith guiding your hand, Arjuna, or is it fear? If it is fear, then you are not practising bhakti yoga.

'With your actions—engage with the world around you as a human, not animal. Animals have no intellect; their flesh is geared towards survival alone. That is why they are fettered by the law of the jungle (matsya nyaya) using their strength and cunning to stay alive. Humans have intellect and yearn for meaning beyond survival. They have the unique ability to empathize with this need in others too for they can sense the soul encased in all flesh. Humans alone of all living creatures can reject the law of the jungle and create a code of conduct based on empathy and directed at discovering the meaning of life. This is dharma. To live in dharma is to live without fear. To live in dharma is to act in love. To live in dharma is to have others as a reference point, not oneself. Function therefore in this war not like that insecure dog that barks to dominate and whines when dominated, but like that secure cow, that provides milk freely and follows the music of the divine. Do you fight this war to break the stranglehold of jungle law in human society, Arjuna? If not, you do not practise karma yoga.

'Duryodhana does not subscribe to dharma. All his actions stem from fear. He helps those who comfort him; he rejects those who threaten him. He behaves like a beast guarding his territory; but he is not a beast, he is human, very much capable of shattering this delusion. His refusal to do so makes him demonic, deserving of no pity. Your own refusal to fight also deserves no pity. It has its roots in fear, in a lack of empathy for the world. Rather than save the world from the likes of Duryodhana, you would rather comfort your ego that is terrified by the price demanded by this war. Your nobility is a delusion;

it very cleverly masks your insecurities. That is not acceptable. The fight is not out there, Arjuna, it is inside you. Do not surrender to a situation that nurtures the ego. The war is not for you, Arjuna, but for civilized human conduct. Remember, the point is not to win or lose the war, the point is not to kill enemies and acquire their lands; it is to establish dharma and in doing so discover the soul.

'That is why I am here, Arjuna, on earth, as your charioteer: to establish dharma, to remind humans of their humanity, to show the intellect that path that leads to the soul, and away from the ego. Every time humans feel purposeless and meaningless and in fear succumb to the ego, I descend to set things right. This has happened before. This will happen again. And I will keep coming.'

Arjuna realized his friend was no ordinary man. Prostrating himself before Krishna, he said, 'Show me who you really are.'

Krishna then showed Arjuna who he really was. In that battlefield, between the armies of the Kauravas and the Pandavas, a vision unfolded for Arjuna alone.

Krishna's form expanded so that it stretched from above the sky to the bottom of the sea. He was as resplendent as a thousand suns. From his breath emerged countless worlds. Between his teeth were crushed countless worlds. In him Arjuna saw all that was, is and will be—all the oceans, all the mountains, all the continents, the worlds above the sky and the worlds below the earth. Everything came from him, everything returned to him. He was the source of all Manavas, Devas, Asuras, Nagas, Rakshasas, Gandharvas, Apsaras, of all forefathers and all descendants. He was the container of all the possibilities of life.

The sight made Arjuna aware of the enormity of the cosmos and his relative insignificance. He felt like a grain of sand on a vast endless beach. If Krishna was an ocean, this moment, this war, was but a wave. So many waves, so many opportunities to discover the sea. This war, this life, his rage and his frustrations, everything in this world was a pointer to the soul.

'Remember, Arjuna,' said Krishna, 'he who says he kills and he who says he is killed are both wrong. I am both the killer and the killed. Yet I cannot die. I am your flesh and your soul, that which changes and that which does not change. I am the world around you, the spirit inside you and the mind in between. I am the measuring scale, the one who measures and that which is measured. I alone can bend the rules of space and time. I alone can shatter the web of karma. Realize me. Become a master of your intellect as a charioteer masters his horses and you will realize it is not about the war, it is not about fighting or

not fighting, it is not about winning or losing, but it is about taking decisions and discovering the truth about yourself. When you do this, there will be no fear, there will be no ego; you will be at peace, even in the midst of what the deluded call war.'

- The Bhagavad Gita is the most popular Hindu scripture because in it God speaks directly to man.
- The Gita was first translated into English in 1785 by Charles Wilkins under the patronage of the then Governor General, Warren Hastings. It reached Europe and was translated into other European languages like French and German. It was these translations that made the Gita so popular. The founding fathers of the Indian nation state read the Gita for the first time, not in a regional Indian language, or Sanskrit, but in English.
- One of the earliest translations of the Gita was the Marathi Dnyaneshwari by a young ascetic called Dnyaneshwar who challenged the caste hierarchy when he broke away from tradition and made the wisdom accessible to the common man in the language of the common man. Many other sages since have ensured the

wisdom of the Gita reach the common man through song and stories. Few except the educated elite, until the 19th century, had read the original Sanskrit.

- Sages have equated the Vedas with grass, the Upanishads with cows that chew on the grass and the Bhagavad Gita as the milk squeezed by Vyasa from the udders of these cows. In other words, the Bhagavad Gita captures the essence of Vedic wisdom. The Vedic hymns are dated to 2000 BCE while the Bhagavad Gita in its current form is dated to 300 CE, a testimony to the consistency of the thought which is considered sanatan, or timeless.
- At the end of the Bhagavad Gita is a war led by God himself. Does this make the Gita a scripture that propagates war? A reading of the Gita shows that the song is concerned neither with violence nor with non-violence. The song neither condones nor condemns war. The point is to look at the root of any action. What is the measuring scale that makes one war noble and another war ignoble? Wherefrom comes the desire to fight or not to fight? Is the motivation power or love? Is one indulging the ego or seeking the soul?
- From India came the idea of zero to the world of mathematics. This notion may have its roots in philosophical discussions where man's insignificance in the cosmic framework is constantly highlighted. When contrasted against infinity, every moment of life, howsoever wonderful or miserable, is reduced to zero.
- The day the Bhagavad Gita was narrated is celebrated as Mokshada Ekadashi, the eleventh day of the waxing moon in the month of Margashirsh (Nov–Dec). Elsewhere in the epic, it is suggested that the battle took place in autumn, not winter, in the month of Kartik (Oct–Nov) around Dasshera and Diwali.
- Rationalists wonder how such a long discourse took place with two impatient armies on either side. Since this was a discourse by God, the rules of space and time did not apply. What seems like a long discourse to humans, must have taken place in the blink of an eye on the battlefield.
- The purpose of life is to grow—materially, intellectually and emotionally. Unfortunately, the Kauravas focus only on material growth. By embracing Krishna, the Pandavas are offered intellectual and emotional growth, besides material growth, that has the power to help them break their own self-imposed limitations.

BOOK FIFTEEN

War

'Janamejaya, in the battle, fathers, teachers, brothers and friends were all killed, so that delusion could be replaced with wisdom.'

Bloodbath

Krishna's song had changed Arjuna's perspective of the battlefield. This was not Kuru-kshetra, where war was about property or vengeance. This was Dharma-kshetra, where Arjuna would triumph over his fear, guilt and rage.

Arjuna picked up his magnificent bow, the Gandiva, and requested Krishna to take him towards the enemy lines. As the chariot rolled, Arjuna's banner with the image of Hanuman fluttered against the blue sky. The deep sound of Devdutt, Arjuna's conch-shell, filled the air, joined by the sound of Panchajanya, Krishna's conch-shell. Together, they announced the start of the war.

Far away, in the palace of Hastina-puri, the blind king and his blindfolded wife heard Sanjay describe the scene thus: 'Then commenced the battle between your sons and your nephews, O monarch, which was as fierce and awful as the battle between the Devas and the Asuras. Men and crowds of chariots and elephants, and elephant-warriors and horsemen by thousands, and steeds, all possessed of great prowess, encountered one another. Resembling the roar of the clouds in the season of rain, the loud noise of rushing elephants of fearful forms was heard. Some chariot-riders, struck by elephants, were deprived of their chariots. Routed by those raging beasts other brave combatants ran off the field. Well-trained chariot-warriors, with their shafts, dispatched to the other world large bodies of cavalry and the footmen that urged and protected the elephants. Well-trained horsemen, O king, careered on to the field, surrounded the great

chariot-warriors, and struck and slew the latter with spears and darts and swords. Some combatants armed with bows surrounded great charioteers and dispatched them to Yama's abode, the many united battling against individual ones.'

As the sun reached the zenith, he said, 'Those warriors, O monarch, longing to take one another's life, began to slay one another in the battle. Throngs of chariots, and large bodies of horses, and teeming divisions of infantry and elephants in large numbers, mingled with one another, O king, for battle. We beheld the falling of maces and spiked bludgeons and lances and short arrows and rockets hurled at one another in that dreadful engagement. Arrow showers terrible to look at coursed like flights of locusts. Elephants approaching elephants routed one another. Horsemen encountering horsemen, and chariots encountering chariots, and foot-soldiers encountering foot-soldiers, and foot-soldiers meeting with horsemen, and foot-soldiers meeting with chariots and elephants, and chariots meeting with elephants and horsemen, and elephants of great speed meeting with the three other kinds of forces, began, O king, to crush and grind one another.'

At the end of the day, when the soldiers withdrew to their battle camps, this is how Sanjay described the battlefield: 'The earth, covered with blood, looked beautiful like a vast plain in the season of rains covered with red flowers. Indeed, the earth assumed the aspect of a youthful maiden of great beauty, attired in white robes dyed with deep red. Variegated with flesh and blood, the field of battle looked as if decked all over with gold. The field, O monarch, indented with the hoofs of the steeds,

looked beautiful like a beautiful woman bearing the marks of her lover's nails on her person. Strewn with those fallen heads that were crimson with blood, the earth looked resplendent as if adorned with golden-coloured lotuses in their season. Many steeds with garlands of gold on their heads and with their necks and breasts adorned with ornaments of gold, were seen to be slain in hundreds and thousands. And strewn with broken chariots and torn banners and brilliant umbrellas, with shredded chamaras and fans, and mighty weapons broken into fragments, with garlands and necklaces of gold, with bracelets, with heads decked with earrings, with headgears loosened off from heads, with standards, with the undercarriage of upturned chariots, O king, and with traces and reins, the earth shone as brightly as she does in spring when strewn with flowers.'

- In the Vishnu Purana, the earth-goddess in the form of a cow complains to Vishnu that she has been milked so terribly by the greedy kings of the earth that her udders are sore. Vishnu promises to teach the greedy kings a lesson; as Parashurama, Ram and Krishna he will spill their blood on the earth so that like a lioness, the earth can drink their blood. Thus the battle at Kuru-kshetra is preordained by cosmic events. It is a sacrifice to quench the thirst of the earth-goddess and restore the earth's splendour.
- Every warrior on the battlefield has a conch-shell trumpet. The sound of the conch-shell indicated the strength and stamina of warriors, and served as a warning to their opponents. Yudhishtira's conch-shell was called Ananta-vijaya, Bhima's was called Poundrya, Nakula's was called Sughosh and Sahadeva's was called Mani-pushpak.
- The descriptions of the war and renditions in art suggest a crowded battlefield covered with millions of fighting warriors. Vedic wars, in all probability, were

primarily duels where the chief warriors of opposite sides confronted each other. Each warrior, mounted on a chariot, was accompanied by elephants, horses and foot soldiers, who were there more to cheer the warrior, demonstrate his power and mock the opponent rather than actually fight. Poets added their imagination to the reality to create a grand, mesmerizing epic.

Sacrifice for victory

For nine days, they struggled. The sun rose, arched across the sky, and plummeted down the horizon, watching brother kill brother, friend kill friend. Hands were cut, heads smashed, stomachs torn, eyes gouged out—but there was no victory in sight. The ground was wet with blood, the air filled with the stench of rotting corpses. Day after day young men hurled themselves into battle, their energies stoked by the beating drums and the songs of charioteers and the commands of their generals. By evening, a few returned bruised and maimed, impatient for the sun to rise again.

In the silence of the night, servants who had waited in the battle camps all day collected the bodies of their masters lying dead or maimed on the battlefield. Kuru-kshetra was thus prepared for the next onslaught at dawn. By the time the land was cleared, the sun appeared on the horizon: there was no time to dispose of the dead, who were then simply piled up in heaps on the rim of the battlefield, their dead eyes watching the continuing carnage.

At first, it seemed the Pandavas would win. Then the battle moved in favour of the Kauravas. The old leader of the Kauravas proved to be an astute general. Under his command, the warriors successfully pushed the Pandava army back. But young Dhrishtadyumna was an able commander too. He matched the size of the Kaurava army with nimbleness; his instructions ensured that his army stood its ground and his soldiers did not lose heart.

As the days passed, it was clear that the two sides were equally matched. Victory eluded either. Strategies which worked at dawn failed by dusk. For every attack, there was a counterattack. Every astra was matched with an equally powerful astra from the opposite side. If the Pandava side included Rakshasas in their army, so did the Kauravas; if there were elephants on the Kaurava side, there were elephants on the Pandava side. Frustration built up. Hope was like a mirage, appearing for a few hours each day, and then disappearing. Amidst the war cries and clanging of weapons, it was clear to all that this war would not end soon.

'Perhaps if we sacrifice to Kali, the goddess of the battlefield, a worthy warrior, she might reveal how this war may be won,' said Krishna on the ninth night. The oracles were consulted and they agreed. A warrior with thirty-two sacred marks on the body would be ideal, they said.

Only three men on the Pandava side had such marks: Arjuna, Krishna and a warrior called Iravan. The Pandavas could not sacrifice Arjuna and would not sacrifice Krishna and so all eyes turned to Iravan.

'Who are you?' asked Arjuna.

'Your son,' said Iravan, his eyes gleaming with excitement. But Arjuna had no memory of fathering a son such as him. Iravan explained, 'My mother is the Naga princess, Ulupi, who you married long ago.'

Iravan had come to Kuru-kshetra despite his mother's protests. 'It is his war, not yours,' she had said. But Iravan longed to meet his father and yearned for glory.

Arjuna barely remembered Ulupi yet hugged Iravan as a son, for every warrior who joined his side, for whatever reason, was precious. If it meant being father to a man he did not even know, so be it. 'If you are truly my son, you should not have any hesitation in allowing yourself to be sacrificed to Kali,' said Arjuna.

Iravan realized he could not say no. 'But I have one condition,' he said, 'Let me not die a virgin. Let me have a wife, who will weep for me when I die.'

In keeping with the rules of the ritual, it was mandatory to fulfil the last wish of the sacrificial victim. The Pandavas were obliged to get Iravan married but no woman was willing to be Iravan's wife. Who would want to marry a man doomed to die at sunrise? When all attempts to get Iravan a wife failed, Krishna came to the rescue in a way no one could imagine.

Krishna took the female form known as Mohini, married Iravan, and spent the night with him as his wife, bringing great delight to his heart. The next day when Iravan was beheaded at dawn, Krishna wept for him as his widow. No widow had ever wept for a man as Krishna did for Iravan.

- The Sanskrit epic is generally silent on the son of Arjuna and Ulupi who is identified as Iravan. The tale of Iravan's human sacrifice comes from north Tamil Nadu's oral traditions where Iravan is worshipped as Kuthandavar, a form of Shiva.
- Iravan's sacrifice is re-enacted each year ritually where he becomes the divine husband of all men who have womanly feelings. Such men are known locally as Alis and they are today identified as homosexual transvestites, who often castrate themselves and spend their entire lives as women, separate from mainstream society. Through Iravan's mythology the existence of those who call themselves Ali is acknowledged, explained and validated.
- It is said that Iravan had this great desire to see the conclusion of the war. Divining this, Krishna placed his severed head on top of a tree, breathing life into it, so that he could witness what followed in the war from that vantage position.

A woman on the battlefield

The Pandavas knew that as long as Bhishma was alive, they would not win. But the Pandavas were reluctant to hurt Bhishma; he was like a father to them, the only father they knew. Arjuna released many arrows at Bhishma, but none that posed any real threat.

An angry Krishna jumped off the chariot one day, picked up a loose chariot wheel and ran towards Bhishma. Arjuna realized Krishna was so irritated with the way things were moving that to bring the war to a conclusion, he was willing to break his own vow of never raising weapons against anyone at Kuru-kshetra. Arjuna ran after Krishna, and begged him to stop. 'I will kill Bhishma,' he promised.

But therein lay the problem: how does one kill Bhishma, who had been given the boon by the gods that he could choose the time of his own death? Krishna said, 'Maybe he cannot be killed, but surely we can put him out of action by pinning him to the ground so that he can move not a single limb.'

'That is impossible so long as he holds his bow,' said Arjuna.

'Then make him lower his bow,' said Krishna with a smile, knowing fully well that Arjuna was finding excuses to avoid the unpleasant task.

'Bhishma will never lower his bow on the battlefield,' said Arjuna.

'Will he hold his bow even when facing a woman?' asked Krishna slyly, reminding all of the female form he had taken to be Iravan's wife.

'But women are not allowed to enter the battlefield,' argued Arjuna, still focusing on problems rather than solutions.

'Is Shikhandi a woman or a man?' asked Krishna, referring to Draupadi's elder brother.

Shikhandi's story was a peculiar one. She was born a woman but her father, Drupada, king of Panchala, was told by oracles that later in life she would acquire the body of a man. 'In her last life,' they said, 'she was Amba, the eldest daughter of the king of Kashi, and it is her destiny to be the cause of Bhishma's death.' So Drupada raised his daughter as a man. He even gave her a wife. On the wedding night, Shikhandi's wife ran screaming to her father, Hiranyavarna, king of Dasharna, complaining that her 'husband' had the body of a woman. Hiranyavarna raised an army, laid siege to Drupada's kingdom and threatened to raze it to the ground to avenge the humiliation of his daughter. To save Panchala from war, Shikhandi decided to kill herself. She ran to the forest where she encountered a Yaksha called Sthuna. On hearing of her situation, the Yaksha offered Shikhandi his manhood. 'Use it to prove to your wife and her father that you are a man but return it tomorrow,' said the Yaksha. Shikhandi took the Yaksha's manhood and did all that was necessary to prove to his wife that he was no woman, forcing his father-in-law to beat a hasty retreat. When Shikhandi returned to the forest the next day to return her temporary manhood, the Yaksha said, 'My king, Kubera, lord of the Yakshas, ruler of Alakapuri, was not pleased when he learnt how I let you use my manhood for a night. He has cursed me that my manhood will return to me only at the end of your life.' Shikhandi was overjoyed. Born a woman, he had now become a man and would stay so till the day he died.

All those who knew this tale wondered if Shikhandi was man or woman. Is gender defined by the truth of birth or by the truth of this moment?

Krishna said, 'If you, Arjuna, believe Shikhandi is a man, you can take him into the battlefield on your chariot. But if Bhishma believes Shikhandi is a woman, he will lower his bow and complain that you have breached the rules of war. That will give you an opportunity to overpower him.'

'That is unfair,' said Arjuna.

'That's a matter of opinion,' said Krishna.

And so on the tenth day of the battle, Shikhandi mounted Arjuna's chariot and challenged Bhishma to a duel. As expected, Bhishma refused to fight one who was born with the body of a woman. He lowered his bow. Arjuna who stood behind Shikhandi immediately shot hundreds of arrows at Bhishma.

Duryodhana watched in horror as Arjuna's arrows ripped through the great warrior's limbs and torso. The great leader of the Kaurava army fell from his chariot, and fell to the ground. The arrows that had pierced every inch of his flesh suspended him between sky and earth.

News of Bhishma's fall spread across the battlefield like wildfire. All the soldiers lowered their weapons in respect. Bhishma was the great patriarch of the Kuru clan respected by all. They gathered around him and wept on seeing him so pinned to the ground.

An ordinary man would have died of these injuries. But Bhishma was no ordinary man. 'I can choose the time of my death and the time is not now. The rising sun moves in the southern direction along the eastern horizon, and the moon wanes with each passing day. I shall wait until this changes and die at an auspicious time after the winter solstice, when the sun rises each day closer to the Pole Star, only in the bright half of the lunar month when the moon is waxing.'

Thus ended the tenth day of battle, with the Kaurava army losing its great leader.

- Though the Pandavas invoke Durga, goddess of war, before the battle, they still hesitate to allow a woman to fight beside them. In the epic age, killing a woman was considered the worst of crimes, equal to killing a Brahman, keeper of wisdom, and a cow, source of wealth, because to kill a woman was equal to killing a mother.
- Bhishma's defeat marks the end of an old and noble era when rules of war were respected. The days that follow witness the gradual breakdown of all principles.
- Arjuna's arrows suspend Bhishma between the earth and the sky because he is rejected by both in death. This is because Bhishma cannot be identified clearly either as a householder or as a hermit. Moreover, though born a man he lives like a non-man, meaning he neither fulfils his obligations as a son nor partakes the benefits of being a son: he does not marry, does not father children, does not inherit his father's kingdom and, in the end, dies because of a woman. Bhishma also carries the burden of letting his family bloodline die because of his vow; his half-brothers turn out to be weaklings who die childless. Vyasa thus draws attention to the terrible consequences of what may appear to be a very noble sacrifice.
- In a way, Bhishma practices adharma. He breaks the code of ashrama-dharma that demands that men retire when their children are old enough to take care of themselves. He refuses to let go and allow his family to fend for itself. Taking advantage of the fact that he can choose his death, he refuses to die, or retire, or detach himself from his household.
- The time when Bhishma is pinned to the ground falls in the period before the winter solstice when the Pitrs or ancestors are close to the earth according to the traditional calendar system. Bhishma, who chose never to give birth to a child, perhaps is ashamed to meet his ancestors and so chooses to die in the next half of the year after the winter solstice when the Pitrs pull away from the earth.
- Both the stories of Iravan's marriage and Shikhandi's participation deal with sexual transformation and gender ambiguity. Both these events take place on the ninth night and tenth day, which is midway between the eighteen-day battle. Until their occurrence, the battle is indecisive. Only after these events occur does the battle approach a conclusion. Thus the ninth night marks the shift from binary logic to fuzzy logic, where lines are not so clearly drawn between points of view.

Drona's onslaught

On the eleventh day, Drona became the leader of the Kaurava army. Duryodhana told Drona, 'The first great warrior to die on this battlefield is a Kaurava, not a Pandava. This is a great blow to our morale. You must kill a great Pandava too, preferably Yudhishtira.'

Drona swore to do so. Unlike Bhishma, who showed great restraint in his battle strategies, and whose intention was primarily to push the Pandavas back with the least harm, Drona's strategies were directed at causing maximum damage.

He dispatched the charioteers of Trigarta known as the Samsaptakas against Arjuna and a vast legion of elephants led by Bhagadatta, king of Pragjyotisha, against Bhima. 'With Arjuna and Bhima thus distracted, the eldest Pandava, left unguarded, will be easy to capture,' said Drona.

Bhima tried his best to push back Bhagadatta's elephants. But they were more than a match for him. He decided to retreat.

The sight of Bhima's chariot retreating filled the Pandava army with gloom. Arjuna saw this and felt he should subdue Bhagadatta first and then deal with the

Samsaptaka charioteers. So Krishna pulled out the chariot and moved towards Bhagadatta and his elephants. 'No, go back. First Samsaptaka and then Bhagadatta,' he said first. Then he said, 'No, maybe first Bhagadatta and then Samsaptaka.'

Realizing Arjuna's dilemma and rising stress, Krishna said with a smile, 'You can defeat both. One at a time or simultaneously. I have faith in you.'

Thus reassured by Krishna, Arjuna raised his bow and first showered arrows in the direction of the Samsaptakas. The arrows hit dozens of horses, smashed hundred more chariots and killed thousands of riders. As the horses fell on top of each other and the broken chariots piled up, there was complete confusion among the great Samsaptakas. Arjuna had single-handedly destroyed this legion which had sworn either to destroy Arjuna or be destroyed by him.

Arjuna then turned to Bhagadatta. As the chariot moved towards Bhagadatta, the great warrior stood on top of his elephant and released a dreaded weapon—the Vaishnav-astra. Arjuna raised his bow to counteract the effects of this astra. But Krishna came in between and bore the brunt of the missile. As soon as the missile touched him it turned into a garland of flowers.

'Why did you take the weapon upon yourself, Krishna? I could have destroyed it myself,' said Arjuna arrogantly.

Krishna replied, 'No, you could not. This weapon was given to Bhagadatta by his father, who had received it from his mother, the earth-goddess, who in turn had received it from me when in an earlier incarnation, in the form of a boar I had raised the earth from the bottom of the sea. No creature in this world, but me, its creator, could withstand the power of the Vaishnav-astra. That is why I took the brunt of the weapon.'

Arjuna apologized for his arrogance. And then he turned his attention to Bhagadatta. With one arrow, he split open the head of the elephant on which Bhagadatta rode. With another, he ripped open Bhagadatta's chest. As the two fell, so much blood spurted out that it felt like it was raining blood.

And while Arjuna was defeating the Samsaptaka charioteers and Bhagadatta's elephants, Bhima ensured that Yudhishtira was well protected, foiling Drona's plans.

Shakuni led the forces of Gandhara against Arjuna. With his arrows, reverberating with the power of chants, he conjured up darkness and torrential rains. Arjuna retaliated by releasing magic missiles of his own: he destroyed the darkness with light and the rains with dryness. Shakuni finally had to give up and withdraw from the battlefield.

A warrior called Shrutayudha tried his best to defeat Arjuna but failing to do so, hurled his mace at Krishna. This mace was a gift of the sea-god Varuna and could not be used against an unarmed warrior. As Krishna was unarmed, the mace bounced off Krishna's chest and struck Shrutayudha and killed him on the spot.

- Despite hearing Krishna's Bhagavad Gita, Arjuna struggles with his attachments and prejudices. This repeatedly manifests in his hesitation and indecisiveness on the battlefield. Growth is thus not a one-time activity; it is a process where decisions to overpower the beast within have to be taken every single moment.
- The stories of the Vaishnav-astra and Shrutayudha show us that the Pandavas are clearly under divine protection. Krishna's presence ensures that Arjuna can do what he is supposed to do on the battefield, unhurt.
- The Pandavas and the Kauravas fight each other with astras: these were not just ordinary arrows. These were missiles charged with the power of magical hymns. There were different types of astras, each one containing the power of one or many gods. There were the Brahma-astra, Vishnu-astra and Pashupat-astra containing the power of Brahma, Vishnu and Shiva respectively. There were the Agni-astra, Vayu-astra and Indra-astra, reverberating with the power of fire, wind and rain respectively. The descriptions of the effect of these weapons have led to speculations that the ancients were probably familiar with nuclear technology and that astras were really nuclear warheads.

Death of Abhimanyu

As the twelfth day drew to a close, Krishna noticed that just as Arjuna had hesitated to strike down Bhishma, who he considered to be like a father, he hesitated to strike down Drona, who was his teacher. 'In battle there are no sons or fathers or uncles or teachers. There are only soldiers who fight for dharma or adharma,' said Krishna. But Arjuna's heart was filled with too much regard for his teacher to be so detached.

Drona, meanwhile, angry at his failure to harm even a single Pandava, after two days of intense fighting, came up with a terrifying plan on day thirteen.

He had observed that Krishna constantly kept Arjuna away from Karna, who had, after the fall of Bhishma, finally entered the battlefield. The reason for this was as follows:

As long as Bhishma led the Kaurava forces, Karna had not stepped into the battle. When it was time for him to finally enter, after Bhishma's death, an old man came to him, at dawn, begging for alms. As was his nature, Karna said, 'Ask and it shall be yours.' The old man immediately asked Karna for his earrings and armour that had been part of his body since the day of his birth. They clung to his body like flesh and were impermeable to any weapon. Giving them up meant giving up his advantage in the battlefield and letting himself be vulnerable. Without a second thought, Karna decided to part with his divine gifts—cutting them out like bark from a tree using a very sharp knife. The old man, who was none other than Indra, king of the gods, and father of Arjuna, acted out of love for his son. As he watched the blood gush out of Karna's ears and chest, he felt overwhelmed by Karna's selflessness. He revealed his true identity and said, 'I salute you, son of Surya. Your charity has no parallel. I give you a gift. A celestial spear that never misses its mark. But you can use it only once. Use it wisely.' Karna decided that he would use this spear to kill Arjuna. Divining this, Krishna never let Arjuna come within Karna's line of sight from the moment the latter stepped into the battlefield.

'Let your chariot be next to mine,' said Drona to Karna, thus ensuring that Krishna would move Arjuna to the other end of the battlefield. Drona then organized his soldiers in the dreaded battle formation called Chakra-vyuha where the soldiers encircle and entrap the enemy. Only Arjuna knew how to break this formation but with him on the other side of the battlefield, Drona was able to trap some of the major warriors of the Pandava army within the Chakra with great ease.

Suddenly surrounded by the Kaurava army, Yudhishtira cried out for help, but Krishna blew his conch-shell simultaneously so that Arjuna heard nothing. 'How do we break this battle formation? How do we escape?' asked a nervous Yudhishtira.

Abhimanyu, Arjuna's young son by Subhadra, newly married and barely sixteen, said, 'I know how to break the battle formation so that you can escape.' His eyes were wide with excitement at this opportunity to fight great warriors in this great war.

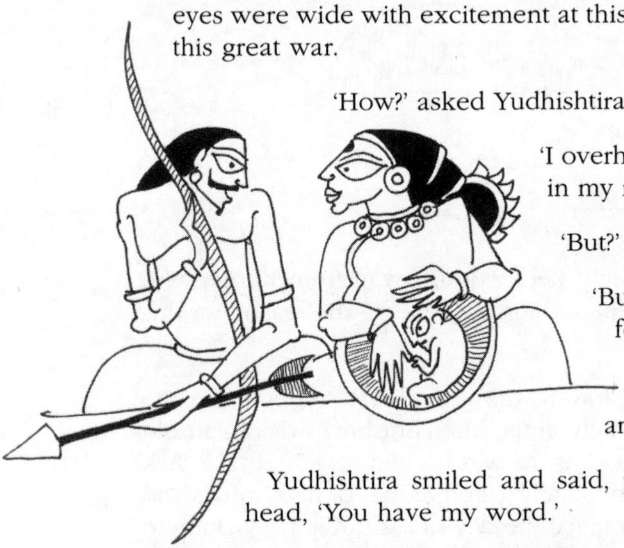

'How?' asked Yudhishtira.

'I overheard father describe it when I was still in my mother's belly. But . . .'

'But?'

'But, while I know how to breach the formation and help all of you escape, I do not know how to escape from it myself. You will have to come back and get me.'

Yudhishtira smiled and said, placing his hand on the young lad's head, 'You have my word.'

Abhimanyu immediately set about breaching the Chakra formation and to the amazement of everyone around, Drona included, the formation was breached and the Pandava warriors were able to slip out.

Then gathering reinforcements, Yudhishtira turned around to rescue Abhimanyu, only to find his path blocked by Jayadhrata and his army. Drona, meanwhile, managed to close the Chakra breach and Abhimanyu was trapped inside.

Abhimanyu found himself surrounded by all his uncles and cousins, Duryodhana, Dusshasana, Lakshman, Kritavarma, Kripa, Karna, Drona, Ashwatthama, each one armed, each one moving menacingly towards him. 'But is it not against the rule of war for many warriors to attack a single warrior simultaneously?' asked Vikarna.

'They broke the rule first by getting a woman to fight Bhishma,' said Drona, justifying his decision.

Abhimanyu fought back bravely. They broke his bow, so he raised a sword. They broke his sword, so he picked up a spear. They broke his spear, so he picked up a chariot wheel. He was able to kill Duryodhana's son, Lakshman. But Dusshasana's son was able to strike him on the head with a mace. Before he could recover his senses, the other warriors jumped on him like wild dogs on a young antelope and cut him to pieces mercilessly.

Outside the Chakra, all Yudhishtira could do was hear Abhimanyu's piteous cries for help. He could do nothing except glare at Jayadhrata who smiled in triumph.

- Abhimanyu's death holds great significance because he is the first member of the Pandava family to be killed by the Kauravas.
- The play *Chakravyuha* by Manoranjan Bhattacharya, with lyrics and music by Kazi Nazrul Islam, first performed on 23 November 1934, gives a modern twist to the tale of Abhimanyu when he and Duryodhana's son, Lakshman, make a pact to share the kingdom between themselves, irrespective of what their elders do, if they ever become heirs to the throne.

- There are many folktales attempting to explain why Krishna allowed Arjuna's son to die so. One states that in his former birth, Abhimanyu was a demon and had escaped being killed by Vishnu by taking birth as Arjuna's son. Another states that Abhimanyu was actually the son of Chandra, the moon-god, who had been allowed by his father to stay on the earth for sixteen years.
- At various times during the battle, the supreme commander organized his troops into special formations known as vyuhas. Each formation had a specific purpose; some were defensive while others were offensive. Furthermore, each formation had specific strengths and weaknesses. The formations that were encountered are as follows:
  - Krauncha vyuha—Heron formation
  - Makara vyuha—Dolphin formation
  - Kurma vyuha—Turtle formation
  - Trishula vyuha—Trident formation
  - Chakra vyuha—Wheel or discus formation
  - Padma vyuha—Lotus formation

Before sunset

'You let my son die,' cried Arjuna. He blamed Yudhishtira for abandoning Abhimanyu and Krishna for purposefully taking his chariot to the far side of the battlefield.

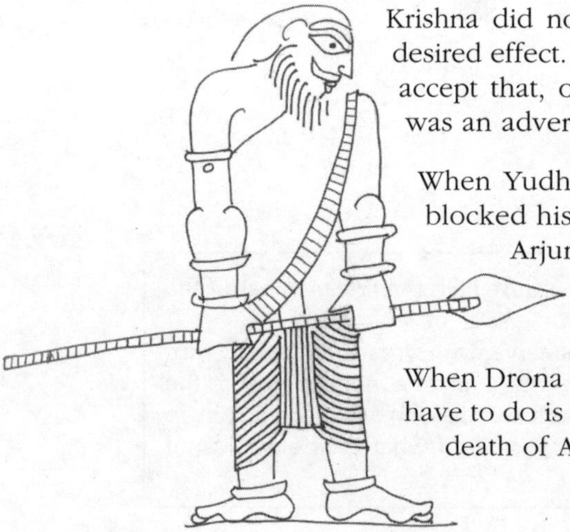

Krishna did not protest. The death of Abhimanyu had the desired effect. Arjuna was filled with rage and was forced to accept that, on the battlefield, Drona was no teacher. He was an adversary.

When Yudhishtira informed Arjuna how Jayadhrata had blocked his way when he had tried to save his nephew, Arjuna directed all his rage against Jayadhrata. 'I swear that if I do not kill Jayadhrata before sunset tomorrow, I will burn myself alive.'

When Drona learnt of Arjuna's oath, he was happy. 'All we have to do is protect Jayadhrata till sunset and it will be the death of Arjuna.'

The entire Kaurava army was positioned between Arjuna and Jayadhrata on the fourteenth day of battle, their sole aim to protect the son-in-law of the Kaurava household from death until sunset.

No matter how hard Arjuna tried, he could not find Jayadhrata. Arjuna fought fiercely, releasing hundreds of arrows that shattered the chariots and standards and weapons of the soldiers who stood between him and Jayadhrata, but they kept pouring in like waves of locusts, determined to block Arjuna's progress until nightfall. Arjuna was a lion determined to get to his prey. The Kauravas were like wild elephants equally determined not to let him have his way.

A point came when the horses of Arjuna's chariots were too exhausted to chase Jayadhrata. While Arjuna kept the enemy at bay with his fierce shafts, Krishna stopped the chariot and unyoked the horses. Krishna said that the horses needed water. So Arjuna, pausing for a moment, turned away from the surrounding enemies and shot an arrow in the ground and caused water to gush out. Arjuna then resumed fighting, keeping the enemy at bay, and allowing the horses to drink this water and refresh themselves. Soon, the four white stallions were ready to pursue Jayadhrata once more.

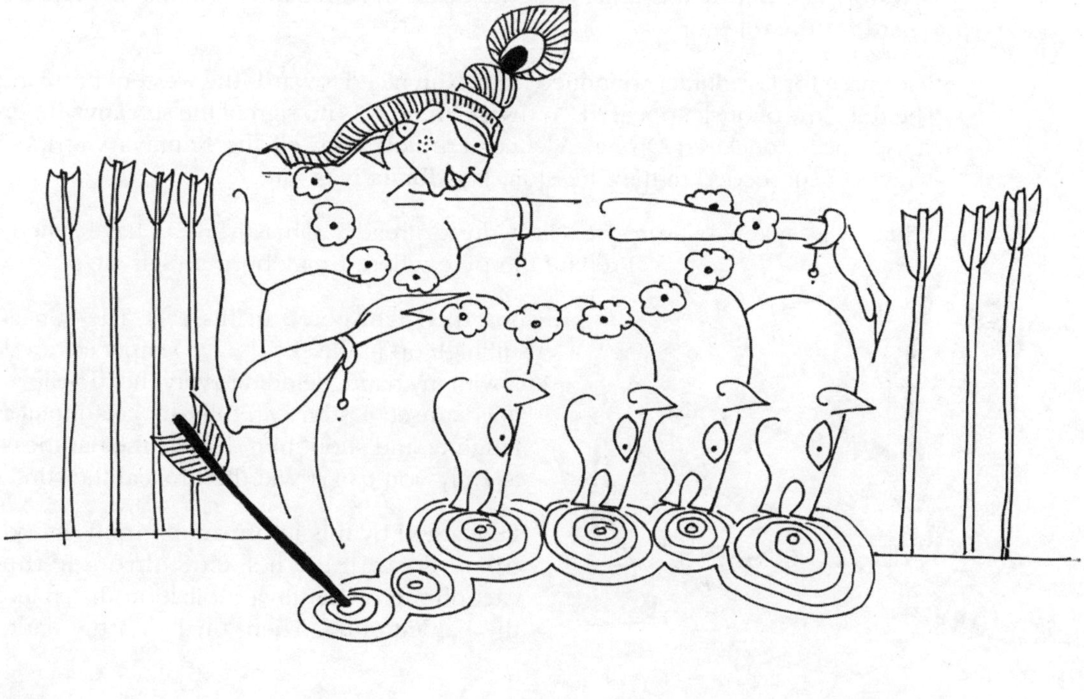

Arjuna saw Bhurishrava, who fought for the Kauravas, pinning Satyaki, the Yadava, to the ground and about to strike him dead with a sword. The rivalry between the two was well known—it had started when Satyaki's grandfather, Sini, had defeated Bhurishrava's grandfather, Somadatta, and would end only when Bhurishrava had avenged that defeat by killing Satyaki. But when Bhurishrava attacked Satyaki, he was tired and unarmed. Arjuna, already irritated by his failure to find Jayadhrata, released an arrow to save Satyaki. The arrow severed Bhurishrava's upraised arm. Bhurishrava cried foul, for it was against the code of war to interfere when two warriors were in a duel. As Bhurishrava expressed his outrage to Arjuna, Satyaki recovered his senses. Without realizing that his enemy was in conversation with his saviour, Satyaki picked up a sword and swung it to behead the armless and distracted Bhurishrava. The assembled warriors condemned Arjuna and Satyaki for such a cowardly act. But by this time, after the death of Abhimanyu, Arjuna had lost all regard for the rules of war.

The chase for Jayadhrata continued as the sun raced towards the western horizon. The red glow of dusk appeared. And soon there was no sign of the sun anywhere. 'It is sunset,' declared Drona. A cheer erupted from all the Kaurava warriors. They had succeeded in their mission. Jayadhrata was safe.

Arjuna was taken by surprise, 'Is it dusk already? Oh Krishna, I have failed. Prepare the pyre where I may burn myself alive.'

Krishna then whispered in his ear, 'The sun is still high up in the sky. I have simply covered it with my hand, deluding everyone to believe it is sunset. Listen carefully to Jayadhrata's laughter and shoot him dead in the darkness as only you can. I will then reveal the sun.'

Recharged by this information, Arjuna stood up and strained his ears through the cacophony of Kaurava jubiliation that filled the battleground. Then, finally, in the dark, he heard the unmistakable peal of Jayadhrata's laughter. Arjuna released the arrow and the arrow hit its mark. Before Drona could cry that it was adharma to fight after sunset, Krishna uncovered the sun. It stood high above the horizon.

Jayadhrata's father, Vriddhakshatra, who had become a hermit long ago, had obtained a boon from the gods to protect his son. It was said that whosoever caused Jayadhrata's head to fall on the ground would have his own head burst into a thousand pieces. To prevent this from happening, Krishna caused Arjuna's arrow that had severed Jayadhrata's neck to carry his head through the sky and drop it on Vriddhakshatra's lap. Finding his son's severed head on his lap, an alarmed Vriddhakshatra stood up. The head rolled to the ground and Vriddhakshatra's head burst into a thousand pieces. Thus the boon obtained by the father to protect his son turned against him, thanks to Krishna's intervention.

- The death of Abhimanyu makes the war more personal for Arjuna. Thus while the Bhagavad Gita motivates Arjuna to enter the battlefield, the wisdom of God's discourse fails as the days pass. Arjuna does give in to his fears and attachments, much to Krishna's exasperation. This was perhaps Vyasa's way of drawing attention to how even God's discourse need not bring about permanent transformation.
- Bhurishrava kicks Satyaki on his head because his grandfather, Somadatta, had long ago been treated so by Satyaki's grandfather, Sini. Thus there were many underlying agendas that brought warriors to the battlefield of Kuru-kshetra. Often, the Kaurava–Pandava conflict was just an excuse.
- According to the Indonesian retelling of the epic, Bhurishrava, who is killed by Satyaki during the war, is the son of Shalya. He is an impolite and arrogant man, cursed to be so by his own maternal grandfather, who Shalya hated and killed.
- The Drona Parva informs us that at one point Satyaki comes face to face with Duryodhana and the two start weeping, lamenting the state of affairs. When they were children, they were the best of friends. And now, circumstances had caused them to fight on opposite sides.
- In the epic, there are several occasions when Arjuna takes the dramatic vow of burning himself to death if he fails to succeed. This vow is taken when he promises to save the dying children of a Brahman, when he proclaims to Hanuman

that he can build a bridge of arrows across the river, and finally in the battlefield when he declares his intention to kill Jayadhrata before sunset. One wonders if this was Vyasa's way of showing Arjuna's bravado and tendency to be dramatic.

After sunset

After the death of Jayadhrata just before sunset on the fourteenth day of battle, Drona was so angry that he ordered his troops to continue fighting even after the sun had set. Duryodhana and Karna reminded Drona that this was against the code of war. Drona replied, 'If Krishna can make the day night, why can't we consider night day?'

And so the Kauravas did not lower their weapons even when the sun set and the battlefield was covered with darkness. To help warriors see in the dark, Duryodhana ordered some soldiers to drop their weapons and carry lamps instead.

Soon, there were lamps along the entire length of the Kaurava army. The light of the lamps bounced off the golden armours and gleaming weapons of Karna and Drona and Duryodhana and Kripa. They looked magnificent. It seemed as if stars had descended on earth and were moving menacingly towards the Pandavas determined to annihilate them. The exhausted Pandava army was taken by surprise and suffered many casualties.

Then Arjuna organized his army to carry lamps as well so that they too could see in the darkness and fight back. Seven lamps were placed on each elephant, two on each horse and ten on each chariot. Thus illuminated, the Pandavas fought back, refusing to let darkness overwhelm them.

On this night, Drona slew his enemy, Drupada, father-in-law of the Pandavas, as well as Virata, the king of Matsya, who had sheltered the Pandavas in the final year of their exile.

Watching Drona take advantage of the darkness, Krishna turned to Bhima and said, 'Summon your son, Ghatotkacha, born of the Rakshasa queen, Hidimbi. A Rakshasa is invincible at night. Let him and his hordes fight for the Pandava army is exhausted.'

Bhima did as told and Ghatotkacha came when summoned. At night, he looked tall and ferocious with his long, sharp, razor-like teeth and claw-like nails. He had the Kaurava forces running for cover in no time. Anticipating this move from the Pandavas, Drona had summoned another Rakshasa to support the Kauravas. His name was Alamvusha.

Alamvusha, tall as a mountain, challenged Ghatotkacha for a duel. They rushed at each other like wild elephants. Such was the force with which they struck each other that it produced sparks of fire. The two armies watched in the flickering light of lamps the two demons fight on behalf of the two human armies. In the end, Ghatotkacha prevailed as he managed to choke Alamvusha to death.

A desperate Duryodhana then turned to Karna. 'Ghatotkacha fills our army with fear. We must destroy him. I beg you to use the spear Indra gave you against this Rakshasa. We have no other choice.'

Karna had planned to use the spear against Arjuna, but compelled by Duryodhana, he hurled it at Ghatotkacha. Ghatotkacha screamed as the spear ripped open his chest. Such was his cry that all the elephants and horses on the battlefield stood still. He then kept tottering, swaying back and forth, like a tree in the forest that is about to fall to the floor. He did not want to die before looking at his father one last time.

Krishna shouted, 'Don't fall on the Pandava side. Increase your size and fall on the Kaurava side. Crush as many of your father's enemy as you can. Serve your father thus even in death.' Ghatotkacha nodded his head. He stretched himself until his head touched the sky. He then threw himself on the Kaurava army crushing hundreds of soldiers, horses, chariots and elephants under him. Bhima howled as he saw his son fall. Duryodhana was happy to see Bhima cry, but the happiness lasted only until he was told of the vast numbers of Kaurava soldiers Ghatotkacha had claimed in death.

Only Krishna was happy with this incident. With Indra's spear gone, Arjuna had little to fear from Karna. And the death of Ghatotkacha would have the same impact on Bhima as the death of Abhimanyu had on Arjuna—now, the battle was personal.

The battle continued through the night until Arjuna realized that half his soldiers were asleep or so drowsy that they had begun letting themselves be killed or had taken to killing each other, too tired to distinguish friend from foe. He directed all his troops towards Drona forcing him to leave the battlefield. With Drona driven out, the fighting stopped. The soldiers, with no energy to return to their battle camps, collapsed wherever they stood and slept along with their horses and elephants, amidst the debris of broken chariots and dead warriors.

- There are Rakshasas who fight for the Pandavas and Rakshasas who fight for the Kauravas. Thus the Rakshasas, though feared for their strength, and disdained for their barbarism, are accepted as allies.
- That Krishna is an opportunist is reinforced in this tale when he encourages Bhima's demon son to inflict maximum damage on the enemy while dying.
- The night battle where exhausted soldiers have lamps in one hand and weapons in the other is a metaphor for the extent of human rage. When angry, all rules collapse, all good sense vanishes and the beast of vengeance takes over.

A teacher beheaded

All eyes now turned to Drona. How does one defeat a great warrior like him, the Pandavas wondered. Krishna said, 'All his motivation comes from his obsessive love for his son, Ashwatthama. Perhaps we must take away that motivation or at least let him believe that the cause of all his actions no longer exists. Let us tell him, Ashwatthama is dead.'

All the Pandavas around Drona kept telling each other, 'Ashwatthama is dead.'

A distressed Drona refused to believe them. He turned desperately towards Yudhishtira, the most honest man in the world, and asked, 'Is that true?'

Yudhishtira turned to Krishna. Krishna smiled a compassionate smile, for he could hear the unspoken arguments that Yudhishitra was having with himself: Was truth so important? What if a lie could end a war? Wherefrom came his desire to tell the truth? To look good or to do good? With a heavy heart, Yudhishtira decided to speak his first lie, a little white lie. 'Yes, Ashwatthama is dead,' he said, and then, as an afterthought, he murmured, 'Maybe it was an elephant, or maybe it was a man.' But in the din of the battle the devastated father did not hear the murmur.

Yes, an elephant called Ashwatthama had died, killed by Bhima on Krishna's instructions. Yudhishtira knew this very well and still he told his teacher that he was not sure if the Ashwatthama referred to by his warriors was a man or an animal.

This plan of Krishna's had the desired effect. A shaken Drona lost the will to fight. He even lost the will to live. He stopped his chariot, alighted, put down his weapon and sat down in deep meditation ready to die.

'Kill him. Kill him,' shouted Krishna. But Drona was a teacher, a Brahman. To kill him was the greatest crime in all of Aryavarta. The soldiers hesitated. Krishna shouted, 'He was merely the son of a Brahman. But he lived as a Kshatriya for wealth and power and vengeance. Let him die as a Kshatriya on the battlefield.'

Thus instructed by Krishna, Dhrishtadyumna, son of Drupada, commander of the Pandava forces, raised his sword and in one sweep severed the neck of Drona.

When Ashwatthama saw the beheading of his father who had laid down his weapons, he was so outraged that he released the Narayana-astra. It was a dreadful missile that spat out fire and covered the sky in the form of dark serpents with giant fangs. 'It will destroy us all,' said Yudhishtira.

Krishna said, 'Do not fear. Just drop your weapons and alight from your chariots. Do not fight it. Just salute it respectfully. It will not harm you.'

All the soldiers fighting for the Pandavas did as told, all except Bhima, who in his rashness, rushed towards the son of Drona on his chariot, mouthing profanities, whirling his mace. The Narayana-astra enveloped him with fire and the dark, fanged serpents would have surely destroyed him had Arjuna and Krishna not rushed to his rescue. They forced him down from his running chariot and pulled the mace from his hand. Bhima was at first furious at being stopped. But then he saw how the Narayana-astra withdrew. It would not harm anyone who was not armed and hostile.

Ashwatthama was outraged at the failure of his dreaded missile. 'Shoot it again,' said Duryodhana, impressed by the power of this weapon. 'Avenge your father's death.'

'I can't,' said Ashwatthama. 'The Narayana-astra can be used only once. If I use it again, it will turn against me.'

- In Vedic India, it was important to uphold varna-dharma and ashrama-dharma. The former meant sticking to the profession of the father. The latter meant behaving as per one's stage in life. Drona breaks the varna-dharma by living like a warrior rather than a priest. Bhishma breaks the ashrama-dharma by not getting married and enabling his father to shun retirement. Thus, for all their nobility, the two generals of the Kaurava army are responsible for the breakdown of dharma as much as Duryodhana.
- Yudhishtira's chariot never touches the ground until he utters the only lie of his life—that he is not sure if the Ashwatthama killed is a man or an elephant. This act of Yudhishtira makes him human. Brings him down to earth, literally.
- Since Drona is a Brahman, by killing him, Dhrishtadyumna bears the burden of Brahma-hatya-paap, the sin of killing a priest, a terrible sin in the Hindu world.

A person who does so loses his right to be a member of society. In mythology, only Shiva is allowed to perform this act. The epic equates Dhrishtadyumna with Shiva. Attempts are made to downplay this event. It is said that by the time Dhrishtadyumna's sword severed Drona's neck, his life had already left his body. So there was no killing. Just the decapitation of a lifeless body.

A fight between brothers

Drona was dead. Who would lead the Kauravas now? 'It can only be the charioteer's son,' said Dhritarashtra to Gandhari as Sanjay concluded the narration of the fifteenth day of battle.

Kunti who sat behind the couple overheard this. She could not bear the idea that her sons would now be fighting their own elder brother. She had to stop this. The younger five would not understand, but the elder one would—he was wiser and perhaps, kinder. In the dead of the night, Kunti left the palace in Hastina-puri and made her way to the battlefield. Dawn was yet to break when she reached the Kaurava battle camp in Kurukshetra. She saw Karna meditating in preparation for the war. He looked strange, stripped of his magical earrings and armour; his ears still bled and his chest was still raw. This was her son, her firstborn, the one who was abandoned at birth. With her heart filled with love and trepidation, she addressed him for the first time in her life. 'Son,' she said.

Karna raised his head and recognized Kunti. Glances were exchanged between mother and son. A lifetime of unspoken emotions gushed forth. Karna bowed. 'The charioteer's son salutes the mother of the Pandavas,' he said. The sarcasm in his voice was like a poisoned barb.

'Forgive me,' said Kunti, tears in her eyes.

'Forgive me,' said Karna, apologizing for his pettiness. She was after all barely a child when she had borne him. 'What can I do for you? It is almost daybreak. I always grant the wish made to me at this time of the day.' He paused. It dawned on him why she had chosen to meet him and acknowledge him as son so late in his life. 'Perhaps that is what you came here for. A boon? That's what you want, isn't it? You came here not to give love to your outcast firstborn but to collect charity from the charitable charioteer's son.'

The truth was grating. Kunti nodded her head shamefacedly. 'I do not want brother to fight brother,' she said, 'Abandon the Kauravas, take your rightful place among your family, and let there be peace.'

Karna pulled his shoulders back, took a deep breath and declared rather forcefully, 'Peace for whom? Them or me? I will never abandon Duryodhana. Ask for anything else but that.'

'I do not want my sons to die.'

'Who do you refer to? The ones born after marriage, or the one born before?' Kunti wanted to shout, 'All,' but a despondent Karna continued, 'The world knows you as mother of five sons. At the end of the war, I promise you that you will still have five sons, including one great archer, either Arjuna or me.' Karna turned away from Kunti. He did not want her to see his pain. It was time for war. Dawn broke. Conch-shells could be heard. Kunti slipped away unnoticed, wanting to bless Karna but resisting the urge. How could she wish him victory against the sons of Pandu?

Duryodhana approached and, amidst great fanfare and cheering, declared Karna the leader of the Kaurava armies. To mark the occasion, Duryodhana appointed Shalya as Karna's charioteer and with excitement told his dear friend, 'All your life, the kings of the earth called you a charioteer who is supposed to serve warriors and kings. Now, ride into battle as a warrior with a king serving you as a charioteer.'

This made Karna happy but soon he realized having Shalya as charioteer was not a good idea. Rather than energizing him with encouraging words, as charioteers are expected to, Shalya kept praising Arjuna and demoralizing Karna.

Karna noticed that Krishna steered Arjuna's chariot away from his own, avoiding a confrontation with him. So Karna decided to focus his energies on the other Pandava brothers. He defeated Nakula and Sahadeva in a duel. He then defeated Bhima and finally defeated Yudhishtira in a duel. He could have killed each one of them but, in keeping with the vow he made to Kunti, he let them go alive. The only son of Kunti he would kill was Arjuna.

Before he set them free, Karna wanted to hug the Pandava brothers and tell them that they were his younger brothers, that they shared the same mother. But Karna restrained himself. Instead, he said, 'I give you your life in charity.'

Karna's words seared the soul of the Pandava brothers. They realized they owed their lives to a man they hated, one who they considered nothing more than an ambitious servant.

The encounter with Karna so shattered Yudhishtira that he lost all will to fight; he had to be carried away from the battlefield by Nakula and Sahadeva. Arjuna saw this from afar and out of concern told Krishna, 'Take me back to the battle camp. I think my elder brother is hurt.'

'No, do not worry about him. I think we should focus on Karna. He must be tired after fighting your four brothers. Look, there is Bhima doing his duty and fighting the enemy. You must too.'

'No, no. I insist. Let us return to the battle camp. I must see my brother,' said Arjuna. So Krishna turned the chariot around and made his way to Yudhishtira's tent.

On seeing Arjuna, Yudhishtira beamed. 'You have returned alive before sunset. Karna must be dead. Tell me, how did you kill that wretched charioteer's son? Tell me, how did you kill that venomous friend of Duryodhana's?'

Arjuna replied, 'No, Karna is not dead. I just came here to check if all is well with you.'

Hearing this, Yudhishtira lost his temper, 'You coward. You come here to check on me instead of fighting and killing Karna. How could you? Are you telling me that Bhima is all alone on the battlefield fighting the Kauravas while you are here in my tent displaying false concern for me? I think you came in here because you are afraid to face the man who is perhaps a greater archer than you. I think you are afraid of Karna, despite having the great Gandiva as your bow and the great

Krishna as your charioteer and the great Hanuman atop your chariot. I am ashamed of you. Fie on you, on your bow Gandiva. Give your bow to someone more worthy so that he may kill Karna.'

Arjuna's blood boiled as he heard Yudhishtira speak so. 'How dare you speak to me like that? How dare you insult my bow like that? How dare you suggest that someone else wield my bow?' In fury, hissing like an angry snake, he picked up a sword and rushed towards Yudhishtira, intent on striking him. Nakula and Sahadeva threw themselves on Yudhishtira to protect him from Arjuna's wrath. Krishna caught hold of Arjuna's hand and pulled him back. Everyone in the battle camp was shocked to see this—never before had they seen the Pandava brothers fight so.

'What are you doing, Arjuna?' asked Krishna. Then turning to Yudhishtira, he said, 'What are you doing, Yudhishtira? Has the war taken away all good sense? Rather than fighting your enemy, you are now turning against each other? What is happening?'

Krishna then told the brothers the story of Valaka. A hunter called Valaka shot an arrow at a creature he saw drinking water from a forest pond. Only after he released the arrow did he realize that the creature was blind. He regretted releasing the arrow but it was too late—the arrow hit the target and the blind animal was dead. As Valaka approached the animal, full of remorse, flowers fell upon him from the sky and the Devas appeared before him to thank him. They said, 'This blind beast you feel sorry for is actually a demon that was planning to destroy the world. By killing him you have saved the world. 'Thus,' said Krishna, 'sometimes an action we think is wrong turns out to be right.'

Krishna then told the brothers the story of Kaushika. Kaushika was a sage. One day, he saw four people running into his hermitage and hiding behind a tree. Pursuing them was a fierce-looking man, who asked Kaushika if he had seen four men running before him. Kaushika, who always spoke the truth, nodded his head and pointed to their hiding place. The fierce-looking man was actually a dacoit and he found the four men he was chasing behind the tree. He killed them and

took away their belongings. For this act, Kaushika was dragged to hell. 'Thus,' said Krishna, 'sometimes an action we think is right turns out to be wrong.'

The reason for telling these stories was to calm the angry brothers and to tell them that sometimes things are not what they seem. Arjuna should not assume that words spoken under stressful situations were real. His brother was just angry and did not mean to insult him or his bow. One should have faith in one's friends and family and not let one harsh word break the bond of trust.

Hearing Krishna's words, Arjuna calmed down. 'But I had taken the vow of killing anyone who insulted my bow. I must keep my promise.'

Krishna said, 'You can kill your brother physically by harming his body or emotionally by insulting him. Why don't you choose the second option?'

Arjuna took that option and insulted Yudhishtira as a weakling who had gambled away his fortune and his wife. Then Arjuna said, 'Oh, when a younger brother insults his elder brother, he is not fit to live. I feel like killing myself.'

Once again, Krishna came to Arjuna's rescue. 'You can kill yourself physically by harming your body or intellectually by praising yourself. For when a man praises himself, it is intellectual suicide.'

So Arjuna decided to kill himself intellectually. He praised himself as the greatest of archers. And having embarrassed himself so, he thanked Krishna for finding clever ways to overpower awkward situations.

Arjuna then apologized to his brother. Yudhishtira apologized too. Both realized they were overreacting to the situation. 'Let us forget this ugly event. Let us focus on our duty. Let us restore justice. Let us kill Karna,' they said. All issues resolved, the brothers returned to the battlefield ready to fight once more.

- As the war progresses, stress takes it toll. Vyasa describes many arguments in both battle camps. Karna and Shalya abuse each other until Duryodhana intervenes. Satyaki argues with Dhrishtadyumna forcing Bhima to restrain both parties. Karna argues with Kripa and comes to blows with Ashwatthama.
- This episode reveals Krishna's ability to twist and turn the rules by looking at them from various angles. Here he divides the human body into physical, emotional and intellectual components and prescribes ways of killing each of these bodies. Insulting the other destroys the other's emotional body; praising oneself destroys one's intellectual body.

Wheel of Karna's chariot

On the seventeenth day, all energies of the Pandava camp were directed against Karna. Arjuna shot dead Karna's son, Vrishasena, hoping to make Karna feel the pain he experienced when Abhimanyu was killed. Other sons of Karna were also killed by other Pandava warriors. Karna refused to mourn for his sons; he continued battling, determined to do his duty, help his friend, and kill that one brother of his, the one who taunted him all his life, the one who he was determined to hate—Arjuna.

At long last, Karna came face to face with Arjuna. With his arrows, Arjuna was able to create a force that pushed Karna's chariot back a hundred yards. Karna's arrow was able to push Arjuna's chariot barely ten yards and yet every time Karna did so, Krishna praised him ecstatically.

An envious Arjuna asked, 'But why do you shower him with praises when I push his chariot back by a hundred yards while he pushes mine barely ten yards?'

Krishna replied, 'Look carefully, Arjuna. On Karna's chariot stand two men. But on your chariot sit Nara and Narayana and on your banner sits Hanuman. Surely pushing his chariot is easier than yours.'

Karna shot arrow after arrow at Arjuna. At one point a serpent entered his quiver. This was the Naga Ashwasena whose family had been killed by Arjuna when he set ablaze Khandava-prastha. Arjuna's arrows had pierced his mother but he had survived, for he was then still in her womb. He was determined to avenge the killing of his family so he turned himself into an arrow in Karna's quiver. Karna mounted this arrow and shot it at Arjuna. Realizing that this was no ordinary arrow, Krishna pressed his feet against the floor of the chariot causing it to sink to the ground. As a result, the arrow, which could have split Arjuna's head, struck and split Arjuna's crown. Arjuna was taken by surprise, as his beautiful crown fell to the ground. He wondered who was the greater archer—he or Karna? 'It is not so much the archer as much as it was the arrow that caused your crown to fall,' said Krishna reassuringly.

The Naga Ashwasena then ran to Karna and told him to shoot him again. Karna did not recognize the serpent. When he learnt that the serpent had taken the shape of his previous arrow, Karna said, 'It is beneath my stature as warrior to shoot the same arrow twice. Find some other way to avenge your family. I do not need a Naga's help to kill Arjuna.'

Rejected by Karna, Ashwasena rushed towards Arjuna to kill him on his own. But he was no match for the great archer and was killed by a single dart. Arjuna, his crown shattered, tied a white cloth around his head and resumed his battle with Karna.

The duel between Karna and Arjuna continued all day until just before the sun was about to set, Karna's chariot wheel got stuck in the ground. At that moment, Karna knew he would soon die.

Long ago, Karna had incurred the wrath of Bhoo-devi, the earth goddess. He had come across a little girl who was crying as she had dropped her glass of milk on the ground. To make her happy, Karna collected the milk-soaked soil and squeezed the milk back into the glass. This cheered the little girl but Bhoo-devi was not amused. She cursed Karna that she would one day squeeze him just as he had squeezed milk out of her. And on that day, Karna would surely die.

Parashurama, Karna's guru, had taught Karna a magical formula that could make a chariot pull itself out from the earth. Karna could not remember this formula no matter how hard he tried. He then remembered the curse of his guru: 'Because you duped me into teaching you, you will forget what I taught you the day you need it most.'

Karna asked Shalya to release the chariot wheel. Shalya refused saying that as a king he had never done such a chore. So Karna had no choice but to get down from the chariot and release the wheel himself. This was certain death for he would have to, in front of his enemy, lower his weapons and turn his back. 'It is against the rule of war to strike an unarmed man in battle,' said Karna before getting down to the task of releasing the wheel.

As soon as his back was turned, Krishna told Arjuna, 'Shoot him. This is your only chance.' Arjuna hesitated, knowing that it was dishonourable to kill an unarmed, helpless man. To force Arjuna to action, Krishna taunted, 'He is surely not as helpless as Draupadi was when they disrobed her in public.' Thus reminded of that fateful day, Arjuna released his arrow which ripped through Karna's heart.

That day, it is said, the sun set faster to mourn for his son. Far away, in the Pandava battle camp, Kunti wept for her eldest son, the son she could never publicly acknowledge. The charioteers of the Pandava army and the charioteers of the Kaurava army, all stopped to mourn for that son of a charioteer who belonged nowhere. Duryodhana was inconsolable in his grief. Karna was dearer to him than his own brothers. He, who had not wept at the fall of Bhishma and Drona, broke down when he heard that his dear friend was no more. Even the death of his son was not as painful as the death of Karna. Suddenly, victory had no meaning. What was victory without Karna by his side?

- The story of Ashwasena reminds us how Arjuna's past deeds return to haunt him in the battlefield. He is saved because of Krishna. But his descendant Parikshit is not so lucky for the Naga Takshaka succeeds where the Naga Ashwasena did not.
- Karna realizes the folly of having a king as charioteer when Shalya refuses to pull out the wheel claiming it to be beneath his royal dignity. Thus a decision taken to please the ego turns out to be dear in the long run.
- It is ironical that Karna seeks to disown his charioteer legacy, and become a warrior, while Krishna embraces his role of charioteer whole-heartedly, refusing to become a warrior in Kuru-kshetra.
- When Vishnu took the form of Ram, he took the side of Sugriva, son of Surya, and killed Vali, the son of Indra. As Krishna, Vishnu clearly sides with Arjuna, the son of Indra, against Karna, the son of Surya. Both Vali in the Ramayana and

Karna in the Mahabharata are shot in the back. Thus balance is achieved across two lifetimes.

- Just before Karna was about to die, Krishna came to him disguised as a priest and asked him to give him some gold. A dying Karna broke his jaw and gave his teeth to Krishna, saying his teeth were covered with gold caps. Thus till his dying breath, Karna remained daan-veer, the great hero of charity.
- In Yakshagana, the bards say that in their previous life, Arjuna and Krishna were Nara and Narayana and they were called upon by the Devas to destroy an Asura who was blessed with a thousand impenetrable armours. To destroy each armour, one had to gather the strength of a thousand years of tapasya. It took another thousand years of fighting to actually break the armour. Nara and Narayana came up with a plan. While Nar meditated Narayana fought, and while Narayana meditated Nar fought. Thus, together they were able to destroy 999 armours of the demon. Before Nar could destroy the final armour, the demon hid behind the sun. At that time, the world came to an end. When the world was reborn, the demon took birth on earth as Karna while Nara and Narayana took rebirth as Arjuna and Krishna. Arjuna had to complete the task left unfinished. He was obliged to use his arrow against Karna and finally destroy the 1000-armoured Asura. So it was ordained.
- The three commanders of the Kaurava army—Bhishma, Drona and Karna—were students of Parashurama. They were killed on Krishna's advice. Parashurama and Krishna were both forms of Vishnu on earth.
- Karna was such a generous soul that it is said that he once broke down his house to provide wood to a man on a wet, rainy day so that the man could cremate his son.

Death of Shalya

Shalya, brother of Madri, maternal uncle of Nakula and Sahadeva, was tricked by Duryodhana into fighting for the Kauravas. He was further humiliated by being forced to serve Karna as a charioteer. Shalya did whatever he was told without protest, earning the respect of both the Pandavas and the Kauravas. Finally, on the eighteenth day, he was asked to lead the Kaurava forces. With a heavy heart, he took this responsibility but promised that his personal feelings would not come in the way of his duty.

Krishna told Arjuna that Yudhishtira must fight Shalya, the last great general of the Kaurava army, alone. 'Why?' asked Arjuna. Krishna did not reply.

Locked within Shalya's body was a great demon whose strength kept multiplying when confronted by an aggressive being. The more aggressive the opponent, the stronger was Shalya's demon.

Yudhishtira was, however, not an aggressive man, certainly not when it came to Shalya. On the final day of the battle, he came face to face with Shalya. Instead of approaching him violently, he approached with great love and affection. This caused Shalya's demon to lose strength; faced with Yudhishtira's gentleness, the demon kept dividing rather than multiplying itself. Finally, the demon ceased to exist. Shalya and Yudhishtira faced each other alone.

Yudhishtira then picked up his spear and with not a shred of anger or hatred in his heart, hurled it at Shalya and killed him on the spot. With this, the last great leader of the Kaurava army ceased to be. Victory now certainly belonged to the Pandavas.

Realizing that defeat was imminent, Shakuni came up with a plan. He realized that Bhima, Arjuna and Yudhishtira were all leading the army. The rear flanks were unprotected. He rallied his soldiers from Gandhara and ambushed the Pandava army from behind.

The sons of Kunti turned around on hearing the commotion and saw what the cunning Shakuni was up to. It was difficult for them to go to the rescue of the army at the rear. Yudhishtira shouted to the sons of Madri, who were stationed closer to the rear end of the army, 'My brothers. I know you mourn your uncle who has just died. But we need you to wipe your tears and fight that wicked Shakuni who fights like a cowardly fox from the rear. Else all that is gained will be lost.'

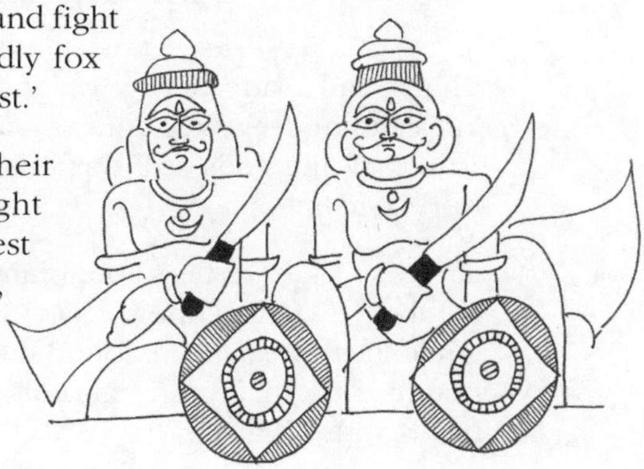

Nakula and Sahadeva immediately raised their swords and attacked Shakuni. A great fight followed. In the end, Sahadeva, the youngest and most silent of the Pandava brothers, managed to strike down and kill Shakuni. Sahadeva was happy for the day which saw the killing of his maternal uncle also saw the killing of Duryodhana's maternal uncle. And while his maternal uncle was innocent and had been duped to fight for the enemy side, Shakuni was no innocent—his skill with the dice had caused the Pandavas to lose their fortune over thirteen years ago.

- Bhishma commands the Kaurava army for ten days. Drona commands it for half that, five days. Karna commands it for half Drona's duration, that is two days. Shalya commands it for one day, that is half Karna's. Thus, it is a downward spiral, evident quite mathematically.
- The Pandavas have to fight father (Bhishma), teacher (Drona), brother (Karna) and uncle (Shalya) to defeat the Kauravas. They have to break free from all attachments that bind them.
- The story of the demon in Shalya's body that multiplied itself when confronted with an aggressive being comes from the Indonesian telling of the epic.
- While in the Indian epic, Bhanumati, the wife of Duryodhana, is princess of Kalinga, she is the daughter of Shalya in the Indonesian epic. She was in love with Arjuna but Arjuna asked her to marry the man her father had promised her to—Duryodhana. As Shalya is the father-in-law of Duryodhana, he is obliged to fight on the side of the Kauravas.
- After the death of Shalya and his son in the war, the kingdom of Madra is left with no ruler. In keeping with Shalya's wishes, the kingdom is passed on to his nephews, Nakula and Sahadeva.
- The sons of Madri do not play a significant role in the war except during the killing of Shakuni.

Fall of ninety-nine Kauravas

Bhima had made a vow on the day of the gambling match that he would kill each and every Kaurava. And he fulfilled this vow with a ferocity that scared all the gods and demons who witnessed the war on the battlefield of Kuru-kshetra.

Each day, like a restless lion, Bhima killed a few of the hundred brothers. As their numbers dwindled, the sons of Gandhari did their best to avoid Bhima, but like a relentless predator he found them, hiding behind chariots and elephants, and pounced on them and, ignoring their piteous pleas for mercy, smashed their heads with his mace.

The other Pandavas resisted the urge to strike down any son of Gandhari, even when presented with a suitable opportunity, so as to ensure Bhima fulfilled his terrible vow. And so as the war progressed, Gandhari and Dhritarashtra wept, as Sanjay informed them of the growing list of their dead sons.

Bhima found it quite difficult to kill Vikarna. Though a Kaurava, he had never agreed with Duryodhana and had openly opposed his brothers in the gambling hall. But when it was time to fight, he stood by his brothers out of a sense of loyalty. For that he was highly respected by the Pandavas. When Vikarna died, all the Pandavas wept. Krishna, however, did not weep. 'Dharma must be valued over family or friends,' he said.

Killing Dusshasana who had disrobed Draupadi in public gave Bhima the most pleasure. Bhima pinned him to the ground and ripped out his bowels with his bare hands. He then invited Draupadi to wash her hair with Dusshasana's blood so that she could, in keeping with her vow of vengeance taken long ago, bind her hair.

Watching the blood-soaked Bhima washing Draupadi's hair with blood, tying it with Dusshasana's entrails, and decorating it with his heart, many concluded that Bhima was for Draupadi what Bhairava was for Shakti—the guardian who beheads

all those who look upon the earth with eyes of lust. The heads of the Kauravas were his war trophies. Their blood, his warpaint.

On the eighteenth day, only one Kaurava was left to kill. The eldest, Duryodhana.

- In parts of Tamil Nadu, such as Dindigul, where Draupadi is worshipped as a goddess, processions enacting various episodes of the Mahabharata are taken out over eighteen days of the Draupadi Amman festival. The sequence of events enacted follows the sequence found in the 13th century Tamil version of the Mahabharata written by Valliputtur Alwar. Along with the procession, there is a discourse by a storyteller as well as a grand sacred play called Terukkuttu which is very much like the Ramleela of North India, only based on the Mahabharata.
- The epic does record the names of all the hundred Kauravas. They are (in no particular order):

1. Duryodhana (also called Suyodhana, before he turned villain, say some texts)
2. Dusshasana
3. Dussaha
4. Jalagandha
5. Sama
6. Saha
7. Vindha
8. Anuvinda
9. Durdharsha
10. Subahu
11. Dushpradarshan
12. Durmarshan
13. Durmukha
14. Dushkarn
15. Vivikarn
16. Vikarna
17. Salan
18. Sathwa
19. Sulochan
20. Chithra
21. Upachithra
22. Chitraksha
23. Charuchithra
24. Sarasana
25. Durmada
26. Durviga
27. Vivitsu
28. Viktana
29. Urnanabha
30. Sunabha
31. Nanda
32. Upananda
33. Chitrabana
34. Chitravarma
35. Suvarma
36. Durvimochan
37. Ayobahu
38. Mahabahu
39. Chitranga
40. Chitrakundala
41. Bhimvega
42. Bhimba
43. Balaki
44. Balvardhan
45. Ugrayudha
46. Sushena
47. Kundhadhara
48. Mahodara
49. Chithrayudha
50. Nishangi
51. Pashi
52. Vridaraka
53. Dridhavarma
54. Dridhakshatra
55. Somakirti
56. Anudara
57. Dridasandha
58. Jarasangha
59. Sathyasandha
60. Sadas
61. Suvak
62. Ugrasrava
63. Ugrasen
64. Senani
65. Dushparajai
66. Aparajit

67. Kundasai	79. Kradhan	90. Kundhabhedi
68. Vishalaksh	80. Kundi	91. Viravi
69. Duradhara	81. Kundadhara	92. Chitrakundala
70. Dridhahastha	82. Dhanurdhara	93. Dirghlochan
71. Suhastha	83. Bhimaratha	94. Pramathi
72. Vatvega	84. Virabahu	95. Veeryavan
73. Suvarcha	85. Alolupa	96. Dirgharoma
74. Aadiyaketu	86. Abhaya	97. Dirghabhu
75. Bahvasi	87. Raudrakarma	98. Mahabahu
76. Nagaadat	88. Dhridarathasraya	99. Kundashi
77. Agrayayi	89. Anaaghrushya	100. Virjasa
78. Kavachi		

Below the belt

Every day, before marching into the battlefield, Duryodhana would go to his mother and ask for her blessings and she would say, 'May the right side win.' Duryodhana knew that his mother's word always came true, so he begged her to say, 'May my sons win,' but she refused to say so.

But after Bhima had killed ninety-nine of her sons, Gandhari's maternal instincts got the better of her. 'Righteous or not, Duryodhana is still our son,' Dhritarashtra told her.

So Gandhari instructed Duryodhana to take a bath before the crack of dawn and come before her totally naked. 'I will open my blindfold for the first time since the day of my marriage and look upon you. My eyes, shut for all these years, are filled with the power of my piety and fidelity. Every part of your body that I gaze upon with my first glance will become impervious to weapons.'

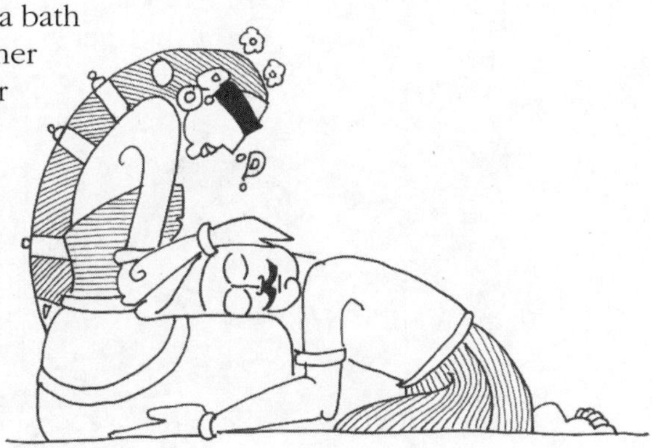

Accordingly, Duryodhana removed his clothes, took a bath and walked naked towards his mother's chambers. On the way, he saw Krishna emerge from the darkness Krishna looked at his nakedness and laughed, 'Have some shame. Mother or not, a grown man must at least cover his private parts.'

An embarrassed Duryodhana took a banana leaf and tied it around his waist covering his thighs and genitals. When he came before his mother, she opened her blindfold and saw her naked son. But when she discovered that he had covered some parts of his body, she began to cry, 'Oh my son. That part of your body that you have covered will remain vulnerable. And that will be your death.'

In fear, Duryodhana ran and hid inside a lake on the far side of the battlefield. Bhima and the other Pandavas spent the eighteenth day, after the death of Shalya, searching for the eldest Kaurava. So long as he was alive, the war was not over. They finally found him hiding inside the lake. 'Come out, coward,' shouted Bhima.

'I am no coward,' said Duryodhana, rising up. 'I was just resting my tired limbs so that they can kill you without much effort.'

As Krishna and the Pandavas watched, Bhima and Duryodhana prepared to duel. They were like two wild elephants in heat. Their eyes were red and their massive arms, covered with sweat, shone like pillars of gold in the afternoon sun. Both these warriors had learned the art of mace warfare from Krishna's elder brother, Balarama. Both were equal in strength. Sure enough, try as he might, Bhima could not subdue Duryodhana. He managed to defend himself deftly, moving his limbs swiftly each time Bhima swung his mace.

As the maces clanged, Bhima turned to Krishna in despair.

Krishna looked straight into his eyes and then slapped his thigh close to his genitals. Bhima realized that this is where Krishna wanted him to strike Duryodhana. But was that not against the rules of war? But Bhima never questioned Krishna's wisdom. He swung his mace and smashed it where Duryodhana least expected it: below the waist, breaking his thighs and crushing his genitals.

'This is foul play,' cried Duryodhana as he fell to the ground. But neither Bhima nor Krishna apologized. 'Adharma, adharma,' shouted Duryodhana. He called out to his teacher, Balarama, 'Come, see, how instigated by your brother this student of yours breaks the code of war to kill me, your favourite.'

Balarama appeared on the battlefield at that very moment and saw the smashed thighs of Duryodhana. Enraged, he raised his plough and threatened to kill Bhima. Bhima bowed his head to receive the blow when Krishna came in between. 'Those who live by the law of the jungle die by the law of the jungle,' said Krishna, his voice cold. Balarama saw the dispassionate truth of that statement and lowered his plough.

Duryodhana lay on the ground, unable to stand up or raise his head, bleeding to death, surrounded by all the victors. He mourned his tragic end while the Pandavas let out whoops of victory and jeered their fallen cousin. Bhima, unable to contain his joy, jumped on Duryodhana's head and began to dance.

'Stop,' cried Krishna in outrage. 'How can you humiliate him so? He is your brother, a king, a warrior. Has he not been punished already? Must you not be gracious in victory?'

A shame-faced Bhima lowered his head and followed his brothers to their battle camp where Draupadi, unable to contain her excitement, was busy making preparations to celebrate this great victory.

As they moved away, Duryodhana called out from behind them and said, 'All my life I have lived as a prince in the palace and today I die like a warrior on the battlefield. You have spent most of your lives in the forest, like beggars and thieves, hiding in fear, and now you inherit a world of corpses. Who has lived a better life than me? Who has died a better death than me?'

- The story of Gandhari's failed attempt to make her son invulnerable to weapons is similar to the Greek tale of the sea nymph Thetis dipping her son Achilles in the river Styx, so that most of his body except the part she held—his ankles—became impervious to weapons.
- Kuru was an ancestor of the Pandavas and he had tilled the land that came to be known as Kuru-kshetra or the field of Kuru. He had used the bull of Shiva, god of asceticism, and the buffalo of Yama, god of death, to pull the plough. He used his own flesh as the seed, thus pleasing the gods who offered him a boon. He asked that the gods allow any man who died on this land into paradise.
- Bhasa in his play, *Urubhangam*, dated 100 CE, introduces a character not known in the epic, Duryodhana's young son, Durjaya, who on seeing his father wants to sit on his lap but is stopped as Duryodhana's thigh is broken. The fallen villain, full of remorse, advises his son to serve his victorious uncles, the Pandavas, well.
- In Tamil Nadu, the eighteen-day war is ritually enacted during the Terukkuttu performance, in which a giant image of Duryodhana lying on the ground is made out of the earth. On the right thigh is placed a pot full of red fluid. This pot is smashed at the end of the performance by the actor playing Bhima who goes into a frenzied trance. After this ritual, the crowds swarm to take fistfuls of the mud used to make Duryodhana's image; kept well, it is supposed to protect grain from getting lost or spoilt in granaries.
- The gap between 'what is mine' and 'what is not mine' is an artificial construct, not a natural phenomenon that is created and can be destroyed by the human mind. The animal mind, the Kaurava mind, is unable to fathom this and hence tenaciously clings to land and is filled with rage and fear till the very end. Krishna's focus is to help the Pandavas outgrow the territorial beast within and realize the divine potential. But it is not easy. Though Krishna helps Bhima defeat Duryodhana, he is unable to teach Bhima empathy for the enemy. For him, Duryodhana remains 'not mine'. Unless there is empathy and inclusion, dharma cannot be established. Bhima reduces the war to a tale of revenge rather than looking at it as a stimulus for inner transformation.
- The Kauravas are villains in the epic only because they refuse to outgrow the animal desire to cling to territory and dominate like an alpha male. Krishna helps the Pandavas undergo the transformation, but as events unfold, one realizes there is a huge gap between the intention and the implementation.
- Duryodhana is worshipped as a benevolent deity in Har-Ki-Doon Valley in Uttarakhand. Wooden temples dedicated to the epic villain are found there.

Talking head

The sun set for the eighteenth time since the start of the war. The victorious Pandavas returned to the battle camp where they were greeted by a very happy Draupadi who showered upon them fragrant flowers.

Arjuna waited for Krishna to alight from the chariot. But Krishna showed no signs of doing so. This annoyed Arjuna for in keeping with tradition, the charioteer gets down first and only then the archer. An exasperated Arjuna got down from the chariot while Krishna continued to sit. As soon as Krishna alighted, the chariot burst into flames.

Krishna then informed Arjuna that his chariot had long ago been destroyed by Drona. Arjuna realized that the only thing that kept the chariot going was Krishna's presence. Krishna's apparent act of disrespect was meant to protect him. So long as Krishna sat on the chariot, it did not burst into flames. Arjuna, smug in victory, thus learnt a lesson in humility. Without Krishna by their side, the Pandavas would never have won.

Soon, the battle camp was filled with the sound of revelry. The soldiers danced and sang as food and wine were served. In the midst of the victory celebrations, a dispute arose among the soldiers as to who of all the Pandavas was the greatest warrior on Kuru-kshetra? Was it Arjuna who killed Bhishma and Karna? Or was it Bhima who killed all the hundred Kauravas?

'If the answer is so important to you, why don't you ask the talking head?' said Krishna.

The talking head was Barbareek, the son of Ahilawati, a Naga princess, who claimed his father was Bhima. There were many who believed that his father was not Bhima but Bhima's son, Ghatotkacha.

Barbareek had come to Kuru-kshetra armed with just three arrows. 'With one, I can destroy the Pandavas. With the other, the Kauravas. And with the third, Krishna,' he said boastfully.

To test his skill, Krishna asked him to shoot all the leaves of a Banyan tree. Everyone watched with wonder as a single arrow released from Barbareek's bow pierced all the leaves on the tree and then hovered over Krishna's foot which Krishna had slyly placed over a fallen leaf.

'On which side do you plan to fight?' asked Krishna, impressed by the great warrior.

'On the side of the loser,' said Barbareek, 'for only then am I invincible.'

The reply disturbed Krishna. If Barbareek was invincible only when he was on the losing side, he would always support one army until the time it was losing. As soon as his contribution made that side stronger, he would cross over and join the other side. When the Kauravas would be winning, he would fight against them and when they would be losing, he would fight for them. As a result, the war would never reach a conclusion.

To prevent such an eventuality, Krishna came up with a plan. 'Will you help me?' asked Krishna, 'I feel helpless against this warrior who threatens the world.'

Barbareek who could never say no to the helpless replied, 'Who is it? Tell me and I shall destroy him.'

Krishna immediately showed Barbareek a mirror. 'Give me the head of this warrior, I beg you.'

Barbareek realized he had been tricked by Krishna but he could not say no. So he severed his head from his body and offered it to Krishna. His only regret was that he would die without witnessing the war of Kuru-kshetra. Divining this, Krishna breathed life into Barbareek's head. He would see all and hear all, but never be able to participate in anything.

At first, Barbareek's head was placed on the ground. But each time he found something funny on the battlefield and laughed, he would push back hundreds of galloping war-chariots simply by the force of his laughter. So Krishna placed his head on top of a hill from where he had a panoramic view of the war. 'He surely has seen more of the war than anyone else. He will answer your question best,' said Krishna to the Pandava army.

When the soldiers asked the talking head who the greatest warrior in Kuru-kshetra was, he gave a very strange reply, 'Bhima? Arjuna? I saw neither. In fact I saw no warrior. All I saw was the Sudarshan Chakra of Vishnu whizzing past and cutting the heads of unrighteous kings. And the blood spilt consumed by the earth who spread out her tongue in the form of Kali.'

When the Pandavas asked for an explanation, it said, 'Long ago, Vishnu took the form of Prithu, who said that as king he would treat her as a cowherd treats a cow. To ensure harmony between human culture and nature, he established the code of civilization known as dharma based on discipline, generosity and sacrifice. Pleased, the earth took the form of Gauri, the mother, who nourishes life on earth with her bounty. Kings were appointed on earth to institute and maintain dharma in their respective kingdoms. Unfortunately, as the years passed, the kings forgot their primary role as custodians of dharma. They used their power to plunder the earth. An anguished earth, in the form of a cow, went to Vishnu weeping and reminded him of his promise. Vishnu was furious when he saw how the greed of kings had made her udders sore and broken her back. He swore to teach the kings of the earth a lesson. He would descend to earth as Parashurama and Ram and Krishna and kill all those who followed adharma. He told the gentle Gauri to turn into the fearsome Kali and quench her thirst with the blood of all those who greedily squeezed out her milk. Thus, this war is not just about the Pandavas and Kauravas, it is about man's relationship with the earth. The talking head, placed above the battlefield, saw the violence with a perspective that was much wider than of those in the battlefield.'

A silence descended on the Pandava camp. They realized neither the war nor the victory was their own creation. Both were products of destiny. The celebrations resumed but they were muted. The Pandavas won not because they were better warriors; they won because God wanted them to.

- The tale of Barbareek is part of oral tradition in Kerala and Andhra Pradesh. In Rajasthan, he is worshipped as Khatu Shyamji, he who always fights for the loser. The talking head invites everyone to view the war from a wider cosmic perspective. We realize that the war is not merely about two cousins fighting over their inheritance; it is simultaneously about God creating a cosmic balance. No event takes place in isolation; it the culmination of various historical and geographical events. Likewise, current events have a profound influence on the history and geography of the future.
- In some traditions, the talking head belongs not to Barbareek but to Iravan, son of Arjuna and Ulupi.

BOOK SIXTEEN

Aftermath

'Janamejaya, in those eighteen days, Gandhari lost all her children and so did Draupadi.'

Death of Draupadi's children

Eighteen days had passed. Eighteen armies had fought. Over one billion, two hundred and twenty million people were killed. Less than twenty-four thousand survived. Of these, only three had fought for Duryodhana: Ashwatthama, son of Drona, Kripa, teacher of the Kuru princes, and Kritavarma, the Yadava.

The three sat in the darkness, close to the lake where Duryodhana lay dying, hearing sounds of the revelry emerging from the Pandava camp. 'We may have been defeated but they have not yet won,' said a tearful Ashwatthama unable to bear the sound of laughter and merrymaking.

'You display such spirit, Ashwatthama!' Duryodhana groaned, 'Though born in a family of priests, you display greater spirit than a warrior. You are indeed fit to lead an army.'

Bowing his head, his eyes burning with rage, the son of Drona said, 'Make me the commander of what is left of your army and I will destroy the Pandavas if it costs me my life.'

'Do it, if you can,' whispered the dying Duryodhana, surprised at the rage that burned in his heart even though death stared him in the face. A much pleased Ashwatthama struck the earth with his sword.

'How do you plan to destroy the victors?' asked Kripa, 'We are only three and they are so many.'

'I don't know,' said Ashwatthama, gritting his teeth, 'but I will. I surely will.'

As the sun set, the three survivors saw an owl land on a tree that stood next to the lake and slowly kill a hundred crows sleeping on its branches. 'That is how,' exclaimed Ashwatthama, leaping up in excitement.

Sensing Ashwatthama's murderous intention, Kripa said, 'An attack while they are asleep! That is not appropriate. It is against dharma.'

'Was it not against dharma to let a woman into the battlefield? Was it not against dharma to kill a man who puts down his weapons? Was it not against dharma to kill a man by striking him below his waist? The Pandavas never cared for dharma. Why should we?' So saying Ashwatthama silently proceeded towards the Pandava battle camp. After some hesitation, Kripa and Kritavarma followed him.

While Kripa and Kritavarma kept watch, Ashwatthama entered the section where the warriors from Panchala slept, his sword unsheathed. At the entrance he found Shiva, the God of destruction, appearing not like the benevolent Shankara but as the fearsome Bhairava, covered in blood with a garland of heads around his neck.

Bowing to Shiva, Ashwatthama entered the Pandava enclosure and found there the brothers of Draupadi, Shikhandi and Dhrishtadyumna, sleeping. He raised his sword and hacked them to death. 'There I have avenged Bhishma and Drona,' he said. He then beheaded five warriors who he assumed to be the Pandavas.

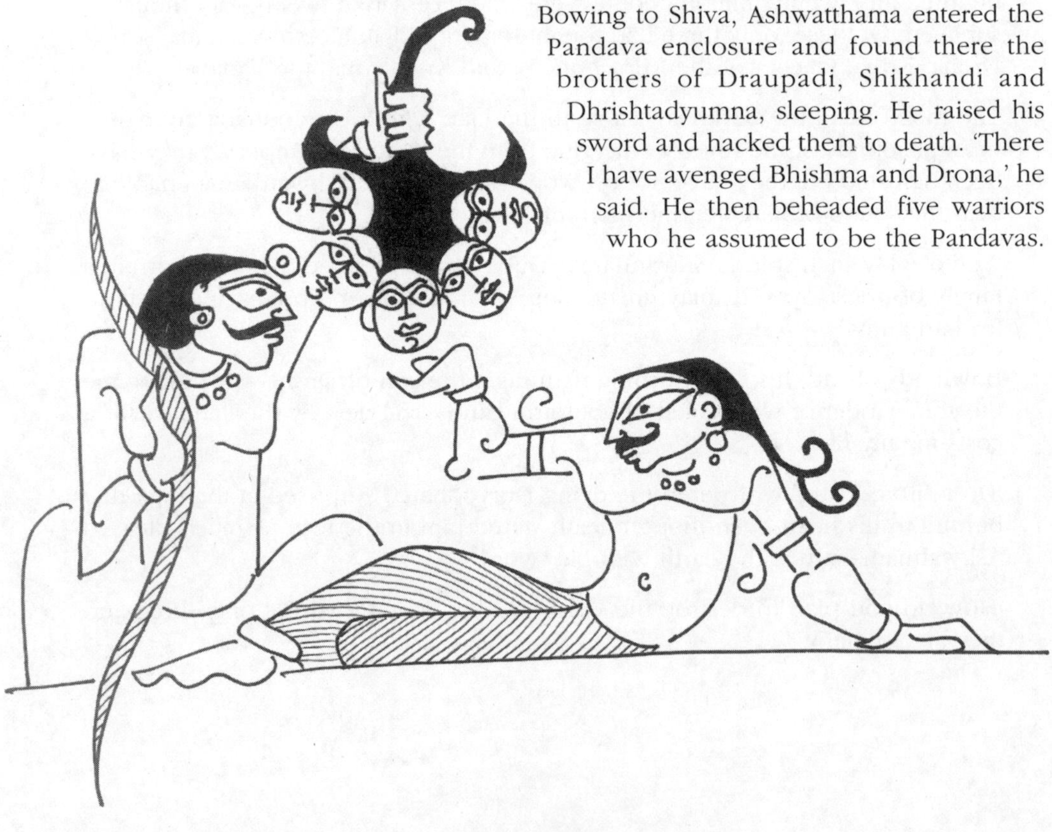

'There I have avenged all the Kauravas.' He then set fire to the Pandava camp. Those who tried to escape were shot dead by Kripa and Kritavarma.

Ashwatthama presented the severed heads to Duryodhana and exclaimed, 'Blessed by Shiva, I have managed to behead the five Pandava brothers.'

Duryodhana found this hard to believe. 'Show me the head of Bhima,' he said. When it was presented, Duryodhana held it between his palms and crushed it like a coconut. 'No, this is too weak to be Bhima's head. Who have you killed, Ashwatthama?' asked Duryodhana.

Kripa looked at the heads closely. 'These are not the Pandavas. They are young faces, children in fact. Oh Ashwatthama, blinded by rage, you have killed the five sons of Draupadi,' he cried. Ashwatthama did not know what to say.

Duryodhana let out a cry, 'Are we now reduced to killing children? When will this stop? When we are all dead? This is madness. The Pandavas will rule over a city of corpses. Yes, Ashwatthama, I may have lost but no one has actually won.' With those anguished words, Duryodhana breathed his last.

Rule of war	Rule breaker	Victim
No woman shall fight in the battlefield	Pandavas (Arjuna)	Bhishma
No single warrior shall be attacked by many	Kauravas (Drona)	Abhimanyu
No fighting after sunset	Pandavas (Arjuna)	Jayadhrata
No one shall interfere in a duel	Pandavas (Satyaki)	Bhurishrava
No killing of animals	Pandavas (Bhima)	Ashwatthama (the elephant)
No spreading of misinformation	Pandavas (Yudhishtira)	Drona
No killing of people who have laid down arms	Pandavas (Dhrishtadyumna)	Drona
No archer shall fight one who has lowered the bow	Pandavas (Arjuna)	Karna
No one shall strike below the waist	Pandavas (Bhima)	Duryodhana
No attacking people who are asleep	Kauravas (Ashwatthama)	Sons of the Pandavas

Ashwatthama cursed

The sun rose to a terrible sight: charred bodies of the entire Pandava army and the headless remains of Draupadi's brothers and sons. Thousands of vultures circled the skies above. The cawing of crows filled the horizon. Only seven warriors survived: the five Pandavas and the two Yadavas, Krishna and Satyaki.

'My children,' screamed Draupadi. 'Oh, heavy is the price of tying my hair.'

When the tears stopped, the demon of vengeance reared its ugly head. 'Who did this?' she asked. Dhrishtadyumna's charioteer who had seen it all informed how Ashwatthama had attacked the sleeping warriors without mercy like an owl feasting on crows at night. 'I want his head,' said Draupadi.

'No,' said Krishna. 'Let us stop this spiral of vengeance. Once, Ashwatthama came to Dwaraka and asked me for my Sudarshan Chakra. Since he was a Brahman, I was obliged to hand it over to him. He tried to lift it with his left hand and then with this right. Having failed both times, he started to weep. I asked him why he wanted this weapon of mine, a weapon that no one dared ask from me—neither my friend, Arjuna, nor my son, Pradyumna. He said he wanted it because he knew it was the most powerful weapon in the world. He wanted to use it against me and thus become the greatest warrior in the world, feared by all. Such was his nature. Even though he was born in a family of priests, his father's upbringing transformed him into an ambitious monster. He craves power but does not know how to wield it. Neither a Brahman nor a Kshatriya is he. Killing him will serve no purpose. Bring him alive.'

Scouts were sent to look for Ashwatthama. When Ashwatthama realized the Pandavas were looking for him, he raised his bow and shot the missile known as Brahma-astra. As the missile approached, Arjuna raised his bow and released another Brahma-astra to neutralize the first.

As the arrows moved towards each other, darkness enveloped the horizon. Fierce winds began to blow showering dust and gravel everywhere. Birds croaked madly, the earth shook, scorched by the terrible violent heat of these two missiles. Elephants burst into flames and ran to and fro in a frenzy. Horses crumpled to the ground and died. Each approaching missile released ten thousand tongues of flames towards the other, both determined to destroy.

'Recall your astras,' cried Krishna, appealing to the warriors. 'Your weapons will scorch the earth and destroy all life.' Other Rishis, including Vyasa, who saw the two fiery missiles hurtling towards each other, begged the two warriors to listen to Krishna.

Realizing the seriousness of the situation, Arjuna immediately withdrew the missile back to his quiver. Ashwatthama, however, did not know how to pull the missile back. So he redirected the weapon towards the wombs of the Pandava women. 'May it kill all the unborn descendants of the Pandavas. Thus, I shall wipe out the race of those who killed my father and my friend,' he said.

A furious Krishna stood before Abhimanyu's widow, Uttari, and took the impact of the horrific missile on his body, preventing it from harming the unborn child in her womb, the last and only fruit of the Pandava tree.

Krishna then turned to Ashwatthama, and uttered a deadly curse, the only curse to leave the lips of God, 'Ashwatthama, so terrible has been your action that even death will shun you for three thousand years. For that period your wounds will fester with pus and your skin will be covered with boils forcing you to contemplate on the nature of your crime.'

On Ashwatthama's head was a jewel that brought him great luck. This was taken away from him and given to Draupadi, who gave it to Yudhishtira. Ashwatthama was then driven away from civilization, deemed inauspicious for all mankind.

- Many scholars believe that the description of the weapons released by Ashwatthama and Arjuna suggest that the Rishis of ancient times were familiar with, or at least visualized, nuclear weapons.
- Abortion is traditionally considered the worst of crimes in Hinduism not only because it involves the killing of an unborn innocent but also because it denies an ancestor a chance to be reborn. To make matters worse, Ashwatthama who tries to induce miscarriage in the Pandava women is a Brahman by birth, obliged to protect life. That is why the punishment meted out to him by God is worse than death. He is forced to live and suffer. It is said that even today if one listens carefully to the wail of the waves or the howl of the wind, one will hear the mournful cry of Ashwatthama, the baby-killer, too ashamed to show his face to man.
- Ashwatthama embodies what happens when the rules of varna are not obeyed. Born to a priest, he was supposed to live as a priest as per ashrama-dharma. But instead he chose to be a warrior, not to protect the weak but to harness power. That is why he is not shown any mercy by Krishna. He embodies the fall of civilization and the height of human rage and greed.
- Draupadi is depicted as helpless and angry in the Mahabharata of Vyasa, wailing and weeping when her brothers and sons are killed. In regional lore, however, Draupadi is reborn as different heroines who are not so passive. She is Bela in the Hindi medieval epic, Alha, who commits sati after her warrior husband is killed in battle. Draupadi is also reborn as Virashakti in folklore of north Tamil Nadu where armed with five sacred objects (a drum, a bell, a whip, a trident and a box of turmeric) she fights demons much like Durga.

Kunti's secret

The cry of orphans rent the air as they ran desperately looking for the remains of their fathers. The old blind couple, Gandhari and Dhritarashtra, entered the battlefield accompanied by their hundred daughters-in-law, now widows.

The women ran searching for their husbands. They found headless torsos, cut hands and crushed legs, dogs chewing on the tongues of great warriors, rats nibbling on the fingers of archers. The stench of rotting flesh was unbearable.

The Pandavas saw their mother, Kunti, wandering among the dead Kauravas. 'Who are you looking for, mother?' asked Yudhishtira.

'Karna,' she said.

'Why that charioteer's son?' asked Arjuna.

'Because he was your eldest brother. My firstborn,' said Kunti, finally unafraid to face the truth.

At first, the words did not sink in. When they finally did, Arjuna went weak in the knees. He realized he had killed not only Bhishma, who was like a father to him, and Drona, who was his teacher, but also Karna, who was in fact his brother. 'Did he know?' asked Yudhishtira. Kunti nodded her head. This made Arjuna feel even worse.

She told her sons how out of childish curiosity she had used Durvasa's magic formula that compelled the sun-god to give her a child. She told them how Karna had promised never to harm any of her sons except Arjuna. 'With or without Arjuna, you can always tell the world you have five sons,' he had said.

The Pandavas remembered how Karna never killed them in the war despite having ample opportunities to do so. Now they realized why. They felt miserable. Victory had come to them stained in their brother's blood. 'Oh, may no woman ever again be able to keep such secrets from the world,' said Yudhishtira.

'Why did you not tell us?' asked Arjuna.

'If she did, would you have fought him? And if you had not fought him, the Kauravas would not have been defeated and dharma would not have been established,' said Krishna, who had overheard the conversation. But this logic did not take away the gloom that descended on the surviving sons of Kunti.

- After revealing the truth of Karna's origin, the relationship between Kunti and her sons was never the same again. They were angry with her. She had abandoned her own child to save her reputation. She had allowed them to hate him all these years. But for her silence, Karna would not have been treated so unjustly by the world.
- Through Karna, Vyasa reiterates that our knowledge of the world is imperfect based on perceptions and false information. We are surrounded by Kuntis who hide the truth in fear. We are surrounded by Karnas, villains who are actually brothers.

Rage of elders

Krishna advised the Pandavas to go and pay their respects to the parents of the Kauravas. 'But be careful, Bhima. Beware of Dhritarashtra's pent-up rage. When he tries to embrace you, place an iron image of yourself before him.'

Bhima did as advised. Dhritarashtra embraced the iron pillar with such force, thinking it was Bhima, that the iron image was crushed as if it was made of soft clay. Such was the intensity of the blind king's rage against the man who had killed his sons.

The deed done, Dhritarashtra started to cry. 'What have I done? In rage, I have killed the son of my brother who was like a son to me.'

But Gandhari knew that Bhima was still alive. She sensed his breath. 'Once again, Krishna protects the Pandavas,' she said bitterly.

As the sons of Pandu approached her, Vidura whispered in her ear, 'Gandhari, control your rage. If you curse these men, the earth will be left with no kings.'

And so as the Pandavas fell at her feet, Gandhari forced herself to bless them. As she did so, her eyes filled with tears swelled so much that her blindfold was pushed away and she managed to steal a glance at Yudhishtira's big toe for a moment. That one glance was so fiery that it turned Yudhishtira's big toe blue. With that glance, all of Gandhari's rage dissipated.

When Draupadi came to Gandhari, she hugged her and wailed, 'Both of us are left with no children. What can we mothers do but cry?' Draupadi broke down and hugged Gandhari tightly.

Gandhari sensed Krishna's presence beside her. 'Why did all my children have to die?' she asked. 'Could you not spare even one?'

'It was not I who killed your sons,' said Krishna, his voice full of compassion.

'It was your fate and theirs. Long ago, while cooking rice, you poured the hot water into the ground outside your kitchen destroying a hundred eggs laid by an insect. That insect cursed you that you would witness the death of all your children as she did hers.'

'But that was an innocent act of a child,' protested Gandhari.

'Such is the law of karma. Every action, howsoever innocent, has a reaction, that one has to experience if not in this life, then in the next,' said Krishna.

Krishna then told the tale of a king called Nriga, whose cow, given away to a Rishi, had managed to slip back into the royal cowshed and was given away a second time to another Rishi. Though this was done unintentionally, the two Rishis who claimed the same cow were so angry with Nriga that they cursed him and he was reborn as a lizard.

- Rage needs expression. Dhritarashtra expresses it by crushing the iron effigy of Bhima while Gandhari expresses it by burning Yudhishtira's toe with a glance. Once expressed, rage dissipates and reason returns. One is advised in many parts of India to eat sugar when angry, just like Gandhari did, so as not to end up cursing the Pandavas.

- In Andhra Pradesh, women are advised never to pour hot water on the ground like Gandhari. The water must be allowed to cool or mixed with cold water before it is poured out.
- In Orissa, it is said that Gandhari sat on a rock crushing the eggs laid under it by a turtle. The mother turtle cursed Gandhari which is why she was destined to lose all her children.
- The epic speculates on the origin of death. One day, Brahma, God who creates all living creatures, realized that all his children were reproducing and their numbers were multiplying and the earth was groaning under their weight. And so he created the goddess of death called Mrityu. This goddess, however, refused to kill any living creature. She did not want to carry the burden of such a terrible act. Brahma reassured her that she would carry no such burden. 'Death will be the direct result of merits and demerits earned by living creatures in their lifetime. You will merely oversee the transition. The burden of death shall be borne by those who live.' Thus all creatures die not because of external factors but because of their own karma.

Gandhari's curse

Krishna knew that his erudition would not take away the pain in Gandhari's heart. Despite his words, she kept crying. The sun set. The wailing widows of the Kuru clan decided to return to the palace as the horizon was filled with vultures and crows and dogs and ghosts waiting to feed on the dead. 'Come mother,' they cried out to Gandhari. 'We shall return tomorrow and cremate our sons and husbands.'

'You proceed. I shall not leave my children. Let me comfort them as they lie unloved on this battlefield.'

Krishna said, 'Go home. This pain will be forgotten when you have a greater pleasure or a greater pain.'

'No,' said Gandhari angrily, 'What do you know of my pain? You have not been mother to a hundred sons.' Realizing that the blindfolded mother of the Kauravas was determined to spend the night in the battlefield, the rest decided to leave her alone and return to the city.

That night the air was filled with the sound of hungry dogs and vultures and crows. Gandhari swung her walking stick to keep them away from the bodies of

her sons. She felt sorry for her miserable situation. She was angry with the Pandavas. She was angry with Krishna. She was angry with life.

At midnight, she began experiencing pangs of hunger. So great was the hunger that she could think of nothing else but food. Suddenly she smelt a mango. It came from above her. Desperate to eat this mango, she made a pile of stones, climbed on it and stretched out her hand to reach the fruit. The mango was delicious. As soon as she ate the mango, the hunger pangs abated. Gandhari's senses returned. She felt the stones that she had climbed to pluck the fruit. They did not feel like stones at all, but like the bodies of men. Her sons! Gandhari realized she had made a pile of her own children's corpses to pluck the fruit which satisfied her hunger.

'Oh Krishna,' she cried, 'now I know the power of maya: that which deludes you to be unhappy can be overpowered by another delusion that causes greater unhappiness. Oh Krishna, did you have to use such a cruel way of teaching me the truth? Wicked one, I curse you. I curse you that you too will feel the pain of losing your loved ones. May you watch helplessly as your children, your grandchildren, and your entire clan kill each other. And may you, great God, die like a beast at the hands of a common hunter.'

The next day, the bodies of the warriors were put in a great pile. There was not enough wood to burn them. So the broken war chariots with the wheels and banners were used as fuel and the pyre set alight. The flames rose high up to the heavens. The pyre was so bright that many felt the sun had descended on earth.

- Since God takes birth as a mortal, he needs to live like a mortal, earn demerits that will be the cause of his death. Vyasa reminds us that all actions have positive and negative repercussions. In establishing dharma, Krishna kills many people. They may be villains according to one measuring scale, but according to another measuring scale they are the beloved sons of doting mothers. So while Krishna is blessed for restoring faith in justice, he is also cursed for breaking a mother's heart. What may seem like a good deed from one point of view may not be seen as one from another point of view. Thus does Vyasa reflect on the complexity of life where even the goodness of God is challenged by man.
- In many ways, Gandhari is the reason for the Mahabharata war. She chose to blindfold herself and so never really saw the truth about her children. Perhaps if she had not blindfolded herself and felt self-righteous about it, she would have been a different mother, a less indulgent mother, and the story would have taken a different, less violent, turn.
- It is simplistic to imagine that the Pandavas are good and the Kauravas are bad and so Krishna sides with the former. Pandavas are willing to change; they want to

outgrow the beast within them. The process of change is difficult—the Pandavas have to suffer exile, kill loved ones and lose their children, in the process of gaining wisdom. The Kauravas cling to their kingdom like dogs clinging to a bone. They refuse to change. Hence, they die without learning anything. Krishna is the teacher. But the onus of learning rests with the students.

Marital alliances between the clans of Yadu and Kuru

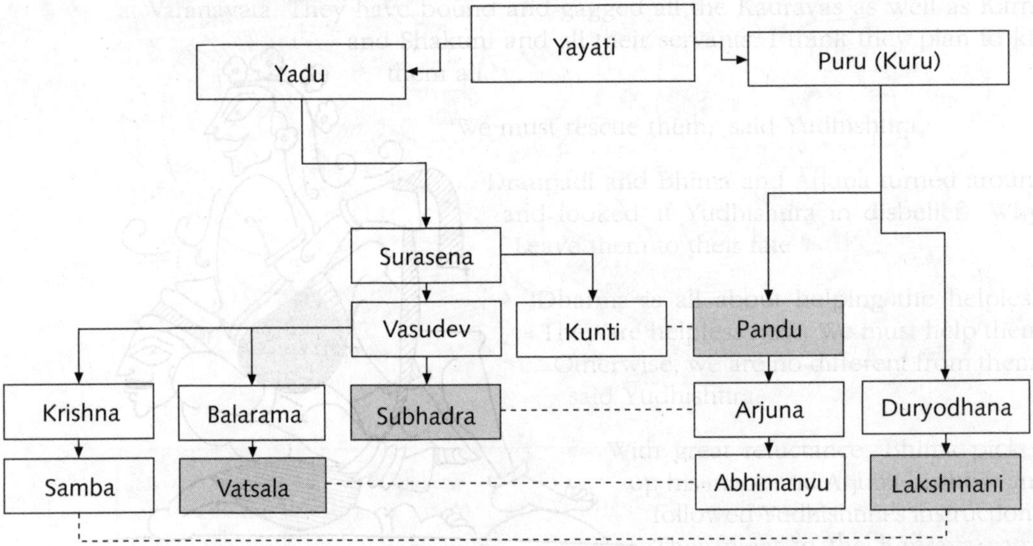

BOOK SEVENTEEN

Reconstruction

Janamejaya, knowledge must outlive death, so that the next generation is more enlightened.’

Yudhishtira's coronation

And then it was over: The war, the burning of the bodies, the immersion of the ashes in the river Ganga, and the long period of mourning. It was time to end the wailing, and the fasting. It was time to bring the flowers, raise the banners and light the kitchen fires. It was time for Hastina-puri to crown its new king, Yudhishtira, son of Pandu, grandson of Vichitravirya, great grandson of Shantanu.

But the eldest Pandava had lost all interest in kingship. 'I am a murderer,' he cried. 'My hands are soaked with the blood of my family. When I sit on a pile of corpses, how can I drink the cup of success? What is the point of it all?'

Arjuna said, 'The point of life is to compete and excel in the playground of life.'

Bhima said, 'The past is gone. Don't think about it. Focus on the present, the future, the food we shall all eat and the wine we shall all drink. That is the point of it all.'

Nakula said, 'The point is to make wealth and distribute it to the poor and the wise and the deserving.'

Sahadeva, as usual, said nothing. Nor did Draupadi, still mourning her five sons.

Vidura spoke solemnly to his nephew, 'Everybody dies—some suddenly, some slowly, some painfully, some peacefully. No one can escape death. The point is

to make the most of life—enjoy it, celebrate it, learn from it, make sense of it, share it with fellow human beings—so that when death finally comes, it will not be such a terrible thing.'

A Charvaka, one who does not believe in the existence of anything spiritual or metaphysical, shouted from the city square, 'Yes, Yudhishtira, life has no point at all. So enjoy every moment for there is no tomorrow, no life after death, no soul, no fate, no bondage, no liberation, no God. Be a king if it makes you happy; don't be a king if it does not. Pleasure alone is the purpose of life.'

None of this pacified Yudhishtira. He paced the palace corridors all day and lay awake on his bed at night, haunted by the wail of widows and orphans. No one understood his pain. 'Perhaps I must become a hermit. Find serenity in the forest.'

It was then that Krishna spoke, 'Yes, Yudhishtira, you can renounce the world and become a hermit and achieve peace, but what about the rest of the world? Will you abandon them?' Yudhishtira did not know what to say. Krishna continued, 'A hermit seeks meaning for himself but only a king can create a world that enables everyone to find meaning. Choose kingship, Yudhishtira, not out of obligation but out of empathy for humanity.'

'Why me?' asked Yudhishtira.

'Who better than you? You, who gambled away your kingdom, can empathize with the imperfections of man. You, who silently suffered thirteen years of exile, know the power of repentance and forgiveness. You, who saw Duryodhana reject every offer of peace, know the power of the ego and the horror of adharma. You, who had to lie to kill your own teacher, know the complexities of dharma. Only you, son of Kunti, have the power to establish a world where the head is balanced with the heart, wealth with wisdom, and discipline with compassion. Come, Yudhishtira, with your brothers by your side, be Vishnu on earth.'

Yudhishtira needed no more persuasion. He realized what it meant to be king. He agreed to wear the crown.

In the presence of all elders, he was made to sit on the ancient seat reserved for the leader of the Kuru clan. Milk was poured on him and water. He was given first a conch-shell trumpet, then a lotus flower, then a mace and finally the royal bow.

The priests said, 'Like Vishnu, blow the trumpet and make sure the world knows your law. Reward those who follow it with the lotus of prosperity and discipline those who don't with a swing of your mace. And always stay balanced—neither too tight nor too loose—like the bow.'

Everyone bowed to the new king. It was the birth of a new era, an age where dharma would be reinstituted by the five Pandavas with the guidance of Krishna. Filled with hope, the people cheered their new king as he rode into the streets dressed in white and gold on a cart pulled by a hundred oxen. Conch-shell trumpets blared from the eight corners of the city. Flowers were showered on him on every street. The war seemed a distant memory. It was an impressive sight, worthy of the great Kuru clan.

- The coronation ceremony in ancient times paralleled the ceremony in which a stone statue was transformed into a deity in temples. The ceremony was aimed to bring about a shift in consciousness. Just as it enabled a stone to become divine and solve the problems of devotees, it enabled an ordinary man to think like God—more about his subjects and less about himself.
- One must never forget that during Yudhishtira's coronation, each and every Pandava is aware that all their children are dead—Abhimanyu, Ghatotkacha, Iravan, Barbareek, even the five sons of Draupadi. The only surviving heir is unborn, resting in the womb of Abhimanyu's widow, Uttari. Thus, it is not quite a happy occasion as some storytellers like to project.
- Dharma is not about winning. It is about empathy and growth. Yudhishtira knows the pain of losing a child. He can empathize with his enemy rather than gloat on their defeat. In empathy, there is wisdom.

Bed of arrows

When the coronation ceremonies drew to a close, Krishna advised the Pandavas, 'Go and seek the blessings of your granduncle. Let him share with you the secret of peace and prosperity before he dies.'

Life was slipping away slowly for Bhishma as he lay on the bed of arrows, but he was eager to share all he knew with the new king. 'Give me some water first,' he said.

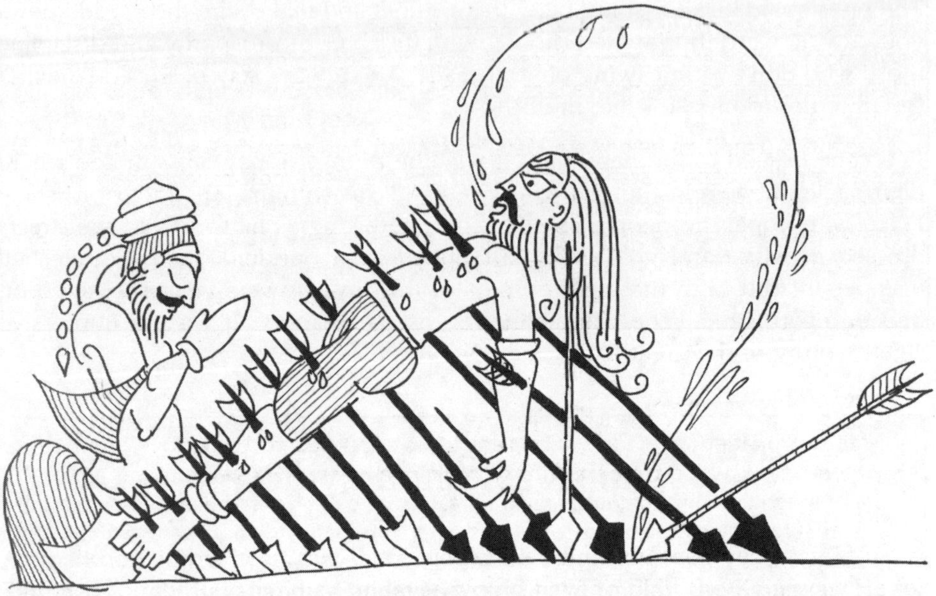

Arjuna immediately shot an arrow into the earth and water gushed out, leaping into the mouth of the dying patriarch.

His thirst quenched, Bhishma told Yudhishtira, 'Life is like a river. You can struggle to change its course but ultimately it will go its own way. Bathe in it, drink it, be refreshed by it, share it with everyone, but never fight it, never be swept away by its flow, and never get attached to it. Observe it. Learn from it.'

Bhishma told Yudhishtira about the human condition. A dove, pursued by a hawk, asked a king called Sivi to save it. As soon as the king offered it protection, the hawk shouted, 'What will I eat then?' Sivi then offered the hawk any other dove to feed on. 'That is not fair to the other birds, is it, O king?' asked the hawk. The king then offered his own flesh, equal in measure to the dove's weight. 'How much flesh can you give king? Sooner or later, you will die, and the dove will have to fend for itself. Unless one creature dies, another creature cannot survive, that is the natural cycle of life,' said the hawk. 'Was I wrong to save the dove?' wondered the king—his inner voice said he was not. So what must a man do? What must a king do? Save doves and let hawks starve or save hawks by allowing them to kill doves? At that moment, the king realized how different man was from animal. Animals spent their entire lives focused on survival. Humans could look beyond survival, seek meaning in life, harm others to save themselves, help others by sacrificing themselves. Humanity was blessed with a faculty that enabled it to empathize and exploit. It was this unique faculty that allowed humans to forsake the jungle and establish civilization.

Bhishma told Yudhishtira about human society. Humans, unlike animals, were blessed with imagination. They could foresee the future, and take actions to secure it. Often attempts to secure the future led to hoarding; need gave way to greed. With greed came exploitation. King Vena plundered the earth to such a degree that the earth, tired of being so abused, ran away in the form of a cow. The sages then had Vena killed. Vena's son, Prithu, pursued the earth-cow crying, 'If you don't feed them, my subjects will die.' The earth-cow retorted angrily, 'Your subjects squeeze my udders until they are sore. They break my back with their ambition.' Prithu then promised that he would establish a code of conduct based on empathy, rather than exploitation, which would ensure the survival of humanity. 'This code of conduct will be called dharma,' said Prithu. By this code, the earth became a cow while kings became the earth's cowherds ensuring there was always enough milk for humans as well as the cow's calves.

The conversation between Bhishma and Yudhishtira went on for many days. At first, everything seemed like the ramblings of a dying man. Later, everything made great sense. Yudhishtira learnt many things—history, geography, law, polity, economics and philosophy, the idea behind the strange tales of gods, demons and humans.

Yudhishtira had many questions. Bhishma answered each of them. At one point Yudhishtira asked, 'Who gets greater pleasure in life? Man or woman?'

'Not all questions have answers, Yudhishtira. No one knows what you ask, except perhaps Bhangashvana, an ancient king, who was cursed by Indra to turn into a woman. He was the only creature on earth who knew sexual pleasure both as a man and a woman. And only he had children who called him "father" and children who called him "mother". Only he knew if a man has greater pleasure during sex or a woman. Only he knew if the call of "father" is sweet or if the call of "mother" is sweeter. The rest of us can only speculate.'

Finally, Bhishma told the Pandavas about God. 'Our merits create fortune. Our demerits create misfortune. Merits bring us joy. Demerits bring us sorrow. We are thus fettered by karma. Karma binds us to the material world, compels us to be born and compels us to die. No one can change this, except one. That one is God. Pray to God to cope with the fetter of karma.'

Following this, Bhishma began chanting the thousand names of God. As he mouthed these words, the Pandavas noticed that the sun was now on its northerly course along the horizon. It was time for Bhishma to die.

- In both the Ramayana and the Mahabharata, at the end of the war, there is a scene of discourse before death. In the former, Ram requests Ravana, his learned opponent, to share his wisdom before he dies. In the Mahabharata, the Pandavas request Bhishma to share his wisdom. The idea behind both episodes is that, unlike wealth, knowledge does not outlive death, hence has to be passed on to the living so that it is not lost forever.
- There is little difference between the latter part of the Shanti Parva and the whole of the Anushasan Parva. In both, Bhishma is sharing his knowledge on various topics including death and immortality, ascetic life and householder's life, peace and conflict, rebirth and liberation, space and time, health and disease, duty and desire.
- The Mahabharata is among the first Indian scriptures to move away from ritualism and abstract speculation and propagate devotion. In it, divinity is not nirguna (without form) but saguna (with form). Both the Mahabharata and Ramayana identify God as Vishnu, the worldlier form of God, because both these epics are concerned with worldly issues like property and conflict.
- The practice of chanting God's name to invoke God's grace can be traced to the Mahabharata. Bhishma identifies God as Vishnu and chants the thousand names of Vishnu or Vishnu Sahasranama before he dies, each name describing an attribute or a feat of the divine. In the chant, he identifies Krishna as Vishnu on earth, thus transforming Krishna from a mere hero and statesman to a very personal form of the divine.
- Many communities in South India observe Bhishma Ekadashi on the eleventh day of the waxing moon in the month of Magh (Jan–Feb) to mark the occasion when the Vishnu Sahasranama was revealed to the Pandavas.

Death and rebirth

At long last, eight days after the full moon that followed the end of the terrible war, Bhishma breathed his last. He was at peace: all his knowledge would outlive him. It was up to the new king to make use of it.

Bhishma's cremation was attended by all the surviving kings and warriors of the land. He was not just an elder of the Kuru clan; he was the last representative of the old order. His death symbolized the end of an era. For the Pandavas, Bhishma's death was a personal tragedy; he was the only father they knew.

But the sorrow was short-lived for a few weeks after Bhishma's cremation, Abhimanyu's widow, Uttari, went into labour. The whole palace was abuzz with excitement as her water broke. All the women of the palace, from Draupadi to Gandhari, rushed to the side of this young girl to help her give birth to the one who would be the last surviving member of the Kuru clan.

Uttari heaved and the women around her waited with bated breath. The child slipped out. It was a boy. Everyone smiled. But then the midwife exclaimed, 'The baby is not crying! The baby is not moving! I think he is stillborn.'

Hearing this, all the Kuru women began to wail. Was this household cursed? Was it doomed to wither away and die?

The wail of the palace women reached Krishna's ears. He rushed to the women's quarters and took the newborn into his arms. 'Don't be afraid, child,' said Krishna, 'the world is not such a terrible place.'

Coaxed by Krishna's comforting voice and his gentle touch, the young prince opened his eyes and smiled. Krishna returned the smile and then presented him to the world. 'Behold, Parikshit, the first of the next generation.'

- Bhishma died after fifty-eight days. Scholars are not sure if the fifty-eight days are to be calculated from the first day of the war, from the last or from the day Bhishma was shot. What is clear is that he died after the sun enters the house of Capricorn (Makara Sankranti), following the winter solstice, after which days get longer and warmer. Thus the war took place in winter, in the darkest and coldest days of the year. This could be taken as factual or symbolic, indicative of the end of an era and the collapse of a great household.

- B.N. Narahari Achar has determined the date of the war using Planetarium software, beginning with Krishna's journey to Hastina-puri and ending with Bhishma's death. He concludes that Krishna left on 26 Sep 3067 BCE, reaching Hastina-puri on 28 Sep and leaving Karna on 9 Oct. A solar eclipse occurred with the new moon on 14 Oct, with Saturn at Rohini and Jupiter at Revati exactly as given in the epic. The war began on 22 Nov 3067 BCE. Bhishma expired on 17 Jan 3066 BCE (Magh Shukla Ashtami), the winter solstice occurring on 13 Jan 3066. It must be kept in mind that 5000 years ago, the date of the winter solstice was very different from what it is today; the current night sky is different from the one seen by our ancestors.
- Bhishma is believed by many to have died on the eighth day of the waxing moon in the month of Magh (Jan–Feb) following Uttarayan, the northern movement of the rising sun. Since he left behind no offspring, he is forever trapped in the land of the dead. Since there is no food in the land of the dead, even today, priests across India perform funeral rites and offer him rice cakes on Bhishma-ashtami.

Horse sacrifice

Parikshit's birth restored the smile on Yudhishtira's face. His family would survive.

To mark this joyful event, Dhaumya, still the family priest of the Pandavas, and now the royal priest, proposed that the Pandavas perform the sacrifice of the royal horse known as Ashwamedha. This would involve letting the royal horse loose and allowing it to roam freely for a year, followed by the army. All the lands it would traverse unchallenged would come under Pandava rule. On its return, the horse would be sacrificed so as to symbolically transfer to the king all the power and glory gathered on the year-long journey.

The idea so excited his brothers that Yudhishtira agreed to the proposal. The priests divined that the most suitable horse for the ceremony could be found only in the city of Bhadravati in the stables of king Yuvanashva. Bhima set out to fetch the horse accompanied by his grandson, Meghavarna, son of Ghatotkacha and his nephew, Vrishadhvaja, son of Karna. At first Yuvanashva refused to part with the horse but after much debate and some display of force by Karna's son and magic by Ghatotkacha's son, he agreed.

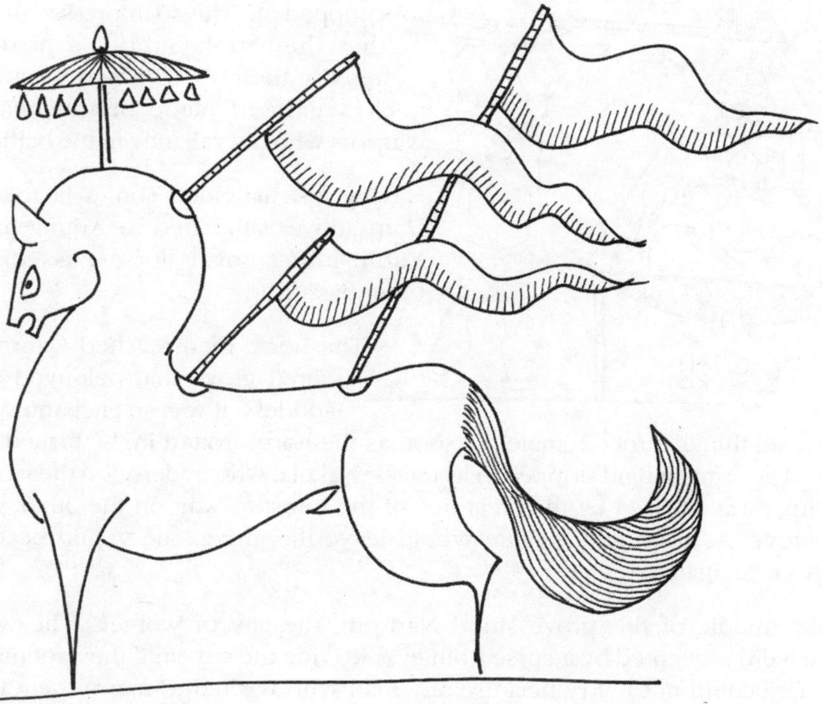

After the horse was brought to Hastina-puri, the yagna began and after due ceremony the horse was let loose into the wilderness beyond the city frontiers to the sound of chants, drums and conch-shell trumpets. Arjuna led the army that followed the horse. He was accompanied by Nakula. Bhima and Sahadeva stayed back to watch over Hastina-puri while they were away.

When the horse reached Champaka-puri, it was met with opposition. Its king, Hamsadhvaj, was so determined not to accept Yudhishtira as overlord that he declared that whosoever in his kingdom did not fight Arjuna would be boiled in oil. Unfortunately, when the army gathered at the gates, the youngest son of the king, Sudhanva, was nowhere to be found. He was busy making love to his wife. Since he made his wife's pleasure his priority, the king ordered that he be boiled in oil. Sudhanva's wife begged for mercy. When none was forthcoming, she prayed to Krishna, who had saved Draupadi in her time of need. Krishna responded and the hot oil miraculously had no effect on Sudhanva.

Suratha, the eldest son of Hamsadhvaj, led his father's army against Arjuna. He fought so ferociously that his body continued to fight even when his head was

chopped off. This so impressed the gods that they took Suratha's head and offered it to Shiva who wears round his neck a garland made of the heads of warriors who die valiantly in the battlefield.

Having lost his eldest son, a heartbroken Hamsadhvaj submitted to Arjuna and let Yudhishtira's royal horse pass through Champaka-puri.

The horse then reached Gaurivan, a sacred grove that belonged to the Goddess. It was an enchanted grove where all things turned female. As soon as the horse trotted in, he turned into a mare. The army behind stopped in its tracks. Nakula, who understood the language of birds, was advised by the creatures of the forest to wait on the other side of the grove. As soon as the mare would leave the grove, she would become a horse once again.

In the middle of this grove stood Nari-pur, the city of women. The women there were prevented by a curse from ever leaving the city until they got married, but they could not marry because any man who wished to marry them turned into a woman as soon as he entered the enchanted grove. The trapped and frustrated queen of the city, Pramila, caught hold of Yudhishtira's sacrificial horse, now mare, as soon as he reached the gates of Nari-pur. 'She shall pass and Yudhishtira shall become my overlord only if Arjuna accepts me as his wife,' she said. Her words reached Arjuna through the animals of the forest who spoke to Nakula. Arjuna was at first angry by such a demand but then discretion prevailed and he consented. A joyful Pramila emerged from the enchanted grove along with the mare. The mare became a horse and she became Arjuna's wife. 'Go to Hastina-puri and wait for me till I return,' said Arjuna to his new wife. Pramila agreed and Arjuna resumed his journey as guardian of Yudhishtira's sacrificial horse.

Yudhishtira's horse then crossed Sindhu where Arjuna was welcomed by Dusshala, the only sister of the Kauravas and the wife of Jayadhrata, and her son. Jayadhrata had helped in the killing of Arjuna's son, Abhimanyu. But now all was forgiven. Arjuna hugged his cousin sister with love and blessed her son.

Arjuna then crossed Gandhara, where he was welcomed by Shakuni's sons. Here too there was no more anger against the Pandavas. Bygones were bygones.

Finally, Arjuna reached the sea where the horse was able to walk on the waves. Arjuna was pleasantly surprised when even he was able to walk on the waves. Arjuna realized this was because of the spiritual powers of Rishi Bakadalbhya, who lived on a lagoon nearby. The sage told him a story, 'I once performed tapasya and compelled Indra, king of the gods, to appear before me. I asked him if he accepted that I was stronger than him. He said yes, but there is one greater. I asked him to take me to that greater being. He took me to Brahma, the father of all living things. He had four heads. I asked Brahma if he was the greatest being in the world. He said no, for there was someone greater. I asked him to take me to that greater being. He took me to a Brahma who had eight heads. I asked this eight-headed Brahma if he was the greatest being in the world. This eight-headed Brahma said no, for there was someone greater. I asked him to take me to that greater being. He took me to a Brahma who had sixteen heads. This Brahma took me to a Brahma with thirty-two heads who took me to a Brahma with sixty-four heads. Thus we went to meet many more Brahmas, each greater than the previous ones. And finally, we came to a Brahma with a thousand heads who said that greater than him was Vishnu, who reclines on a serpent that lives in the ocean of milk. And that Vishnu walks the earth as Krishna. Hearing this, I realized how insignificant a creature I was in the universe and how foolish. That day my ego was shattered and I attained bliss. Since that day, people have been able to walk on water when they come near my hermitage.'

After hearing the Rishi's tale, Arjuna returned with the horse to the shore. As the journey continued, the horse was captured by Mayurdhvaj. The only reason Mayurdhvaj did this was because Arjuna would follow the horse. If he captured Arjuna, then Krishna would come to the rescue of Arjuna. Mayurdhvaj knew that Krishna was Vishnu, God on earth. Being a great devotee, he wanted to see Krishna in person, hence this elaborate plan. This plan worked and Krishna did come to his city in search of Arjuna. After falling at Krishna's feet, Mayurdhvaj released both Arjuna and the horse.

- Jaimini's version of the Mahabharata is different from that of his master, Vyasa's. It focuses more on Yudhishtira's Ashwamedha after the war, on the reconciliation with the children of enemies (the sons of Karna, Jayadhrata, Shakuni) and on the value of worshipping Krishna as God. Known as Jaiminiya-ashwamedha, this work has inspired many folk stories, a few of which are narrated in the chapter above.

- Rishi Bakadalbhya is associated with walking on water or crossing water. He taught Ram rituals that would enable him to cross the sea and reach the island of Lanka, where Ravana, king of the Rakshasas, had confined Sita. The same rituals are performed every year on Vijaya Ekadashi which falls on the eleventh day of the waxing moon in February–March.

Babruvahana

After conquering many lands, the horse of the Pandavas reached Manipur where it was stopped by its ruler, a young man called Babruvahana, who turned out to be Arjuna's son by Chitrangada, princess of Manipur.

Babruvahana welcomed his father, who he had never met before, and would have let the horse pass through the city when Arjuna said, 'This is unbecoming of a warrior's son. Challenge me. Fight me. Don't give in so easily.' In deference to his father's wishes, Babruvahana raised his bow and to everyone's surprise turned out to be more than a match for his father. He very ably destroyed the arrows released by his father and it took a lot of effort on Arjuna's part to destroy the arrows released by his young son.

Then, after hours of fighting, the unthinkable happened—an arrow that left Babruvahana's bow ripped through Arjuna's heart killing him instantly. Chitrangada let out a cry and Babruvahana was shattered for he never intended to harm his father. He hugged the lifeless body of Arjuna and began to wail.

Suddenly, there appeared on the scene a Naga woman. Her name was Ulupi. She was the mother of Iravan, sacrificed on the ninth night of the war. 'You have done nothing wrong, Babruvahana,' said Ulupi, 'Your father brought this upon himself. You were but an instrument of destiny. Your father killed his granduncle, Bhishma, who was like a father to him. For that shameful act, Bhishma's mother, the river-goddess, Ganga, cursed Arjuna that he would die at the hands of his own son. That curse has just expressed itself through your arrow. But fear not. I bring with me Naga-mani, a magical gem from the realm of serpents that has the power to bring the dead to life.' Ulupi placed the magical gem of serpents on Arjuna's fatal wound and, to Babruvahana's utter astonishment, the wound healed itself.

Arjuna then started to breathe. He opened his eyes as if waking up from a deep sleep. Arjuna looked at Ulupi but failed to recognize her for years had passed since the night they had spent together. A heartbroken Ulupi silently withdrew to her subterranean realm.

After spending many days with Chitrangada and Babruvahana, it was time for Arjuna to return to Hastina-puri with the sacrificial horse. Mother and son let him go with a heavy heart.

As soon as the horse entered Hastina-puri, it began to neigh happily. All the Rishis were surprised. 'Why does it laugh so? Does it not know that it will be killed at the altar?' Nakula heard what the horse had to say and revealed that the horse was happy because unlike other horses that had been sacrificed in earlier Ashwamedha yagnas and had ascended to the paradise of the gods after their death, he would go to a higher heaven, located even above Swarga.

'What is this heaven located even above Swarga?' asked Yudhishtira.

The Rishis replied, 'It is a secret known to few. We do not know it. Maybe, one day, O king, if the gods find you worthy enough, the secret will be revealed to you.'

- In a Bengali folk retelling of the Mahabharata is the tale of one of Arjuna's many jilted wives who takes the form of the arrow which Babruvahana shoots to kill his father. Later, she regrets her action and begs the gods to restore Arjuna to life.
- In Jaimini-bharata, Babruvahana has to go to the land of the serpents, following directions given by Ulupi, to fetch the magical jewel himself. He succeeds but only after many adventures in Naga-loka.
- The Naga princess Ulupi's love for Arjuna remains unrequited. He has no recollection of her. But still she forgives and saves him.
- Arjuna's death at the hands of his son washes away the demerit he himself earned when he killed his foster father, Bhishma.

Start of Kali yuga

Yudhishtira's Ashwamedha yagna was the grandest yagna in human memory. No expense was spared. All the Rishis who conducted the yagna and chanted the mantras were given food, clothing and cows.

In the midst of the ceremony, two farmers came to Hastina-puri and begged Yudhishtira to settle a dispute. One of the farmers had sold his land to the other. The following day, while ploughing the field, the new owner stumbled upon a pot of gold buried under the ground. He went to the old owner and offered it to him saying, 'I bought the land. However, what lies beneath it still belongs to you.' The old owner refused to take the pot of gold saying it now belonged to the new owner who had found it.

Yudhishtira, impressed by the charitable nature of the two farmers, did not know how to settle this case. So he sought Krishna's advice. Krishna suggested that the farmers leave their pot of gold with the king and return after three months. The two farmers agreed.

As they left, Yudhishtira looked at Krishna quizzically. What would happen after three months, he wondered. Krishna replied, 'In three months the same two farmers, who were so willing to give away the pot of gold today, will return and fight furiously to be its sole owners. On that day, you will find it easier to settle the case as you will see greed in their eyes instead of generosity, outrage instead of compassion. Three months later, Yudhishtira, your yagna will conclude and the Kali yuga will dawn. A new age will dawn where nothing will be as it was. Only a quarter of the values instituted by Prithu at the dawn of civilization will survive. Man will live for pleasure, children will abandon responsibility, women will be like men, men like women. Humans will copulate like beasts. Power will be respected, justice abandoned, sacrifice forgotten and love ridiculed. The wise will argue for the law of the jungle. Every victim will, given a chance, turn victimizer.'

Three months later, the two farmers returned and, as foretold, fought over the pot of gold. It was now very easy for Yudhishtira to settle the dispute: he divided the gold into three equal portions. One portion was given to each farmer and the third portion was kept by the king as fee for the judgement.

After sacrificing the royal horse and completing all the ceremonies, the Rishis who conducted the Ashwamedha were about to leave when they saw a mongoose, half of whose body shone like gold, enter the sacrificial hall. It jumped into the

fire-pit, rubbed its normal side on the charred remains of the ritual, and then left the altar with a disappointed look.

When asked by the Rishis why he looked so unhappy, the mongoose said, 'Half my body turned into gold long ago when I rolled on the remains of a ritual. I hoped the other half would turn to gold when I rubbed against the remains of this ritual. But it has not happened.' Everyone was curious to know of the earlier ritual which was clearly greater than Yudhishtira's. 'It happened over three months ago. A poor family starved to death as they happily gave up their meagre meal to guests who arrived at their doorstep unannounced. I rubbed my body on the leaves on which the food was offered. And to my surprise, my skin turned to gold. But the remains of this grand Ashwamedha yagna have failed to have a similar effect.'

The Rishis realized that Yudhishtira's sacrifice, though grand, was less about charity and more about royal power. Hence, it was a lesser ritual.

Dhaumya, guru of the Pandavas, divined that before the war all of dharma rested with the Pandavas. A quarter with Yudhishtira, a quarter with Arjuna, a quarter with Bhima and a quarter between Nakula and Sahadeva. Draupadi, who is the Goddess, and Krishna, who is God, had managed to harness them together. But with the dawn of Kali yuga, this would not continue. Arjuna would submit to conceit, Bhima to gluttony, Nakula to pleasure and Sahadeva to arrogance. Only Yudhishtira would cling tenaciously to his quarter of dharma. That dharma would sustain the world through the final quarter of the world's lifespan. And when that would be abandoned, Pralaya would follow. The waves of doom would engulf civilization and the world would cease to be.

- Kali yuga refers to a time when man lacks the spirit of generosity. Life becomes all about taking and hoarding. This is seen as the prime cause of any strife.
- In the Bhagavad Gita, God says that whenever the world is full of adharma, he descends to restore dharma. One would therefore assume that at the end of God's stay on earth, the world returns to primal perfection. It is however not so. Adharma may be seen as disease and dharma as health. God restores the health of the world from time to time but he cannot prevent the ageing of the body. By defeating the Kauravas, Krishna enables the Pandavas to restore order in the world. But this does not stop the arrival of the Kali yuga, the fourth quarter of the world's lifespan, the age before the world's death. We will all die eventually but this should not stop us from living healthy lives. In the same way, the eventual collapse of an organization should not stop leaders from striving to uphold order.

BOOK EIGHTEEN

Renunciation

'Janamejaya, there are many kinds of victory, and only one where everyone wins.'

The elders renounce the kingdom

Yudhishtira's reign was peaceful and prosperous. As the years passed, memories of the war faded away. Everyone took joy in watching young Parikshit grow up to be a fine young man.

Dhritarashtra and Gandhari continued to stay in Hastina-puri and Yudhishtira did his best to keep them comfortable and happy. Unfortunately, Bhima was not so forgiving.

Every time the family sat down to eat, Bhima would crack his knuckles and slap his arms and discuss in detail how he killed each of the Kauravas. Every time Dhritarashtra bit into a bone while eating meat, Bhima would say, 'That's exactly the sound I heard when I broke Duryodhana's thigh.' Every time Dhritarashtra sucked a juicy marrow, Bhima would say, 'That's what Dusshasana's last gasp sounded like.'

Unable to bear his brother being treated so, Vidura would say to Dhritarashtra, 'Have some shame. Leave this place where you are given no respect.'

Dhritarashtra would reply, 'Where will I go?' and suffer his humiliation silently.

An exasperated Vidura one day narrated a story, 'Once a man lost his way in the forest and fell into a pit. As he fell, his feet got entangled in some vines and he was suspended head down. Above, the sky was dark. He heard the wind howl. On the edge of the pit he saw a herd of wild elephants trumpeting wildly. Down in the pit were hissing hundreds of venomous serpents. Rats were gnawing the roots of the vine to which he clung like a jackfruit ripe for the picking. Suddenly, through the corner of his eye, he saw bees humming around a bee hive. A drop of honey fell from the beehive. Forgetting the terrible situation he was in, the priest stretched out his hand to collect a drop of that honey. At that moment, fear of storms, elephants, rats and serpents, and imminent death escaped him; all that mattered was the sweet taste of honey.'

Hearing this, Dhritarashtra realized that it was not the absence of his eyes, but his attachment to palace comforts, that prevented him from seeing the truth of his pathetic situation. At long last, he gathered the courage to renounce all things worldly and walk out of the palace. 'Come, Gandhari, let us go,' he said.

Gandhari obeyed. Vidura followed them. So did Kunti, realizing it was time for her generation to let go.

Yudhishtira tried to stop his mother, but failed. 'I am tired, son,' she said. 'Time to move on.'

For many years, the elders wandered in the woods meeting Rishis, appreciating from them the meaning of life. Then one day, Vidura died. His life breath

slipped away as he meditated. Another day, Gandhari had a vision of all those killed in the battle, dressed in white, bedecked in jewels, smiling, with no sign of sorrow or anger on their faces. This made her happy.

Shortly thereafter, a fire broke out in the forest. 'Run,' said Dhritarashtra sniffing the smoke.

'Why?' asked Gandhari.

Why indeed? And so the older generation of the Kuru clan sat still and let the wall of flames encircle and engulf them.

- The dharma-shastras divide life into four parts. The first, brahmacharya, prepares one for the world. The second, grihastha, is the time to enjoy the pleasures and powers of the world. The third, vanaprastha, is the time to retire from the world passing on all wealth to the children and all knowledge to the grandchildren. The fourth, sanyasa, is the time to renounce all things worldly. The characters in the Mahabharata from Pratipa to Dhritarashtra retire from society and renounce the world after completing their worldly duties. Thus only the young are allowed to enjoy the fruits of the earth, while the old contemplate on it.
- Vyasa is well aware how the old are treated by many families especially when they do not have children of their own and when all their power is gone. Yudhishtira symbolizes how things should be, while Bhima personifies the grudges the youth bear towards the older generations for actions in the past that have left them scarred for life.
- Sanjay followed his master to the forest and died with them in the forest fire, such was his loyalty to the old, blind king.
- Despite learning from Krishna the value of outgrowing the beast within man, the Pandavas cling to their grudges after the war, like dogs clinging to bones. No lesson is permanent. Wisdom thus is always work in progress.

End of the Yadus

In Dwaraka, meanwhile, the Yadavas decided to gather on the shores of the sea at Prabhasa to make offerings to all those who had died in the war at Kuru-kshetra. During the ceremony an argument erupted between those who thought the Pandavas were righteous, and those who felt the Kauravas had been wronged.

'The Kauravas pounced on Abhimanyu like dogs pounce on a lamb separated from its herd!' said Satyaki, leading the group that supported the Pandavas.

'Yudhishtira lied to kill Drona, Arjuna shot an unarmed Karna and Bhima struck Duryodhana below the waist!' said Kritavarma, who led the group that supported the Kauravas. He also reminded Satyaki how he attacked and killed Bhurishrava unfairly.

Before long, the argument turned into a brawl, the brawl into a battle and the battle into a full-fledged civil war. Krishna and Balarama watched in helpless horror as their brothers, friends, cousins, sons and grandsons lunged at each other.

In a bid to save their clan, the two brothers hid all the weapons of the Yadava warriors. But such was the fury that the Yadavas, unable to find any weapon, started striking each other with blades of reeds growing along the shore.

These were no ordinary reeds. They had sharp, serrated edges and pointed tips. They were born of iron dust pounded out of an iron pestle.

Years ago, Samba, son of Krishna, had played a prank on a group of sages. To test their spiritual prowess, he went to them disguised as a pregnant woman and asked if the unborn child was male or female. 'Not male, not female, but an iron bar is what you carry in your body,' growled the Rishis not amused by Samba's trick, 'One that will destroy all the Yadavas.'

Sure enough, an iron mace ripped itself out of Samba's thigh. A terrified Samba pounded it to dust which he then cast into the sea. The sea rejected this iron dust and tossed it back to the shores of Prabhasa, where it turned into the deadly reeds that the Yadavas plucked to strike each other with.

In a few hours, struck by the deadly blades of grass, the bodies of hundreds of slain Yadavas, young and old included, covered the shores of Prabhasa. It was impossible to distinguish who sided with the Pandavas and who with the Kauravas. Satyaki was dead. Kritavarma was dead. It was like another Kuru-kshetra. Krishna and Balarama could do nothing to save them.

Thus did Gandhari's curse fulfil itself.

- Krishna's son, Samba, is portrayed in the scriptures as an irresponsible lout, perhaps to inform us that the child of a great man need not be a great man; greatness is not transmitted through the generations. Every man ultimately makes or destroys his own legacy.
- A game of dice leads to the carnage at Kuru-kshetra. An argument leads to the carnage at Prabhasa. Ultimately, all wars can be traced to the simplest of quarrels where man is eager to overpower rather than indulge the other.
- Krishna's family does not escape Gandhari's curse. Thus even God surrenders to the law of karma. By making man the master of his own destiny and the creator of his own desires, God makes man ultimately responsible for the life he leads and the choices he makes. God does not interfere with fate; he simply helps man cope with it.

Death of Krishna

Watching the destruction of his family, a distraught Balarama lost all interest in life. He let his life breath slip out of his mortal body in the form of a serpent.

With Balarama gone, Krishna realized it was time to end his mortal life. He sat under a Banyan tree, crossed his left foot over his right leg and started shaking it as he reminisced about his life: his journey from Vrindavan through Mathura and Dwaraka to Hastina-puri and finally Kuru-kshetra.

As he was doing so, the sole of his left foot was struck by a poisoned arrow shot by a hunter who, seeing it through a thicket, mistook it to be the ear of a deer.

The arrowhead was the only piece of the iron mace that Samba had been unable to pound into dust. The hunter had found it in the belly of a fish. The poison took effect and soon, even Krishna's life breath slipped away.

While all the Yadavas crossed the Vaitarni and entered the land of the dead awaiting rebirth, Krishna returned to the heaven known as Vaikuntha, located even above Swarga, and took his place as Vishnu, God who sustains the universe. Balarama was already there as the thousand-hooded serpent of time, Adi-Ananta-Sesha, ready to receive him in his great coils.

- In the cyclical Hindu world, all that is born must die. Even Krishna must experience death since he experienced birth. But Krishna's death is not a normal death; he returns to his heavenly abode, Vaikuntha, after shedding the mortal flesh he acquired at the time of his birth. Such is not the case with other creatures. After death, they move into another life and forget their past life. This is because during their time in the world, they are involved in various activities that generate karma; they are obliged to experience the reaction of their actions in one life time or another. Krishna, being God, does not perform actions that generate karma; his actions are neither paap nor punya. They generate neither demerit nor merit. His actions, full of awareness and detachment, are part of leela, the divine performance.
- According to one folk tale from North India, in his previous descent as Ram, God had shot a monkey called Vali in the back while he was busy engaged in a duel. Vali protested against this unfair action and so God caused him to be reborn as Jara and allowed him to strike him dead when he descended as Krishna.
- In Prabhas Patan, on the sea coast of the state of Gujarat, stands a tree that has been identified as the descendant of the Banyan tree under which Krishna was fatally injured.
- The Banyan tree is a sacred tree for Hindus because of its long life which has made it a symbol of immortality.

Fall of Dwaraka

No sooner did Krishna's father, Vasudeva, hear of the calamity at Prabhasa than he died of a broken heart. Soon, a vast field of funeral pyres lined the shores of the sea. The Yadava women let out a wail as they mourned their dead. The sound of their mourning reached the heavens and even made the Devas cry.

Some women leapt into the funeral pyres, unable to bear the thought of living without their husbands. Others lost all interest in worldly life and retired into the forest to live as mendicants. Those who still clung to life turned to Arjuna who had rushed from Hastina-puri on hearing of the great civil war in Dwaraka. But he came too late; there was hardly anything left of the Yadava clan to save.

Then the sea rose and lashed against the walls of Dwaraka. It started to pour and rainwater flooded the streets of the island city dissolving its very foundations. Before long, the walls started to crumble. The widows and orphans had to scramble out and make their way to the mainland on rafts and boats.

Arjuna decided to take the few survivors with him to Hastina-puri.

But the misfortunes continued. On the way, they were attacked by barbarians who abducted many of the women and children. Arjuna raised his Gandiva and tried to protect them but he was outnumbered. The great Gandiva which could destroy hundreds of warriors with a single arrow now seemed powerless. Arjuna realized that he was no more the archer he used to be. His purpose on earth and that of the Gandiva had been served.

Overwhelmed by his helplessness before the rising tide of fate, humbled before the raging storm of circumstances, Arjuna fell to his knees and began to cry uncontrollably.

When the tears dried up, it dawned on him that Gandhari's curse, which had destroyed Dwaraka and its people, had its roots in the war at Kuru-kshetra. And that war would not have happened if they had simply restrained themselves and not wagered their kingdom in a game of dice. Arjuna realized, that in a way, he was responsible for the fall of Dwaraka. This was the great web of karma that connects all creatures in a single fabric. He begged for forgiveness for his part in the sorrows of all mankind.

In response, the clouds began to rumble and in a flash of lightning Arjuna saw a vision: a gurgling, happy child sucking its butter-smeared big toe as it lay on a Banyan leaf cradled by the deadly waves that were destroying Dwaraka. In the midst of destruction, this was a symbol of renewal and hope.

Arjuna finally understood the message given to him by God. Life would continue, with joys and sorrows, triumphs and tragedies rising and falling like the waves of the sea. It was up to him to respond wisely, enjoy simple pleasures unshaken by the inevitable endless turmoil of the world.

He took the surviving Yadavas and gave them a home in Mathura, where in due course, Vajranabhi, son of Aniruddha, grandson of Pradyumna, great grandson of Krishna, would rise as a great king.

- Archaeologists have found traces of an ancient port city in the coast near modern Dwaraka dated to 1500 BCE, the time when a great city-based civilization thrived on the banks of the Indus across what is today Punjab, Sindh, Rajasthan and Gujarat. It is a matter of speculation if the characters of the Mahabharata inhabited these vast brick cities.
- Vajranabhi asked artisans to carve images of Krishna based on descriptions given by Abhimanyu's wife, Uttari. But the description was so grand that each artisan could capture only part of the beauty in each image. These images were lost to the world for centuries and later discovered by holy men who enshrined them in temples. The image of Srinathji at Nathdvara is said to be one such image.

Renunciation of the Pandavas

It was finally time for the Pandavas to retire. Parikshit, born after the bloodbath of Kuru-kshetra, was now old enough to rule Hastina-puri. The forest beckoned Yudhishtira. 'Let the younger generation enjoy life while we try and make sense of ours,' he said.

Crowning Parikshit as king, and distributing all their cows, horses, vessels, jewels and clothes among their subjects, the Pandavas left Hastina-puri dressed in clothes of bark.

They walked north towards the great snow-clad mountain whose peak touches Swarga. 'Let us climb Mandara,' said Yudhishtira. 'If we have truly upheld dharma in our lives, then our bodies will not die. We will enter the realm of the gods with this flesh.' His brothers agreed. Even Draupadi followed. So began the long and arduous journey of five old men and one old woman on a path that was narrow and steep to the realm of the virtuous high above the sky.

Suddenly, Draupadi slipped and fell. She cried out but no one turned around to save her. Then Sahadeva slipped and fell. No one turned around to help him either. Then Nakula slipped and fell. Then Arjuna. And finally Bhima. Yudhishtira stood his ground, and continued walking up the path.

Yudhishtira had refused to turn and help anyone. 'I have renounced everything,' he told himself, 'Even relationships.' He surmised that they had died because Yama did not find them worthy enough to enter Swarga with their mortal bodies. Each one of them had a flaw: though she was supposed to love all her five husbands equally, Draupadi preferred Arjuna, desired Karna, and manipulated Bhima; Sahadeva's knowledge had made him smug; Nakula's beauty had made him insensitive; Arjuna had been envious of all other archers in the world; and all his life Bhima had been a glutton, eating without bothering to serve others.

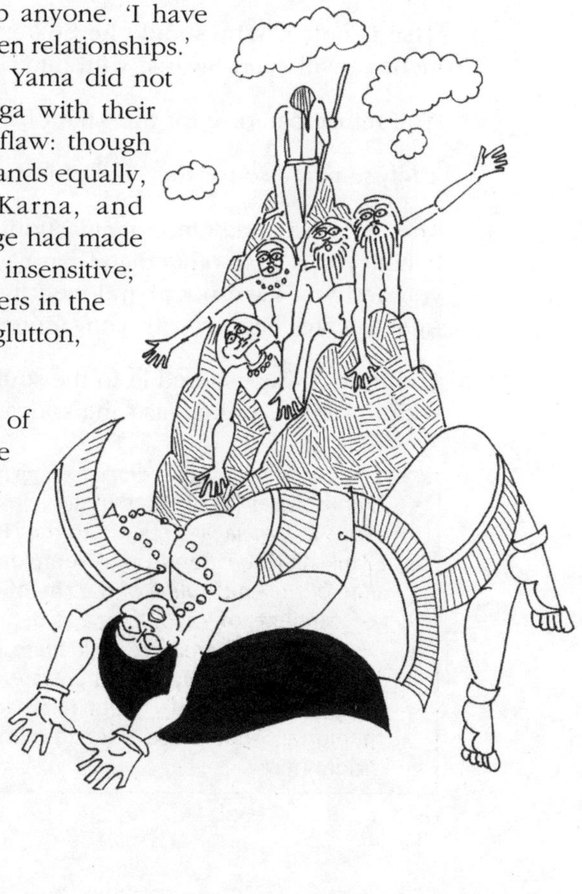

At long last, Yudhishtira reached the peak of Mandara. He found himself before the gate of that garden of unending delights known as Amravati.

'Come inside,' said the Devas spreading out their arms. 'But keep that dog out.'

'Dog?' asked Yudhishtira, sounding surprised. He turned around and found a dog behind him, wagging his tail. Yudhishtira recognized it from the streets of Hastina-puri. It had followed

him all the way, surviving the cold and the perilous journey.

'Dogs are inauspicious. They wander in crematoriums and eat garbage. They are not welcome in Swarga.'

The dog looked at Yudhishtira with adoration and licked his hand. Yudhishtira's heart melted. 'I have given up everything, but this dog has not given up on me. He has survived this journey with me. Surely, he too has earned the right to paradise, as I have. You must let him in,' he said.

'No,' said the Devas.

'That is unfair. Why should he be kept out and I taken in? We both have equal merits. I will enter Swarga with him or not at all.'

'You refuse paradise for the sake of a dog!' exclaimed the Devas.

'I refuse paradise for the sake of justice,' said Yudhishtira, firm in his resolve.

The Devas smiled. 'Once again Yudhishtira you display your integrity. This dog behind you is none other than Dharma, god of righteous conduct. He has followed you and you have not abandoned him. That is why only you have earned the right to enter heaven with your mortal body.'

Yudhishtira was ushered in to the sound of conch-shells. Apsaras showered him with flowers. Gandharvas sang songs to his glory.

- Parikshit has Naga blood in his veins since his grandmother Subhadra is a Yadava. Thus Janamejaya is related to the Nagas.
- Parikshit is the grandson of Subhadra. He thus has the blood of Yadu. Thus, at the end of the epic, rulers of the city of Hastina-puri are not descendants of Puru but descendants of Yadu, long ago denied the throne of Yayati.
- Vyasa says all creatures kill themselves eventually because of merits lost and demerits earned. By logic therefore, one who earns no demerit cannot die. Such a person can potentially rise up to paradise without dying. In other words, he becomes immortal. That is the ultimate aim of all spiritual practice. That is the aim of Yudhishtira.

- Dogs are considered inauspicious in Hinduism as they are associated with Yama, the god of death, and Bhairava, the fearsome killer form of Shiva. Dogs represent attachment and bondage because they are territorial and possessive of their masters. They constantly seek attention and validation. They therefore become the symbol of neediness, insecurity, attachment and ego, contrasted against the cow which is the symbol of the serene soul.

Kauravas in Swarga

As soon as Yudhishtira stepped into heaven, he saw the hundred Kauravas, Duryodhana and Dusshasana included, standing beside the Devas looking radiant and blissful. They too spread out their arms to welcome Yudhishtira. Yudhishtira recoiled in disgust. 'How did these warmongers reach Amravati?' he asked angrily.

The Devas replied, 'They were killed on the holy land of Kuru-kshetra. That has purified them of all misdeeds and earned them the right to enter Amravati. Surely, if heaven is good enough for your dog, it is good enough for your cousins.'

The explanation did not satisfy Yudhishtira. 'And my brothers? And my wife? What about them? Where are they? Are they here too?' he asked.

'They are not here,' replied the Devas placidly, refusing to pay any attention to Yudhishtira's rising rage.

'Where are they?' Yudhishtira demanded.

'In another place,' said the Devas, taking no notice of Yudhishtira's impatience.

'Take me to them,' said Yudhishtira, determined to get to the bottom of this.

'Certainly,' said the Devas who led Yudhishtira out of Swarga, down from the sky, along the slopes of Mandara, through a crevice deep under the earth to a realm that was dark and gloomy and miserable. There, Yudhishtira heard cries of pain and suffering. It was everything Amravati was not. He realized it was Naraka, the realm of misery.

'My brothers are here?' cried Yudhishtira in disbelief.

In response, he heard the moans of his brothers, including Karna. 'Yes, we are here,' they said in unison.

Bhima, Yudhishtira knew, was paying for his gluttony, Arjuna for his envy, Nakula for his insensitivity, Sahadeva for his smugness and Draupadi for her partiality. But Karna? Why him? Had his elder brother not suffered enough in life? 'Karna promised Kunti to spare four of her five sons despite knowing that Duryodhana relied on him to kill all five Pandavas. He is paying for breaking his friend's trust,' clarified the Devas rather matter-of-factly. Yudhishtira felt everyone's pain and started to weep. 'Shall we go back to Amravati now?' asked the Devas.

'No, no. Please don't go,' Yudhishtira heard his brothers cry. 'Your presence comforts us.'

'Well? Shall we leave?' asked the Devas impatiently.

'Please stay,' Yudhishtira heard Draupadi plead. She sounded so lost and tired and anxious and afraid.

Yudhishtira could not bring himself to move. Tears welled up in his eyes. How could he return to Swarga and leave his family here? He took a decision. 'No. I will not leave Naraka. I will stay here with my wife and my brothers. I will suffer with them. I refuse to enter Amravati without them.'

The Devas laughed. Rising up in the air, glowing like fire flies, they said, 'Oh, but we thought you had renounced everything?'

'What do you mean?' asked Yudhishtira, suddenly uncomfortable.

'Did you not renounce all worldly ties when you entered Swarga? Wherefrom, then, comes this attachment? You are as attached to your hatred as a dog is attached to its master.'

Yudhishtira argued, 'How can Amravati open its gates to the Kauravas, those murderers, and not to my family which has always followed the path of righteous conduct? Even Krishna fought against the Kauravas!'

'Do you feel we are taking sides, Yudhishtira?' asked the Devas.

'Yes,' snapped Yudhishtira, looking at the dark misery all around him. Surely, his family who had established dharma on earth did not deserve this. This was so unfair.

'You have given up your kingdom and your clothes, son of Dharma, but not your hatred. You killed the Kauravas in Kuru-kshetra and ruled their kingdom for thirty-six years! Still you have not forgiven them. You, who turned your back on your brothers on your way to Amravati, recalled them the instant you saw the Kauravas in heaven. This display of love is nothing but a reaction, retaliation. You cling to your anger, Yudhishtira. You still distinguish between friend and foe. You refuse to let go and move on. How then do you hope to truly attain heaven?'

Suddenly, a vision unfolded before Yudhishtira. The Virat-swarup of Krishna. 'Behold within God,' a voice boomed, 'all that exists. Everything. Everyone. Draupadi and Gandhari. The Pandavas and the Kauravas. All possibilities. The killers and the killed.'

At that moment, Yudhishtira realized he was not the great man who he thought he was. He had not really overcome his prejudices. Only when there is undiluted compassion for everyone, even our worst enemies, is ego truly conquered. Realization humbled Yudhishtira. He fell to the ground and began to weep.

Led by the Devas, Yudhishtira then took a dip in the Ganga and rose enlightened, purified, refreshed and truly liberated, with the sincere desire to forgive and accept the Kauravas. There was no more hatred. No more 'them' and 'us'. No more 'better' and 'worse'. There was only love. Everyone was one.

'Jaya!' shouted Indra. 'Jaya!' shouted the Devas. 'Jaya!' shouted the Rishis. For Yudhishtira had won the ultimate victory, victory over himself. Now he would ascend to a heaven higher than Swarga. Now he would ascend to Vaikuntha, the abode of God.

- The epic ends not with the victory of the Pandavas over the Kauravas but with Yudhishtira's triumph over himself. This is spiritual victory or Jaya. This is the ultimate aim of the great epic.
- The phrase 'Jaya ho' is a greeting and the phrase 'Jaya he' is part of the Indian national anthem.
- Merit can be earned in many ways. It can be earned through acts of charity, by performing religious rituals, by bathing in holy rivers or by dying in holy places. One such holy place which purged all demerit and provided merit was Kuru-kshetra. Another one is Kashi, on the banks of the river Ganga, which is why people still go to Kashi to die.
- Unlike Biblical traditions, Hindus have more than one heaven. There is Swarga and Vaikuntha. Swarga is the paradise of Indra where all desires are fulfilled. Vaikuntha is God's heaven where one is free of all desires.

EPILOGUE

The End of the Snake Sacrifice

Vaisampayana concluded his narration. The serpents were still suspended above the sacrificial fire and the priests were still around the altar impatient to conclude their ritual. The blazing fire had by now reduced to a flame. All eyes were on the king.

'I am confused,' said Janamejaya. 'Who is the hero of this tale? Who is the villain?'

'Who shall we call villain, my king? Duryodhana, who refused to share even a needlepoint of land? Yudhishtira, who gambled away wife and kingdom? Bhishma, who prevented Dhritarashtra from becoming king just because he was blind? Shantanu, who sacrificed his son's future to satisfy his own lust? Or is it Gandhari, for blindfolding herself to her son's many faults? Or maybe Krishna, who had long ago promised the earth-goddess to rid the world of unrighteous kings? You decide who is hero and who is villain,' said Vaisampayana.

Janamejaya had no reply. He recollected the many forces that influenced the flow of the tale: boons and curses and manmade laws. There was no hero or villain in the epic, just people struggling with life, responding to crises, making mistakes, repeating mistakes, in innocence or ignorance, while trying to make their lives meaningful and worthwhile. 'Why then do you call this tale "Jaya"? There is no real victory.'

'There are two kinds of victory in this world,' said the storyteller-sage, 'Vijaya and Jaya. Vijaya is material victory, where there is a loser. Jaya is spiritual victory, where there are no losers. In Kuru-kshetra there was Vijaya but not Jaya. But when Yudhishtira overcame his rage and forgave the Kauravas unconditionally, there was Jaya. That is the true ending of my tale, hence the title.'

'Though defeated in battle, the unrighteous Kauravas go to Swarga, while the victorious Pandavas end up in Naraka. It makes no sense.'

Astika spoke up, 'For merits earned one goes to Swarga. For demerits earned one goes to Naraka. In the book of accounts, measured at the end of a lifetime, the Kauravas had been cleansed of all demerit by being defeated on a sacred land, while the Pandavas fell short on merit as the war had not purged them of their prejudices. Hence, it was Swarga for one and Naraka for the other.'

'It does not feel right.' said the king.

'You see only one lifetime, my king,' said Astika. 'Stay in Swarga is not for eternity, nor is stay in Naraka. Eventually, after exhausting merits and demerits, the Kauravas will fall and the Pandavas will rise. Both will resume their journey through the cycle of rebirths. Once again they will be born and once again they will die. Once again they will earn merit, or demerit. Once again they will attain either Swarga, or Naraka. This will happen again and again until they learn.'

'Learn what?'

'What Yudhishtira learnt—the point of existence is not to accumulate merit, but to attain wisdom. We have to ask ourselves—why do we do what we do? When we truly accept the answer, we break free from the cycle of births and deaths, and discover the realm beyond Swarga, Vaikuntha, where there is peace forever.'

'I thought the Pandavas did what they did for dharma,' said Janamejaya, suddenly unsure.

'If that had been true, then Vijaya over the Kauravas would also have been accompanied by Jaya over self. Following Krishna's directive, they did defeat the Kauravas and ensured the overthrow of forces who pursued the law of the jungle. This was good for the world, but had no impact on the Pandavas themselves. There was remorse but no wisdom. External victory was not accompanied by internal victory. In the absence of spiritual insight, the Pandavas gloated over the Kaurava defeat which is why they went to Naraka.'

'What was the insight that eluded my forefathers?' asked Janamejaya.

'That conflict comes from rage, rage comes from fear, and fear comes from lack of faith. That lack of faith which corrupted the Kauravas continued to lurk in the minds of the Pandavas. It had to be purged.'

The image of Krishna, serving as Arjuna's charioteer, singing the song of wisdom before the war, flashed through Janamejaya's mind. 'If you have faith in me, and in the karmic balance sheet of merit and demerit, then you will have no insecurity,' he heard Krishna say.

The lotus of wisdom bloomed in Janamejaya's mind. 'I too have no faith,' he admitted. 'That is why I am angry with the serpents and frightened of them. That is why I delude myself with arguments of justice and vengeance. You are right, Astika, this snake sacrifice of mine is not dharma.'

Astika smiled, and Vaisampayana bowed his head in satisfaction: the king had finally inherited the wisdom of his forefathers.

An expression of peace descended upon Janamejaya, the son of Parikshit, the grandson of Abhimanyu, the great grandson of Arjuna. He finally took his decision. 'Shanti,' he said. 'Shanti,' he said again. 'Shanti,' he repeated a third time.

Shanti, peace. This was the king's call to end the Sarpa Sattra.

Astika burst into tears. Janamejaya had overpowered his fear and abandoned his rage. No more serpents would be killed. 'Shanti, shanti, shanti,' he had said. Not peace in the outer world. That could not happen as long as man felt insecure. This was a cry for inner peace.

Let us all have faith. Let us all be at peace—with ourselves, our worlds, and all the rest there is.

Shanti. Shanti. Shanti.

- The Nagas may have acted in fear and rage but Janamejaya does not have any excuse. As human, he has a larger brain and can imagine the possibility of outgrowing animal instincts. That is the journey towards the divine. That is dharma.
- The Mahabharata is not as much concerned with the war as it is with the root of conflict. Conflict is the result of greed exhibited by Duryodhana, and outrage exhibited by Yudhishtira. Both greed and outrage stem from insecurity; insecurity is the result of a poor understanding of, and a lack of faith in, one's true nature and the true nature of the world around us. The Veda says that as long as we do not accept life for what it is, as long as we try to control and change things, there will always be conflict. Conflict ends when we realize that beyond tangible material reality, there is intangible spiritual reality.
- Astika boasts that he is responsible for ending the massacre of the serpents. To humble him, his uncle, Vasuki, king of the Nagas, introduces him to Sarama, the mother of dogs, who reveals that when the sacrifice started, Janamejaya and his brothers had thrown stones at her children, wrongfully accusing them of licking the sacrificial offerings. For this, Sarama had cursed them that the sacrifice would be interrupted. So it was not Astika's protest, but Sarama's curse, that perhaps stopped the Sarpa Sattra. No one person can ever take credit for a moment in this cosmos.
- A Bengali folktale informs us that Janamejaya asked Vyasa why he was not able to convince his ancestors from not going to war. Vyasa replied that excited people never listen to such logic. To prove his point, he advised Janamejaya not to marry the beautiful woman he had recently fallen in love with. Janamejaya married the woman nevertheless and ended up with a sexually transmitted disease. The king realized that he was no different from his ancestors when it came to taking advice.
- All Hindu rituals end with the chant 'Shanti, shanti, shanti' because the quest for peace is the ultimate goal of all existence. This peace is not external but internal. It is not about making the world a peaceful place; it is about us being at peace with the world.
- Among Hindu literatures, the Mahabharata is classified as Itihasa. Itihasa is not history, as is conventionally believed; it means 'an account of life as it was, is, and always will be'. Itihasa is that which is timeless or sanatan. The sages therefore consider the Mahabharata to be the fifth Veda, the final whisper of God.

The Idea Called Dharma

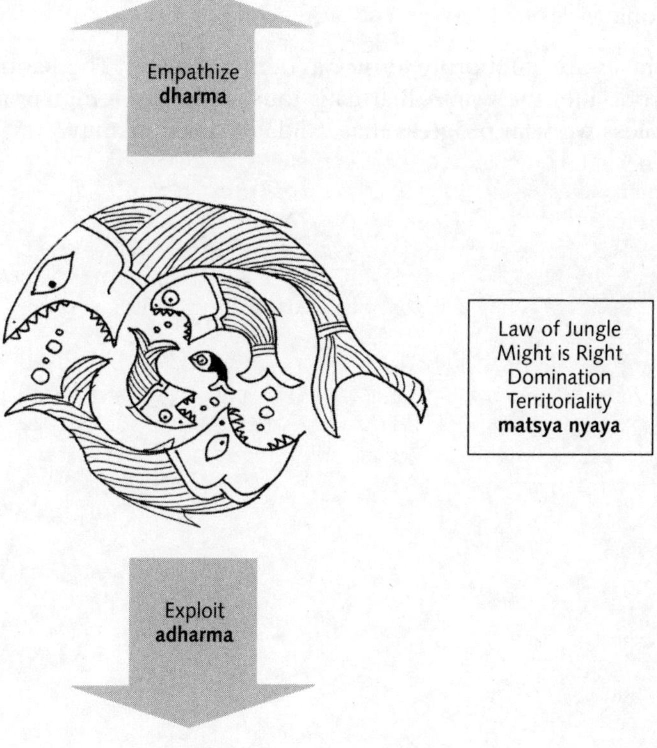

The fear of death makes animals fight for their survival. Might becomes right as only the fit survive. With strength and cunning territories are established and pecking orders enforced. Thus, the law of the jungle comes into being. Animals have no choice but to subscribe to it. Humans, however, can choose to accept, exploit or reject this law.

Thanks to our larger brain, we can imagine and create a world where we can look beyond ourselves, include others, and make everyone feel wanted and safe. We can, if we wish to, establish a society where the mighty care for the meek, and where resources are made available to help even the unfit thrive. This is dharma.

Unfortunately, imagination can also amplify fear, and make us so territorial that we withhold resources, exploit the weak and eat even when well-fed. This is adharma. If dharma enables us to outgrow the beast in us, then adharma makes us worse than animals. If dharma takes us towards divinity, then adharma fuels the demonic.

The Kauravas are stubbornly territorial before the war. The Pandavas struggle to be generous after the war. Adharma is thus an eternal temptation, while dharma is an endless work in progress that validates our humanity.

Acknowledgements

- Bodhisatva, who explained to me the difference between the words Jaya and Vijaya
- My driver, Deepak Sutar, who is also an artist, who helped me shade many of my illustrations
- Rupa, who read many of my drafts and whose expressions told me what works and what does not work
- Works and people that have inspired and informed this retelling: A. Harindranath (Internet resources on the Mahabharata), Akbar the Great (paintings of the Razmnama and the Persian translation), Alf Hiltebeitel (research on Cult of Draupadi), Bhandarkar Oriental Research Institute (Critical Edition), Bhasa (play *Urubhangam* in Sanskrit), B.R. Chopra & Rahi Masoom Raza (teleserial *Mahabharata*), C. Rajagopalachari (Mahabharata retold), Chitra Banerjee Divakaruni (novel *Palace of Illusions* in English), Dharamvir Bharati (play *Andha Yudh* in Hindi), Gajendra Kumar Mitrai (novel *Panchajanya* in Bengali), Iravati Karve (essay collection *Yuganta*), Jean-Claude Carrières & Peter Brooks (play *Le Mahabharat* in French), John Smith (Mahabharata translation), K.M. Munshi (novel *Krishnaavatar* in English), Kabi Sanjay (Bengali Mahabharata), Kamala Subramanium (Mahabharata retold), Kisari Mohan Ganguli (Sanskrit Mahabharata translation in English), Krishnaji Prabhakar Khadilkar (play *Kichaka-vadha* in Marathi), M.T. Vasudevan Nair (novel *Second Turn* in Malayalam), Mpu Sedha & Mpu Panuluh (Javanese Mahabharata titled *Kakawin Bharatayuddha*), Niranatt Sankara Panikkar (Bharatamala, Mahabharata in Malayalam), Perum Devanar (Tamil Mahabharata), Pradip Bhattacharya (essays in Boloji.com), Pratibha Ray (novel *Yagnaseni* in Oriya), R.K. Narayan (Mahabharata retold), Ramasaraswati (Assamese Mahabharata), Ramdhari Singh Dinkar (epic poem Rashmirathi in Hindi), Ramesh Menon (Mahabharata retold), Ratan Thiyam (theatre performance Chakravyuha), S.L. Bhyrappa (novel *Parva* in Kannada), Sarala Das (Oriya Mahabharata), Shivaji Sawant (novel *Mrtiyunjaya* in Marathi), Shyam Benegal (film *Kaliyug* in Hindi and teleserial *Bharat Ek Khoj*), Teejan-bai (Pandavani performance) and William Buck (Mahabharata retold)

Bibliography

Abhisheki, Janaki. *Tales and Teachings of the Mahabharat*. Mumbai: Bharatiya Vidya Bhavan, 1998.

Bhattacharji, Sukumari. *The Indian Theogony*. New Delhi: Penguin Books India, 2000.

Coupe, Lawrence. *Myth*. London: Routledge, 1997.

Banerjee, Debjani, trans. Bishnupada Chakravarty. *The Penguin Companion to the Mahabharata*. New Delhi: Penguin Books India, 2007.

Dange, Sadashiv Ambadas. *Encyclopaedia of Puranic Beliefs and Practices*, Vols 1–5. New Delhi: Navrang, 1990.

Danielou, Alain. *Gods of Love and Ecstasy: The Traditions of Shiva and Dionysus*. Rochester, Vt.: Inner Traditions International, 1992.

_____. *Hindu Polytheism*. Rochester, Vt.: Inner Traditions International, 1991.

Eliade, Mircea. *Myths, Dreams, and Mysteries*. London: Collins, 1974.

Flood, Gavin. *An Introduction to Hinduism*. New Delhi: Cambridge University Press, 1998.

Frawley, David. *From the River of Heaven*. New Delhi: Motilal Banarsidass, 1992.

Hawley, J.S. and D.M. Wulff, eds. *The Divine Consort*. Boston: Beacon Press, 1982.

Hiltebeitel, Alf, ed. *Criminal Gods and Demon Devotees*. New York: State University of New York Press, 1989.

Hiltebeitel, Alf. *Cult of Draupadi*, Vol. 1. Chicago: University of Chicago Press, 1988.

Hopkins, E. Washburn. *Epic Mythology*. New Delhi: Motilal Banarsidass, 1986.

Jakimowicz-Shah, Marta. *Metamorphosis of Indian Gods*. Calcutta: Seagull Books, 1988.

Jayakar, Pupul. *The Earth Mother*. New Delhi: Penguin Books India, 1989.

Kinsley, David. *Hindu Goddesses*. New Delhi: Motilal Banarsidass, 1987.

Klostermaier, Klaus K. *Hinduism: A Short History*. Oxford: Oneworld Publications, 2000.

Knappert, Jan. *An Encyclopedia of Myth and Legend: Indian Mythology*. New Delhi: HarperCollins, 1992.

Kosambi, Damodar Dharmanand. *Myth and Reality*. Mumbai: Popular Prakashan Pvt. Ltd, 1994.

Mani, Vettam. *Puranic Encyclopaedia*. New Delhi: Motilal Banarsidass, 1996.

Mazumdar, Subash. *Who Is Who in the Mahabharata*. Mumbai: Bharatiya Vidya Bhavan, 1988.

Meyer, Johann Jakob. *Sexual Life in Ancient India*. New Delhi: Motilal Banarsidass, 1989.

O'Flaherty, Wendy Doniger, trans. *Hindu Myths*. New Delhi: Penguin Books India, 1975.

_____. *Origins of Evil in Hindu Mythology*. New Delhi: Motilal Banarsidass, 1988.

_____. *The Rig Veda: An Anthology*. New Delhi: Penguin Books India, 1994.

O'Flaherty, Wendy Doniger. *Sexual Metaphors and Animal Symbols in Indian Mythology*. New Delhi: Motilal Banarsidass, 1981.

_____. *Śiva: The Erotic Ascetic*. London: Oxford University Press, 1981.

Pandey, Rajbali. *Hindu Samskaras*. New Delhi: Motilal Banarsidass, 1969.

Pattanaik, Devdutt. *Devi: An Introduction*. Mumbai: Vakil, Feffer and Simons, 2000.

_____. *Goddess in India: Five Faces of the Eternal Feminine*. Rochester, Vt.: Inner Traditions International, 2000.

_____. *Hanuman: An Introduction*. Mumbai: Vakil, Feffer and Simons, 2001.

_____. *Indian Mythology: Tales, Symbols and Rituals from the Heart of the Indian Subcontinent*. Rochester, Vt.: Inner Traditions International, 2003.

_____. *Lakshmi, Goddess of Wealth and Fortune: An Introduction*. Mumbai: Vakil, Feffer and Simons, 2003.

_____. *Man Who Was a Woman and Other Queer Tales from Hindu Lore*. New York: Harrington Park Press, 2001.

_____. *Shiva: An Introduction*. Mumbai: Vakil, Feffer and Simons, 1997.

_____. *Vishnu: An Introduction*. Mumbai: Vakil, Feffer and Simons, 1999.

Sen, Makhan Lal. *The Ramayana of Valmiki*. New Delhi: Munshiram Manoharlal, 1978.

Subramaniam, Kamala. *Srimad Bhagavatam*. Mumbai: Bharatiya Vidya Bhavan, 1987.

_____. *Mahabharata*. Mumbai: Bharatiya Vidya Bhavan, 1988.

_____. *Ramayana*. Mumbai: Bharatiya Vidya Bhavan, 1992.

Varadpande, M.L. *Mahabharata in Performance*. Clarion Books, 1990.

Walker, Benjamin. *Hindu World*, Vols 1 and 2. New Delhi: Munshiram Manoharlal, 1983.

Watson, Duncan. *The Mahabharata: Chapter by Chapter Summary of the Great Indian Epic*, as an aid to finding passages within the original 18 volumes (14 December 1992). Downloaded from the Internet on 3 April 2007.

Wilkins, W.J. *Hindu Mythology*. New Delhi: Rupa, 1997.

Zimmer, Heinrich. *Myths and Symbols in Indian Art and Civilization*. New Delhi: Motilal Banarsidass, 1990.

YOU MAY ALSO LIKE

YOU MAY ALSO LIKE